A SPECIAL QUEST

"You have awakened the warrior within me, my Flower, but it is also true that you have awakened the woman within yourself. The time has come for us both to pursue a vision quest.

"We will travel to a sacred cave in the foothills. During the journey, from this night forward, and until the end of the quest, we will not eat or speak. Taking only water to sustain our physical lives, we will partake of only spiritual nourishment."

Desert Rain listened with wide-eyed wonder. She had heard of such journeys. Several times the warriors of her people would set out on vision quests. They would tell briefly of their journey around the campfires after their return. They would tell of seeing visions. She remembered one young brave telling of his vision, his purpose, regarding his place among the people. He told of following his spirit guide through a maze of visions. It was never proper to reveal one's spirit guide, but sometimes the visions were described in detail in order for the shaman to help interpret what the warrior had seen. But, she had never heard of a woman seeing a vision quest, and she said as much.

Spirit Walker spoke firmly, resolutely. "You are a warrior, my Flower. The quest is yours to seek."

DESERT RAIN

SPIRIT WALKER

LEISURE BOOKS NEW YORK CITY

A LEISURE BOOK®

September 2001

Published by

Dorchester Publishing Co., Inc.
276 Fifth Avenue
New York, NY 10001

ISBN 0-8439-4919-8

The name "Leisure Books" and the stylized "L" with design are trademarks of Dorchester Publishing Co., Inc.

Printed in the United States of America.

Visit us on the web at www.dorchesterpub.com.

For the REAL Desert Rain,
who has brought joy and love to my life,
a rain to quench my thirsty soul.
It is in her arms that I take my rest and comfort from this
day forward.

I would also like to thank my son, KickingHawk,
for his love and support.

ACKNOWLEDGMENTS

Back in late 1997, I was a very depressed "wannabe" writer. After receiving several rejection notices for the first book I had written, I wandered into an AOL chat room to vent my frustration. It was in that Writers Café that I met a very special lady; her name was Madeline Baker. From that first meeting, a close friendship grew. She was working on a book of her own at the time and invited me to take a look at her progress. She asked for my input. It was a great honor for me to assist such a widely published author. She fanned the flame of desire in me that drove me to write and though I had never attempted a romance novel before, she encouraged me to do so.

We finished *Spirit's Song,* the book she was writing, and she graciously dedicated it to me. Then she allowed me to help her with her next book, *Apache Flame.* I was hooked. This book was originally an idea I presented to her. After I described the opening scene, she informed me that she thought that I should write the book. Frankly, I was afraid to attempt the project, but she was absolutely adamant.

I owe a debt of gratitude to her for giving me the heart I needed to complete this work. I will forever be grateful for her support and assistance (she read and edited every chapter). Mandy, I tip my headdress to you as one of the greatest friends of the Apache Nation and the finest Historical Romance writer in the business.

FOREWARD

Dear Reader,

This is a very special book. I can honestly say that I don't think there's ever been one like it . . . an Indian romance written by an Indian man who is the embodiment of my own native amercian heroes.

I had the pleasure of reading this book from the beginning, and it was a wonderful adventure. I fell in love with SpiritWalker, and lost myself in the love story, and in the lore and legends of the Apache.

So, sit back and prepare to be swept into a time when a man's word was his bond, and honor meant more than life.

Madeline Baker

INTRODUCTION

It is my great pleasure to introduce you to my ancestors. This book is about a distant relative, an Apache warrior—The Spirit That Walks as a Man.

I was raised to appreciate those who have gone before me. I was taught that the history of my People is to be cherished and passed on from generation to generation. The loves, losses, happiness, and sorrows of the past are an important part of who we are today. They are the components that influence our spirts and our hearts—that which makes us human.

This book is written so that you might share in the history of the Apache Nation. The events portrayed are a mixture of historical facts and fictional creations. Many of the characters are real, but some have been created to flesh out the story. My intent is that you will feel what it was like to dwell among the Apache, to live under the fear and trepidation that influenced the decisions that were made in the late 1800s.

In the book, you will meet the several different bands of the Apache. The Jicarilla Apache are one of the easternmost bands. Their name, meaning "little basket," was derived from the expertise of their women in making baskets of all sizes, shapes, and colors. Conversely, the Chiricahua were one of the westernmost bands. The Central Chiricahuas were known as Chokonen. The Eastern Chiricahuas were known as the the Gileños because they lived mostly along the Gila River in Arizona. Though the bands were different in some ways, they were alike one important way—they were Apache.

There is no attempt to portray any group of people as villainous or treacherous. Any enlightened person knows that the men and women of long ago made judgments and decisions based upon the information available to them. I seek to judge no one person or group. I only seek to tell the story of the conflict between the Apache, the Anglos, and the Mexicans. There were heroes and villains in all races, and so there are in this book. It is my intention to bring these three groups together, in harmony.

I hope that you will enjoy the journey of Desert Rain and Spirit Walker, remembering that as a descendant of Spirit Walker, and bearing a variation of his name, I am proud to be able to use him as my main male character in my solo book.

I hope you enjoy reading these pages as much as I enjoyed writing them.

Desert Rain

The land was parched and dry,
There was no life within.
The sun had scorched the barren plains,
The soil was cracked and thin.
My life was in a similar state,
With troubles, toils, and pain.
I felt the heat of endless days,
Void of nurturing rain.

I never saw the cloud come in,
I never saw the signs.
Perhaps my eyes were inward turned
From the loneliness of time.
I was prepared to bear the heat,
To brave the harsh terrain.
I did not need the joy of love,
I could live without the rain.

I held my head high as I walked,
With confidence I strode.
I stalked the trails of time and space,
Though it was a lonely road.
I fell among the thorns of life,
I lay lifeless on the plains.
My lips were dry, my spirit gone,
I prayed for a drop of rain.

Just when it seemed I'd breathed my last,
Just when all hope had fled,
Just when my heart had turned to dust,
My feet had turned to lead,
There in the west arose a cloud,

SpiritWalker

Its beauty would not wane.
It left a fragrance on the air,
The sweet, sweet smell of rain.

It was on your lips and in your hair,
It was in your eyes of brown.
A love I never knew to seek,
Was the very one I found.
You rained your kisses on my brow,
My spirit rose again.
I felt my strength returning from
These golden drops of rain.

My life has changed in many ways,
This warrior's been reborn.
My eyes are bright, alive with love,
That in your heart was formed.
Your arms gave life, your lips gave breath,
Your love erased the pain.
You brought new life to quench my thirst,
You are my Desert Rain.

Chapter One

It was a beautiful night. The moon was full, the spirits were high, the Indians danced. Desert Rain took it all in, a smile curving her mouth as she watched the young braves circle the crackling fire. She felt Arm Bow squeeze her tightly beneath the buffalo robe that engulfed them. This was as close as they had been able to get in three days and she felt as if they were sharing the same skin, becoming one person. She laughed softly. She was so happy.

She had missed her new husband while he was away on the hunt. It seemed that he had been gone forever, even though he had only been gone three days. It had been a necessary hunt and she knew he'd had to go, but they had only been married a week when the time arrived for the first hunt of the spring.

She glanced at her tall, muscular husband. Arm Bow was young and strong. His long black hair teased her face as he bobbed his head to the beat of the ceremonial drum. He was the one many young maidens had sought for companionship, but he was hers now. How had she gotten so lucky?

He had always told her that it was her eyes that first attracted him to her. He said they shone brighter than the Dog Star. She had never been so happy in her life. He filled her days with joy. Just watching him joking and cavorting with his friends made her laugh. He filled her nights with love. She knew they were the envy of many in the encampment—maybe that was the real reason for the light in her eyes.

"Arm Bow, dance with us!"

Arm Bow looked up at his friend and smiled. "Ai, Cloud Maker, should I leave the warmth of this robe to dance with you?"

Cloud Maker smiled a wide, toothy smile. "I think the robe is not what brings you such warmth, my brother."

Desert Rain's cheeks flushed red and she dipped her head in embarrassment.

Cloud Maker stepped forward and extended his hand. "Come on, Bow, you must dance. You had a big part in the hunt so you must tell your story."

"I'll be right back, Rain. Wait for me." Arm Bow kissed his wife on the forehead and stepped from the robe. He took Cloud Maker's arm and approached the other dancers.

Desert Rain watched her husband tell his story in dance. She watched as his lean, tanned body danced around the fire circle. The yellowish flames turned his skin to copper as he acted out his part in the hunt.

Someone tossed Arm Bow a stick as he began the old dance. He acted out the part of the trackers, bending low as he shuffled around the fire. Using the stick, he pretended to point out the tracks of the elk they were seeking. He used the stick like a cane as he pointed to one spot and then another, reversing direction, and reversing again to illustrate the long time they had spent in tracking. The drums beat steadily on and Arm Bow's dance became more frantic as he imitated the warriors' joy as the elk were spotted. He began to run and jump around the fire to demonstrate the dispersal of the hunters. Suddenly he dropped to the ground. Crawling on all fours, he acted out the stealthy approach he had taken. He raised to one knee, the stick standing in for the bow that had given him his name. He pulled the imaginary bow string back and released it with a deliberate motion.

The rest of the warriors suddenly burst into dance. Sweeping Arm Bow up in their frenzy, they circled the fire, whooping and dancing with more fervor now. The last story having been told, all that was left was the victory dance, a dance of thanksgiving to *Usen* for arranging a bountiful hunt.

Desert Rain's eyes lit the night.

The dancing was over and the flames of the once raging fire were dying. Arm Bow once again snuggled with Desert Rain beneath their robe tipi.

"Let's walk a little before we sleep." Desert Rain whispered.

"Walk? Is that all that's on your mind?"

Arm Bow's impish grin made her smile and she gave him a mock slug on the arm. "It may be if you do not behave yourself."

Arm Bow threw aside the robe and stood up. "We will walk then."

Desert Rain held tightly to Arm Bow's hand. It had always amazed her that the hand that caressed her so gently could turn to iron in battle. It was his gentle way with her that had won her heart. She knew that as a young warrior married into her clan, he had responsibilities. He had to help to defend the others, to supply meat from the hunts, but he always had time to walk with her and talk with her. She knew he was the warrior of her heart.

"The moon is so beautiful tonight," she whispered.

"Yes, the old man is very clear tonight."

Desert Rain laughed, recalling the story of the old man who had been banished to the moon. His image could be seen as he

17

carried his wikiup across the face of the glowing ball of light. It was one of her favorite childhood stories.

"Where shall we walk tonight, my sweet Rain?"

"Can we walk the high trail? I would love to look out over the valley. The moon is so full and the night is so pretty. I would love to see the valley in this light."

Arm Bow smiled and took his wife in his arms. "Yes, we will walk the high trail." Gently his lips met hers.

"It's alive, isn't it?" Desert Rain asked, as they looked over the valley from the top of the high trail.

"It is alive. It lives and breathes, like you and I. The valley enjoys the night just as we do."

"Listen. I hear NightHawk screaming for her mate."

"Yes, but she must be careful. I hear Coyote the Trickster answering her call."

Desert Rain laughed. She pulled away from Arm Bow and gave a shrill cry.

Arm Bow smiled as Desert Rain imitated the call of the NightHawk perfectly. He replied with Coyote's howl.

Desert Rain turned and began to run away from the trail. Arm Bow pursued her, knowing that she would not run far. It was a game they had played often.

She ran into the trees, pretending to be NightHawk as she fluttered on the night winds.

Arm Bow loped, pretending to be the Trickster weaving through the maze of trees.

Desert Rain suddenly fell to the ground, in a place they knew so well that it felt like home. It was a large patch of tall green grass, their secret place.

Arm Bow stepped from behind a tall pine. He crept toward her, imitating Coyote stalking his prey. She laughed louder now and feigned fear as the Trickster approached. Then he leapt onto her.

They rolled in the soft grass. Desert Rain beat on his broad shoulders as they fought in the moonlight. Arm Bow wrapped his arms around her, rolling over and over, enjoying the warmth of her soft, delicate body.

He looked up at her when they finally came to rest. She lay on top of him, breathing heavily. "I love you, Desert Rain." He pulled her mouth to his.

She kissed him willingly, deeply, as if life itself depended on this one kiss.

His hands slid her tunic over her shoulders and he rolled her gently to the side. She was the most beautiful creature in the forest and he meant to make her feel that way.

Wiggling out of her tunic, Desert Rain released the rawhide cord that held Arm Bow's breechclout in place. He was full of desire and she meant for him to know the fulfillment of that desire like never before.

She thrilled at his lips on her breasts as he pressed his body down on top of her. She felt his passion as it moved from her loins, into her stomach, up through her bosom and leapt from her throat in a soft purr. She was in the clutches of the Trickster, and that was where she meant to stay.

Later, Desert Rain watched the stars as they twinkled above her, encircling the moon in a necklace of white. She still felt the warmth of the love they had made. "Aren't the stars wonderful?"

Arm Bow glanced at his wife. The starlight played across her body. "They delight in your beauty."

Desert Rain smiled and snuggled closer to his strength, her hands moving along his thighs, caressing him softly, lovingly. "Sing for me. Will you sing for me?"

Arm Bow immediately began his song. It was a song that Desert Rain had heard many times, but she never tired of it. His voice was beautiful and it melted her heart.

You give the moon its light, you give the stars their shine.
The sun cannot rise without your smile.
The wind whispers your name to the pines, and they bend to
your will.
The leaves dance at the sound of your voice, and the deer leap
for joy.
You give the birds their song, they sing of your beauty.
You are the song on the midnight wind.

Desert Rain rolled over to face her husband, taking his manhood once again in her hand. "Make love to me again, my husband. Love me forever."

"I will, my sweet. And I will love you forever."

Chapter Two

Arm Bow awoke with a start. He and Desert Rain had slept longer than usual. The camp was already alive with activity. He shook his head and wiped the sleep from his eyes. They had gotten back to their tipi late last night from their adventures on the high trail.

Desert Rain rose from her sleep as she too heard the commotion in the encampment. "What's happening?"

"I don't know," Arm Bow replied as he pulled his breechclout around him and began to tie the leather thong at his waist. "I will find out."

Arm Bow stepped into the morning light. By the looks of the sun he had slept till almost noon. Children ran around the encampment screaming for others to follow them. There were so many people yelling that he couldn't determine exactly what was happening, but it was clear that there was indeed an emergency.

Arm Bow grabbed one of the children as he ran by. "What is it? What's happened, Small Bear?"

"It's Beaver Tail! We were crossing the rock bridge to get to the berry patch. Halfway across, Beaver Tail fell!"

"Did he fall to the bottom of the ravine?"

"No. He's hanging on, but he can't last long. We must hurry!"

Arm Bow released the boy and ducked back inside his tipi.

"What is it? What's happened?" Desert Rain asked.

"One of the children has fallen from the rock bridge. I must go to help."

Arm Bow grabbed his moccasins and started back toward the tipi flap.

"Aren't you going to take your rope?"

Arm Bow stopped and looked back at the sturdy rawhide rope he had twisted together while on the hunting trip. "No, I know those rocks well. They are too rough and jagged—they'd chew the rope to shreds."

"Well, be careful, my husband."

Arm Bow glanced at his adoring wife. "I will, my sweet Rain. I will be careful."

He headed out again through the tipi flap.

Beaver Tail clung to the rock like a spider on its web. He chanced a look down only once, and the fear that gripped him only made him more determined to never let go.

He spoke to himself, trying to imagine what his grandfather would say if he were still alive and here to help him. *Hold on, Beaver Tail. Your friends will bring help. They would never let you fall. Hold on, it will not be long.*

He looked up, tempted for a moment to try climbing higher, but fear gripped his heart once again and he squeezed the rocks tighter than ever. "I am not doing so well, my Grandfather," he whispered. "Not so well at all."

Hold on, Beaver Tail. You will become a valiant warrior, do not fear.

Beaver Tail closed his eyes. He could see his grandfather's smiling face. How he missed him. But the old man had always promised to be there for him. Even death could not part their spirits.

Beaver Tail heard movement on the rocks above him, then a voice. "Beaver Tail, where are you?"

"Down here! I'm here!" the boy shouted as loudly as his small lungs would allow.

"Help is coming! Hold on!" Crow Woman shouted.

Arm Bow ran toward the rock bridge. He could see many children, some women, and a few men running ahead of him. It was times like this that his people truly demonstrated their love for their children. Children were a precious gift from *Usen*. They were to be cherished and loved. Each member of the tribe was responsible for each other's children, and the young ones were taught respect for their elders and their ancestry. That was the way of *Teneh*, the People, and Arm Bow took it to heart. Some day, he hoped to have children with Desert Rain and he would want the others to care for his offspring as he cared for theirs. He ran harder.

Crow Woman was standing on the edge of the rock bridge, pointing out to the others where she had heard Beaver Tail answer her call. Arm Bow pushed to the front of the crowd. "Crow Woman, keep the children away from the bridge. I'll climb down and bring Beaver Tail back up with me."

A young warrior stepped forward. "I will help."

Arm Bow smiled at his best friend. He and Cloud Maker had themselves crossed this rock bridge as youths. They knew every inch of it. They had both been fascinated by the legend of the bridge. Many moons ago, there had been a great drought upon the land. The animals scavenged for food, but the fruits and berries had dried up and not much could be found. Across the wide ravine, the animals noticed a large, luscious patch of berries, but couldn't reach it. Even Hummingbird was too weak to fly the distance across the ravine. All seemed lost, until Fox stepped forward with an idea. He had every animal gather stones and throw them into the ravine. As the pile of stones rose higher and higher, a rock bridge began to form, until they were able to step out on the rocks and cross to the berry patch.

Arm Bow knew that it was this berry patch that tempted all children to cross the bridge. He also knew that they were not supposed to cross it by themselves, but that had never stopped him and Cloud Maker, and it obviously hadn't stopped the children this morning. He patted Cloud Maker on the shoulder and the two men set off across the bridge.

"Beaver Tail, are you there?" Arm Bow yelled.

"I'm here! I'm here!" the frightened boy shouted in return.

"I'm coming down for you!" Arm Bow sat down on the edge of the bridge, looking for any sign of the stranded boy.

"What shall we do?" Cloud Maker asked.

"I'll climb down to the boy. I think I know the rocks well enough to bring him up."

Cloud Maker smiled. "I remember, Bow. I remember the day you were challenged to climb down the rocks and into the ravine. No one thought you could do it. No one thought you *would* do it."

Arm Bow looked up at his friend. "Fond memories we have, my friend."

"Yes, fonder still since you did not die." Cloud Maker laughed out loud then and slapped his friend on the top of his head.

"Arm Bow! Be careful!"

Arm Bow turned at the sound of Desert Rain's voice as she cried from the edge of the bridge.

Arm Bow stood up. "I will, my love! Don't worry about me!"

He turned once again to his friend. "Cloud Maker, take care that Rain does not come out onto the bridge. Care for her, my friend. I will return."

Cloud Maker nodded. "Hand the boy up to me. All will be fine."

Arm Bow turned and began to climb down the steep pile of stones. He realized immediately that some things had changed since he last descended to the ravine below. The rocks had shifted and settled with time. Some were rough, some smooth, some loose, some firm. As Arm Bow climbed, he dislodged several small rocks, which fell tumbling to the valley floor. He tried not to let any of them fall in Beaver Tail's direction, but he wasn't sure exactly where the boy was. Each time a stone was dislodged, Arm Bow would yell, "Rock!" in order to warn the boy to keep his head down.

He moved slowly, carefully, as precisely as possible. He kept his body in control at all times, not wishing to become off-balanced in the descent. The rocks slipped beneath his feet and he grabbed a larger rock for stability. "Beaver Tail! Where are you?"

"Here! I'm here!"

Arm Bow could tell that the young boy was tiring quickly, his voice getting increasingly weaker. "Hold on, Beaver Tail! I'm coming!"

"I know," the boy called faintly. "Grandfather said you would come."

Finally Arm Bow caught sight of the boy. He was straddling a large boulder that jutted out from the side of the rock structure. He was hugging the rock, slumped over it like a warrior asleep on his pony. The boy wasn't looking around, wasn't moving. Had he fallen farther? Was he still alive? "Beaver Tail! Beaver Tail! I'm right above you! I'm coming!" The child moved slightly, but he didn't answer. Arm Bow had to reach him, and quickly.

Beaver Tail could hear Arm Bow scrambling on the rocks overhead, but fear was taking its toll on his young muscles. He began to shake as every muscle twitched in his arms, his legs, his abdomen. "I cannot hold on much longer, Grandfather. I'm so frightened," he whispered.

I'm here, Beaver Tail. You are not alone.

His grandfather's voice made him look up. He smiled as he looked into his grandfather's wrinkled face. "Thank you, Grandfather. I knew you would come to rescue me."

You must turn loose of the rock, my son.

"But I cannot. I will surely fall."

No, you will not fall. I am here. Take my hand.

Beaver Tail looked to the valley below, then back up into the eyes of his grandfather. "I'm not afraid now, Grandfather. Am I a warrior now?"

Soon, Beaver Tail. Very soon. Take my hand.

For the first time since his fall, Beaver Tail felt no fear at all. He reached up to take his grandfather's hand. It was strong and firm and lifted him easily from the rock ledge. "Thank you, Grandfather. I knew you would come."

Arm Bow smiled broadly. "Well, my little warrior, I'm not quite old enough to be called grandfather, but you may call me uncle."

"Yes, uncle," Beaver Tail said as he collapsed into his rescuer's arms.

Struggling for balance, Arm Bow hugged Beaver Tail closely to his bosom and began his ascent.

Chapter Three

Dancing Waters pushed her way to the front of the crowd that had gathered at the edge of the rock bridge. "My son! My son!"

Desert Rain turned at the cry of Beaver Tail's worried mother. She knew Dancing Waters had been washing at the creek when her son fell. Her husband, Black Beaver, was a tracker and was out locating elk for the next hunt. Desert Rain's heart went out to the frightened woman. She felt a mother's sorrow at the thought of losing a child. Someday, she hoped to have children of her own. There could be no better father than Arm Bow, who would risk his life to save another's, she thought as she watched Dancing Waters fall sobbing into Crow Woman's open arms.

"Do you have the boy?" Cloud Maker yelled down to Arm Bow.

"Yes, I have him!"

Cloud Maker turned to the onlookers at the edge of the bridge. "He has the boy! He's safe!"

A cheer went up from the crowd. Desert Rain could feel the pride swell in her chest. There would be songs written of Arm Bow's courage. Songs that would be sung around the campfires at night. Arm Bow's name would be known by all of her People. It might even be spread abroad to other clans, other tribes, even other nations. She beamed with pride and patted Dancing Waters on the back for comfort.

Arm Bow struggled up the rocks, still holding Beaver Tail in his arms. "You are a very brave boy, Beaver Tail."

"Thank you, uncle. My grandfather gave me strength."

"Yes, your grandfather was a great warrior. A noble elder. You are the seed of his loins, that is sure."

Beaver Tail smiled, but it disappeared quickly as Arm Bow's right foot dislodged a stone and the two of them fell hard against the side of the rock bridge. Arm Bow struggled for better footing.

When he had better settled himself, he addressed Beaver Tail again. "Little warrior, I'm afraid we cannot make the climb this way. I need for you to help me. I cannot do it on my own."

"What can I do, uncle?"

Arm Bow smiled at the boy, trying to alleviate his fears. "You must climb onto my back and hold on with all your strength. Wrap your legs around my waist and hold onto my shoulders. Can you do that?"

Beaver Tail looked up into Arm Bow's smiling face. It was Arm Bow's calm countenance that gave him courage this time. "Yes, uncle. Yes, I can."

"You are indeed your grandfather's seed, Beaver Tail. He is very proud of you."

"Can you see them?" Desert Rain yelled from the edge of the rock bridge.

Cloud Maker looked once again over the side of the bridge,

then turned back to the onlookers. "Not yet! But I hear them climbing on the rocks just below me!"

Desert Rain saw Dancing Waters bite her lower lip. Beaver Tail was the woman's only son, the spitting image of her husband. Dancing Waters cast a glance at Desert Rain, as if asking her to help Arm Bow's efforts somehow.

Desert Rain met the glance and gave Dancing Waters a wide smile. "Don't worry, my sister, Arm Bow will see that Beaver Tail is safe. I know he will."

"He is very brave," Dancing Waters said. "I shall never forget his kindness."

Desert Rain smiled. He was not only kind, he was hers, and she was proud.

Arm Bow clung to each handhold with all of his strength. Having the boy on his back made the climbing easier, but it took a toll on his stamina. He moved slowly, deliberately, making sure that every handhold, every foothold, was secure before reaching for another. His breath was coming in short gasps now, and he was climbing on sheer will power. He had to make it to the top. The life of the boy, not to mention his own, depended entirely on himself. He could not fail. He climbed on.

"I see them!" Cloud Maker yelled to the crowd. "They are just below me! It won't be long now!"

Another cheer went up from the people.

"Climb, my husband!" Desert Rain yelled, hoping that it would urge her husband on to success. Her voice echoed through the canyon.

"I'm . . . I'm . . . climbing, my love. I'm climbing." Arm Bow said weakly as he reached for another handhold and pulled the two of them up the rock wall.

Beaver Tail clung tightly to Arm Bow's back as he watched

the muscles in the warrior's shoulders and arms strain in turn with each pull. They were making progress, but it was slow. Beaver Tail looked up and could see, now and then between the rocks, the face of Cloud Maker looking down from above.

"I see Cloud Maker. I see him." the young boy said.

"How far . . . up . . . is he?"

"Not far. He's reaching down."

Arm Bow reached up and pulled hard.

"You are not far, my brother. I see the boy's head." Cloud Maker said, trying to encourage his friend.

Arm Bow heard Cloud Maker's call, but was too weak to answer. He had to save his strength for climbing. He was getting weaker. He could feel the strength leaving his body with each pull of his arms, each push of his legs.

"I see them! I see them!" Cloud Maker yelled. "Arm Bow, you are not far from the top now."

Arm Bow looked about him at the rocky outcropping. He might not be far from the summit, but he was in a tricky situation. A sharp overhang was between him and his goal. He desperately sought a way around it. "Beaver Tail . . . can you . . . see over . . . the rocks? Can you . . . see Cloud Maker?"

Beaver Tail looked skyward. "Yes, I can see him."

"Can you . . . reach him?"

Beaver Tail hesitated a moment. "No, I don't think I can."

"If you . . . stood . . . stood on my shoulders . . . could you reach him?"

"I don't think so, uncle. Not yet."

Arm Bow glanced above him, looking for a way to gain a little more height. If he could just get a little higher, if Beaver Tail could just reach Cloud Maker's arms, if he could just get Beaver Tail off his back, he felt sure he could make it. "Cloud Maker!"

"I'm here, my brother."

"Cloud Maker . . . reach for the boy. I'm going . . . to try . . . to hand him . . . up to you."

Cloud Maker turned toward the crowd of onlookers. "I need some men over here! Quickly!"

Before Cloud Maker had finished speaking, three young warriors raced to his side.

"Form a human chain. One of you hold my ankles. I'm going to reach for the boy."

The three men did as they were told. Lying flat on the ground, each man grabbed hold of the ankles of the man in front of him, beginning with Cloud Maker as he stretched over the side of the rock bridge.

"Arm Bow, hand the boy up to me!" Cloud Maker shouted over the rocks.

Arm Bow placed his right foot on a large rock he had spotted. He would have to push himself up with this one foot in order to grab a handhold above him. He felt sure if he could reach that handhold, he could pull them high enough for Cloud Maker to reach Beaver Tail's hand. He tensed the muscles in his right leg and pushed.

His hand barely got a grip on the handhold, as the rock beneath his right foot gave up its hold on the rocky ledge. Suddenly all of his weight, and the weight of the boy, fell full on his left arm. He grunted, and every muscle tightened in his arm as he sought desperately to hang on.

Arm Bow's feet scrambled for a foothold, but it was futile. The rocks were too loose, the footing unsure, and he swung to his right before reaching up. His right fingertips found a small rock and gripped it tightly. "Climb, Beaver Tail . . . climb up my back!"

The frightened boy looked up at Cloud Maker, hanging over the edge of the rock bridge, and began to climb Arm Bow's back.

He managed to get to his knees on the warrior's shoulders.

"Grab the rocks . . . stand up!" Arm Bow instructed, panic in his voice. He could feel his strength ebbing, and could tell that the rock under his right hand was giving way. He knew he didn't have long.

Beaver Tail reached for the rocks overhead, placed his right foot on Arm Bow's right shoulder and pushed. He stood up.

Cloud Maker reached to his full length. "I can't reach him! I can't reach him! I have to slide further out over the edge," he shouted to the warrior holding his ankles.

Arm Bow's arms began to twitch violently and the rock shifted suddenly beneath his right hand. "Hurry! Hurry, Cloud Maker!"

Cloud Maker shifted further over the edge. "Reach for my hand, Beaver Tail! Reach up, higher!"

Beaver Tail stretched, the tips of his fingers meeting with the tips of Cloud Maker's. He felt Arm Bow's body shift beneath him. Fear struck him like lightning and he suddenly leaped upward. Cloud Maker grasped the boy by both forearms and held on tightly.

The force of the boy's leap was enough to pry the rock under Arm Bow's right hand from its perch. Arm Bow's full weight once again transferred to his left arm, which gave up its strength immediately.

Cloud Maker screamed in terror. "No! No!"

As Arm Bow cleared the side of the bridge and plummeted toward the valley below, one word escaped from his lips, one word hung on the wind. "Rainnnnnnn!"

Chapter Four

Desert Rain turned quickly at hearing her name. Her heart froze. She looked toward the men lying prone on top of the bridge. Cloud Maker was pulling with all of his strength and suddenly Beaver Tail popped over the side and onto the rocks beside Cloud Maker. But something was wrong; something was terribly wrong. Feeling a sudden sense of urgency, she began to run.

The warrior holding Cloud Maker's ankles pulled him back from the edge, then released his hold, grabbed the boy, and pulled him away from the side of the bridge. Cloud Maker rolled in agony, his eyes shut tightly. He covered his face with both hands, rolling in the pain of the moment. "No! It cannot be! No!"

The three warriors who had formed the human chain rose to their feet in disbelief. One of them held the trembling boy tightly in his arms. Desert Rain approached quickly and the other two warriors stepped in front of her to keep her from approaching the edge.

One of the men grabbed her. "Rain, there is nothing more that can be done."

Cloud Maker sat upright. "Rain!" He quickly rose to his feet, made his way to her side, and enveloped her in his arms. "Rain, Arm Bow is gone. He fell. There was nothing we could do to save him."

"No. No. It cannot be so. Not Arm Bow. Not my Arm Bow." She began to sob violently, her shrieks of woe piercing the very walls of the valley.

She struggled toward the edge, but Cloud Maker held her tightly. "I cannot let you go. I promised. I promised to watch after you."

Cloud Maker had led the party of warriors sent to recover Arm Bow's body. It had taken a long time for them to reach the badly broken body at the valley floor. It had taken even longer for them to bring the body back to the encampment.

Desert Rain had been taken to her tipi by her mother, Wind Song. Arm Bow's parents were from another clan, so runners were sent to inform them of the tragedy.

Though Dancing Waters had received her son again, safe and sound, her joy was bittersweet. She sat in front of her lodge, weeping, as she held Beaver Tail in her arms.

The encampment resounded with the wails of warriors and women alike. The sorrow was thick. The loss of a young warrior was almost unbearable to the entire clan.

The clan chief, Five Dreams, entered the sweat lodge with the elders. The holy men offered up their prayers for the spirit of their fallen brother. Chants rose and fell. The birds ceased their singing. The camp mourned.

Desert Rain barely felt the weariness of the long walk to the valley floor. She had followed the funeral bier as her husband's body was carried from the encampment to the place where he had fallen. She had requested that he be buried on the spot where he gave the last measure of loyalty to his people. She stood, watching, as the bier was lowered into the earth and covered with dirt and rocks.

The wailing of the mourners was almost more than she could stand. She felt her knees buckle, felt herself begin to fall. Suddenly there was someone there, holding her up, holding her tightly. She felt another's tears mix with her own. She looked up. "Cloud Maker. Oh, Cloud Maker. My Arm Bow is gone. He's gone."

Wind Song leaned against a willow backrest outside of her daughter's tipi. It was a beautiful morning, but she was not yet ready to enjoy its beauty. It had only been two days since her handsome son-in-law had met an untimely end. Her daughter, still mourning, refused to eat, refused to leave her tipi, refused to talk.

Wind Song knew her daughter's grief. It had only been five summers ago that her own husband, Sees the Way, had been trampled by buffalo while hunting. She too had thought her heart would burst with grief.

She had been married to Sees the Way for almost two years before she bore him a child. Their firstborn, Yellow Dog, was married now, living with his wife's clan along the Gila River. Their second child, Broken Branch, also a son, was as yet unmarried. He had been away tracking elk when Arm Bow fell. Their youngest child, their only daughter, Desert Rain, was now nineteen summers old, just a tender flower. But that tender flower suddenly had been plucked by the roots and dashed against the rocks of despair. She now lay grieving for the love of her life.

Wind Song remembered her daughter's whirlwind romance. The summer of love began for Desert Rain when they attended the gathering of the clans in the Chiricahua Mountains. It was a time of reunions and the making of new friends, a time when mothers visited their sons and their families. The old men traded stories and bragged of their exploits. The children played and competed in games of skill. The young warriors raced their ponies and wagered on the winners. Trading was welcomed by all and virtually anything could be bartered away. The women talked of the hardships of the long winter, the joy of spring, and their delight in their children. That had been two summers ago—a joyous time for them all.

Desert Rain had always been a shy child, never one to speak out of turn or get into much mischief, so it had been somewhat surprising when Wind Song observed her daughter walking with a young man. They had seemed completely oblivious to everyone around them as they wound their way through the encampment, talking, even laughing, together. What a handsome couple they had made. He was tall and slender in build, but the muscles in his arms and legs showed the strength of a warrior. His smile was warm, his demeanor charming, his gait determined, but Wind Song saw much more than that. This young man had something no one else had. He had the heart of her youngest child. Desert Rain was smitten.

"Mother, I've met a young man," her daughter had said to her that evening.

"So I see. He is very handsome."

"And brave, my mother. I was told that he faced a bear last summer and carries its claws in his medicine pouch."

"Oh, my. He *is* brave."

"Yes, he is. And handsome too."

The old woman had chuckled as her daughter plopped to the ground and let out a deep sigh. There was no mistaking young love.

Wind Song hadn't been surprised the next summer when the young warrior came to ask for her daughter's hand in marriage.

The dowry was set, but Arm Bow wouldn't settle for giving only two ponies. He promised twice that.

The winter had only just passed when Arm Bow entered the Jicarilla encampment and approached Wind Song's tipi. He led not four, but five ponies. The wedding was arranged and they were joined in marriage. That had been but two weeks ago, and now he was gone.

The midnight moon was high in the sky as it cast its shadow on the form of the young woman walking the high trail. Her gait was slow, her face veiled in sorrow. Desert Rain's feet shuffled forward, but she was not focused on her steps. There was something heavier on her mind. She had to talk to Arm Bow. She needed to see his face, feel his touch, hear his song. She walked on.

The night wind blew Desert Rain's hair across her forehead as she looked skyward. The stars shone, but they seemed dimmer somehow, the moon not as bright. She opened her mouth and let out the cry of the NightHawk.

Desert Rain lowered her head and the tears flowed again. She jumped when from the valley floor came the lonely howl of a coyote.

Sinking to her knees, she sobbed uncontrollably, hopelessly. After a while, she once again lifted her face to the midnight sky. "My husband, you always said that my skin was as soft as the desert rain and that that is why my father gave me that name. My husband, touch me now. I need to feel your touch. My husband, I want to hear your song. I need to hear your song."

It may have been her imagination, but it didn't matter to Desert Rain. When the wind blew gently across her face, she felt the caress of Arm Bow's loving hands. As the wind moved through the trees, she could hear his sweet voice, *You give the moon its light, you give the stars their shine. . . .* Yes, it was his voice. She listened and smiled for the first time since his fall. . . . *You are the song on the midnight wind.*

Chapter Five

"Rain! Desert Rain!"

Desert Rain opened her eyes at the sound of her name. She recognized Cloud Maker's voice immediately. Why was he calling her now? She looked around. The infant morning sun shone through the trees, illuminating the small patch of grass on which she lay. She smiled. It was the secret place she had shared with Arm Bow.

Her memory returned to her a little at a time. She had walked the high trail last night. She remembered giving the call of the NightHawk and hearing the answering call of the Trickster. Arm Bow had chased her to their secret place and they had made love all through the night. And now she lay naked on the grass of their secret place. Only, she was alone. Where had he gone? Suddenly, she remembered—Arm Bow had fallen. He was no more, and it had been merely a dream.

"Desert Rain, are you here?" Cloud Maker called again.

She rose quickly, grabbed her tunic, and began to dress. She couldn't let Cloud Maker find her here. Not here. No one must know of this secret place. It belonged only to her and Arm Bow. She wouldn't share it with anyone.

Tugging on her moccasins, she ran quickly into the trees and headed for the high trail.

"Desert Rain, where have you been?" Cloud Maker asked as the young woman stepped from the trees and onto the trail.

"Walking," she said quickly.

"Your mother is worried about you. She went to your tipi this morning and found you missing. Everyone is out looking for you."

"I just needed to walk. To think."

Cloud Maker approached her and placed a hand on her shoulder. "I understand, Rain, I have felt the same way since . . . since . . ."

"Well," Desert Rain interrupted, "I think we had better get back to the encampment. I don't want my mother to continue worrying about me."

"Yes. Let's return."

They turned and started down the trail.

The days were long, but the nights were even longer. Desert Rain found herself crying most of the time. Everything she saw reminded her of her loss.

Tradition dictated that all of Arm Bow's possessions be distributed to those he loved. When Wind Song came to the tipi to help her daughter with this difficult task, she found Desert Rain sitting in the center of the tipi, sobbing, rocking back and forth with grief.

One at a time, Wind Song collected Arm Bow's belongings. Desert Rain couldn't bring herself to help with the gathering and there was only one item she seemed interested in—her husband's bow.

"Mother, see that Cloud Maker receives the bow."

Wind Song picked up the bow and examined the fine weapon. It was made of bodark, the best of all woods for a bow. It was perfectly carved and beautifully painted with black and red designs. "It is very nice," she remarked, turning the bow over in her hands.

"Yes, it was made for my husband when he was very small. His father made it strong and sturdy. My husband told me that it required so much force to pull the bow that it took him years to build up the strength. When he managed the task, his father not only gave him the bow as a gift, but also bestowed upon him his name—Arm Bow."

Wind Song gasped. It was forbidden to speak the name of one who had passed on to the After World.

Desert Rain sensed her mother's discomfort at the mention of the name. "It's all right, Mother. He doesn't mind. I speak to him every night. He is still with me."

Wind Song's concern was evident. She silently gathered the rest of the items and left the tipi.

"I'm worried about your sister, my son."

Broken Branch shifted nervously on the floor of his mother's tipi. "I know that Desert Rain still grieves, *shima*, but it has only been a few days since her husband's death."

"It is not so much her grieving, my son. I fear for her mind. She speaks crazy words."

Broken Branch had always adored his little sister. They were closer in age than were he and his older brother Yellow Dog. As children, Broken Branch and Desert Rain had been practically inseparable. He could clearly see his mother's concern. "What words does she speak, my mother?"

"She talks of speaking to him constantly. She mentions his name often to me."

Broken Branch flinched at this information. Speaking the name of the deceased was strictly forbidden. The name died with the individual unless a descendant was called by the same name before the original name holder died. This was troubling.

"I shall talk to her. She will listen to me, I'm sure."

"I hope so, *ciye*. I hope so."

Broken Branch waited until the next day to visit his sister. He approached Desert Rain's tipi and shook the closed flap. "Hello, my sister."

He waited politely outside of the tent flap, respecting Desert Rain's privacy, but when she didn't answer, he shook the flap once again. "Hello, my sister. It is I, Broken Branch."

He waited. When no answer came, he pulled back the flap and peered inside. She wasn't there. He entered the tipi and looked around. There was hardly anything left inside. His heart sank. A chill ran up his spine. He darted back through the flap, running across the encampment, shouting *"Shima! Shima!"* He had a feeling his sister was not coming back.

Desert Rain was walking. She didn't know where she was going, she didn't know how long it would take to get there. She was just walking. The memories of the life she had spent with Arm Bow had become too grievous for her to bear. "I can't stay in this place!" she had whispered to herself in the night. She had packed a few things in a leather pouch and left. Now, she was walking.

In the moonlight she skirted a finger ridge and descended to the woodlands below. Once on the plains, she had turned north and walked till the morning broke.

She moved through the forest silently as the miles passed on. She had been taught, as a young child, to appreciate the Earth

Mother, *Terte*. Earth Mother was kind to her children, but must be respected. It was for that reason that *Terte* grew thorns and thistles that tore the skin and reminded one that she was not defenseless, nor unable to provide punishment for her children if they disobeyed her will. It was this punishment that Desert Rain sought. She must have deserved such punishment to have been afflicted with so much grief, she thought. The thorns tore her skin, ripping her tunic, as she moved among the mesquite trees. She never flinched.

Desert Rain stood on the edge of a large open field, lined on all sides by towering pines. She had not eaten in three days, yet she was not excessively hungry. However, thirst parched her throat. She needed water and her survival instinct was getting stronger.

She glanced around the meadow, lush with budding wild-flowers. A flicker above the trees caught her eye. Butterflies. Hundreds of them fluttered to the east. Where there were butterflies, there was water. She headed east.

She approached the small creek carefully. Water was needed by all kinds of animals, some of which were predators—mountain lions, snakes, bears, Comanches. She stood for a moment observing her surroundings. When at last she determined that it was safe, she moved to the water's edge.

Kneeling near the babbling brook, she dipped her hand into the cool water and brought the life-giving liquid to her lips. She dared not bend over and drink directly from the brook, for she must be constantly aware of everything around her. She couldn't chance a predator catching her unawares.

She drank handfuls of the clear water as she watched the rainbow trout leap in the spring. The day was waning and she knew she had to find shelter before nightfall. She stood and moved upstream.

★   ★   ★

"Geez, Clem, how far do we have to walk?"

"Shut up, Laird, we're almost there."

"Well, I hope it's worth the trip. My feet ain't gonna like walkin' all this way for nothin'. We shoulda just brung the horses."

"You idiot, you know we couldn'ta rode through that dense thicket to get to this creek. We'da had to take the long way around. It woulda taken us hours longer."

"Yeah, but I sure don't cotton to walkin'."

"Laird, you are one lazy son of a bitch, you know that?"

"I cain't help it, Clem. I was born that way." He laughed.

When they reached the creek, Laird could see the abundance of fish that populated the stream, but saw no sign of what he was really after. "So, where's the beaver?" he asked the tall man in buckskins.

Clem turned to face his small friend. "Don't worry, there's some around. Look at them wood chips."

Laird glanced in the direction Clem was pointing. On the ground near the creek was a patch of wood chips lying beside the pointed stump of a willow tree. Clem grinned. It was a sure sign of beaver.

They were getting ready to set traps along the edge of the water when Clem first spotted the small moccasin tracks. "Look. Injuns."

Laird nodded and knelt beside Clem. "Yeah, but that ain't no Injun buck's track. That's a squaw's print."

"You sure?"

"Yeah, I'm sure. Ain't no buck got a foot that small. And look at the trim at the toes. Yep, that sure is a squaw's moc."

Clem stood up. Cautiously he surveyed the area around the track. " 'Pears she's alone. I don't see no other tracks anywhere around."

Rising, Laird took a look around as well. "Yep. Don't see

hide nor hair of anyone else. What'cha think she's doin' out here alone?"

Clem smiled. "I don't know, but I know what she's gonna be doin'. Come on, let's get back to the camp and get our horses. We'll come back in the mornin' and track her. Might be fun." He pounded Laird on the back and laughed.

"Yeah, might be at that."

The two men disappeared into the trees.

Chapter Six

The trappers broke camp as the sun's light crested the nearby mountains. Clem saddled the horses while Laird loaded their meager belongings onto the lone pack mule.

"Make sure you tie them things down good, Laird. It's gonna be a rough ride. We can't take the same trail to the creek that we took last night. Too much mesquite brush to deal with. We'll have to take the long trail around."

Laird grunted. "I know that. I ain't stupid."

"I was just sayin'."

"Well, just make sure my cinch is tight. I don't want to go slippin' off on them rocks."

"You won't. Just mind what you're doin'."

It was noon when the two men reached the moccasin tracks they had discovered the evening before. They approached with caution, not knowing if more Indians might have passed this way in the night.

Laird searched the ground around the small tracks, finding no other sets of prints but their own. "Ain't nobody else been here," he said with a smile. "Looks like we got 'er all to ourselves."

"Think you can track 'er?" Clem asked.

"Don't see why not. I figure she'll stay near the water. I say we ride wide on this side of the creek, 'case she strays a might. She definitely won't be crossin', the other side's thick with mesquite bushes, it'd tear 'er to pieces."

"Yep. That's what I was thinkin'."

Turning to the left, away from the creek, the two men rode on.

Desert Rain had spent the night in a grove of willows near the creek's border. Though it was pleasant lying under the stars all night long, she slept fitfully. She woke often, thinking she heard Arm Bow calling her name. It wasn't their secret place, but it seemed he knew where to find her.

In the morning hours, she followed the stream, walking against the current. Something about the creek was comforting. It could have been the calming sound of the water rushing over the rocks, gurgling as it swirled between the larger stones. It could even have been the pleasing sight of the fish as they fanned their tails at the morning sunlight. Whatever it was, she felt at peace along its shores.

The afternoon sun beat down on her head and shoulders. She stopped often to drink at the edge of the stream, which seemed to grow wider as she traveled north along its banks. Though she still hadn't eaten, she felt no need for nourishment. She had heard that some of the Old Ones, when they felt that they had outlived their usefulness, when they knew they were nothing but a burden on their family during the winter months, would wander off into the snow to die. She had heard that they felt no hunger in their grief, that they were simply escorted into the After World by beings more wonderful than words could tell. Maybe that was her fate. She wondered what it would be like. It didn't matter though. If she could just see Arm Bow there, just feel his caress, hear his song, she'd be happy to stay in the After World forever.

She lay down beside the stream and closed her eyes. She slept.

"You are well, my sister?"

Desert Rain's eyes opened at the sound of the strange voice. She stared up into eyes so dark, so deep, so bright that she could see her own reflection.

He was a handsome man with the body of a warrior. There were streaks of gray in his black hair, which trailed down his back and blew freely in the breeze. His smile was warm and friendly. He was speaking the language of her people. She felt no fear.

"Yes, uncle," she replied, using the customary term of respect for an elder.

"You have traveled far."

"Yes, far. Where am I?"

"Do we ever truly know where we are?"

What a strange answer, she thought. "Who are you?" she asked cautiously.

"A friend. Only a friend. I have come to help you."

Desert Rain sat upright. "Help me? Are you going to take me to the After World?"

The man laughed. "No, my child. I am not."

"My husband. Did he send you?" The man's eyes were piercing. She awaited his reply anxiously.

The warrior glanced over his shoulder, downstream. "Yes," he said hurriedly. "He told me to tell you to go to the waterfall. It's just ahead of you. You will see it just beyond the bend. You will be safe there."

Desert Rain looked upstream. She could hear the faint sound of the waterfall, but saw no sign of it from where she sat. "I will," she said. When she turned back to face the strange man, he was gone.

She stood and looked up and down the bank of the fast-running stream. There was no sign of the warrior. He was gone. Had he ever really been there?

She began walking upstream.

Clem sat on his horse, just inside the tree line, his right hand holding the reins to the pack mule. Hearing a noise from the direction of the creek bed, he moved his mount forward a little to get a better look in that direction.

It wasn't long before Laird came into view. Clem relaxed, relieved it was his friend and not an Indian approaching.

"Well?" Clem asked impatiently.

"She's still following the creek. My guess is, we'll catch up with her real soon. Let's go."

Desert Rain stood on the edge of the mountain stream, watching the water cascade over the falls. The water fell like a curtain and beat relentlessly on the rocks below. Mist rose like steam and covered the vegetation on each side of the spring with a fine sheen. It was one of the most beautiful sights Desert Rain had ever seen.

She chose a large rock on which to sit as she watched the dazzling falls. Why had Arm Bow wanted her to come here, she wondered. What was she to do?

Removing her moccasins, she dangled her feet in the cool mountain stream. The water gently massaged her feet and she lost herself for a time in the comfort it provided. She closed her eyes.

Even the sound of the water falling against the rocks was soothing. She could only imagine what she would be doing if

Arm Bow were here with her. She smiled at the thought of them cavorting beneath the ribbon of water. She brought her hands up, crossed them in front of her, and touched her shoulders. Rubbing gently, she imagined Arm Bow's strong hands massaging her, touching her, loving her. Her hands moved down her own arms, then slowly across her breasts. "I love you, my husband."

Desert Rain opened her eyes and stepped down from the rocks and into the water. She slid her tunic up and over her head. Dropping it into the stream, she bent and pushed it beneath the surface of the water. She washed the garment as well as she could and then moved to the edge of the stream, hanging it on a small bush. Turning back toward the waterfall, she dove into the water.

She swam beneath the surface for a short distance, then broke once again into the late afternoon sun. Her body was adjusting to the coldness of the water and she swam toward the falls. Finding a large, flat rock, she lifted herself onto it.

Beneath the light curtain of water, things looked different. The trees blurred and the rocks took on new shapes. The water poured over her head and shoulders, splashed onto her breasts, her thighs. She stood up, the cold water raising bumps on the surface of her skin. "Touch me, my husband," she whispered.

She felt Arm Bow's hands caress her cheeks ever so gently. She lifted her face and felt his hands move down her neck, tickling the soft underside of her throat. She giggled at the thought. The feeling moved down onto her breasts, sampling the hardness of each nipple. She sighed. His lips were there, his tongue. She felt the passion of his touch. Warmth enveloped her stomach, moved down over her hips. She thrilled at the feeling that now stirred in her loins, gasped as it penetrated to her very core. The excitement was more than she could stand and she screamed in ecstasy.

She laughed then, remembering how her husband had covered her mouth in the tipi on their first night of love. She had looked up at him, eyes wide with fright, wondering what was wrong. He had been so embarrassed by her outburst. The memory of the startled look on his face still made her laugh out loud.

"I told you there was a waterfall." Laird said as the two men came within sight of the stream.

"I said I heard it, Laird. I ain't deef."

"Well, she may have climbed the rocks or somethin'. We need to get closer, I got a feelin' 'bout this."

"Yeah, I got a feelin' too and when we find her, she's gonna have a feelin' herself."

The men approached the waterfall cautiously. Suddenly Laird raised his hand, reining his horse to a halt. "What's that a hangin' on that bush?"

Clem squinted his eyes at the piece of cloth dangling from the small shrub. "Cain't make it out from here. Let's tie off the horses, creep up, and find out."

The two trappers dismounted, securing their horses and the pack mule. They began walking toward the edge of the falls.

She was the most beautiful woman Clem had ever seen. She stood beneath the falls, her body quivering in the cold water. Her breasts were perfectly round, her hips wide and inviting. He had to have her. He would have her.

"Now, that's worth trappin'." Laird whispered.

"Yeah. And I mean to trap it."

"That there's her dress hangin' on that bush."

"Let's go. I gotta get a closer look." Clem walked forward boldly.

As they reached the bush, Clem took the tunic in his hand. "Look here, Laird," he said loudly, "some little lady done went and lost her clothes."

Desert Rain jumped at the sound of Clem's voice. Through the falling water, she could make out the form of two men standing at the edge of the stream. One of them was a large man, the other smaller, thinner. The large man with the beard was holding her tunic in his hand and staring at her intently. They were white men. She'd never seen white men before, never heard their strange language. But one of them was talking loudly. She shuddered, but this time it was fear that coursed through her.

Chapter Seven

Laird glanced suspiciously at his large friend. "Why'd you yell like that? Now she's gonna run for sure."

Clem held the tunic over his head and twirled it like a lasso. "If she does, it won't be too hard to catch a nekkid squaw running through the mesquite trees. Them thorns'd tear her to pieces."

Laird looked across the mountain stream and noted that, even here, the opposite bank was bordered by a thick stand of mesquite brush. He smiled. "Yeah. But what if she climbs them rocks, gets on top of the falls?"

Clem lowered the tunic. "Now that's a thought." He wadded up the damp tunic, tossed it on the rock beside her moccasins, and drew his pistol. "I guess I'll just have to persuade 'er not to."

Laird stood on the bank as he watched Clem step out on a rock cresting the surface of the water. "You ain't goin' after her, are you?"

Clem surveyed the maze of rocks before him. His eyes traced a path, from stone to stone. He was sure they would take him to the boulder on which she stood. "Yep. I kin make it. She ain't gonna come to us, you know."

Desert Rain watched the clumsy man jump from rock to rock, almost falling twice. She glanced around her. She could easily swim to the far shoreline and be away from these dangerous-looking men, but the mesquite trees were thick along the bank. She knew she'd never make it through them. The cliffs were behind her. They were high, but there were plenty of hand and footholds. She turned and began to climb.

"No you don't, you mangy Injun!" Clem yelled. He raised his gun and fired.

Desert Rain flinched at the sound of the Colt's discharge. A rock above her head exploded and splinters of rock and dirt flew in her face. She began to fall, but had enough presence of mind to push herself away from the rocky face. She hit the water hard. Too hard.

Clem was moving faster now. Hopping from rock to rock, he reached the squaw. She was floating face down, not moving.

"Is she dead?" Laird yelled.

Water from the falls soaked the burly trapper as he pulled the girl's limp body from the water and hefted her up onto the rock. He noticed the rise and fall of her breasts. "Nah. She's fine. Nothin' a little lovin' cain't fix."

Laird watched Clem settle the still unmoving girl on his shoulder, and make his way carefully back to the shore.

Clem flung the girl onto the ground. The air rushed from her lungs in a quick burst. She groaned and rolled her head from side to side.

"Now what?" Laird asked.

Clem smiled. "Wha'd'ya think?" He began to remove his wet

53

shirt. "Go on now, I don't need no audience. You can have 'er when I'm done."

"Then what?"

Clem removed his wet shirt, wrung it out, and draped it over the bush that had held the girl's tunic. "You ain't exactly the brightest fella, are ya?" He looked back at the naked form lying on the ground. He unbuckled his belt. "If'n we're lucky, we'll get to use 'er for a month or so. Then we'll either kill 'er afore we go back to town or trade 'er to a Comanch for some beaver pelts."

Laird drew his hand across his rough beard. "Reckon you're right. Well, let me know when you're done. I sure would like to get some of that."

Clem's pants dropped around his ankles. "Yeah." He stepped out of his pants.

Laird turned and started walking back toward the horses. A whooshing sound caught his attention and he whirled in time to see Clem's knees buckle. "What the. . . ."

Clem had his pants in his hand. Wearing only his long johns, he stood facing the water. He was evidently just about to hang his pants on the bush beside his shirt, but something didn't seem right. He was swaying awkwardly. Laird ran toward him. "Clem?" Suddenly the big man dropped his pants on the ground and pitched forward into the stream. His body flipped face up on the water as it was picked up by the fast-moving current.

Laird stopped in his tracks. There was an arrow protruding from Clem's chest, and he wasn't moving. The angle of the arrow meant that it probably came from the top of the waterfall. Laird looked up at the rocks, then dove to the ground. An arrow barely missed his head. He had no time to look again. He rolled, gained his feet, and ran.

Laird was just about to the horses when another arrow whizzed over his head. He heard the mule squeal, then saw it drop to the ground. Only the fletching kept the arrow from going all the way through the animal's neck.

Laird circled Clem's mount, using it for cover from the unseen attacker. He untied his mount just as Clem's horse jumped in pain as an arrow struck its left flank. It bucked violently, trying to shake the arrow loose. Laird swung into his saddle and kicked his horse into a run. He headed away from the waterfall, lying low across the horse's neck.

Desert Rain blinked and tried to remember what had happened. She remembered the two men standing on the banks, the one coming after her. She remembered the rock exploding in front of her. But that was it. Had the men caught her? Had they killed her? Was this the After World?

It was certainly peaceful here, she thought. It was dark. She wondered if it was always dark in the After World, if the moon and stars were the only light in this place. No, that couldn't be. There was a glow off to her right. She turned her head. It was a fire.

She tried to sit up, but something was pressing against her. She moved her hands beneath the heavy garment and touched her sides. She was naked. Perhaps that is the way it is in the After World, she thought. At least the passing had not been painful.

"Arm Bow? Arm Bow, are you here?"

She heard no reply, but a familiar scent brushed her senses. It was the smell of a buffalo robe. She smiled as she felt the fur of the heavy robe that covered her. "Oh, Arm Bow," she sighed.

Gathering the robe around her, she stood up and walked toward the fire. It was warm and friendly. Someone had placed meat on a rock beside some of the embers, no doubt to keep it warm. She noticed the greenish husk of an ear of corn protruding from the ashes. She smiled. "Yes, I am hungry, my husband."

She placed the edge of the robe on the ground, sat on it, and wrapped the rest of it around her shoulders. "Join me, my husband. Join me."

The heat from the morning sun gently nudged her awake. She gave a soft moan and opened her eyes. There is sun here, she mused. She smiled, tossed the buffalo robe aside, and sat up. Her mood shifted as she recognized the stream in front of her, heard the waterfall in the distance. She wasn't in the After World after all. Feeling suddenly aware of her lack of clothing, she looked around frantically for her tunic. It was on a rock not far from her, dry and neatly folded beside her moccasins. She jumped to her feet.

She dressed quickly and slipped into the trees, afraid the men might return. She didn't know why they had left her or where they had gone, but she had to escape, had to get away.

She wound through dense thickets of pine trees, walking quietly, listening carefully. She couldn't be sure she was going in a good direction, but she had to keep moving. Still, she didn't feel as though they had hurt her. She took a little time to run her hands over her body. Her back hurt a little, but other than that there were no bruises or sore places that she could detect. She was sure they hadn't raped her, but why not? What had happened? She rubbed her head, hoping to stimulate her memory.

It was no use. She just couldn't remember what had happened after falling from the cliff. Nothing that is, until she had awakened beneath the buffalo robe, thinking she was in the After World.

As she moved on through a stand of poplars, she wondered about the night before. Had she ever been in the After World or was it just a vision? She remembered the robe, the fire, and the food. Arm Bow had come to her in the night, had made love to her beneath the heavy robe. Or had he? She didn't know what was real anymore. Maybe this is a vision and that was real, she thought. Do we ever truly know where we are?

The sound of a twig snapping startled her, jerking her out of her reverie. She froze in her tracks and slowly turned her head in the direction of the noise. She saw several large hickory trees. And beyond the trees, she saw a man.

She could see that he was picking up sticks, obviously gathering wood for a fire. He was bending over, his back to her. She couldn't see his face, but she recognized his clothing. It was the big man she had seen bounding over the rocks, screaming at her in the white man's tongue. He meant to hurt her. She turned and ran.

She didn't run far, didn't try to. She didn't know where the other man was and, fearful of running into him, she looked for a place to hide. A gap in some thick underbrush offered refuge and she slithered inside. She curled into a ball and peered between the thin branches, hoping to see which way the man would walk. As soon as she could determine which direction he was taking, she would know which way was safest for her. No doubt the other man was waiting at their camp. She strained her eyes for any sign of movement.

It wasn't long before she heard the brush scraping against the man's pants as he walked. She listened carefully, trying to determine his direction of travel. The sound grew louder. He was coming in her direction.

Had he heard her? Did he know where she was? Was she concealed well enough that he would not find her? There was no time to move, no more time to think. He stepped into view.

He was facing her now. She could see his face clearly. She placed her hand over her mouth to stifle her gasp of surprise.

Chapter Eight

Desert Rain stayed motionless beneath the brush. The man was moving toward her, but seemed not to notice her hiding place as he passed to her right. Her heart skipped a beat when she heard him speak. "Come, Little One, let us eat," he said in her language.

The invitation startled her. How had he known she was there? The thing that surprised her most, however, was the kindness in his voice.

She wriggled from her nest. Brushing debris from her tunic, she followed the man deeper into the forest.

Through the trees, Desert Rain could see an open field. The man had stopped in the field and was placing the sticks he had gathered beside a small fire. As she approached, she could see pottery of different sizes containing pieces of meat, ears of corn, and fruit. The man turned and smiled at her. "You are hungry, Little One?"

Desert Rain nodded. He was a fine specimen of an Apache warrior. She remembered his dark eyes, his long gray-streaked hair, his calm voice, but the clothes unnerved her—they were the clothes of the trapper who had attacked her.

The warrior seemed to perceive her uneasiness and began to unbutton the buckskin shirt. "Excuse me, my child, but these clothes are very uncomfortable."

Desert Rain watched as the warrior removed the shirt, revealing a broad, heavily muscled chest. His shoulders were wide, his arms thick. Though he was many years older than her, she couldn't help thinking that he was a very handsome man.

He unbuckled the belt and stepped out of the pants. He wore a traditional breechclout bearing a simple hand-painted design. His legs were equally muscled, thick, and powerful. He was indeed a warrior of experience, for his body showed the marks of many battles. Scars of various sizes and shapes decorated his arms, legs, chest, and back. They were the road maps of courage.

"Why were you wearing such clothing, uncle? They make much noise while walking."

The warrior smiled. "Yes, but how else would you have heard me?"

"I might have run away."

"You might have, but you did not." He turned and strategically placed more sticks on the fire. "As soon as I have a good bed of coals, we shall cook our meal. Make yourself comfortable. It will not be long."

Desert Rain looked about the small clearing. By the fire there were logs on which to sit, handmade utensils for eating and cooking, and on the far side of the clearing stood a small wikiup. The shelter was made of sticks and bark. Parts of it were covered by animal hides. She sat down on a log and waited.

*   *   *

She said nothing while he prepared the noon meal. He was the first to speak as he handed her a bowl filled with corn and a large piece of meat. "This is for you, Little One."

She took the bowl from him, but the aroma was foreign to her. "What is this, uncle?" she asked, pointing to the meat.

"Ah. You have never eaten mule meat before?"

Desert Rain shook her head.

"Well, you will like it. It is not as sweet as deer meat, but it is tender and very nourishing."

They ate in silence for a time, but finally Desert Rain could hold her questions back no longer. "Uncle, who are you? Why are you here?"

The warrior smiled. "Well, Little One, I am only a man. I have lived in these mountains for many years. I have seen many things, experienced many adventures. But I am no one, just a friend."

"Where did you come from? What clan do you belong to?"

"Ah. I am Chokonen."

"I know of them. They are lead by Cochise, a very brave warrior chief."

"Yes, Cochise was a very great chief. Two summers ago he was killed by the blue coats. His son Naiche now leads the people. I left at that time."

"Why are you not with your People? Why do you dwell alone?"

The warrior shifted restlessly as he hesitated to answer. "It is my place to be alone." Suddenly he stood and walked toward the woods.

Desert Rain watched the warrior disappear among the trees, his statement still ringing in her ears. She felt a tear slide down her cheek. Was she destined to the same fate?

*   *   *

60

Wind Song watched with sadness as Broken Branch and Cloud Maker walked toward her. Their demeanor told her that the news was not good.

"My mother," Broken Branch began.

"You have not found her?" Wind Song interrupted.

Broken Branch bowed his head, shame evident on his face. "No, *shima*, we have not found her."

"We tracked her for some distance," Cloud Maker added, "but she disappeared into the mountains. Her step is light. It would be almost impossible to track her over the rocks."

"I see," Wind Song said, standing to her feet. "What will you do now, my son?"

"I cannot rest, my mother. I must find her. I have only returned to gather supplies for what may be a long journey."

Wind Song looked to Cloud Maker. "I will go with him," he said. "I promised her husband that I would take care of her and I mean to keep that promise."

Wind Song stepped forward and embraced the young warrior. "You are a good friend. I know you will find her."

She embraced her son in turn. "My son, I know your love for your sister. You will not fail your own heart. Go with speed."

"I will, my mother."

Desert Rain gathered the cooking vessels from around the fire. The warrior had been right. The mule meat was very tasty—the least she could do to show her appreciation was to clean up a little.

She had just approached the wikiup, looking for water with which to clean the bowls, when she heard a noise behind her. She turned to see a large black bear lumber out of the woods. He sniffed the air and approached the fire. She realized that the few scraps of corn and fruit still lying by the fire had attracted him.

She remained motionless, not wanting to discourage his foraging. She knew that he would most likely eat the food and, if left unmolested, he would leave peacefully. She had no intention of interrupting his meal.

She watched the black bear as he ate. He seemed to enjoy himself immensely. He was sitting now and she couldn't help but imagine that he was smiling, smacking his lips with satisfaction. It was then she saw another movement and turned her head to see the warrior approaching through the trees.

She didn't want to startle their dinner guest by yelling a warning to the warrior, but she also didn't want him to be surprised or, worse yet, attacked by the bear. She opened her mouth to yell when suddenly the warrior ran forward.

"Yah! Yah!" the warrior yelled, waving his arms at the large beast. "Leave us! Leave us!"

The bear raised up on its haunches and stared down at the man. The Chokonen stood his ground, his eyes locked with the bear's. He wasn't backing down and Desert Rain watched as the face-off began.

It seemed like an eternity, but actually lasted only a few minutes. Eventually, the bear lowered himself to the ground, turned, and loped into the forest. The warrior turned toward her. "Are you all right, Little One?"

She nodded. "I'm fine." She looked back toward the woods, but saw no sign of the bear. "Are you a spirit?"

The warrior smiled and began walking toward her. "I am the Spirit Walker. I walk with the spirits of my ancestors. I speak to men and animals as one and fear neither."

"I am pleased to meet you, Spirit Walker. I am Desert Rain."

He stood before her now. "A name befitting your beauty."

She smiled, her head dipping in embarrassment.

"You will find a spring just behind the wikiup," Spirit Walker said, noticing the bowls in her hands.

Desert Rain turned and started around the small structure.

*　　*　　*

Midnight was approaching, and Desert Rain tossed restlessly on the buffalo robe Spirit Walker had supplied for her bed. The wikiup was not large, but it was comfortable enough for the two of them. It was obvious that the warrior was not used to having guests lodge with him, but he had made her feel very welcome, even cared for.

She glanced at the sleeping warrior. He truly was a fine specimen of a warrior. But it was not only his strong body that impressed her. It was his wisdom, his bravery, his wise eyes. She watched his chest rise and fall with the slow, steady breathing of sleep. Slowly she slipped out from under her covering. Silently she slipped out into the cool night air.

She walked out into the clearing, the night breeze caressing her skin like a familiar friend. She inhaled the clean night air deeply into her lungs and stretched. Her senses came awake and she smiled. Turning, she moved around the wikiup and walked down to the spring. It wasn't exactly the same as walking the high trail, but she felt at peace there. The water running over the rocks had always been a pleasant sound to her. She found a rock near the edge of the spring and sat down.

The night was beautiful and she tilted her head to the stars. "My husband, I know that you have sent a spirit to help me. I realize that my despair has brought you great sorrow. My heart could find no reason to go on. I felt my life had ended with yours. But now I realize just how much you love me. You have protected me, delivered me from harm. I know that nothing can harm me as long as you are looking down on me from the After World. I don't know what is real, neither do I care any longer. My husband, tell me what I should do. Tell me how to reach you. Show me your love."

She opened her mouth and gave the call of the NightHawk. The cry echoed through the trees. She lowered her head in despair when no answer came. She was far away from the high trail now. Maybe Arm Bow could not hear her. She stood, facing the spring, and sighed.

The sound came from behind her and she whirled to face the wikiup. It was the mournful wail of the Coyote and it had come from the small shelter. She stood in disbelief. Was Arm Bow inside or was it another vision?

Chapter Nine

Even through the thick walls of the hut, Desert Rain could hear the morning birds singing. She opened her eyes and tried to recall the night before. It had been a strange night. She had returned to the wikiup from the creek, halfway expecting to see Arm Bow waiting for her inside. But when she entered the small dwelling, he was not there. Spirit Walker had been sleeping soundly, so she had merely stretched out on her robe bed and closed her eyes. She had fallen asleep, Arm Bow's name on her lips.

"Uncle," Desert Rain said as they sat around the small fire eating their morning meal, "did you not hear the call of Coyote last night as you slept?"

Spirit Walker looked at the beautiful young woman. "That is not an uncommon thing in these woods. I hardly notice such things anymore."

Desert Rain shifted nervously. She had to know, but was not

sure she wanted to hear the answer. "My Spirit, I heard Coyote's call come from within the wikiup last night. Was it you?"

The warrior smiled at the name. She had called him "My Spirit," a term of possession. It indicated a relationship, a closeness she had not expressed before. "Why would I have done so, my child?"

Desert Rain dipped her head. "I have much to tell you, my Spirit. I have suffered many sorrows, my heart is very heavy."

Spirit Walker reached forward, placing his hand on her arm. "You may tell me what you wish. You can always trust the Spirit Walker."

Desert Rain looked up, saw the depth and warmth of compassion in his black eyes. He smiled. She began her story.

She had just finished explaining how fear had gripped her in the night just four days ago and compelled her to begin on a journey toward the After World, when a light rain began to fall. They hurriedly gathered their personal belongings together and moved into the wikiup for shelter.

Spirit Walker sat down on his robes and picked up a piece of black cloth. He examined the cloth for a moment, then reached over and retrieved a wooden bowl from beneath a pile of pelts. The bowl was filled with beads of different sizes and colors. Taking a needle and some small pieces of sinew, he began to sew a pattern of beads onto the cloth.

He watched Desert Rain as she moved around the wikiup, eyeing the odd items he had hanging on its walls.

"Your husband was good to you?" the warrior asked.

Desert Rain turned to face Spirit Walker as she spoke. "Oh, yes, he was very, very good to me. He used to sing to me on the high trail. Then, we would go to our secret place and . . ." her voice trailed off and her cheeks flushed at the memory she had almost voiced.

Spirit Walker smiled to himself, but did not look up. "I'm sure that he would not want you to seek the After World, my child. He still loves you very much and would not want anything to happen to you."

Tears welled up in Desert Rain's eyes. She knew he was right, but how could she possibly go on without her beloved husband? Who could ever take his place?

She turned back to the decorations on the wall, trying to take her mind off of her sorrow. "What's this?" she asked, pointing to a stained white sash. It hung on the tip of a lance at the back of the hut.

Spirit Walker glanced at the sash and shrugged. "Merely a token of a warrior I once knew."

She approached the curious item. "Is it blood that stains the sash?"

"Yes, the blood of many enemies, the badges of many wars," he said, continuing his sewing.

"The warrior must have been very brave."

"Yes, many have said as much."

Desert Rain turned back to the warrior. Was it pain she had heard in the man's voice? She looked for signs of it in his face, but saw only concentration on the task at hand. "Where is the warrior now?" she asked.

Spirit Walker raised his eyes to meet hers. "He is no more, my child. He is merely a shadow of the man he once was."

Desert Rain looked into the face of the seasoned warrior. It was there, she could see it now in the blackness of his eyes. There was pain, not unlike her own. She knew he was talking about himself.

It was raining in the mountains. Cloud Maker and Broken Branch sought shelter under some large boulders to wait out the downpour. There was no use trying to move through a heavy rain. The horses would slide on the wet rocks, endangering their mission.

"I don't think it will last long," Cloud Maker remarked.

"The clouds are moving quickly across the sky," Broken Branch agreed. "Let us rest while we can and save our strength."

"Yes." Cloud Maker sat down and leaned back against the rear of the natural shelter. "Where do you think Desert Rain is going?"

Broken Branch joined his friend on the ground, his face reflecting his mood. "I know not, my friend. I am concerned that she may wander far. She is in great distress."

"There is much land beyond these mountains. Much area for us to cover. It will not be easy to find her."

"That is so, but we must. We must find her before . . . before . . . someone else finds her."

Cloud Maker wondered at these words. "I feel that something troubles you. Something you have not told me."

Broken Branch hung his head. "Yes, Cloud Maker, there is one thing that worries my heart."

Cloud Maker placed his hand on his friend's shoulder. "Tell me this thing. I must know, that I may be of greater help to you."

Broken Branch looked to Cloud Maker. "There are stories. I have heard them from trackers in other clans. Stories of a man who walks the forests."

"A man? Only one man?"

"No, my brother, not just a man—a spirit."

Cloud Maker blinked his eyes in wonder. "A spirit that walks as a man?"

"Yes, a spirit that walks as a man."

"He is dangerous? What has been said about this spirit?"

"Not much is known about him, but it is said that he was a great warrior. He fought alongside Cochise in many battles. He wore a sash from his left shoulder to his right hip. The sash was white, but bore the blood of many enemies. He carried a lance, but never fought with it. I was told that he would enter the battle on foot. He would stride into the midst of the fight and plant the lance firmly in the ground. Then he would take the sash and bind himself to the lance. From that place he would fight."

"He would fight while bound?" Cloud Maker asked with surprise.

"Yes. He would fight until the enemy was vanquished or turned to run. Only then would he loose himself. Once, I was told, Cochise counted fifteen Comanche lying at the spirit's feet when the battle was done. The spirit's body was red with his own blood as well as that of his enemies, but he was still standing."

"How is it that a spirit bleeds as men do?"

"Oh, he was not a spirit then, he was a man like you and me."

"He must have had a name. What was he called?"

"In those days, they called him only the Walker."

"The Walker." Cloud Maker repeated the name, committing it to memory. "What happened to him? How did he become a spirit?"

Broken Branch stood and moved toward the opening of the overhang. "No one knows exactly. Only that he left the clan and became a hermit of sorts. I have heard that he was killed by Comanche for taking one of their women. I heard also that he was killed by the blue coats when he was found with a white woman. Last summer, I heard that he had simply become one with the Earth Mother and is free to roam at will, even passing back and forth to the After World."

Cloud Maker shook his head in wonder. The rain began to slacken and he rose to his feet. He moved up beside Broken Branch and peered out onto the plains below the mountains.

Broken Branch was staring out onto the plains, squinting his eyes to sharpen his vision. Suddenly he pointed. "There is a rider!"

Cloud Maker followed his friend's gaze. He saw it too, a lone rider out on the plains. Not much detail could be seen except that the rider was wearing buckskins and seemed to be in a hurry. "I see him. Maybe he has seen your sister."

Broken Branch nodded. "Let us ride. We must know."

A light drizzle of rain, and wet rocks beneath their feet, hindered their descent down the mountainside, but eventually they reached the plains below.

"The tracks are deep, they will be easy to follow," Cloud Maker observed.

"Yes, but he has gained much ground. He will be far ahead of us."

Cloud Maker glanced in the direction the rider had taken. "He is heading toward the white man's fort. I don't know that it would be wise to follow him."

Broken Branch had to agree. It would be a dangerous thing to do. The blue coats might misinterpret the actions of two Indians chasing a white man across the plains. The perimeter guards might think their actions hostile and attack, especially since the Apache chief they called Geronimo was actively on the warpath. He said as much to Cloud Maker.

The two men sat in silence for a while, weighing their options. Finally Broken Branch spoke. "I wonder at his haste. Why would he ride so quickly to the blue coats?"

"Perhaps someone was chasing him?"

"But I see no riders in pursuit," Broken Branch countered.

Cloud Maker looked over the rider's back trail. "Can the spirit of the Walker be seen?"

Broken Branch felt a chill climb his spine as he too looked back over the trail. "I think we shall have to backtrack to find out."

Cloud Maker nodded and the two men turned their horses back along the trail.

Chapter Ten

The afternoon found Cloud Maker and Broken Branch following the back trail of the unknown rider. The sky was overcast, though the rains had passed. Some of the tracks were difficult to see, having been eroded by the rains, but luckily the mud was still soft enough to maintain a few of the prints.

"He came from the creek bed ahead," Cloud Maker noted.

Broken Branch nodded as he also caught sight of the creek bed crossing the open prairie. "We will no doubt find his camp soon."

As far as they could determine, the rider's camp consisted of only a small fire. The two Indians dismounted and Cloud Maker began to examine the ashes. There were no small pieces of charred meat or bones among the remains of the fire. "He cooked nothing on this fire, my brother," he concluded a short time later.

Broken Branch was circling, looking for any further sign of

visitors to the camp. "It seems that the rider was concerned only with having light in the darkness."

Cloud Maker turned to face his friend. "What have you found?"

Broken Branch pointed to the ground, just inside the tree line. "He slept here and obviously covered himself with brush. There is an impression where he lay and loose brush all around. He was no doubt trying to stay out of the fire's light, not wishing to be seen, but wishing to see anyone approaching."

Cloud Maker nodded. "He was fearful for his life. We must continue trailing him. It did not begin here."

They reached the creek bed and found that the rider's back trail turned to their left and paralleled the flowing stream. They rode in silence, eyes scanning the ground, the creek, the trees, for any signs that would indicate the apparent danger the rider had felt.

The afternoon wore on, the sun hot overhead. They stopped often to drink from the clear stream and were filling their waterskins when Cloud Maker spotted something unusual on the far side of the creek. In a tangle of driftwood a piece of pinkish cloth could be seen. He quickly pointed it out to Broken Branch.

The two men moved around to get a clearer view of the object on the other bank. The wind shifted in their direction and they caught the unmistakable smell of death.

Broken Branch climbed onto a boulder to get a better view. "It is a man," he stated. "A white man. There is an arrow in his chest."

"An arrow?" Cloud Maker asked in wonder. He knew of none of the People who were currently on the warpath against the whites in this area. "Is it Comanche?"

Broken Branch squinted his eyes, carefully looking over the fletching and shaft. "I'm afraid not, my brother."

"Whose then?"

Broken Branch stepped from the rock and looked solemnly at his friend. "Chokonen."

"The clan of Cochise," Cloud Maker said quietly.

"And the clan of the Spirit That Walks as a Man," Broken Branch added.

The two friends stood staring upriver. As far as they could tell, there were still no other tracks except those of the lone rider. After a while they turned and swung onto the backs of their horses.

Cloud Maker took a look back over their own back trail, a habit that he had found beneficial in the past. Sometimes while tracking elk, the animals would watch from concealment while the Indians passed by, then they would wander into view and graze. But what he saw this time was no elk. A rider was coming on hard. "Broken Branch, look behind us."

Broken Branch turned to see the man riding toward them. The rider was still some distance away, but it would not take him long to catch up with them. "Into the trees, Cloud Maker. We'll set up a defense there."

The two rode into the trees in search of a place to make a stand.

They had selected an area filled with downed cedar trees. The trees, toppled by storms some time in the past, lay in twisted heaps on the ground. They secured the horses behind some standing trees and crept into the midst of the tangle of tree branches and trunks.

Broken Branch was sure that no rider would ever see them before they were able to fire two or three volleys of arrows. He pulled his bow and smiled when he noticed that Cloud Maker held the bow he had received from Arm Bow's possessions. They knelt in ambush, breathing lightly.

It wasn't long before the rider came into sight, moving through the trees. It was an Apache pony, there was no mistaking the markings, but something else about it was familiar. They watched from the cover of the cedars as the pony stepped lightly around the trees, the rider following their tracks carefully.

Suddenly the rider reined his horse to a stop and sat still. Though Broken Branch could see the horse clearly, low-hanging branches obscured his view of the rider. The pony's ears twitched and the animal looked directly into Broken Branch's eyes.

Broken Branch raised his bow and took careful aim.

"Broken Branch! Broken Branch, my brother!"

Broken Branch's fingers froze on the bow string at the rider's shout. "Black Beaver? Is that you?"

The rider urged his horse forward and stopped once again. Sitting proudly on the pony's back was Black Beaver, his long black hair covering his broad shoulders. "Yes, my brother, it is I."

Cloud Maker smiled at Broken Branch in relief. They stood as one and climbed out of the timber.

Black Beaver slid from his pony and approached his two friends. They exchanged greetings.

"I could not let you ride on without me," Black Beaver began. "I felt you might need two trackers to find your sister."

"I appreciate you wanting to help." Broken Branch acknowledged.

Black Beaver nodded. "You know that I owe a debt of gratitude to Desert Rain's husband for saving my only son. The least I could do is to help find his wife and ensure her safety."

Broken Branch placed his hand on Black Beaver's shoulder. "Thank you, my brother. Your skills are welcome."

The three warriors sat among the fallen trees, discussing what they should do. Broken Branch told Black Beaver all they had discovered. When Broken Branch told of his concern about the Spirit, Black Beaver had something to add. "This Spirit that walks as a man has been seen of late, my brother."

"Where?" Broken Branch asked with interest.

"Just north of the mountains, about two day's ride, along the Crooked Water."

"Tell us of this," Cloud Maker prodded.

Black Beaver cleared his throat as if the story had stuck there for a moment. "A small band of Mescalero were tracking game along the river. They found the tracks of a mountain lion near the bank. Making sure to keep track of the mountain lion's prints, so as not to be surprised, they soon noticed that the tracks disappeared."

"Disappeared? How is that possible?" Broken Branch asked.

"There was evidence that the cat had fallen over on the ground. Moccasin tracks were detected approaching the place where the cat had fallen. The tracks deepened and moved away from the site."

"So, someone had killed the cat, picked it up, and carried it away," Broken Branch concluded.

"True," Black Beaver agreed, "yet there was no blood. They continued to follow the man's tracks, in an attempt to discover who he was."

Cloud Maker shifted nervously. He remembered times around the campfire as a child when other boys would tell mysterious stories. The feeling he felt then was not unlike what he was feeling now. "Who was he?"

"They finally caught sight of the mountain lion moving through the brush, except the cat was not moving on his own, he was being carried by a man. The man had long gray-black hair and carried the beast across his shoulders. He was dressed only in a breechclout. But the amazing thing was that the man carried no weapons, nothing with which he could have killed the cat."

"Nothing?" Broken Branch asked in amazement.

"Nothing," Black Beaver repeated.

"How had he killed the cat, then?" Cloud Maker asked.

"They could never determine," Black Beaver answered.

"Perhaps the cat was shot by another," Broken Branch suggested.

"Perhaps, but where was the blood? When the warriors attempted to approach the man, he disappeared into the brush. No further sign of him could be found."

Broken Branch could appreciate the difficulty of such an action. To disappear without trace while carrying a heavy object was indeed remarkable. "Did they not find the cat lying on the ground somewhere?"

"No. There was no trace of the cat or the man. It could only have been the Spirit That Walks as a Man."

The evening was still young when Broken Branch suggested that they make camp for the night. The other two agreed that it would be best to rest a while before continuing. The thought of meeting the Spirit weighed heavily on them all.

Before the fading light had turned the forest into shades of gray, they crawled into their hide bedrolls and tried to sleep. They would need their strength should they enter into battle with the Spirit, Broken Branch mused, though he had no idea what might be required of them.

Desert Rain had spent the day exploring her new home. She followed the creek a little ways in both directions and even found a shortcut to the waterfall.

Spirit Walker spent the morning in the wikiup tinkering with a bead design on the black cloth. It seemed to be important to him, so Desert Rain had left him alone as she set out to get to know her surroundings.

She arrived back at Spirit Walker's clearing just as night was falling. The old warrior was sitting near a small fire. Desert Rain could smell mule meat roasting on the flames.

"Where did you get so much mule meat out here?" she asked as she stepped from the shadows of the trees.

"From the men who tried to take you at the waterfall."

Desert Rain looked at the warrior, feeling somewhat confused by the statement. "You were at the waterfall when those men came after me?"

"Oh, yes, my child. Why do you think I told you to go to the waterfall in the first place?"

"You said that Arm Bow told you to tell me that," she protested.

Spirit Walker picked up a stick and stirred the coals around the fire. "Your husband is indeed watching over you, my child, but it is up to the living to look after the living."

Desert Rain sat on a log and stared wistfully into the fire. "Will Arm Bow never make love to me again?"

She felt Spirit Walker's eyes upon her as he spoke. "Your husband has gone, but he has not forsaken you. He makes love to you with the wind that caresses your cheeks, the stars that light your eyes. But he realizes that a young maiden needs more. She needs a living, breathing lover. Life nurtures life."

As she stared into the flames, watching the tongues of light lick the darkness, her mind wandered back to the campfire just ten days ago. The drum beat, the braves danced, and Arm Bow held her close beneath the buffalo robe, only this time it was all in her mind.

Chapter Eleven

Desert Rain thought the mule meat tasted especially sweet, but maybe it was just that her palate was getting used to this new food. She ate in silence, watching Spirit Walker's graceful movements around the fire. She hadn't asked, but she figured he was probably more than forty summers old. The gray in his hair and the wrinkles on his brow and around his eyes told her so. Though these features marked the years, they indicated far more than that. They were points of interest, like those carefully sketched on a deerskin map. The lines that furrowed his brow were put there by many years of concern and toil—many summers spent squinting under a hot sun, seeking game, reading sign, fighting enemies. The lines radiating from his eyes not only showed his fierce concentration, but also the laughter of many years. She could tell that there was a time when he had been very happy. She wondered about the woman who had made him so, for surely there must have been one.

She placed her empty bowl on the ground beside her feet and shifted on the log. She didn't want to pry, but she had to know. "Uncle, what was her name?"

The question took Spirit Walker by surprise. He looked up. Desert Rain was watching him, her dark eyes filled with curiosity. "Who, my child?"

Her cheeks flushed, but she had to continue now. "The woman . . . your woman. What was her name?"

Spirit Walker turned back and placed another log on the fire. "Does it yet show?"

"Yes, very much. I sense there was a time when you were not so alone."

"Yes, my child, this is so. But that was very long ago."

"What was her name?" she persisted.

"Her name was Follows The Sun."

"That's a pretty name. She was very special to you?"

"That she was. There was a time she was my whole world."

Desert Rain could hear the sorrow in his voice as he spoke. "I'm sorry, uncle, if it pains you to talk of her, I'll ask you nothing further."

Spirit Walker walked over and sat down beside her. "She was not unlike you, my child." He stroked her hair gently as he spoke. "Her hair caught the moonlight, her eyes caused the stars to flicker with joy. Her voice gave wings to the wind. The leaves danced before her every movement."

Desert Rain closed her eyes. She sighed as Spirit Walker's hands ran through her hair. She was listening to his words, but it was Arm Bow's beautiful voice she was hearing. "Was she your song on the midnight wind?" she asked.

Spirit Walker's hand softly touched the side of her cheek. "Yes, my child, she was my song on the midnight wind."

Desert Rain nuzzled against the warrior's tender touch. His hands were gentle, yet strong, his voice rough, yet sweet. She placed her head on his shoulder, felt his powerful arms enfold her. She sighed, deeply, sensuously.

She felt a stirring in her loins as his lips brushed her forehead. Tilting her face toward his, she found his lips with her own. As their mouths met, the passion surged through her like lightning among the clouds. She kissed him hungrily, deeply.

She was so sweet to the taste. Spirit Walker felt a fire that he not felt for many summers. He felt her hand move across his cheek, down his throat, and lightly stroke his chest.

When their lips parted, he chanced to speak. "My child . . ."

Desert Rain quickly placed a finger to his lips. "Please, my Spirit, I am no child."

He hesitated, looking deeply into her dark eyes. "That is truth, my sweet Flower. You are no child."

Once again she pressed her lips to his, once again she felt her passion stir. She hadn't felt that way since Arm Bow had last made love to her. It was that thought that made her pull away suddenly. "I can't, my Spirit. I'm sorry, but I can't."

She looked up into his coal black eyes. There was passion there, but beyond that, there was understanding.

"I know, my Flower," he whispered, "I know." The old warrior stood up and extended his right hand. "Walk with me, my Flower. I shall tell you a story of long ago."

"Oh, would you?" she said. Taking his hand, she leapt to her feet. "My Spirit, would you tell me a story of the warrior who wore the sash?"

"Yes, if you would like."

"I would like that very much."

As they began to walk toward the creek, Desert Rain gripped his arm tightly. He walked tall, head high, and smiled.

"Was he a brave warrior?" she asked as they walked in the darkness along the creek's bank.

"Some say he was one of the bravest," he replied.

"And he was Apache?"

"Ah, yes, a pure-blood Apache. But one of the things he enjoyed most was to travel. He visited many other Nations, learned many other languages."

"Did he ride far?"

"He rode far, yes, but he preferred to walk farther."

"Walk? Didn't he have a horse?"

"Yes, my Flower, but there are some places a man cannot go on horseback. He walked the roughest terrain and found it necessary to hide among the rocks when pursued. He learned to hide quickly, often disappearing without a trace, right in front of his enemies."

"Like a spirit?" she asked excitedly.

"Oh, yes, just like a spirit."

"How did he come to wear the sash?"

"Well, the sash was a gift from a Kiowa warrior named Sitting Bear. Sitting Bear was one of the Ten Bravest among his people. The Ten Bravest all wore the sashes and carried the lances. In battle, they would strike the lance into the ground and lash themselves to it with the sash. The only way one of them could be released from his position was if the enemy fled in retreat or were all dead, or if one of the other of the Ten released him."

"But if the Ten were all bound, how could one release another?"

"When one of the Ten was required to release one of the others, it was usually for burial."

Desert Rain was silent for a while as they walked. The courage of such men reminded her of her husband. She was sure he would have been as brave. "If the warrior was not Kiowa, why did Sitting Bear give him the sash?" she asked at last.

"That is a good story, my Flower. Once the warrior was traveling along the Salt River with two of the Ten—Sitting Bear and White Bear. The Earth Mother was covered in a blanket of snow at that time. They rode along the river heading north, and just before sundown they happened upon a camp of about twenty blue coats. They kept a safe distance, but could hear merriment among the white men. The Kiowa could not understand what was being said, so the Walker decided to sneak closer."

"The Walker?"

"Yes, that is what the warrior was called in those days. He waited till the shadows of night would hide his presence, then approached the blue coats' camp. It was a dark night, from which the moon refused its light. The blue coats never knew he was there. He could see the soldiers dancing around their fire, mocking the People. Some of them danced with scalps on long poles. It was obvious that they had come from a great slaughter."

Desert Rain was speechless. She had heard of such things before. She remembered the story of how this ritual came about. Many years ago, the Mexican government had hunted her people for their scalps. The scalp of a warrior, fourteen years or older, would bring the taker one hundred pesos; a woman's, fifty; and a child's, twenty-five. Her people began to take scalps in return. None of her people kept the scalps for more than a day or so, because they were considered unclean and could not remain in the camp.

"When the Walker returned to his brothers," the warrior continued, "he told them everything he had seen and heard. The blue coats had raided a Cheyenne camp along the Washita River, killing everyone in the camp. They were making fun of the chief because he had been flying the white man's flag above his tipi, thinking that that would protect his camp from attack. After the attack, the main body of blue coats had gone north, but this group was heading southwest toward Fort Sill for supplies.

"Sitting Bear had heard that a band of the southern Cheyenne, led by Chief Black Kettle, had tried to make peace with the white eyes at Fort Sill. He was sure it was this band that was massacred. This made Sitting Bear very angry and he began to put on his war face.

"White Bear reasoned that they should wait until morning to fight the blue coats, as it would be a disgrace for their spirits to wander in darkness should one of the Ten be killed. The three decided to attack at sunrise. It was also agreed upon that they would use only war clubs and spears—the traditional weapons of their ancestors. They believed these weapons held strong magic over that of the blue coats.

"They lay hidden in the trees until daybreak, protected against the cold only by their fur robes. At first light, the three warriors crept forward and, using their spears, killed the two guards. Three other soldiers were killed with clubs as they slept. The camp was awakened and soon the blue coats were pulling their guns and firing. The warriors moved quickly around the group of blue coats, swinging their clubs, running from soldier to soldier. A couple of the blue coats were shot by their own men, so they stopped firing and tried to use their swords.

"There was a time, long ago, when our people first fought with them that the blue coats used their swords with skill. But when the white man began using the Iron That Shoots Fire, they lost their ability to fight hand to hand. Though our brothers were wounded and bleeding, they prevailed in the battle.

"Before turning to their medicine bags, they used the soldiers' swords to dismember the bodies. This was so that in the After World, they could not continue to fight the People. The bodies were then burned so that no trace of the battle could be found by the white man. The equipment was burned as well, but the horses were herded together.

"The horses were taken to a nearby Kiowa-Apache camp and traded for supplies. When they reached Sitting Bear's people, the Walker was presented with a sash in honor of his bravery. He wore the sash from that time forward."

Desert Rain had listened intently as they walked and was only now noticing her weariness. She stopped near a large boulder, overlooking the creek, and climbed up to sit on its top. "How did you come to possess this valuable prize?" she asked as she swung her legs over the edge of the large stone.

Spirit Walker climbed onto the rocks between her and the creek and looked up at her. "Well," he said, "when the Walker became too old to fight, he gave it to me for safekeeping."

Desert Rain reached down and softly touched the warrior's cheek. "I do not think he is too old, my Spirit."

The warrior's eyes had just begun to close at the delicate caress when something moved to his right. With lightning speed, he turned and reached toward the movement with both hands. His fingers curled around the throat of a mountain lion.

Desert Rain screamed when she realized the fate that had almost been hers. Spirit Walker had caught the lion in midair as it leapt toward her, teeth bared. She watched in horror as the big cat brought its hind legs up and began to rake its deadly claws along Spirit Walker's strong arms. The warrior held a death grip on the cat's throat as blood poured from his forearms with each strike of the cat's claws. Spirit Walker gave a blood-curdling cry, then propelled himself and the cat backward into the mountain stream.

Desert Rain jumped from the rock but jerked back in fright when she spotted the rattlesnake. In the dim midnight moon she could just see that the snake was partially eaten. Obviously, the mountain lion had been eating the snake when she had hopped up on the rock and disturbed its meal.

She could hear Spirit Walker thrashing in the water with the big cat but could not see them in the stream. Figuring that the current would take them downriver, she walked along the bank calling the warrior's name.

She was sobbing when the thrashing stopped. "My Spirit!" she cried. "My Spirit, where are you?"

Her heart sank when the cat leaped from the water and landed on the rocks in front of her. She started to run, but stopped when she realized that the cat was laying sprawled on the rock, lifeless.

Then, she saw Spirit Walker's bloody arms reach from the water and grab a large stone. She rushed to help the wounded warrior, but his arms were too slick with blood. He climbed from the water and collapsed on the bank.

Chapter Twelve

The sun was just peeking through the trees when Cloud Maker opened his eyes. He nudged the still-sleeping Broken Branch and looked around for Black Beaver.

Black Beaver was hunched next to a fire and smiled over his shoulder as he heard the two men stir. "Good morning, my brothers," he called. "You are in time to have squirrel for breakfast."

Cloud Maker and Broken Branch rose and moved to the fire. Broken Branch sat down, wiped sleep from his eyes, and examined the meat roasting over the small fire. "You have put your bow to good use already this morning, Black Beaver."

The older tracker smiled. "No, my little brother, I could not chance losing an arrow just to fill your scrawny stomach. I used a rock instead."

Cloud Maker laughed out loud. The thought of an Apache warrior chasing a squirrel with a rock was indeed a funny image.

Broken Branch seemed lost in thought and his friends looked at him wonderingly.

"What is it, Broken Branch?" Cloud Maker asked.

"It just occurred to me how the Spirit That Walks as a Man could have killed a mountain lion without spilling its blood."

"You mean, he could have hit it with a rock?" Black Beaver asked with surprise.

"You killed a squirrel in such a way," Broken Branch countered.

"Yes, but the rock merely stunned it out of the tree. Once it fell, I grabbed it by the tail and hit its head against a tree."

"Could the Spirit not have stunned the cat with a rock, then approached the animal and killed it in another way?"

"There was no blood at the site," Black Beaver reminded him.

"I suppose he strangled it with his bare hands," Cloud Maker said in jest.

"It would take tremendous strength to choke a mountain lion to death," Black Beaver remarked.

"I guess you are right. I don't know why the thought came to me," Broken Branch said. He pulled a piece of meat from the cooked squirrel and began to eat.

After the meal, the three men broke camp. They made their way back to the mountain stream and resumed backtracking the unknown rider.

"Broken Branch, what makes you think that following these tracks will assist us in finding Desert Rain?" Black Beaver asked.

"I cannot be sure. But something had the man running for the blue coats' fort. If it was some of the People, they may be able to help. If it was danger, then it presents danger also to my sister."

They rode on. A few hundred yards upriver they picked up the trail of three horses coming out of the woods. Black Beaver dismounted and examined the tracks closely. After a while he turned back to his friends. "Two horses, both bearing riders. The second rider leads a pack mule."

"Are you sure it's a mule?" Broken Branch asked.

"Yes. The tracks are wide and it follows the second horse exactly."

"Trappers. White trappers," Cloud Maker suggested.

Broken Branch dismounted and approached the second horse's tracks. He knelt beside the tracks for a closer look. "These are the tracks of our unknown rider," he said, standing to his feet once again. "There is a break in the left rear hoof. They are the same tracks."

"So, two riders, one leading a mule, come to the water and turn upstream. Later, the second man flees downstream." Black Beaver concluded.

"The other one must be the man we found floating in the water," Cloud Maker said.

"Yes," Broken Branch agreed, "killed by an Apache arrow."

"A Chokonen arrow," Cloud Maker corrected.

"Yes, Chokonen." Broken Branch turned and swung onto his mount.

The three men paralleled the creek and it was just after noon when they came to another confusing set of tracks. Black Beaver dismounted to examine the find. Broken Branch stepped his horse closer to the trees and dismounted as well. Cloud Maker also slid from his horse to stretch his legs.

"Someone came from the tree line," Broken Branch said, pointing to a couple of small impressions in the ground. "They were on foot, but the tracks were not deep enough to hold up under heavy rains."

"Someone light, then," Cloud Maker noted.

"Here is a moccasin track." Black Beaver stood pointing to a small footprint near the creek.

Broken Branch moved over to examine the track. It was eroded by rain, but just visible enough to make out the entire outline.

"It's small enough to be your sister," Back Beaver acknowledged.

Broken Branch nodded. "Yes, it is. I cannot be sure, but we must find whoever made this track."

Black Beaver moved along the bank cautiously and surveyed the ground with a careful eye. "She too moved upriver, my brothers. Let us continue."

The three Apache warriors mounted once again and resumed their trek upstream.

The three men rode carefully, checking the ground often in case the smaller tracks wandered away from the creek bed. It was nearing dusk when Cloud Maker made another discovery. "Buzzards!" he cried, pointing above the trees to their left.

"Stay here and watch for enemies," Black Beaver said as he stepped from his horse. "When I return, I will tell you what I have found." He disappeared into the brush.

Broken Branch sat on his horse nervously. He couldn't bear to think that his beloved little sister might be lying dead among the weeds, but he couldn't shake the image. He shifted uneasily on his pony, taking in any and all movement around him.

After what seemed like hours, but was actually only minutes, Black Beaver reappeared from the trees. "It is one of the horses and the mule," he said.

Broken Branch breathed a sigh of relief. It was not Desert Rain. She might yet be alive. "How were they killed?" he asked.

Black Beaver raised his right hand. "Each one was shot once through the neck with one of these." There was no mistaking the Chokonen arrow he held in his hand.

"The Chokonen," Cloud Maker stated flatly.

"And he is a deadly shot," Black Beaver added. "The animals were not killed here. They were cut into pieces and placed under some brush."

"He did not want them found easily," Broken Branch noted.

"It is true, he did not," Black Beaver continued. "He also cut pieces of meat from the mule."

"He must have a camp close by," Cloud Maker said. An uneasy feeling crept down his spine and he shifted uncomfortably.

Broken Branch turned his head upstream. "I hear the sounds of a waterfall ahead. Let us move closer and see what we can see from the top of the falls."

The others agreed. The three of them mounted and once again moved on.

It did not take an experienced tracker to spot the small fire. The three men dismounted once again and surveyed the area. Cloud Maker noted that someone had eaten at the fire. There were small pieces of bone and corn husks in the ashes. Broken Branch noted the place where someone, wrapped in a robe, had slept, and Black Beaver found where the mule and horse had originally been killed. When they came together again, they shared what they each had found.

"This is the place where the trappers' problems began," Black Beaver suggested.

"Yes, from here, one of them made his retreat and the other died," Broken Branch agreed. He moved closer to the water's edge and knelt before a huge boulder. "Here!" he cried.

The other two rushed to his side. He was pointing to a well-defined track. It was small, dainty, and definitely a moccasin. "That is my sister's print."

"How can you be sure?" Cloud Maker asked.

"Since my sister was a small child, she has always walked on the outside of her feet." He pointed to the outer edge of the footprint. "This line was made by the beaded edge of the moccasin. It is my mother's design, I am sure of it."

Broken Branch stood and the three men swept the area with their eyes. "She must be close," he said. "I can feel her spirit."

"And so is the Chokonen," Cloud Maker whispered.

Chapter Thirteen

Desert Rain moved through the woods carefully. She had spent the day before caring for Spirit Walker's badly wounded arms. She made do with what she had available, but it was not enough. Neither of them had eaten yesterday, so she also needed to gather some food. In the early morning light, she had collected quite a few berries in a cloth. She was now moving toward the waterfall. She remembered seeing some yarrow near the falls. The root of that plant could be chewed to relieve fevers and headaches. Though Spirit Walker was resting quietly in the wikiup, he often groaned in pain. She would also make a poultice from the mashed roots. Applying the mixture to the wound itself would bring a cooling sensation, purify the blood, and keep out infections. She had to find a way to soothe his agony and this looked like her best hope.

She was nearing the falls when she thought she heard the stamp of a horse. She froze in place, knowing that movement would give her away.

Suddenly, she was jumped from behind. Her attacker's momentum forced her to the ground. She tried to scream, but a hand covered her mouth, while her assailant's other arm circled her shoulders and chest. She struggled, but the grip was too strong.

"Do not cry out, my sister," the attacker whispered.

Desert Rain's eyes widened at the sound of her brother's voice. She shook her head in response to his request.

Broken Branch released his grip, but held her on the ground. "Are you all right?" he asked.

"Yes. How did you find me?"

Broken Branch smiled. "I am a tracker, little sister. You knew I would come."

Desert Rain had to admit that she did know. But she was still surprised at her brother's skills.

"You are in danger here, my sister, we must take you home."

"No," she protested, "I must stay. I am needed."

Broken Branch rolled over and sat up. "Needed? By whom?" he asked, looking about him.

Desert Rain sat up. She reached for the cloth full of berries she had dropped. "My Spirit is wounded. He is in need of healing."

Broken Branch looked at his sister with pity. His mother had been right to worry about Desert Rain's mind, he thought. The strain of losing Arm Bow had caused her to see visions. She now thought of his spirit as a natural man, able to feel pain, in need of healing.

Thinking to humor her, Broken Branch stood to his feet and lifted his sister from the ground. "You are right, dear sister. Let us return to the rancheria and nurse his wounds."

Desert Rain brushed her tunic with her free hand. It was then that Broken Branch noticed the blood staining her clothing.

"You are hurt, my sister? There is much blood."

"No," she repeated. "I told you, my Spirit is injured. He is waiting for me in the wikiup. I must return to him."

They turned at the sound of movement as Cloud Maker and Black Beaver stepped into view.

"You have found her!" Cloud Maker exclaimed.

"Yes, she is well," Broken Branch said hesitantly.

"Then let us return her at once to her mother," Black Beaver suggested hastily.

"No! We cannot go," Desert Rain protested emphatically. "My Spirit is wounded. I must assist him." Suddenly she turned and bolted through the trees.

Broken Branch turned to his friends. "My brothers, she is still in great distress. Her mind is not her own. Bring the horses. I'll leave an easy trail for you to follow." With that, he turned and ran after his sister.

He arrived on the edge of the tree line in time to see Desert Rain enter the wikiup. He paused at the far side of the meadow, not sure what his next action should be.

A few minutes later Cloud Maker and Black Beaver showed up with the horses.

"What is it, my Flower? You are breathing heavily. Who is after you?" Spirit Walker asked as Desert Rain entered the wikiup.

"We have visitors, my Spirit."

Spirit Walker instinctively reached for his bow, but his heavily bandaged arms were cumbersome. He only managed to knock the bow to the floor.

"No, my Spirit, it's all right," she assured him. "There is no danger. They are my clan." She picked up the bow and set it against the wall where it had stood before. Gently she moved his arms back alongside his body and caressed his fevered brow. "It's all right, my Spirit. I am here for you."

"Your clan," Spirit Walker said feebly, "they will take you

from me." Suddenly his eyes brightened. She felt them pierce her very soul. "Go with them, my Flower. Grow. Be brave." With a sigh, he closed his eyes as the fever overcame him.

Desert Rain jumped at the sound of the door flap being thrown back. Broken Branch peered cautiously into the gloom. "I'll not go with you, my brother. I'll not go! My Spirit needs me."

Broken Branch entered the small dwelling and glanced at the old warrior lying on the robe before Desert Rain. "I can see that, my sister. Do not fear, we will help you."

Cloud Maker and Black Beaver waited patiently outside the wikiup. A few minutes later, Broken Branch emerged. "We need herbs to stem a fever. Hodentin and moss for a poultice, and yarrow root for pain," he said hastily.

"Who is injured?" Cloud Maker asked.

"An old warrior. Hurry. He will not live if we do not help him."

Broken Branch ducked back inside the hut as the other two hurried to gather the necessary items.

Broken Branch's gaze roamed over the small hut and came to rest on the sash draped over the lance on the rear wall. "Who is this man, my sister?"

"His name is Spirit Walker. He is a Chokonen warrior."

Broken Branch's heart skipped a beat when he heard the warrior's name. He took a long look at the warrior's face. He did not look dangerous, nor did he look much like a spirit. He looked only like a man, a very sick, weak man.

"Where did you get the bandages?" Broken Branch asked.

"From that pack over there." She pointed, indicating a green pack tossed into a corner of the hut.

Broken Branch moved to examine the pack. Inside were some beans, coffee, sugar, bandages, and other items often carried by trappers. The evidence was adding up, but Broken Branch still could not believe that this injured old warrior was the feared Spirit That Walks as a Man.

Once again he moved to take a careful look at the prone warrior. His chest, stomach, and legs were scarred. In the warrior's thigh, Broken Branch noted at least two scars obviously left by bullets. It was certain the man had seen many battles. For a man of his years, his muscles were well defined. He was no doubt a powerful man.

"How was he injured, my sister?"

Desert Rain looked into her brother's eyes. "Two nights ago, as we talked by the river, a mountain lion leapt to attack me. My Spirit grabbed the cat by the throat. They fell into the stream. My Spirit managed to kill the beast, but not before it clawed his arms terribly."

"He killed it with his bare hands?" Broken Branch was astonished at the feat.

"Yes. To save my life, he risked his own. The cat still lies at the water's edge, behind the wikiup and just upriver." A tear came to her eye as she remembered that night's events. She reached down and tenderly kissed Spirit Walker's fevered brow. "I cannot leave him."

Broken Branch stepped toward the door flap. "I'll see about the others," he said as he left the shelter.

The story was just too incredible for Broken Branch to believe, yet his sister had no reason to lie. He thought of his mother's concern for Desert Rain's mental state and decided he would feel better about the whole thing if he saw the cat for himself.

It didn't take Broken Branch long to spot the large cat's body, sprawled across a boulder on the bank. As he approached, he could see the back legs and stomach of the cat stained red with blood. There was no blood around the mouth, meaning that it was never able to get its teeth on its prey. That would have been the mountain lion's first weapon of choice. He raised the lion's head to examine its neck, but there was no sense in looking any further. Its neck was clearly broken. The skull was intact—it had not been beaten against a rock. Someone had applied enough pressure to snap the lion's neck. Someone with great strength.

Cloud Maker and Black Beaver were just returning with the items they had gathered when Broken Branch stepped out from behind the wikiup. He approached his friends. "I will take these to Desert Rain. You stay here. I have much to tell you."

Spirit Walker was still unconscious when Broken Branch entered the hut. Desert Rain accepted the medicines eagerly and then began to unwrap the warrior's right arm. For the first time Broken Branch could see the distinct, deep gashes caused by the mountain lion's claws. He left his sister to continue her work and went to join his friends.

Cloud Maker and Black Beaver were sitting on the logs around the cold fire. Broken Branch took a seat beside them, and told them all that he had seen and heard—of seeing the sash and lance, finding the trappers' pack, the story of the mountain lion, and the examination of the cat's body. In the end, it was still hard for them to believe that the man who lay dying on the wikiup floor could be the legendary Spirit That Walks as a Man.

"What if it is him?" Cloud Maker asked at last.

There was silence for a moment as each of them weighed the options. "If it is him, I'd say he's more man than spirit," Black Beaver offered.

"This is true, but he was spirit enough to kill a wild cat with his bare hands and man enough to save my sister," Broken Branch added.

"Well, whether he is or is not the Spirit That Walks as a Man, he is an elder of our people and a brave warrior. He deserves our respect and gratitude and therefore our help." Cloud Maker rose from his log chair. "I'll take care of the horses, it will be dark soon."

The three men bedded down around the fire circle. Too

weary to eat, they never even lit the fire, just curled up in their hide bedrolls and went to sleep.

Broken Branch opened his eyes and gazed at the stars. A familiar sound had awakened him. His mind wandered back to days of long ago. He was small, but his sister even smaller. Their father, Sees the Way, was off on a hunt. One night a strange chill entered the tipi that he, his mother, brother, and sister occupied. It gave them all a sickly, eerie feeling. For some reason, Desert Rain began to sing. She had a sweet voice, high and melodious. It was the first time anything like that had ever happened. It turned out to be an omen of death. Their father was trampled in a buffalo stampede the next morning and died. It was her voice he heard singing now, only the words that came from the wikiup were different this time.

You give the moon its light, you give the stars their shine.
The sun cannot rise without your smile.
The wind whispers your name to the pines, and they bend to your will.
The leaves dance at the sound of your voice, and the deer leap for joy.
You give the birds their song, they sing of your courage.
You are the song on the midnight wind.

Chapter Fourteen

"Get up, ye scalawags and biscuit eaters! This ain't no furlough. This here's an Injun hunt. A band of furry-legged squaws could ride in here and scalp the lot of ya."

Captain James J. Jackson, Jr., sipped his morning coffee and smiled as the tough-talking Sergeant Beyer roused his men from sleep. He couldn't help but smile at his first sergeant, who, for all his bluster and hot air, loved his men. And they loved him. The captain knew that they'd follow their sergeant to hell to fight the whole Apache Nation with a fiddle bow if he said they could do it. And that's just about what he had asked them to do.

Captain Jackson looked over at the trapper who was responsible for their being in these woods. He wasn't much to look at, just a scrawny kid, probably not much of a trapper either. He'd come into the fort a few days ago yelling something about a band of renegade Indians who had attacked him and killed his partner. The company commander, Lieutenant Colonel Graffe, had then commissioned Jackson and eleven men to search the area and capture or destroy the renegades. This was their first morning out and they'd seen nothing of concern so far.

Sergeant Beyer snapped a salute as he approached his captain. "All men are present and accounted for, sir."

"Excellent, Sergeant. Call in the perimeter watch and have the men take breakfast. We'll head out in one hour."

"Yes, sir." Sergeant Beyer saluted and turned on his heels.

"Oh, and Sergeant."

"Sir?"

"Send that trapper to me."

"Yes, sir." The sergeant walked away, barking commands, and headed for the trapper.

"Good morning, Mr. Carney," the captain said as the trapper approached.

"Please, call me Laird. Mr. Carney was my pa," the trapper said with a snaggle-toothed grin.

"Fine. Laird. I just want to get a few things straight." Jackson unrolled a military map of the area, placed it on a boulder, and pulled out a charcoal pencil. "You say the area where you and your partner were attacked was right about here?" He pointed to an area on the map that indicated a waterfall along one of the tributaries flowing south from the San Pedro River.

"That's right. They ambushed us from the falls. We was just ridin' along, lookin' to set some beaver traps."

"Beaver traps?"

"Yeah. We was settin' a couple around the falls when this here squaw come moseyin' down to the river. We didn't know it, but she was a decoy for the ambush."

Captain Jackson scratched his head. "Any idea why a band of Apaches would send a squaw into their line of fire just to ambush two trappers?"

99

"Well, we was heavily armed. Maybe they figured we'd drop our guard for a purty woman."

"And they were right?"

"Well, ol' Clem always had an eye for the ladies. Didn't matter much to him if'n they was Injun or not."

"I see. So how many of them attacked you?"

Laird hesitated a moment. "I figure at least a dozen or more."

"A dozen? You saw that many of them?"

"Nah. Ain't no way they'da popped their heads over them rocks. We'd a picked 'em off like jackrabbits. But, the air was full of arrows—from the ridge, the woods, ever'where. Weren't no time for countin', just runnin'."

"Only Clem didn't run quite as fast, is that it?"

"Well, we put up quite a fight. We dropped a couple. I know that fur sure. They shot our mule, then shot Clem's horse out from under 'im. When I looked back, he had about a half dozen arrows in 'im and he was a yellin' for me to go get help. I rode for the fort."

"Surely he couldn't think that he would survive 'til you returned with help."

"No. But Clem and me had an understandin'. If'n one of us was kilt by Injuns, the other one would hunt 'em down and kill 'em like dirty dogs."

"Is that what you're doing now?"

"Yes, sir, I aim to."

"Well, that's quite a tale, Mister . . . uh . . . Laird." Captain Jackson rolled the map and placed it back in its cylindrical case. "Tell me, how is it that these dozen or so Apaches, the best guerrilla fighters ever sired by the western plains, didn't just swoop down on you two on horseback and finish you off?"

"Well, sir, I guess we just kinda caught 'em sleepin'."

"Sleeping?"

"Yes, sir. They wasn't expectin' us to be there, so they didn't have no time to organize."

"But they were organized enough to send out a decoy. Interesting. Well, thank you very much. We'll be leaving soon. Better get some grub."

"Thank you, sir."

Captain Jackson watched the trapper walk away. Every bone in the cavalry officer's body told him the man was lying. That left a bad taste in his mouth, especially when it put eleven of his men in jeopardy. But he would know soon enough. He signaled for his sergeant.

Sergeant Beyer hurried to his captain's side, wiping coffee from the tips of his handlebar mustache. "Yes, sir?"

"Sergeant, we'll continue heading northeast till we hit the river. We'll need to follow it upstream to the falls. You'll need to have men watching all sides for possible ambush. We'll ride in columns of two. That will mean twelve of us, two abreast with one man riding drag. You and I will lead the parade, but I want that trapper right behind you, in case I need to talk to him. Rotate a man in and out of drag every hour. He'll need to keep a good eye on our back trail."

"Yes, sir."

"We'll reach the river this evening and make camp early. We'll reach the falls by afternoon the next day. I don't want to push the men too hard. If the Indians are camped around that area, we'll need the men to be fresh, ready for action."

"I'll see to it, sir."

"Sergeant, mind you watch that trapper. His story has more holes in it than a buckshot squirrel."

"Well, sir, I never quite heard his whole story."

"Walk with me, Sergeant, I'll fill you in," Captain Jackson began to walk and the sergeant fell in beside him.

When the double column of soldiers reached the stream, they headed upriver as planned. It was already well into the evening and Captain Jackson decided to make camp early in order to rest his men. He was just about to give the order when a trooper on the right flank gave a shout. "Sir, look at that driftwood in the river."

The captain, riding in the left front, looked in the direction the trooper was pointing. A pinkish object could be seen floating along with a large clump of driftwood, bouncing along the opposite shore.

"Looks like a body floating," Sergeant Beyer noted.

The captain moved around his sergeant to get a better look. "Take three men and check it out, Sergeant."

"Yes, sir." Turning in his saddle toward the others, Sergeant Beyer issued his orders. "I need a three-man burial detail to follow me across the river. The rest of you draw weapons and provide cover if necessary."

The burly little sergeant kicked his mount into the water and started across. Three troopers followed his lead.

Captain Jackson watched as Sergeant Beyer's men pulled the badly decomposed body from the tangle of debris on the far bank. "Is that your friend?" he asked.

"Reckon it is," Laird replied.

Sergeant Beyer pulled the lone arrow from the corpse's chest and held it aloft. "It's an Apache arrow all right."

Well, at least that much of the trapper's story seemed true, the captain thought. "Any other arrows? Any other wounds?" he asked the sergeant.

"Too hard to tell, sir," Sergeant Beyer answered back. "The body's in pretty bad shape."

"Bury him, Sergeant."

"Yes, sir."

Captain Jackson turned once again to the small trapper. "That man's in long johns. Thought you said you two were setting traps when you were ambushed."

Laird hesitated a moment before replying. "We were. They musta kilt him and took his clothes."

"Suppose you can tell me where the other arrows went. You said he was full of 'em."

Laird shifted nervously in his saddle. Sweat beaded on his forehead. "They musta come out when they stripped him. You know, I bet it was ol' Geronimo hisself what done it."

"Yet they worked his shirt off over that one arrow?" Captain Jackson's face flushed red. "Trapper, not one thing you've told me makes much sense. If Geronimo had wanted you dead, you'd have never reached the fort. When an Apache strips a man, he strips him clean. And no Apache would toss a body in a stream and pollute his own drinking water. What's more, Geronimo wouldn't leave an arrow in a white man's body so that the whole world could figure out who killed him.

"The Apache are smarter than you give them credit for and so am I. If I find out you've been lying to me about this entire affair, I'll tie a bow around your neck, take you into the Dragoon Mountains and deliver you to Geronimo personally. Now, get out of my sight!"

Chapter Fifteen

Desert Rain welcomed the coolness of the late evening. It had been a rough night. Spirit Walker had convulsed in fever, but she had never left his side, continually cooling his brow with a damp cloth. Though the night had been rough, the day was even worse. The heat inside the small dwelling was almost unbearable and only served to add to the wounded warrior's discomfort.

Throughout the day, Broken Branch and the others brought fresh water from the spring. Desert Rain continued to bathe Spirit Walker with the cool liquid. Until she removed his breechclout, she had never seen a grown man's nakedness except for her husband's. Even in unconsciousness, his body was impressive. She fought hard to keep at the task, not wanting to linger on the hint of desire spreading through her bosom. She felt a twinge of guilt, not wanting to desire anyone but Arm Bow.

By evening, exhaustion had overtaken her. When Broken Branch offered to keep watch over Spirit Walker, she reluctantly agreed to get a little sleep. She lay in the opposite corner of the wikiup while Broken Branch sat beside Spirit Walker.

Broken Branch had just begun to doze off when he noticed a change in the warrior's breathing. When he looked down at the old man, Spirit Walker was looking up at him. It felt as if the Chokonen was looking straight into his spirit. Broken Branch remembered hearing that a shaman could look at one's spirit by looking into the eyes. He didn't know if that was true, but if it was, it was happening now. He felt a coldness grip him, but he couldn't look away.

"You are Desert Rain's brother," the man said at last.

"Yes. I am Broken Branch."

Spirit Walker smiled weakly. "You have the same spirit. Your father is very proud of you both."

"Our father is dead."

"I know."

"What else do you know, uncle?"

Spirit Walker's face suddenly went pale. His strength was waning. "I know that one should surrender to fight another day, rather than to die foolishly."

"Words of wisdom, uncle, but . . ."

"Words of life!" Spirit Walker interjected. "You will need to remember them well." Slowly the old man's eyes began to close. "Remember them well," he repeated.

Broken Branch tried to inquire further of the warrior, but Spirit Walker's eyes were shut and his breathing deep. There would be nothing else forthcoming from him tonight.

It had been another rough night, but as the morning dawned, Spirit Walker's fever seemed to be subsiding. Broken Branch led the horses to a large meadow to graze, and returned by late morning. By midday, he was finally able to talk his sister into going to the waterfall with Cloud Maker and Black Beaver. "You will feel better after a bath," Broken Branch had told her. "And you can pick up more yarrow while you are there. I'll stay with Spirit Walker, don't worry about him."

Reluctantly Desert Rain had agreed and followed Cloud Maker and Black Beaver to the falls.

She swam for a while, reveling in the cool mountain water as it washed over her skin. Her tunic would never be shed of Spirit Walker's blood, but it looked a little better after a good washing.

Cloud Maker and Black Beaver kept watch for intruders along the banks while Desert Rain bathed. When she was finished, she climbed onto a boulder in the middle of the white water and enjoyed a little of the afternoon sun.

Cloud Maker challenged Black Beaver to jump from the falls into the deepest part of the river. The challenge was accepted and like two school boys, they began to climb the bluffs, deriding each other's courage.

"Broken Branch."

Broken Branch turned at the sound of his name and once again met the seasoned warrior's gaze. "Yes, my uncle?"

"It is time."

"Time?"

"Time to remember your lesson."

"Which lesson, my uncle?"

"Go to your sister. She needs you now. If you have learned the words of life, she will live. Her life is in your hands." Once again Spirit Walker closed his eyes.

Broken Branch had no idea exactly what the shaman had meant by those words, but suddenly an urgency rose in his heart. He rose hurriedly, ducked through the door of the wikiup, and began running toward the falls.

"I can climb higher, my brother!" Cloud Maker shouted above the noise of the falls.

106

"And I," Black Beaver returned. "When you are tired of climbing, we shall jump."

Cloud Maker looked down from his perch on the rocky cliff. Desert Rain lay on a boulder, drying herself in the sun. Everything around her was still and quiet. He turned back to his friend. "I will not tire till we reach the top, Black Beaver. Let me know when you have grown weary of climbing."

The higher the two friends climbed, the louder the roar of the falls grew in their ears. Cloud Maker halted suddenly, thinking he heard a sound from below. He turned and looked in Desert Rain's direction. She no longer lay languishing in the late afternoon sunlight. She was standing now, hurriedly donning her tunic, looking toward the bank, and yelling frantically. He too looked toward the bank.

Six blue coats lined the edge of the mountain stream. They were on foot with guns drawn. But there was another man, a man who stood out from the rest, a trapper. "Black Beaver, look!" Cloud Maker called to his friend.

"Trooper Sosa!" Captain Jackson called.

A dark skinned young soldier hurried to his side. "Yes, sir?"

"Trooper, you speak a little Apache, don't you?"

"Yes, sir, I do."

"What's she saying, Trooper?"

"She's telling the two men up on the rocks that we're here, basically. I believe the one man just told the other man to look in our direction."

"Seems they're alone, then. Otherwise they would be yelling for others to come to their assistance."

"Yes, sir, it would appear that the two men on the cliff are the only ones around to protect her."

Sergeant Beyer stepped up. "Sir, we've found their weapons lying on the bank. We've secured them. They're unarmed."

"Thank you, Sergeant. Do you have any suggestions about

how to get them off the cliff and into custody?" the captain asked.

"Well, sir. We'll need to call the other men forward, have them ride across the river and cut off that avenue of escape. Then we may have to wait them out or shoot them down."

"Sergeant, I want to avoid shooting these people if it's at all possible. We don't know who they are or if they're even involved in the incident we've come to investigate."

"Oh, I can tell you that much," Laird said as he stepped up beside the captain. "That there's the squaw what was used as a decoy."

Captain Jackson cast a hard glance at the scrubby trapper. "Thought you might say that." He turned again to his sergeant. "Have the men cross the stream. We'll wait 'em out. I don't want any shooting unless we have to defend ourselves. Is that clear?"

"Yes, sir. Clear." Sergeant Beyer turned and gave a sharp whistle.

Six mounted troops rode from the trees. "Ride across to the other bank and keep 'em from escaping. No shooting! Draw your weapons and defend yourselves only."

The six men nodded as one and heeled their horses into the creek.

"They are sending men to the other bank!" Cloud Maker observed.

Black Beaver nodded and looked upward. "Do you think we can reach the top, my brother?"

Cloud Maker also cast a glance upward. "We might finish the climb, but what about Desert Rain? There is no way she will be able to make it."

Black Beaver thought for a moment. "My brother, you must escape to the top of the cliff. I will stay with Desert Rain. Once on top of the rocks, make your way back to Broken Branch."

"What can two of us do against so many blue coats?"

"I will slow them as much as possible as they take us to the fort. You must ride ahead with Broken Branch and rally the People. If you ride hard, you may overtake us before we reach the white man's fort. I will do my best to be a hindrance to them."

"What if they only seek to kill you both?"

"Then they would have already begun the slaughter. No, they want us as captives. I'm sure of it."

"And if we cannot rescue you before you are taken into the fort?"

"You must! That is all. You must."

Cloud Maker nodded, looked skyward, and began to climb.

"What are they saying, Trooper?" Jackson asked.

"The roar of the falls is too loud to hear every word, Captain, but it seems that one of them has decided to try to reach the top of the cliff and go for help," Trooper Sosa replied.

"Well, we can't allow that to happen. If these men are from Geronimo's clan, that could be real trouble. Sergeant!"

Sergeant Beyer once again hurried to Jackson's side. "Sir?"

"Sergeant, we cannot allow that man to reach the top of the falls. Step up on that boulder, in plain view. Let them see you point your weapon straight at him. Trooper Sosa, tell him to come down or we'll shoot him down."

"I hope I can speak it well enough, Captain," Sosa said, a twinge of doubt in his voice.

"So do I, Trooper, for their sakes. Sergeant, step up on that rock. Ready your weapon."

"Yes, sir." Sergeant Beyer climbed up on the rock and did as he was told.

Trooper Sosa glanced once at the captain, then stepped forward and began to shout to the men on the cliff.

* * *

Broken Branch ran through the underbrush. Dodging branches and limbs, he picked up speed. A sense of urgency drove him forward. It was something in Spirit Walker's voice that made him quicken his pace. "If you have learned the words of life, she will live," the old man had said.

Sweat poured from his brow. He jumped a fallen tree, tripped on a branch, scrambled to his feet, and continued his run. He knew he was close, but not close enough. He had to reach the waterfall. Had to get to his sister's side.

Suddenly a single shot echoed from the river. "No!" Broken Branch shouted in disbelief. "My sister! My sister! No!"

Chapter Sixteen

Captain Jackson turned his head as he gave the command for Sergeant Beyer to shoot. Jackson had never liked seeing an unarmed man shot, even if the man was trying to escape. Disgust was evident in his eyes as he sought out the trapper. "You had better be telling me the truth, trapper!" he snapped. " 'Cause if you're not, I'll have your hide!"

Sergeant Beyer lowered his Winchester, watched as Cloud Maker's body tumbled from the cliff. Beyer was a crack shot, the best in the unit. He only hoped his shot was as true as he wanted it to be.

Black Beaver cried out in grief as he heard the shot, saw Cloud Maker fall backward past him and plunge into the river below. Without a second thought, he dove from the cliff face. If Cloud Maker was still alive, Black Beaver had to save him from drowning.

Desert Rain's heart dropped as she witnessed the fate of her husband's best friend. As Cloud Maker's body hit the water, tears welled up in her eyes. Then, there was another splash and Black Beaver was in the water. In seconds, Black Beaver broke the surface cradling Cloud Maker in his arms and swimming for the rocks at the foot of the falls. A deep crease marked the side of Cloud Maker's head, but there wasn't a lot of blood. Desert Rain dove in the water and swam toward her friends.

"Sergeant, let's wait 'em out now," Jackson commanded.

"Yes, sir." Sergeant Beyer stepped from the rock. "I only meant to nick him a might, Captain. I don't think I killed him."

Jackson smiled at the wily sergeant. "Thank you, Sergeant. I have a feeling that they will be of more help to us alive than dead."

Laird was boiling with anger. This insolent captain was spoiling the whole thing. He should have killed these redskins already. What was he hoping to gain by keeping them alive? Still, Laird kept his silence. Though he feared Captain Jackson, he was set on revenge, and by God he would have it. He shook his head and moved away from the captain.

"Sosa, as soon as they get up on the rocks, tell them to come out. Tell them we won't shoot them if they come out peacefully." Jackson instructed his interpreter.

"Yes, sir."

Black Beaver hauled Cloud Maker onto the rocks and assessed his wound. It was a clean abrasion near the left temple. There was more blood since they exited the water, but it appeared that the wound wasn't critical. He would live.

Desert Rain reached the rocks and crawled up beside the two men. "Is he dead?"

"No, he will live. Are you all right?"

"Yes. I am not harmed." She looked back at the men on the bank. "One of them is speaking to us in the tongue of the People."

"I hear him."

"His speech is crude, but I think he is telling us to come out."

Black Beaver looked around him. The soldiers were on both sides of the river and the cliff was too high. There was no escape. He looked back at Desert Rain. "Little sister, we are trapped."

"What can we do, Black Beaver? They have our weapons."

Cloud Maker began to stir in Black Beaver's arms. "We must fight," he said weakly. "We cannot surrender, they will kill us."

Black Beaver looked down at his wounded friend. "We cannot, my brother. We have no weapons."

"We might float down the river," Desert Rain suggested. "The current is strong, the rocks along the stream may hide us."

"We cannot outfloat their horses as they ride the banks," Black Beaver noted. "They will wait for us to come out of the river no matter how far we float."

Cloud Maker sat up, weaving as he tried to regain his composure. "Black Beaver, did you not agree to watch after Desert Rain?"

"Yes, of course I did."

Cloud Maker reached behind him and pulled a slender blade from a sheath at the back of his clout. "Then I will draw them to me. I will keep them busy while you two ride the river."

"No," Desert Rain protested. "You cannot fight them with only a knife. They will surely kill you."

"That is true, but it is the only chance for you to escape," Cloud Maker said.

"This is foolishness, my brother," Black Beaver admonished.

Cloud Maker looked into Black Beaver's face. "I promised my best friend that I would watch after his woman. If I cannot succeed in keeping that promise, I would rather die. Wait for my signal."

He tossed himself into the water and swam toward a large boulder close to the bank.

*　　*　　*

"Captain."

"Yes, Sergeant."

"One of them's coming out," The burly sergeant pointed in Cloud Maker's direction as the Apache climbed up on the boulder.

"Good, maybe we can wrap this up soon."

"I don't think so, sir, he's got a knife. Looks like he's spoiling for a fight."

"That's crazy! He's going to fight twelve armed men with only a knife? What's he saying? Sosa, what's he saying?"

"He's saying that he would rather fight and die than to surrender," Trooper Sosa said over his shoulder as Cloud Maker continued his shouting. "Now, he's singing, Captain."

"Singing? What the hell could he be singing about?"

"It's his death song, Captain." Sosa turned to face his leader. "He's preparing to die and he means to take someone with him."

Captain Jackson turned a solemn face toward his first sergeant. "Sergeant." It was only one word but its meaning was crystal clear.

Sergeant Beyer looked at his captain, then back at the Apache standing boldly on the rock. "Ready arms!" Beyer commanded his men. The troopers shouldered their rifles.

"Wait for my command!" Captain Jackson ordered. He raised his right hand.

Cloud Maker continued his singing as he surveyed the situation. Three men with rifles on the near shore, six others on the opposite shore. He turned to his friends on the rocks. "Now, swim!"

"No! No, Cloud Maker!" Cloud Maker froze in place as he saw Broken Branch run from the trees and onto the shore. "No, you cannot die in this way!"

Captain Jackson stood in amazement at the sight. Another Apache had come on the scene. How many more could there be?

"Grab that man!" Sergeant Beyer shouted, pointing to Broken Branch.

"No, wait!" Jackson ordered, as the nearest trooper began to move in Broken Branch's direction. "Let's see what he's saying. Cover the woods behind us. Sosa, interpret what he's saying."

Sosa raised his own weapon and brought it to bear on this new intruder. "Sir, he's telling them to give up. He's telling them that this is no way to die, that they must live to fight another day."

"My brother!" Desert Rain cried. "My brother, you must escape! Run!"

Broken Branch glanced at the soldiers. "No, my sister, I cannot. They will not kill us, not here, not now."

"How can you be sure of this?" Cloud Maker asked.

Broken Branch looked at his friend. A smile traced his lips. "Our medicine is too strong, my brother. The Spirit will serve us well."

It took some time for Broken Branch to convince the others to surrender peacefully. Soon they were all bound, sitting apart on the banks of the river. Broken Branch hung his head, wondering if he had truly learned a lesson that would save their lives. He couldn't help thinking that if he had ridden for the rancheria, rallied his brothers, he might have had a better chance of saving his sister. He hoped the old man was right, but his heart was heavy with worry.

Captain Jackson stood apart from his men, his sergeant at his side. "Sergeant, I want you to send some men up and down the banks."

"Searching for tracks, sir?"

"Yes, tracks, but there is more, Sergeant. I want them to check for traps. Beaver traps."

Sergeant Beyer was puzzled by the request, but held his peace. "Yes, sir. I'll send them at once."

When he returned from giving the order, he hesitantly confided in his captain. "Sir, I'm a little nervous about staying in this area."

Captain Jackson glanced around him. Heavy woods were on one side and a river on the other. It was a precarious place for them to be in the middle of Apache territory.

"What if more Apache show up?" the sergeant asked.

"I know what you mean, Sergeant. What do you suggest?"

"I suggest that as soon as the men are finished here, we move as far downriver as possible and set up a secure camp for the night."

"Agreed, Sergeant. Prepare the men."

"Yes, sir."

The four captives were bound, hand and foot, and thrown across the backs of four different horses. Each trooper whose horse bore a captive was positioned in the middle of the formation.

Captain Jackson rode at the lead with his sergeant on his left. Jackson's mind was troubled, filled with the knowledge that his scouts had not found one single beaver trap. He tried to reason that maybe the Indians had removed the traps, but more and more he was convinced that the trapper was lying—that there hadn't been an unprovoked attack. The captives he had taken were not even prepared to do battle. He was struggling with his emotions and he wasn't enjoying the fight.

They set up camp just inside the tree line, a little distance off from the edge of the water. Not wanting to draw attention to themselves, they lit no fire. Guards were set on all four sides and the rest of the men bedded down for the night.

Desert Rain lay staring up at the stars, wondering if her friends were asleep. The four captives were left bound and separated, and she wasn't quite sure where the others were. "My husband," she whispered, "I love you so. I know that you are here watching over us. I know that you will deliver us from the blue coats. But I am afraid, my husband. I am so afraid."

Suddenly a light flickered to her right. She turned to look, as one of the guards placed a lit match to the cigarette he held in his lips. A silent gasp escaped her throat as she noticed a shadow standing behind the man. Not merely a shadow, but a shadow with bandaged arms.

Chapter Seventeen

Desert Rain had slept fitfully during the night. The shadow she had seen standing behind the sentry must have been Spirit Walker, yet she had seen no further sign of him, heard no noise to indicate chaos in the camp. She was still awake when the sentries were changed after the first watch. Everything had seemed normal. Perhaps it was just her imagination, just her desire to see her Spirit again. Maybe her hope for deliverance from her captors had caused her mind to play tricks on her.

But now, as the light of early morning bathed the trees in golden hues, there was noise in the camp. She didn't know what was being said, but she could hear the white men speaking in anxious tones.

"Captain! Captain, come quick," a curly-headed trooper shouted.

Captain Jackson came awake with a start and instinctively

reached for his Winchester rifle. He sat up suddenly, assessing the scene around him. Some of the other men were waking from sleep, grabbing their weapons, jumping to their feet.

"What is it? What's wrong?" the captain asked with concern.

The trooper approached with urgency. "Sir." The trooper snapped a salute before continuing. "We have a problem with the horses, sir."

Captain Jackson set his rifle on the ground beside him and began to pull on his boots, relieved that they were not under attack. "What kind of problem?"

"Well, sir." The trooper looked around nervously. "They're . . . they're . . . missing, sir. They're gone."

Jackson looked up in shock. "Gone? What do you mean they're gone?" The captain leapt to his feet and started at a run toward where the horses had been secured. "Bring my rifle, Trooper."

"Yes, sir."

"What's going on here, Sergeant?" Jackson asked as he approached the makeshift horse corral.

Sergeant Beyer stood staring at the piece of rope in his hand. "Someone cut the rope, sir. They've either taken the horses or allowed them to run off in the night."

Jackson surveyed the area cautiously. "Wasn't there a sentry at this post, Sergeant?"

"Yes, sir."

"Well, where is he? What does he have to say about this?"

"I wish I knew, sir. He seems to be missing also."

Captain Jackson stood in stunned silence. Had the guard deserted with the horses? Had he been attacked and killed by Geronimo's raiders in the night? Had the horses managed to break the tether line and escape with the sentry in pursuit? He tried to make sense of the scene before him.

"Sergeant, I want scouts in the woods immediately. Find those horses."

"Already done, sir. I have five men combing the woods right now."

"Good. Assemble the others. We need to talk."

"Yes, sir."

The captain stood tall in front of his men. He looked out over his audience—six troopers, one trapper, four bound prisoners—it wasn't much to work with, but he had to do the best he could. He cleared his throat and addressed his men.

"Men, we have a dire situation here. One of the worst things that can happen to a cavalryman has happened. We have been set afoot." As was often the case, Captain Jackson began to pace as he spoke. "This may seem like an insurmountable problem, but let me assure you that it is not. We are a capable fighting force. If the Apache want a war, we are more than able to meet their challenge. Check your weapons and ammunition. Keep your eyes open. Watch for any movement, any sign of an attack. At the first sign of trouble, shout out a warning. We can and will survive."

The captain hesitated as he approached Trooper Sosa. "Sosa, talk to the captives. Find out if they know anything."

"Yes, sir."

"All right, troops, prepare to move out in one hour. Horses or not, we have to move. We're more than fifty miles from Fort Lowell. That's too deep in Apache territory to be comfortable. Dismissed."

For the first time since their capture, Desert Rain, Broken Branch, Cloud Maker, and Black Beaver were allowed to sit together. They were placed with their feet touching, tied ankle to ankle, their hands secured behind their backs. The camp was awash in activity and it was certain that there was concern among the blue coats.

"What do you think is the problem?" Black Beaver asked in a whisper.

Cloud Maker looked around him. "There are not as many blue coats as before. Do you think the others have ridden ahead to prepare the way to the fort?"

"No," Desert Rain said, "there is more trouble than they know."

Desert Rain's smile seemed inappropriate at such a serious time. Broken Branch had to know why she was so confident. "What is it, my sister? What do you know?"

"I know nothing, my brother, but I have seen him."

"Him? Who?" Cloud Maker asked.

"My Spirit, Cloud Maker. I saw him standing in the shadows last night."

Broken Branch sat up and took notice. Had the old man regained enough strength to follow them this far? If so, did he have enough strength to fight this unit of blue coats?

"Shhh," Black Beaver cautioned. "Someone approaches."

Trooper Sosa stepped up and knelt between Cloud Maker and Desert Rain. He looked from captive to captive, then began to speak slowly in Apache. "*Ya a teh, shils aash.* Hello, my friends."

The man was definitely not Apache, Broken Branch thought. Perhaps he was Mexican, but he was not Apache. Where did he learn to speak the language? Cloud Maker looked into the trooper's eyes. "We are not your friends!" Cloud Maker retorted.

Sosa met Cloud Maker's gaze. The hair on Cloud Maker's left temple was matted with blood. "My friend, you are hurt. I can help you, if you will tell me what I need to know."

"We will never help you," Cloud Maker returned insolently.

"Listen," the trooper continued, "I know that there are more of you out there. How many?"

"Many!" Cloud Maker shouted.

"One," Desert Rain said with a smile.

"One?" Sosa asked in amazement.

"Do not talk to him!" Cloud Maker admonished.

"She means," Broken Branch interrupted, "that you need fear the one who leads them."

Sosa swallowed nervously. "Who is this one? Is it Geronimo?"

Broken Branch noted the sweat beginning to bead up on the trooper's forehead. "He is a brave and cunning warrior. Mightier even than Geronimo. He is able, with his band, to destroy many more men than you have."

"Who is this warrior? What is his name?"

Cloud Maker's stare was clearly intended to tell Desert Rain to let her brother continue the explanation. It was not good if she gave out too much information at this time. But the pride evident in her face showed that she thought of the brave warrior whose very presence had already begun to make the white men shake with fear.

"He is the Spirit That Walks as a Man," Broken Branch said.

"Why has he not shown himself? Why have we not seen him before?" Sosa asked.

Suddenly Black Beaver spoke up. "Have you seen the wind? Have you visited the night lodge of the sun? Have you seen the coyote's call as it rides the night air? No, you have not, nor can you see the Spirit That Walks as a Man. But let me assure you, he is here. You cannot stop what you cannot see."

Trooper Sosa slowly stood to his feet. It was strange, but somehow he knew they were serious about what they had told him. There was someone out there, maybe more than one, but it was the one they spoke about that sent a chill down his spine.

Captain Jackson paced nervously. There was no sign of the men who had been sent out to look for the horses. No sign of the horses. Time was slipping away. The information he had gleaned from the captives was of great concern to him. Sosa had told him about the spirit man. At first, Jackson had dismissed the idea, now he was not so sure. Where were his men? Why had they heard no sound from the woods around them? Six men—the guard and the five searchers—didn't just disappear without making a sound. "Sergeant!" he shouted.

Sergeant Beyer's face revealed his concern as he once again stood before his captain.

"Sergeant, any word on the scouts sent out to find the horses?"

"No, sir. Not a sign of any of 'em."

Jackson shook his head in frustration. "Well, we can't wait any longer. I'm afraid we've made enough mistakes. Lost enough men. Ready the men to move out. Have the captives tied together and placed in the middle of the formation. And I want to see that trapper. Now!"

"Yes, sir." Sergeant Beyer moved quickly and returned with the trapper in tow.

"You wanted to see me, Captain?" Laird said as he shuffled up to Jackson.

"Trapper, what the hell is going on here? Who's in those woods?"

"I don't know, Captain, honest. We was just trappin' beaver and . . ."

"Don't give me that! We checked all over for beaver traps and didn't find a one. You had better tell me the truth, and quick! Personally, I don't care a whit about what happened to you and your partner, but I care a hell of a lot about what happens to my men. As far as I'm concerned you're responsible for the possible slaughter of six United States cavalrymen. I've a good mind to cut those prisoners loose and let them have your scalp."

Laird stared at the ground. It was obvious that the captain was furious. Laird knew he was in deep trouble, but he couldn't change his story. It was too late for that now. It would mean certain retribution from Jackson. "All's I know is that them Injuns are part of the group that attacked us. I know that there squaw was the decoy. Other than that, I don't know what to tell you."

Jackson pointed a disgruntled finger in Laird's face. "Well, I will tell you this, trapper. You are expendable. I won't sacrifice the lives of good men to save your sorry hide. Is that understood?"

"Understood."

Chapter Eighteen

Desert Rain shuffled along behind Broken Branch. They had been walking for hours. She wondered where the horses were, but at least it wasn't just her and her friends who were on foot now. It was hard to understand why half of the blue coats had gone ahead with all of the horses, if that was indeed what had happened. But she couldn't worry about that. She was too busy trying to walk with hobbles on her ankles. Her feet were tied together with a piece of rope that allowed her to move them no more than a foot apart. Her friends were similarly tied. Taking such small steps caused her to have to take more steps than the soldiers. Still, she thought, at least they were all walking now, and Spirit Walker would have an easier time keeping up.

She smiled at the thought of him watching her plight. Though she didn't know exactly where he was at the time, she could feel his dark eyes on her. She knew he was watching from afar, waiting for just the right time. Then, like the warrior he was, he would ride in and rescue them. She could imagine him riding in, reins in his teeth, firing arrows like lightning bolts among the blue coats. Seven arrows, seven dead white men, and they would be free. Then he would ride to her side and slide easily from his pony. He would cut her hands and feet free and take her into his arms. And then they would kiss. After all, the living must look after the living, she thought. That is the way Arm Bow would want it.

She didn't know if she was quite ready to give herself entirely to another man, but if there was ever to be another husband for her, it could be no one with less wisdom or bravery than Spirit Walker. She could feel his hands stroking her hair, his eyes piercing her spirit, his voice soothing her fears. He was there, even now as she walked. Broken Branch had called him the Spirit That Walks as a Man. He certainly was that. He had a certain Apache magic that she had never experienced before. He was gentle. He was kind. He never pressured her, never made her try to forget about Arm Bow. He had merely instructed her in wisdom, made her feel that she was important. She wondered if he thought of her. She wondered if he felt the same way. She wondered.

Suddenly the blue coat behind her pushed her roughly with the butt of his rifle and shouted something in his crude language. She realized that, in her reverie, she had slowed her pace and had fallen further behind her comrades. She took a couple of quick steps and caught up with Broken Branch.

The day was hot and Desert Rain was feeling the toll of their forced march. They had stopped for water only minutes before, so it was unusual that they should stop again so soon. The soldiers seemed anxious to reach their fort, but now they had shuffled their captives to the edge of the tree line, placed two men to watch them, and gathered near the bank of the river. They seemed intent on studying the ground around the bank, and were talking and gesturing about something they had found there.

"There's no doubt about it, Captain, they're Indian ponies," Sergeant Beyer was saying.

Captain Jackson examined the tracks at the edge of the water. They were certainly horse prints, but not the kind one would normally expect to see. There was no clear outline of a horse shoe, not even the distinct impression usually made by the hoof. The edges were blurred and somewhat distorted. Jackson had seen tracks like this before and knew them for what they were. The Apache often tied pieces of cloth or leather around the feet of their horses. The leather served two practical purposes: it kept the horses from chipping their hooves on the rocks of the mountains and it hindered anyone from tracking them effectively.

"Lucky for us that they rode so close to the river. Even Indian-shod horses could be tracked in this soft earth," the sergeant continued.

"Yes. Yes, we were lucky," Jackson remarked. "How many ponies do you reckon?"

Sergeant Beyer looked up and down the bank, making a mental calculation of the tracks. "I'd say at least a half dozen, maybe more. It's hard to tell, the tracks overlap each other quite a bit."

"Sergeant, we do have a serious problem here," Jackson said. "If these Indians are the ones seeking the release of our prisoners, they may be waiting in ambush ahead of us."

"Well, sir, they may just be a hunting party passing by."

"Sergeant, a hunting party would have no need to hide their tracks."

"True, sir, but they were very careless to get so close to the water. If they were intent on getting water and yet hiding their tracks, they would have left the horses at the tree line and approached on foot."

Jackson had to admit that the sergeant did have a point. The

Indians were careless. "Well, Sergeant, you may be right. But let us be even more cautious. Have the men travel with their weapons at the ready. At the first sign of trouble, abandon the prisoners immediately and set up a defensive position. My only concern is the safety of these men. If we lose the captives, so be it."

"What about the trapper?"

"Sergeant, I couldn't care less what happens to that trapper. He's the cause of this whole misadventure. As far as I'm concerned, we've lost the horses and possibly six good men because of him. I hold him completely responsible."

"Well, sir, we do have a responsibility to protect the citizens of Arizona Territory."

"Yes, that we do. But, I have a feeling that this is not a case of protecting an innocent citizen from marauding renegades. In this case, I think we may be dealing with two men who provoked an attack and then came to us to help exact revenge."

"I don't get it, Captain."

"Sergeant, I've been watching the way the trapper has been eyeing the female prisoner. It's the look, the expression of contempt. If she was merely a decoy, his attention would be more focused on the male prisoners. I don't think he's ever seen them before, only the girl."

"What do you think happened, sir?"

"The dead trapper was found wearing long johns, yet there was an arrow in his chest. It's obvious that he was shot after he removed his clothing and not before. The Indians would not have thrown his body into the river. When he was shot, he fell into the river."

"So he removed his clothing to bathe, was shot, and fell into the river," Sergeant Beyer concluded.

"If that's so, Sergeant, why didn't the other trapper simply tells us that? He concocted a whole different story. Why?"

Sergeant Beyer removed his cap and scratched his head. "I don't know, sir."

"Sergeant, a man lies for only one reason—to hide the truth. The truth must be hidden when it is detrimental to the liar."

"What reason would the man have had for removing his clothing by the river if he was not going to bathe?"

Captain Jackson smiled and looked in Desert Rain's direction.

Sergeant Beyer followed the captain's gaze. Silently he placed his cap back on his head.

The night was dark, only the stars flickered in the midnight sky. Laird lay on a blanket, eyes wide open, mind racing. He had overheard the captain and sergeant discussing what was to be done with the prisoners should they be attacked. The captain was just going to release them when he should have killed them on sight. The more Laird thought about it, the more it made his blood boil.

He turned his head, straining his eyes in the darkness to get a glimpse of the Indian captives. They were separated from each other, hands and feet securely bound, defenseless. He began to formulate a plan. He could easily slip over to them in the dark. One by one his knife would do what the captain had failed to do. After slitting each prisoner's throat, Laird would then slip into the trees under the darkness of the new moon. Whatever other Indians were out there, let them have the soldiers. He would hide in the woods and watch the carnage from afar.

He rolled over and silently removed his knife from its sheath. The night was perfectly dark; the guards would never see his movements if he kept low to the ground. He began to crawl forward.

It was hard to see as he crawled along the ground, but he was sure he was heading in the direction of the female captive. She couldn't be much farther away. She was going to be the first to go. After all, he reasoned, she was the one responsible for Clem's death.

In the dark ahead, he could just make out the outline of a

body. It had to be her. He reached forward and pulled himself closer.

It was an Indian all right, but not the female. This one was wearing leggings. He could barely see the outline of fringe on the buckskin shirt. It didn't matter which one was first, he thought, might as well start with one of the bucks.

It would be easy. The Indian's hands were tied behind his back. Laird figured that he would just have to make one clean, deep cut. It would be over quickly. The savage would simply wake up dead.

He was close now. The first one would be out of the way soon. He reached for the Indian lying motionless in front of him, but hesitated as a familiar scent brushed his nose. He recognized the odor immediately. It was the musky smell of gun oil and tanning fluid. He could feel the wind in his face as it blew across the prone figure before him. It was the unmistakable smell of a trapper and it was coming from the Indian's clothing.

Laird swallowed hard. Was he dreaming? It couldn't be true. "Cl . . . Clem?"

The dark figure before him suddenly exploded into motion and then there were two hands around Laird's neck. Strong hands. Deadly hands. The last sound Laird heard was the snapping of bones.

Chapter Nineteen

"Sergeant, Captain, you better come quick."

Sergeant Beyer rolled over, rubbing sleep from his eyes, and looked up at the freckle-faced trooper who had just awakened him. "What is it, Booth?"

Captain Jackson stirred from sleep and listened to the exchange.

"Sergeant, something strange has happened during the night."

Beyer looked over at the captain, then back at Booth. "What thing, Trooper? Spit it out."

"Well, Sergeant, the Indian girl is missing."

"Missing?" Captain Jackson bolted upright.

"Yes, sir. And the trapper. . . ."

"I knew it!" Jackson said, pulling on his boots. "He's taken the girl, hasn't he?"

Beyer sat up and began to pull on his boots as well. "Trooper, I want that trapper found immediately."

"Sergeant," the trooper interjected, "the trapper's not missing. I'm afraid he's dead."

Captain Jackson stood staring at the lifeless form of Laird Carney. He was surely dead, lying with his neck at an unnatural angle. "Tell me what you know, Trooper."

Booth looked at his commanding officer and shrugged. "All we know, sir, is that when we changed the last watch there were still four bodies lying where the captives should have been. In the dark it was impossible to tell which one was which. When I came into camp to wake you and the sergeant, I discovered that the girl was missing and the body of the trapper had been put in her place. I don't know when or how it was done, but whatever happened, happened sometime during the night."

"His neck is broken," Sergeant Beyer remarked as he knelt beside Laird's body and moved the head back and forth.

Broken Branch had first awakened to the sound of the men's voices. He lay still, secretly watching the activities around the body. Relief coursed through him as he realized that it was not his sister. They must have moved her in the night, he thought. He watched as the sergeant moved the head of the trapper back and forth, heard the grinding of broken bones. Suddenly a similar image came to mind. The image of the mountain lion, lying on a rock by the river. Broken Branch had moved the lion's head in the same manner, heard the same noise. Could it be?

He glanced around the encampment, trying not to move any more than necessary. There was no sign of his sister. The count of soldiers indicated that there was only one missing. He knew that two guards had been posted last night. That left two possibilities. The missing blue coat was still at his post or he had taken Desert Rain.

"Wake the men, Trooper. Let's see if anyone noticed anything during the night," Jackson ordered.

"Yes, sir."

Four troopers sat silently before the captain and sergeant. There were only three captives now. Still bound, they were placed to the captain's left as he began to speak.

"Did anyone see anything unusual last night?"

To a man, the answer was a resounding "No."

Sergeant Beyer's face flushed with frustration. "You mean not a single one of you heard a sound, saw a shadow? You mean that that squaw was able to kill the trapper in the middle of the night, free herself and escape, and not one of you noticed anything?"

The sergeant's gaze roamed over the faces of his subordinates, looking for any sign that might tell him that one of them was holding out on him. When it came to rest on Trooper Livingston, Beyer noticed a wry grin curve his lips. "What is it, Livingston? You have something to tell me?"

"No," Livingston offered, "not exactly. I was just wondering if *you* heard anything last night, Sergeant."

The sergeant's frustration turned to anger in a flash. Insubordination was one thing he could not abide. He curled his hands into fists and stepped toward Livingston.

"Sergeant!" Jackson said, placing a firm hand on his first sergeant's shoulder, stopping him in his tracks. "We will not resort to fighting amongst ourselves. I'm afraid Livingston may have a point. *None* of us heard or saw a thing out of the ordinary last night. Whatever happened, and however it happened, must remain a mystery right now. There's only one thing we can do. Bury the trapper and continue toward the fort."

Sergeant Beyer struggled to regain his composure. "What about the Indians? Maybe they can tell us what happened."

Captain Jackson turned to his interpreter. "Sosa, ask them if they know anything. I'm sure they won't tell us even if they know, but ask them anyway."

"Yes, sir."

"Sergeant, bury the trapper. We need to be free from these

133

woods as soon as possible." Captain Jackson turned and started toward his bedroll.

Sergeant Beyer's glare once again fell on Trooper Livingston. "Bury him!"

The sergeant's look of contempt was piercing, but Livingston slowly stood. He brushed dirt from his trousers, looked up at Sergeant Beyer, and smiled. "Yes, Sergeant. Right away."

"Where is my sister?" Broken Branch called out as Sosa approached him.

"I don't know. We don't know. I came to talk to you about it," Sosa replied.

"You are lying!" Cloud Maker yelled.

Sosa knelt beside the three men. "I'm telling you, we don't know."

Black Beaver noted the sincerity in the trooper's voice. Something about Sosa's face made Black Beaver feel that the trooper was worried, puzzled. "My brothers, perhaps Desert Rain has escaped into the night."

"No," Cloud Maker objected, "she would have cut our ropes and freed us as well."

"Would she?" Black Beaver asked. "If she was able to free herself, would she have risked freeing us? Would that not have drawn the attention of the blue coats sleeping around us and of the guards in the woods? I think she would have sought to escape alone, making less noise than four people. I think she would have sought to find the Spirit and let him know of the situation."

"She killed the trapper, you know," Sosa informed them.

"No, she did not," Broken Branch blurted. "She could not have broken his neck. That would have taken great strength."

Sosa's eyes registered his surprise. "How did you know his neck was broken?"

"I have eyes to see, ears to hear. The bones in his neck pop like breaking twigs." All eyes were on Broken Branch as he continued. "I know of only one person who could have done that."

"Who?" Sosa asked with wide-eyed anticipation.

"The Spirit That Walks as a Man."

Captain Jackson was alone with his thoughts. *Why would a band of Indians steal my horses and kill only half of my men the first night, instead of riding in and waging all-out warfare on us? Why would the girl be taken and the trapper killed under cover of darkness, yet none of the other men, including the guards, be harmed?*

It just didn't make sense. The Apache were known for their cunning in battle. They were a crafty lot. In fact, at that very moment, there were thousands of troops hunting Geronimo all over the southwest. Yet even accompanied by four hundred men, women, and children, the crafty Apache was able to elude them at will. Like a ghost in the desert, Geronimo moved across the landscape, leaving no indication of his passing. *Perhaps that is what I'm dealing with,* Jackson mused. *Perhaps it is Geronimo who is playing games with us. Maybe he is the one the captives refer to as The Spirit That Walks as a Man.*

Geronimo surely would know that they were far away from the only truly secure fort in this part of Arizona Territory. The garrison at Fort Lowell was the only thorn in Geronimo's flesh in this whole area. But what would Geronimo be doing this far north? Right now, Jackson knew, there were soldiers scouring the Dragoon Mountains to the southwest. Geronimo had been seen there only about a month ago. Could he have traveled this far north without detection?

Captain Jackson shook his head in frustration. If it wasn't Geronimo, it was someone of equal skill and intelligence. Someone was playing games with him, endangering the lives of his men, and had already taken the lives of six of them. *Games are played with only one rule in mind,* Jackson thought. *To win. Maybe I need to change the rules.*

*   *   *

Desert Rain sat under a longleaf pine, thinking about the night's events. It had all happened so quickly that some of it was still just a blur, but slowly bits and pieces came to mind. Her first memory of last night was that of rolling over and discovering that her hands were no longer tied behind her back. Someone had cut the ropes. She smiled as she remembered hearing Spirit Walker's voice for the first time in what seemed like months. "Quiet, my Flower, I am here to help you," he had whispered.

At first, she had thought that she was dreaming, but when she felt his gentle touch she knew it was real. He had helped her escape the encampment and conceal herself in the brush, telling her where the guard closest to them was, and ordering her to stay there until he came for her. She had waited for a long time, but finally he was there once again. He had told her to hold onto the fringe on the back of the shirt he was wearing—the shirt of the trapper who had tried to capture her by the waterfall. The night had been so dark that she was barely able to make out the trunks of the trees, let alone the branches that would brush against them and signal their passing.

Slowly, but surely, Spirit Walker had moved away from the white man's camp with her in tow. He had moved like a spirit in the darkness. She had found that by keeping directly behind him, holding tightly to his garment, she was able to follow exactly in his footsteps. They had moved more silently than she could ever have imagined, and never once made a noise until they were far from the encampment.

She had fallen into his arms then. She had kissed him. She remembered rolling over and over in the dew-laden grass, kissing him, running her hands through his long hair. She remembered laughing and laughing, delight washing over her like a spring shower. She had run her hands down over his strong arms, and it was then she had felt the bandages beneath the sleeves of the shirt he had worn.

Now, sitting beneath the tree in the morning sun, she couldn't stop thinking of her love for this man. A man who, though he was in great pain, allowed her to roll in joy with him in the grass. A man who had risked his life to save hers, not once, not twice, but three times now. A man who at this very moment was preparing to carry out a daring plan to save her brother, her friends. A man like no other man. A spirit who merely walks as a man.

Chapter Twenty

Desert Rain glanced at Spirit Walker, who sat concentrating on the task at hand. With the eye of a true craftsman, he moved his fingers over bits of lichen and cloth, attaching them together with small pieces of sinew. She wasn't exactly sure of his plan, but she knew it had something to do with the six men who sat tied to the trees opposite the wise warrior.

Six blue coats, tied to six trees. She couldn't help but think of the irony of it all. She and her friends had once been their captives, and now they were hers. She rose slowly and walked toward Spirit Walker.

"How did it happen?" she asked as she approached.

The old warrior glanced up momentarily from his work. "What, my Flower?"

"Those men. How did you manage to capture them?"

"Oh." Spirit Walker smiled as he continued his sewing. "I did not so much capture them as persuade them to join me. You see before you, my Flower, a white man who has now learned never to fall asleep while guarding horses at night, and five white men who have learned never to split up while tracking lost horses." The warrior laughed then, a deep hearty laugh.

Desert Rain couldn't help but giggle as he laughed. It was such a pleasant sound to her ear. She wanted to take him in her arms. She wanted to hold him, caress his face, assure him of his worth. She had sensed so many times during her stay with him that he felt useless, no longer of any value to his people. She wanted to be the one to change that. He was still a warrior, still had the courage of ten men. She wanted him to feel what she knew to be true.

She glanced down at his bandaged arms. "My Spirit, perhaps I should take a look at your arms. The bandages need to be changed."

"There will be time for that later, my Flower. There." He held aloft a long wig made of goat's-beard lichen. "What do you think of this?"

"Well, it resembles a scalp. What is it for, my Spirit?"

"Them. It's for them," he said, pointing and smiling at his prisoners. "They are the war party the blue coats found the tracks of by the creek." Spirit Walker picked up the other items he had fashioned and rose to his feet. "Now, my Flower, grab that bag over there. We have work to do. The other blue coats will be free of the woods soon, turning west toward the fort. We must cut them off before they climb the ridge."

Broken Branch sat silently in the cool mountain stream, wondering about the strange turn of events. They had been traveling along the river and would have been clear of the woodlands soon, entering the vast prairie that would take them to the white man's fort. Suddenly the blue coat leader had sent two of his men across the river. The two troopers were even now sitting on the far shore with their guns resting on their hips. Then the trooper who had spoken to him and his friends often in their own language had come to them and told them that they could enter the water and bathe for the first time since their capture. The interpreter had untied each of the men's hands and feet, and then just stepped away.

At first the three Apache men had been leery of entering the water, fearing a trap. Perhaps they were being set up to be shot. Finally, Cloud Maker said that if they were to be shot, they might as well be clean when they entered the After World. He dove into the water and began to wash the blood from his hair and forehead. The other two decided that they might as well join him.

The troopers had withdrawn, almost as if they were trying to give the captives enough space to talk among themselves freely.

And now Broken Branch sat immersed up to his neck in the cool water. He had to admit that the water felt refreshing as it ran over his aching muscles.

"I don't know what to make of this, my brother," Black Beaver said, wading up beside Broken Branch and taking a seat beside him.

"Nor I," Broken Branch said in return.

Cloud Maker also approached and took a place on the other side of Broken Branch.

"You look much better," Broken Branch said with a sly grin.

Cloud Maker rubbed his wrists. "I am glad to be free of those ropes. But what do you think? Why have they allowed us to bathe?"

"Maybe they want us to attempt an escape so they can kill us," Black Beaver suggested.

"I think not," Broken Branch stated. "They could have done that already. Who would question their word?"

"What then?" Cloud Maker asked.

"Maybe they just want us to be clean when they march us into their fort," Broken Branch said.

Cloud Maker made his way to a boulder sticking up out of the stream. Leaning back on the rock he looked at his friends. "Where do you think Desert Rain is right now?"

Broken Branch glanced over at Cloud Maker. "I assure you that she is with the Spirit That Walks as a Man. I know they are planning to set us free."

"Maybe they rode for the rancheria," Black Beaver said. "They may have already rallied the warriors and are even now riding to our rescue."

"I don't know, the rancheria is at least a day away. It would take too much time to ride there and back. I think my sister is still around."

"I hope they have a good plan," Cloud Maker remarked.

"As do I, my brother. As do I." Broken Branch's gaze swept the tree line, looking for any sign of movement, any sign of the only two people who might save them from captivity.

Captain Jackson stood staring into the forest, his sergeant at his side. "Well, Sergeant, if they're out there, if they're watching, they have to know that we are treating their comrades with courtesy."

"Do you really think that that will buy us any mercy if they decide to attack, Captain?" Beyer asked.

"I'm not asking for mercy, Sergeant, but I refuse to lose any more men just to take these three Indians to the brig at Fort Lowell."

"But even if we give up the prisoners, there is no guarantee they will let us continue to the fort unmolested."

"True, Sergeant, there is no guarantee. However, I know the Apache to be a fair-minded people. If we treat them with respect, they will return the respect in kind. But the Apache also value bravery. If we completely back down and let the prisoners go, they will interpret that as a sign of weakness. We must continue to show that we are intent on doing our duty."

Sergeant Beyer cast a glance ahead of them on the trail. "How long till we hit the prairie, do you think?"

"In a couple of hours we should be turning west toward the fort. Better get ready to move, Sergeant; I'd say we've let them have enough time to see our generosity."

"Yes, sir." Sergeant Beyer turned and began to bark his orders.

It had been nice to be able to sit in the water during the heat of the day. After a while Broken Branch and his friends had been ordered out of the stream. Broken Branch walked up to the man who had released them earlier and held out his hands. It was a sign of bravery, not surrender. Broken Branch was a warrior, not afraid to be bound. The white man's magic could never hold a Jicarilla warrior.

"There is no need to tie your hands, my friend," Trooper Sosa said quietly.

Broken Branch hesitated for a moment. "Why?"

"The captain has ordered me only to place hobbles on your feet. That is enough to keep you from escaping."

Broken Branch placed his hands at his sides and watched as Sosa replaced the ankle ropes.

The woodlands were behind them now. Captain Jackson swung the men to the west and started out across the plains. With any luck, they might run into a patrol from Fort Lowell. It wasn't unusual in these times to see roving patrols on the prairie. But, as much as he tried to convince himself of the possibility, Captain Jackson knew that it wasn't very likely that a patrol would be this far from the fort. Not unless, that is, the commander had sent reinforcements to look for Jackson and his men.

They turned west, starting up a small rise, the sun beaming intense light over the hill's crest. Suddenly the captain gave a command to halt. Sergeant Beyer stepped forward, squinting into the afternoon sun. He heard the murmur rise behind him as his men began to assess the situation. It was not a pretty sight. At the top of the hill, silhouetted by the sun's rays, were eight mounted riders.

"The time has come, Sergeant," Captain Jackson noted.

"I count eight, Captain, but that's only what they're willing to show us. I wonder how many more are in hiding behind the hill?"

The black shapes at the top of the rise sat motionless, the wind blowing through their long hair, moving the feathers tied to their horses' manes. The dark figure on the far right suddenly raised his right hand.

"They're greeting us, Captain. Seems they may want to talk," Sergeant Beyer suggested.

"Maybe so," Captain Jackson agreed. He raised his right hand in response. "I'm going forward, Sergeant. Hold the men here. Watch the captives. Be silent, but be vigilant. Let's not make any rash decisions. Wait for my return." Jackson handed his rifle to the sergeant, then removed his saber from its scabbard. Ceremoniously, he held the saber aloft, then plunged the tip into the ground at his feet, hoping that the Apache would take it as a sign of peace.

"Be careful, Captain," Beyer said as Jackson began walking up the hill.

"Count on it."

Desert Rain watched as Captain Jackson stepped forward and walked alone up the small rise. Spirit Walker started his mount forward at a walk to intercept the cavalry officer before he got close enough to make out the identity of the riders on the ridge.

A smile curved Desert Rain's lips as she glanced along the row of riders to her right. It was truly a funny sight to see six cavalrymen, stripped to the waist and wearing wigs of lichen on their heads. They were indeed mounted, but their horses were hobbled, making it impossible for them to run. The men were gagged to keep them from crying out, but Desert Rain noticed something peculiar about the captured troopers. They were very cooperative.

Not once had even one of them hesitated to do anything that they were asked to do. There was a special bond between them and their captor. Somehow Spirit Walker had earned their trust. Maybe it was because he had insured that they always had plenty of food and water. He had treated them with kindness and had talked to them often in their own language.

Now these same men sat on their horses as if they were truly Apache warriors. Tall and proud, they watched as Spirit Walker and Captain James Jackson met face to face on the plains before them.

Chapter Twenty-one

Captain Jackson watched the barrel-chested warrior approach. He sat proudly on the back of Jackson's own horse. The Apache's visage was firm. A thick black stripe bridged his nose and underlined each eye. Captain Jackson recognized the traditional war face of the tribe the white man called the Chiricahua. A broad, whitish cloth crossed the old warrior's chest like a sash, and both arms were carefully wrapped in beaver pelts. The Apache carried only one weapon, a lance decorated with six eagle feathers.

Spirit Walker brought his mount to a halt several yards in front of the captain. He raised the lance slowly, then suddenly tossed it with force into the ground at the officer's feet. Captain Jackson never moved, not so much as a twitch. Spirit Walker smiled, but only inwardly. The blue coat leader was brave, he thought. Throwing a leg over the head of his horse, Spirit Walker slid from its back and landed deftly on the ground below.

The captain looked surprised when Spirit Walker addressed him in English. "What is your name, blue coat?"

"Captain James Jackson, U.S. Cavalry."

Spirit Walker stepped up and placed his hand on the lance. "Captain James Jackson, U.S. Cavalry, you have captured some of my men. I want them back."

"It's not that easy."

"Not that easy? Do you not have the power to release them? I wish to speak to the man who has the power." Spirit Walker yanked the lance from the ground and turned to leave.

"I have that power, but I wish to speak to the Spirit That Walks as a Man. I hear that he is your leader. I will speak to no other."

Spirit Walker stopped in his tracks and turned slowly to face the captain once again. He examined the officer's face, looking for any sign of fear. The captain stood tall and met Spirit Walker's gaze with determination. The Apache knew that courage was not the absence of fear, but rather the control of it. The captain was exhibiting that control.

Spirit Walker stepped forward, stopping directly in front of Jackson. "I am the Spirit Walker. I have the power to take your life and the lives of your men. I demand that you release my brothers."

The warrior's eyes were piercing, but Jackson held his gaze. He knew that the Chiricahua leader was speaking the truth, but he also knew that sometimes running a little risk could bring great rewards. "I have heard that the Spirit That Walks as a Man is a great and wise leader. Surely he would not expect me to give up my prisoners without a guarantee of safety."

"Guarantee? You expect me to guarantee your safety, when you have come into my home and captured my men without reason?"

"I came because some of your men attacked innocent civilians along the river. I came for no other reason•than justice."

"Justice! Two trappers attempt to attack one of our women. Do you call that justice? Are we merely dogs for your entertainment?"

"No, but the words of the trappers are not the same as your words."

Spirit Walker laughed. "You have no trappers, Captain James Jackson, U.S. Cavalry. They are no more."

"And how would you know that, unless you had something to do with their deaths?"

"I had everything to do with their deaths," Spirit Walker said proudly. "I shot the big one from the top of the falls as he stood beside the river. He died quickly for trying to force one of my sisters."

It wasn't hard for Captain Jackson to believe that the warrior was telling the truth. That was exactly the conclusion he had come to only the day before. He had always felt that the prisoners under his charge were never involved in that incident. The first trapper had it coming and he knew it, but he had to know about the other trapper. He had to know how Laird Carney had died. "And what of the other one?" he asked.

"I broke his neck in the night," Spirit Walker said confidently.

"The night the girl escaped?"

"The night I took the girl back."

"Why did you kill the trapper if you only came for the girl?"

"The trapper would have killed all of my people. Crawling in the night, he wanted to kill them all. I had to kill him before he killed them."

Captain Jackson looked the Apache up and down. "I get the feeling that you would have killed more of us that night if you'd had the chance."

Spirit Walker's gaze dropped to the captain's hip. "You are wearing your pistol."

It had not even crossed the captain's mind that he was still

147

wearing his Colt revolver on his right hip. It was the typical cross-draw holster, government issue. The cavalry officer's first weapon had always been the saber, worn on the left hip. Since the saber was wielded in the right hand, the holster had been designed so that the pistol could be cross-drawn by the left hand. It had become such a part of Jackson's uniform that he had completely forgotten to remove it. Slowly Jackson moved his hands away from his sides in a show of peace. Did Spirit Walker believe this to be a trap?

"Draw your weapon, Captain James Jackson, U.S. Cavalry. Draw your weapon."

Jackson's mind was racing. What was the Chiricahua up to? Was there death in his words? The captain remained motionless.

Spirit Walker stepped backward one pace, planted the lance once again in the ground, and raised his hands in surrender. "Draw your weapon. Experience the magic of The Spirit Walker. Draw it!"

Slowly Captain Jackson's left hand began to move toward his right hip. Undoing the flap of the Army-issue cross-draw holster, he reached inside and removed the pistol.

"Shoot me!" Spirit Walker shouted. "Shoot me with the white man's magic. You cannot hurt me!"

Either the old man is crazy or he knows something I don't, Jackson thought.

Desert Rain watched in horror as Captain Jackson raised his revolver and leveled it at Spirit Walker's head. What had happened? What had gone wrong with the plan?

"Ready arms!" Sergeant Beyer yelled to his men. "Looks like we've got trouble."

Sweat traced a path across Captain Jackson's forehead. This could be the beginning of the end for him and his men, or it could be their salvation. Was it worth the chance? The Apache's eyes were unblinking, and showed absolutely no fear whatsoever. What did he know that Jackson didn't know? Jackson knew that if he was going to save his men, he must show no fear as well. He held his breath and slowly squeezed the trigger of the Colt. The metallic click signaled an empty chamber. The captain exhaled his relief.

Spirit Walker reached into the pouch at his hip, withdrew a handful of bullets and tossed them in the dirt at the captain's feet. "I could have killed you in the night, Captain James Jackson, U.S. Cavalry. I chose rather to remove death from your weapon."

Jackson spoke in astonishment. "How were you sure that I had not reloaded my weapon?"

Spirit Walker smiled once again. "If you had, you would have known that using that weapon would have brought death to you and your men—a risk without reward."

Captain Jackson lowered the pistol and slowly placed it back in his holster. "You are indeed wise, my friend. I wish that you were wise enough to return the lives of the six men you have taken."

"Captain James Jackson, U.S. Cavalry, I have the power to restore life for life. Return to me my men."

Jackson searched the Apache's deep eyes. There was an honesty in the warrior's demeanor. "You have my word, Spirit Walker. I believe your words."

Stepping forward, Spirit Walker extended his right arm toward the officer. "You have my word that you may pass safely back to your fort."

Captain Jackson extended his right arm and Spirit Walker gripped the officer's forearm firmly. "It is the way of life and the way of death," the warrior stated flatly. "I give you my words of life."

Jackson smiled. "I am honored to have met face to face with

the Spirit That Walks as a Man. You also have my words of life."

"*Ashoge, shils aash*. Thank you, my friend."

"Sergeant, release the prisoners," Captain Jackson said as he approached his men.

"Sir?"

"I said, release the prisoners."

"But, sir, if we release them now, what's to keep those savages from killing us outright? After all, they've already killed six of our men."

Jackson placed a comforting hand on the sergeant's shoulder. "Sergeant, I believe we are about to see a miracle. Trooper Sosa, release the prisoners and tell them they are free to go."

Desert Rain watched as Spirit Walker rode casually toward her. "My Spirit. I was so worried. I thought I had lost you."

The warrior smiled. "No, my Flower, our time has just begun." He slid from the back of his horse and approached the soldiers who sat mounted before him.

One after the other, he cut the hobbles from their horses' rear legs. "You are free to go," he said in English. "Tell your leader that the other horses will be waiting for him here. We will allow you to return to your fort safely."

Captain Jackson watched as his former prisoners made their way up the small grade. He was actually relieved that it was over.

"Sir?"

"Yes, Sergeant?"

"Sir, six of the warriors are moving our way."

The sergeant was right, they were moving. Jackson watched carefully as six of the eight riders started down the hill in his direction.

"What do we do, Captain?" the sergeant asked.

Jackson pulled his saber from the ground, wiped dirt from the blade, and slid it back into its scabbard. "We wait, Sergeant, we wait."

Desert Rain slid from her pony and embraced Broken Branch. "You are well, my brother?"

"Yes. We are all well."

Cloud Maker and Black Beaver agreed, each in turn hugging Desert Rain.

Black Beaver approached Spirit Walker. "Uncle, we have heard many stories about the Spirit That Walks as a Man, but none of them tell of your true wisdom. Will you not return with us to our People?"

Spirit Walker glanced at Desert Rain. "Will you stay with me for a while?"

Desert Rain smiled. "I will, my Spirit."

"Sister, you cannot. Mother will be so worried if I do not return with you," Broken Branch protested.

Desert Rain stroked her brother's face lightly. "My brother, you will tell her that I am safe. That I am happy. That I will be home to see her soon. Tell her that I am safe in the hands of my Spirit."

"There are your horses," Spirit Walker said. He pointed to nine horses grazing comfortably, though hobbled, on the backside of the hill. Three of them were Apache ponies, the others wore the white man's brand. "Take your horses from among the others and return to your People. Allow the blue coats to return safely to their fort. I will bring Desert Rain to her mother soon."

Broken Branch approached the old warrior. "Uncle, I have learned to trust your words. We will wait for you to come to us."

"Well, I'll be damned," Sergeant Beyer exclaimed as the faces of the men riding toward them came into view.

Captain Jackson smiled broadly. They had been fooled. The six Apache warriors were merely six troopers dressed as warriors on six cavalry horses shod with leather boots. What a sight, he marveled. What a sight!

Chapter Twenty-two

The evening was beginning to lose its light as Desert Rain followed Spirit Walker through the forest. She couldn't help thinking how smoothly he moved through the trees. Many times she had looked at the ground as he walked ahead of her, but was never able to see a single track that would indicate his passing. His pace was steady, his breathing easy, and it was obvious he had spent many years traversing these woodlands.

"My Spirit," Desert Rain called.

Spirit Walker stopped and looked back at his companion. "Yes, my Flower?"

"My Spirit, I do not think that we are making our way back to the wikiup. Should we not be turning farther to the north?"

Spirit Walker smiled. "You are very perceptive, Flower. But we are not going back to the wikiup."

"Where are we going then, my Spirit?"

"Come, we will camp soon and I will explain it to you. There is a spring ahead. We will stop there for the night."

Desert Rain nodded, and Spirit Walker moved on.

Desert Rain sat with her feet in the cool water of a nice stream, fed from an underground spring. She had been walking for days and her feet ached for relief. She glanced over her shoulder at Spirit Walker, who was busy laying a fire for the night. The large bundle he had strapped to his back lay in the brush now. She wondered what it contained, but figured she would know soon enough.

A little later, Spirit Walker simply walked off into the woods. Desert Rain sat quietly by the fire, watching it flicker in the gray darkness of dusk. She thought of the man who had so captivated her heart. He was quiet, mysterious, the very economy of motion. He never seemed to waste time, never seemed to be idle. He reminded her of . . .

A tear came to her eye as she remembered her short life as the wife of Arm Bow. Though it had only been for a few days, she had never known such love as his. She tried to imagine his face, his voice. She struggled to hear his song. She knew he still loved her, knew he was watching over her. She knew that it was Arm Bow who had sent Spirit Walker to help her through her grief.

"My husband," she whispered, "what am I to do now? What is the meaning of my life? Am I to be alone? Am I to wander in isolation like my Spirit? Tell me, my husband. Tell me what I am to do."

"You must undertake a vision quest."

Desert Rain jumped at the sound of the voice. It was not her husband's, but she knew they were his words. She peered into the darkness, barely making out the form of Spirit Walker as he moved through the trees and into the fire's light. He held two squirrels in his hands.

"Now we shall eat," he said with a smile. "Then we shall talk."

Spirit Walker skinned, gutted, and roasted the squirrels over the fire without saying another word. When he finally handed

Desert Rain a piece of the cooked meat, she ate hungrily. It was the first fresh meat she had eaten since she was captured by the blue coats.

After the meal, Spirit Walker placed a few more sticks on the fire. "Now we shall talk, Little One."

Desert Rain looked at her benefactor. She trusted him, respected him. She knew he would have the answers. He would tell her what she must do, how she must continue with her life. She listened intently.

"You have awakened the warrior within me, my Flower, but it is also true that you have awakened the woman within yourself. The time has come for us both to pursue a vision quest. We will travel to a sacred cave in the foothills. During the journey, from this night forward, and until the end of the quest, we will not eat or speak. Taking only water to sustain our physical lives, we will partake of only spiritual nourishment."

Desert Rain listened with wide-eyed wonder. She had heard of such journeys. Several times the warriors of her People would set out on vision quests. They would tell briefly of their journey around the campfires after their return. They would tell of seeing visions. She remembered one young brave telling of his vision, his purpose, regarding his place among the People. He told of following his spirit guide through a maze of visions. It was never proper to reveal one's spirit guide, but sometimes the visions were described in detail in order for the shaman to help interpret what the warrior had seen. She had never heard of a woman seeking a vision quest, though, and she said as much.

Spirit Walker spoke firmly, resolutely. "You are a warrior, my Flower. The quest is yours to seek."

"I don't know how. What do I do? What will happen on the quest and how will I know when it is over? If I cannot speak to you, my Spirit, how will I know these things?"

Spirit Walker stood, walked over, and sat down beside her. Taking her hand, he began to explain. "Little One, I cannot tell you of your quest. A vision quest is a very personal thing. I can only tell you that we shall reach the cave in three days. Before entering the cave, I will light a fire and we will prepare to enter at last light. When we enter the cave, you will follow me through the tunnels and to a sacred area. There, I will light a central fire and give you a tonic. After you drink the tonic, you will begin to see visions. Observe those visions carefully. Listen to your spirit guide. You will find your heart, your mission, your spirit."

"I am afraid." Desert Rain hung her head. She was ashamed of being afraid. Spirit Walker had told her that she was a warrior, but she didn't feel very much like a warrior right now.

Spirit Walker lifted her chin gently. "I, too, my Flower. I, too."

Desert Rain couldn't believe her ears. She had seen him face death more than once. He had stared down a bear. He had strangled a mountain lion with his bare hands. He had boldly looked into the barrel of the white man's magic. She had never seen any evidence that he was ever afraid of anything. Perhaps courage was not the absence of fear. Perhaps it was the mastering of fear, she thought. The idea made her smile.

Spirit Walker bent forward and kissed her. It was so gentle, so reassuring. Warmth spread through her as she kissed him back, wanting him to take her, to possess her. To make her his. The feeling in her breasts was almost overwhelming.

Spirit Walker eased away from her, his fingertips gently brushing her cheek. "When the quest is finished, we will know."

"We will know?"

"Yes. We will know what is to be done. You must be strong."

She did not understand his words entirely, but she had watched in awe as this mighty warrior had exhibited his wisdom time and time again. Who was she to doubt his words now? She nodded. She would do her part, whatever that should be.

"We will begin at sunrise. Sleep now," he said softly.

★   ★   ★

Three days of walking, three days of silence, three days of hunger, and yet Desert Rain was holding up better than she had thought she would. Aroused from sleep this morning, she noticed that even the hunger pangs had subsided. Now, in the early evening, she wasn't hungry at all. She was tired though, so tired. Tired of walking. Tired of making camp, breaking camp, and then walking some more. She was so weary, but Spirit Walker had promised her that they would reach the cave in three days, and this was the third day.

Silently and without warning, Spirit Walker stopped and removed the pack he had strapped to his back. He put the large bundle down and began to pick up sticks from the ground around him. Though Desert Rain felt like collapsing from exhaustion, she remembered that he had told her about building a fire before they entered the sacred cave. She began gathering wood as well.

As she walked the area, picking up as much dead wood as she could find, she casually looked about her for signs of the cave's entrance. There was a small hill, made up of rocks of various sizes, and that was the only conceivable place for the opening to be. Yet she saw nothing out of the ordinary. Just rocks. Rocks upon rocks, rising to a small hill. There certainly could be no large cave inside a hill that small. Either Spirit Walker had been exaggerating about the size of the cave or they were only making camp for the night. Her vow of silence kept her from asking the questions that plagued her.

Spirit Walker had gathered three separate piles of wood. She understood that one was to be the fire he had previously mentioned, but she couldn't help wondering about the other two piles that were set off to the side. After the piles were established, Spirit Walker removed bits of rawhide from his pack and tied the two separated stacks of wood into bundles.

She sat wearily at the base of a tree and watched as Spirit Walker shaved a piece of cedar bark into long thin strips. Balling the strips of cedar and tossing them lightly in the air and catching

157

them, he blew the dirt and debris away from the fibers. He placed the cedar ball onto another piece of bark and struck a well-aimed spark onto it with two pieces of flint. The ball leapt into flame.

Before long Spirit Walker was bathed in the yellowish glow of a roaring fire. Desert Rain, not knowing what else to do, remained at the base of the tree and watched her warrior with wonder. He was so focused on what he was doing that he never even looked to see that she was still there. Perhaps he can sense where I am, what I'm doing, she thought. He was truly a man of mystery, and that was one of the things that drew her to him.

He rummaged through the large pack, which she knew held sleeping robes. Now, he withdrew a bowl and a couple of small pouches. In the bowl, he mixed a reddish powder with other powders. She could only guess what they were. Before long, he began to use the reddish mixture to paint his face. He applied a heavy coat to his forehead, then lightning designs on both cheeks.

She had wanted, many times during the trip, to remove the beaver pelts he had wrapped around his wounded arms. She wanted desperately to see how his injuries were doing. She wondered if he was healing properly. Her questions were answered as he removed the pelts and tossed them on the ground beside him. His arms were streaked with raw scars. They looked painful, but he seemed not to notice.

Suddenly he began a low guttural chant. They weren't words as such, more like noises of various pitches and tones. Then he began to dance. There was no drum beat, but he didn't seem to need one. His feet, pounding the hard-packed soil, kept a perfect rhythm. She watched with interest as he moved to the north, reached into a small pouch, and tossed a handful of powder into the air. He repeated this ritual to the south, east, and west. She had watched this ceremony several times before as warriors prepared for their vision quests, appealing to the four winds for assistance.

Whirling, the dancing warrior tossed a handful of the powder into the fire, which immediately erupted into a ball of flames, towering above the muscular Apache. Spirit Walker danced over to his pack and removed a bag, hung it around his neck, and picked up the beaver pelts. Dusting both pelts thoroughly with the powder he had thrown into the fire, he removed a flaming branch, and began to wrap the pelts around the burning end of it. The branch burned brighter and brighter as the pelts were wrapped tighter and tighter around its tip.

From the other side of the fire's light, Desert Rain watched as the warrior approached one of the stacks of wood, bent over, and picked it up. Placing it on his shoulder, he looked at her for the first time since they had stopped. She followed his gaze to the other stack of wood; then he turned and began walking toward the rocky hill.

Chapter Twenty-three

Desert Rain walked over to the bundle of wood lying on the ground, and picked it up. It was light enough for her to heft it onto her shoulder, so she did, and then quickly followed Spirit Walker.

She followed the wise warrior around and between two large boulders and entered a crevice in the side of the hill. Many times, she found it necessary to turn sideways in order to squeeze between some of the huge rocks that bordered the trail they followed into the hillside. Suddenly they were standing before a small opening.

Stooping, Spirit Walker entered the opening in the rocks. As Desert Rain bent to enter, she could see a path sloping down at a steep angle. She slid, rather than walked, into the tunnel. She could understand now how the small hill could conceal a large cave.

After a while the tunnel leveled off and she was walking once again. Spirit Walker's pace was relentless, but she kept within the light of his torch as best she could.

The tunnel was quiet except for the eerie sound of water dripping from overhead. The air was stagnant, musky, cold. She felt her skin bristle at the cold as she walked deeper into the mouth of the cave.

She knew she should be paying better attention to the twists and turns they were taking through the maze of tunnels, but she was beginning to feel the effects of the journey. Three days without food, being constantly on the move, and not sleeping well had begun to take their toll on her stamina.

The torch Spirit Walker carried illuminated rock walls ingrained with changing hues of green, blue, and red, streaked with ingrained yellow and white veins.

After a while the walls around Spirit Walker disappeared. She knew immediately that he had entered a large cave. She followed the ball of light that surrounded the Apache warrior as he made his way across the vast expanse of the underground room.

When Spirit Walker stopped and dropped the wood he carried onto the cave floor, she added hers to his. He handed her the torch and stooped to arrange an appropriate firelay. When he was finished, he reached up and took the torch from her hand. He placed the burning branch carefully into the stack of wood, setting the entire pile afire. Spirit Walker stepped back, then threw a handful of powder onto the flames.

The eruption of fire from the wood pile illuminated the cave. Drawings of different scenes decorated the walls. Battle scenes, hunting scenes, and scenes of village life intermingled with each other like a huge calendar of events from long ago. Only a few words could be seen among the drawings. Most of the words were names. She speculated that they were names of ancestors who had entered the cave and scratched the images into the limestone of the cave's walls. Black marks along the base of the walls indicated that fires had been lit in order to see what was being etched.

Her gaze swept the walls, then slowly returned to the floor of the cavern. A sigh of wonder escaped her lips as she looked upon the most beautiful piece of art she had ever seen. It was a large sand art design in the center of the floor. Untouched by surface winds, the multicolored grains of sand lay perfectly in place. It wasn't a scene, wasn't an image of anything recognizable. It was made up of concentric circles, interlocking rings, squares, triangles, and wavy lines. It was a wonderful, complex design. She wondered what it meant and who had created it.

As a defense against the cold, she wrapped her arms around herself and moved closer to the fire. Spirit Walker didn't seem the least bit effected by the temperature. Calmly, he moved to a small pool of water near the wall. Reaching into the bag hanging around his neck, he withdrew a small wooden bowl. He knelt and dipped the bowl into the mineral water. Standing, he reached into the bag and removed another little deerskin pouch. As he turned and began walking in her direction, he poured the contents of the pouch into the water, placed the pouch back into the bag, and stirred the water with his finger.

Spirit Walker handed the bowl of liquid to Desert Rain. She took it from him and, remembering his words, drank as she had been instructed. Her vision began to blur almost immediately and she stumbled backward. Before she realized what was happening, she was sitting on the floor of the cave, watching as Spirit Walker returned to the water and once again filled the bowl. Her eyelids began to flicker and she caught only portions of movement from that point on. She watched him drink the liquid.

The temperature in the cave seemed to be rising. She sat warm and peaceful now, eyes closed, smiling. It was such a comforting feeling. No worries, no cares interrupted her thinking. Her senses seemed sharper. She could hear every drop of water, even above the crackling sound of the fire. She could smell the wood smoke, taste the salt of her own sweat as it trickled onto her lips.

She had no idea how long she sat with her eyes shut, or what happened during that time. But she gasped in wonder when slowly she opened her eyes. There before her, the scenes from the cave's walls sprang to life. She watched in sadness as her people were routed by the Comanches and forced to move farther west. She watched her people in battle after battle against their foes. In one scene she watched the white eyes as they poured from their wooden fort onto sacred hunting grounds. She watched the Old Ones as they chased large herds of buffalo across the plains and over steep cliffs. Watched as the women swarmed over the critically injured beasts, killing, skinning, and cutting them into manageable pieces to be taken back to the village. The scenes flashed in her mind, but she felt as if she were actually a part of the action. She was there, she could smell the odors, hear the noises, feel the emotions of every battle, every hunt.

After a while, her gaze wandered back to the fire and lingered on the warrior dancing before her. Was he a spirit from long ago? He was broad-shouldered and muscular. Scars dotted his massive chest, streaked his mighty arms, marked his thick legs with the signs of war. He wore only war paint and danced with enthusiasm. Sweat glistened on his body as he circled the fire. There was no doubt about his masculinity, no doubt about his power and importance. Desire rose within her, elevating her body's heat. Standing, she removed her tunic and moccasins.

The rock floor felt cool and slick beneath her feet. She joined the warrior and danced with him in the heat of the flames, felt the fire of her desire burn brighter and hotter within her. She felt as if she were moving through time, flying through space. She was light and carefree, sailing on the wind.

Then she saw another man, not dancing, just standing in front of her, smiling, as her naked body swayed to the beat in her head. He was handsome, strong, and young. Immediately she ceased her dance. It was Arm Bow. He was here. They could begin their lives together again.

"My husband!" she cried, her eyes filled with tears of joy.

"My Desert Rain, you are more beautiful now than ever."

Her heart bursting with love, she ran into his arms. As his powerful arms enclosed her, she sighed. "I have missed you so, my husband. Have you come for me?"

"No, my wife. I cannot take you with me."

Desert Rain's mind recoiled at his words. "But, my husband, we belong together. I must go with you."

"Rain, there is so much more for you to do here. You cannot come with me."

Sadness gripped her heart and her tears flowed freely. "My husband, I cannot continue without you. I have no desire to go on without your love."

He held her shoulders gently. "You will not be without my love, Little One. You will not. My love will be with you forever. You will always be my Song on the Midnight Wind."

She smiled through her tears. "I'm here to seek my spirit guide, you know."

"I know. I have come to show him to you."

"You have?"

"Yes, my sweet Desert Rain."

Desert Rain looked around her with anticipation. "Where is he, my husband? I want to see my spirit guide."

"You have both seen him and known him, my love."

The questioning look on Desert Rain's face came straight from her heart. She couldn't understand this strange saying. "How is that possible?"

"I am your spirit guide, Desert Rain. It is I who shall watch over you."

"You, my husband? You are to be my spirit guide?"

"Yes. From this time forward I shall guide you through your life."

"You will come to me, my husband? You will talk with me and advise me as I journey to the After World?"

"No, I cannot. I will send a messenger on the winds. My messenger will show you the path you should take. When you need me, you have only to contact my messenger and I will answer."

"Messenger? What messenger?"

"You will know. When the eagle and the hawk fly together as one, you will know."

Desert Rain turned and walked away from the fire. In frustration she sat on the stone floor. "I do not understand these words. I am confused, my husband."

He was standing before her as she sat cross-legged on the ground. His legs were thick and powerful, just as she had remembered. But there was something about them that she had not remembered—a dark indention in his right thigh—the unmistakable scar of a bullet wound. She reached out and touched it.

He was so real, his muscles so firm, he couldn't possibly be a spirit. She gripped his leg, wanting to be close to him, wanting to feel him, never to let him go. She kissed his thigh softly. She wanted to taste him, wanted to please him. Maybe that would make him stay. Maybe he wouldn't leave her if she could only show him how much she needed him.

He stood naked before her and she rose to her knees, kissing his stomach, touching him, running her hand over his manhood. His desire was evident and she felt his hands stroking her hair, caressing her cheek as she tasted him.

Then he lowered her onto the floor. She closed her eyes as she felt his lips on her breasts. His tongue was warm and wet, his kisses gentle and thrilling. She arched her back and moaned as she felt his hand move down her flat stomach and on to the most sensitive part of her body. His fingers were strong and firm.

Her breathing came in short gasps, her body undulating with pleasure.

He kissed his way up the soft part of her throat, over the delicate curve of her chin, and onto her lips. His kisses were deep and caring. She felt the waves of passion overwhelm her, colors exploding in her mind. She wanted to cry out in ecstasy, but his lips held her in check.

As her body relaxed, his lips pulled away from her own. She opened her eyes slowly. "Take me," she whispered. But it was Spirit Walker who stood over her, looking down upon her naked form.

"It is time for us to leave, my Flower," he said softly.

Chapter Twenty-four

Desert Rain opened her eyes and stared up at the afternoon sun. The events of the night before were somewhat fuzzy in her mind. She remembered entering the cave and drinking the liquid she had been given. The visions she had seen came back to her in bits and pieces, but she remembered seeing Arm Bow and talking with him. She remembered touching him, tasting him, the touch of his hands and lips on her body. Even the afternoon sun could not match the warmth she had felt then.

She remembered Spirit Walker leading her out of the cave once she had dressed. She had been so tired, yet it amazed her that the gray light of dawn was cresting the trees when they emerged from the opening. They had fallen asleep shortly after exiting.

As she gazed at the white clouds that now drifted across the sky, she couldn't help but remember the words Arm Bow had said to her. "When the eagle and the hawk fly together as one, you will know," he had said. What did it mean? She had never seen those two birds of prey flying side by side. It would indeed be a sight to see—almost a miracle.

She looked around her, wondering where Spirit Walker had gone. There was no sign of the warrior. She sat up, alarmed that he might have left her or that something had happened to him in the night. A rustling in the trees caught her attention and she looked to the top of a tall poplar tree over looking the hill. Perched on a branch of the tree sat a red-tailed hawk.

"You are awake, my Flower." She turned at the sound of the warrior's voice. He rounded the rocks of the hill and smiled, holding aloft a rabbit. "Let us eat."

Desert Rain had learned that the warrior's custom was to cook and eat in silence. Only after they had eaten would he entertain questions. She waited patiently until the meal was finished. "Do we return now to your wikiup?" she asked at last.

Spirit Walker looked into her eyes. "No, we do not. You must now return to your People."

"But why, my Spirit? I wish to stay with you."

Spirit Walker stirred the remains of the cooking fire with a stick in an effort to kill any still-burning embers. "You must return. You cannot continue your life's journey unless you first return to the path."

Desert Rain knew exactly what the warrior meant. But she was afraid to return to her People, afraid of the emotions that would overtake her when she entered the tipi that had been home to her and Arm Bow. It was as if she had died in that life and had been reborn in this one. She couldn't bear to suffer anew the pain of her past memories. There was only one way she could endure such grief. "Will you go with me, my Spirit?"

Spirit Walker met her gaze and slowly shook his head. "No, my Flower, I cannot. I have memories of my own to deal with."

Desert Rain rose to her feet, tears filling her eyes. "But, my

Spirit, I cannot go alone. I would rather stay with you. Please, don't make me leave without you."

"You will never be without me, Little One." He stepped toward her, placing his hands on her shoulders. "You have seen your vision. I have seen mine. We must follow our visions."

"I know my vision, my Spirit. I do not know yours, but I feel we are meant to be together. Last night, I saw my husband. He came to me for the last time. He said that he would not come again. It was his way of releasing me back to the land of the living. I feel that he was releasing me into your care."

Spirit Walker turned and walked back to the smoldering fire. "I cannot help you. I must seek a sign."

"A sign? What kind of sign?"

"I cannot tell you. I will know when I see it. Until then, I can say nothing. I will tell you that I, too, have seen a past love."

"Don't you see? Your woman has released you to me as well." As soon as the words left her lips, she wondered where the thought had come from. She didn't know how she knew it, but something inside of her had caused her to believe what she was saying. "Our spirits have touched. We were meant to be together."

Spirit Walker turned to face her again. "You are so beautiful, Little One. So tender and young. I am old. I could never give you the things you need. You are like a flower growing in the desert. It would not be right to pluck up and remove the one thing that gives the desert its beauty."

Slowly she approached the warrior. "You are not old, my Spirit," she said as she ran the back of her palm along his cheek. "You are wise. You are kind. I have never known a gentler spirit than yours. I know that you would not leave a flower to grow in the parched earth of the desert. Soon its beauty would fade and the flower would die. I know that you would remove the flower carefully. You would make sure the flower had enough water and nourishment to survive. You would plant it in a safe place where it would be protected and loved. That is you, my Spirit. And I need you."

"My Flower, I will make you this promise. As soon as I see the sign that was promised, I will come to you. I will visit you and your People."

It was all she could ask of him. She could see the resolution in his eyes. She kissed him, pressing herself against his firm chest. She felt his strong arms enfold her, felt the heat of his lips on hers. She closed her eyes. It was so comforting to be in his arms and though he had never said it, she knew he loved her.

Spirit Walker pulled away slowly. "Can you find your way back to your People?"

She looked around her. "I don't know. I don't really know where we are now."

Before Spirit Walker could speak, there was a flutter of wings overhead. Desert Rain looked skyward. The hawk she had seen earlier had taken to the air. With a cry, the dark-colored bird drifted casually toward the south.

Desert Rain smiled. "Yes, my Spirit, I know where my People are. I need only follow the hawk."

Spirit Walker looked deep into her eyes. "The hawk?"

"Yes. My husband said that he would send a messenger to lead me on my journey. I know in my heart that it is the hawk."

Spirit Walker turned and walked away from her a couple of paces before turning to face her once again. "What else did he tell you?"

"I don't know what I am allowed to say about my vision. I have never experienced a vision quest before."

"You may describe the vision, but it is best that you keep the identity of your spirit guide a secret. One's spirit guide is a very personal matter, but sometimes it is necessary to have a shaman help you understand the visions you have seen."

"Then I can tell you that I, too, was given a sign."

"A sign?" He moved closer to her.

"Yes, my Spirit." There was something in Spirit Walker's voice, some suspicion. Could it be that he sensed something that she had missed? "He told me. . . ."

Before she could complete her sentence the hawk's cry sounded from overhead once again. She looked skyward. "My hawk has returned," she said with a smile. "Perhaps she is anxious for me to follow her."

Spirit Walker watched as the hawk drew a lazy circle on the clouds. The hawk rode the wind with grace, her wings barely moving as the currents carried her along. Perhaps she was hunting, circling in an effort to spot prey on the ground. If it were true, she would soon make her dive, catching her meal in her talons. Suddenly she caught an updraft and rose higher in the sky.

"She waits," Desert Rain whispered.

"Perhaps you should go with her, my Flower."

"No, my Spirit, she waits for another," she said, pointing toward the circling hawk.

Spirit Walker followed her gaze. From the east, another bird was approaching. The second bird was bigger than the hawk, with a larger wing span, a broader tail—the unmistakable outline of an eagle. It took a long leisurely ride on the swirling currents of the afternoon breeze. The hawk cried loudly, but made no attempt to fly away. Instead, she circled beneath the eagle. Flying in the shadow of the larger bird, the two appeared as one from the ground.

Desert Rain gasped. "It is the sign! It is the sign I was to look for. The eagle and the hawk fly together as one."

Spirit Walker looked at her with wonder. "The eagle and the hawk?" he asked incredulously.

Desert Rain could not stop watching the birds dance above her. They were fascinating in their grace and beauty. Though the hawk stole the wind beneath the wings of the eagle, the larger bird still seemed to find enough lift to keep him above her. The hawk seemed to know that she must beat her wings now and again in order for the eagle to maintain his height. She was actually creating the wind that kept him aloft. "Look, my Spirit," Desert Rain said with glee. "They leave together toward the south."

Spirit Walker watched the two birds sail out of sight, then turned again to Desert Rain. "I have something for you."

"You . . . you do?" She watched as the warrior picked up his pack and reached inside. He removed a black piece of cloth that she recognized at once as the cloth he had been working on in his wikiup—the one onto which he had been meticulously sewing a bead design.

"It is to be worn in your hair," he said, holding the pattern up for her to see against her hair. The black cloth disappeared against her jet black hair so that only the bead design could be seen.

"It's a hawk!" she exclaimed. "It's beautiful! My Spirit, will you tie my hair back with it?"

She turned her back and he gently pulled her hair back and fastened the cloth around the single ponytail.

"How does it look?" she asked.

"Beautiful. So beautiful."

She turned to face him again. "Thank you, my Spirit. How did you know?"

"I did not know," he said. "I felt."

Moving to his pack again, he reached in and pulled out a two-feather headdress. "Let us fly together to the south," he said as he fastened the eagle feathers in his hair. "I, too, have seen my sign."

Chapter Twenty-five

"She's coming! Desert Rain returns!"

Wind Song heard the children yelling the glad tidings in the encampment. Hurriedly she left her tipi. "What are you saying?"

Beaver Tail ran up to her, his breath coming in short gasps. "We saw them. Desert Rain returns from the north!"

Wind Song's heart leaped within her. Her daughter had returned. "Broken Branch. You must find Broken Branch. Tell him his sister returns."

Beaver Tail nodded and ran off in the direction of Broken Branch's tipi.

Broken Branch stood beside his mother as Desert Rain and Spirit Walker walked into the encampment. Wind Song ran to her daughter, embracing her, tears streaming down her face. "You have returned, my daughter. My heart leaps with gladness."

"Oh, Mother, I am so happy to see you. I have missed you much."

Broken Branch, well aware of the curious stares that accompanied Spirit Walker's entrance into the compound, approached the warrior with reverence. "Thank you, uncle, for returning my sister to her people. Tonight, we will dance in celebration. You will join us?"

"Dance?" Desert Rain's countenance fell.

She didn't expect a dance, but she should have known they would want to celebrate her homecoming. She knew she couldn't stop them from dancing, but what would she do? How could she endure it? The last dance she had attended with her people was the dance she had shared with Arm Bow. The sadness almost overwhelmed her. She reached for her only consolation. "My Spirit, you must be there. I need you."

Spirit Walker looked into her tear-filled eyes. "I will be there for you, my Flower."

"Good," Wind Song replied. "Now, my daughter, let us talk. We have much to discuss about what has happened."

Desert Rain looked about the compound. Not much had changed in the time she had been gone. She had to admit that she was anxious to catch up on things that had happened in her absence. There was only one thing that caught her eye as being different. "My mother, where is my tipi? It is not there."

"I know, my daughter, I had Broken Branch remove it. I thought it best that you stay with me."

Desert Rain smiled. Her mother always knew her daughter's heart. Wind Song had shared her sadness, had done everything to comfort her. Now she had taken precautions to insure that her return would be as painless as possible. Desert Rain threw her arms around her mother's neck and squeezed. "Oh, *shima*, I love you so much."

*　　*　　*

Spirit Walker walked across the rancheria with Broken Branch. It was customary for him to give his regards to the clan chief, and the Chokonen meant to do just that. "Where is your chief?" he asked as they walked.

"I will take you to him. He is anxious to see you. I have spoken of you often to him."

"You are doing well?"

"Yes. Well. I see your arms are still healing. You should let Old Stone look at them. He is a powerful medicine man."

Spirit Walker looked down at his red-streaked arms. They were still very tender, but he felt no pain at the moment. "Perhaps later. How are the others?"

Broken Branch smiled. "Cloud Maker never tires of telling the story of our adventures among the blue coats. The story grows with each telling. He is well, as is Black Beaver."

"This is good news. You have seen no more of the blue coats?"

"No. All has been peaceful since our return, but I do sense that Five Dreams is expecting trouble. I know not why."

"Five Dreams?"

"Yes, our chief. He has been restless for the past couple of days. Two days ago, a runner came to him from another clan. After they had talked for a while in private, the runner left. Five Dreams has been speaking with the elders in the sweat lodge every day since then. I feel a foreboding spirit."

"Yes, I have felt it."

"You have felt it? Since you arrived or before?"

"Since I have arrived. Three days ago, while undertaking a vision quest, I saw a vision concerning the *Pinda-lick-o-ye*."

Broken Branch stopped in place and faced the old warrior. "You have seen a vision about the white man? Are we in danger here?"

"I cannot tell," Spirit Walker said resolutely. "I must speak to your chief and elders."

"Let us hurry then." Broken Branch moved quickly toward the center of the rancheria, Spirit Walker close behind him.

*   *   *

It was the wisdom gleaned from years of hardship and constant toil that Spirit Walker saw in the old chief's eyes. Five Dreams sat in his usual place against his willow backrest in front of his tipi. He nodded as Broken Branch approached with Spirit Walker.

"*Ya a teh, Chies*. Greetings, chief," Spirit Walker said in salutation.

Five Dreams stood and extended his right arm. "I have heard amazing stories of the Spirit That Walks as a Man," he said as he took Spirit Walker's forearm.

"I am honored to meet with such a wise chief as Five Dreams."

The old chief smiled. "Let not age be mistaken for wisdom, *shils aash*."

"We must talk. We have much to discuss."

"Yes. I suggest that we meet in a short while in the sweat lodge. Broken Branch will prepare you for the meeting."

Broken Branch nodded in response. "Come with me, Spirit, we will prepare in my tipi."

Spirit Walker ducked through the opening of the sweat lodge. Chief Five Dreams sat enveloped by the steam rising from the heated rocks in the center of the lodge, smoking his favorite long-stemmed pipe. Spirit Walker took a seat directly across from the chief. Five Dreams handed him the pipe.

Spirit Walker took a long drag on the pipe, exhaled the smoke, and waved the smoke over his head in traditional fashion. He bathed in the smoke for a moment before the chief spoke. "You walk in the spirit of the Old Ones."

"I walk with their spirits, this is true. One can never replace the Old Ones, only seek to please them."

"True enough, *shils aash*; still, one must know the Old Ones to walk with them."

Spirit Walker handed the pipe back to Five Dreams. "Tell me of your name."

Five Dreams was surprised at the Spirit Walker's boldness, for he knew only too well the power of one's name. It gave a certain amount of control to the one who knew the meaning of one's name, and so was never given out freely. Five Dreams examined Spirit Walker's face carefully. The stories he had heard about the famous warrior had been told around campfires for so many years, it was often thought that no such man really existed. To reveal one's name so soon after meeting was indeed troublesome to Five Dreams, but perhaps it was time. Perhaps this was the man who should know and perhaps there was no time to consider the matter further. After all, they had more serious matters yet to discuss.

"I am called Five Dreams because I have seen five visions. Two have already come to pass, three are as yet unfulfilled."

Spirit Walker met the old chief's gaze. He realized the honor the chief had just bestowed upon him in revealing the meaning of his name. He would not hesitate to reciprocate. "As the Spirit Walker, I hear the spirits of my ancestors speaking to me about things to come. They have enabled me to move as a spirit in the forests, to hide as a spirit in the darkness, to see as a spirit without light."

"And what do the spirits say about things to come?"

"There is trouble. I see trouble with the blue coats. Soon."

"I have seen this trouble as well."

"Five Dreams, tell me of your visions. I feel that we may share the same one at this time, but I must know of the five."

The chief nodded. Somehow, he knew it was necessary to reveal them at this time. "Many years ago, I saw five dreams. The first was of the coming of the *Pinda-lick-o-ye*. I saw them blowing across the desert as grains of sand in a storm. They could not be stopped, nor could their number be counted. This has come to pass."

Spirit Walker nodded.

"In the second vision, I saw the People gathered together—some in chains, some bound with ropes, but all were prisoners. They were forced to eat foods that were strange to the taste. They had no horses, no weapons. They had no dignity. They wore strange clothing and spoke a strange tongue. They were the People who were no people."

"The captivity of the reservations?"

"Yes. Our People suffer so now. Only a few of us still roam our homelands, and yet, we are not free. We must hide. We cannot freely show ourselves. We cannot hunt as we once did. The buffalo are no more. Our lives have been reduced to that of prisoners."

Spirit Walker's head dropped in grief as he listened to the chief's words. It was true that not many of the People were left on the plains, and those who were left were not able to be free. He recalled the days when the People moved with the buffalo, raised their sons and daughters to be warriors, hunters, shamans. They roamed from horizon to horizon, gathered together for protection and comfort. Those days seemed far away now.

"The first two have come to pass, but there are three to come," the old chief continued. "The third vision is one of inward destruction among my People. Brother turning against brother, father against son. I see some of our People riding with the blue coats, betraying those they once called friends. I see yet others riding the way of the warrior, but without respect to any chief. Without conscience, without considering the consequences of their actions, they kill and raid at will. In this vision, the two chiefs who would make peace are dead. I feel the other chiefs will make only war."

Spirit Walker knew that the two chiefs Five Dreams spoke of were Mangas Coloradas and Cochise. The last hope that the Apache had had was the treaty that Cochise had made two years earlier. When Cochise died, so died the treaty. Spirit Walker once again met the chief's gaze. "And the fourth?"

Chief Five Dreams took a deep breath. "I see death. But it does not come here, *shils aash*. I see death in a foreign land. A land of strange trees and much water. The water is bitter and tastes like the Salt River, but cannot be crossed for its size. Our People die there, but their cries are ignored. They die without hope." He extended the pipe once again.

Spirit Walker reached forward and received the pipe from Five Dreams. Puffing smoke into the air, he wondered if he really wished to know the last and final vision.

Five Dreams did not wait to reveal the last vision. "The fifth and final vision is the loss of our identity. I see our children's children departing from the teachings of the Old Ones. No longer do they sit at the feet of the tribal elders and listen to the stories of Coyote the Trickster. They no longer concern themselves with the knowledge of the Earth Mother. They no longer speak the language of their forefathers. It is this last vision that grieves me deeply. It takes my spirit into the darkness of the night, causing it to wander without sight, without purpose, without a desire to see the morning sun."

Spirit Walker handed the pipe back to the chief. "We have much to do, Five Dreams. We must do our part to help our People."

The chief nodded. "Yes, *shils aash*, let us talk about the things we can change and not about those we cannot."

"I will tell you this, we will soon see the coming of the third vision. Let us prepare."

Chapter Twenty-six

Desert Rain sat in the familiar surroundings of her mother's tipi. Wind Song served venison and ashcakes, and the two of them ate in silence.

When the meal was finished, Wind Song spoke. "You have been gone for so long, my daughter. I am so glad you have come home to us. I did not want to think that I might have lost you forever."

"I did not know how to handle my grief, *shima*."

"I know, my daughter. I did not know how to help you. When your father died, I felt the same grief. It was as if my heart had been cut from me and I no longer desired to go on. But I had three children to care for, and that gave me strength."

"I have no children, *shima*."

"No, but you have family. Family that cares for you and loves you more than you could know. We want you to stay with us. We will care for you."

"That is kind, my mother, but I am not a child as I once was. I have undertaken a vision quest."

"What?" Wind Song's surprise was evident. "My daughter, only warriors do such things."

"Yes, I know. My Spirit has told me that I am a warrior."

"I see." Wind Song rose and began to clear away the leftover food and utensils. "What do you know of this man? The one you call 'Spirit.' "

"What do the spirits tell you?" Five Dreams asked as he puffed smoke from his pipe into the air.

"I do not understand the meaning of the vision entirely yet," Spirit Walker admitted. "I see them coming. The ones called 'The Nameless Ones.' They head south into the land of the *Nakai-ye*."

"Into Mexico?"

"Yes."

"Are they our People?"

"Yes. They are led by a woman."

Desert Rain spoke for a long time about Spirit Walker. She told her mother of his bravery, his wisdom, his cunning. She finished with the daring rescue of Broken Branch, Cloud Maker, and Black Beaver. "He is the most wonderful man I have ever known," she concluded.

Wind Song sat silently for a moment. "My daughter, for years I have heard tales concerning this man. I have heard that he has been responsible for many evil deeds."

"It is not true, my mother! It cannot be! He is not evil!"

"My daughter, you must understand that I only seek to protect you."

"I don't need you to protect me from him. I love him, *shima*."

"You don't know what you're saying."

"I do know, my mother. I know that my heart longs to be with him. I long to be his wife."

"You are still in grief, my daughter. You are not thinking clearly. It is only because you have so recently been widowed that you feel a need for another man."

"No!" Desert Rain stood in defiance. "I love him. Not because I am still grieving for my husband, but because my husband has released me to him."

Wind Song placed her face in her hands and began to sob quietly. "I do not understand this thing."

Desert Rain knelt beside her mother and hugged her closely. "I shall tell you of my vision, my mother. It will help you understand."

Five Dreams blew another puff of smoke into the air as Spirit Walker continued his explanation. "A group of our People, led by a woman, will flee to Mexico, but there are more to come," Spirit Walker warned.

"But you said that this vision may have something to do with my third dream?" the chief asked as he handed the pipe to Spirit Walker.

"Yes. The 'Nameless Ones' will be followed by those who ride the warrior path. Those who come after them will take the *Netdahe* oath and they will not turn back from it."

"Netdahe?" Five Dreams recognized the word immediately. It was a word that dated all the way back to the time when the Spaniards first began to conquer Apachería. The word literally meant "death to all intruders," but had become a vow of absolute defiance against anyone who was not of the People. Some had taken the vow upon reaching manhood and had begun the path of war against the whites as well as Mexicans. They often died needlessly, recklessly endangering the innocent members of the tribe who desired to live in peace.

"A struggle rises in my chest," Spirit Walker said, handing the pipe back to Five Dreams. "I understand the mind of the *Netdahe*. My heart beats with theirs. I have fought in defense of our People and lands for many summers. I have seen the atrocities inflicted on our People by the whites and Mexicans. I have seen our children killed, our women raped, our old men cut down without mercy. These eyes have seen much pain. I can understand the grief that drives them to revenge. One that I loved very much was killed by the Mexicans. I was at Kas-Ki-Yeh."

The chief knew the story of the massacre at Kas-Ki-Yeh well, but had never met anyone who had actually been there at the time. He knew that Chief Juh had once camped near the Mexican village and sought to trade turquoise for food and whiskey. The Mexicans called the village Janos, but the Apache called it Kas-Ki-Yeh. While the men were away from the rancheria one morning, the women and children were murdered by the Mexican cavalry. In the eighteen years since that massacre, one man had led the people in relentless vengeance against the Mexicans—a man who had lost his wife and children in the raid—Goyathlay, "The One Who Yawns." The white man called him Geronimo.

"Will you ride with the *Netdahe?*" the chief asked solemnly.

"I ride for the People."

Five Dreams nodded. "So let it be."

Broken Branch was waiting outside as Five Dreams and Spirit Walker exited the sweat lodge. The chief raised his hand in greeting. "Take our guest and prepare him for the dance tonight. He will be our guest of honor."

Broken Branch nodded a response, then turned to Spirit Walker. "Come, we will prepare in my tipi."

Wind Song listened carefully as Desert Rain explained her vision, yet it was all too foreign for her to comprehend. She watched Desert Rain as the young woman walked about the tipi relating the details. Though Wind Song didn't understand, one thing was sure—Desert Rain understood it completely. Desert Rain was her daughter and Wind Song listened carefully.

When Desert Rain had finished her explanation, Wind Song stood to face her. "My daughter, your journey has been filled with wonder. I do not understand these things, but this I know, you are my daughter and you have your whole life ahead of you. I trust your heart, my daughter. I will rejoice in your decision."

"Oh, Mother! I love you so much." Running to her mother, she wrapped her arms lovingly around Wind Song's small frame.

Wind Song wiped tears from her eyes as she stepped back from her daughter. "Now, we must prepare for the dance."

As darkness fell across the compound, Desert Rain watched the lighting of the ceremonial fire. Seven singers gathered around a huge drum, carved from a single stump and covered with a dried piece of buffalo hide. The singers circled the drum, each holding a long-handled stick. Each singer took great pride in his drumstick. Each stick was intricately carved with a design identifying its owner. The hitting of the drum by seven different men had to be carefully practiced so that the beat was maintained, yet each man was allowed to rest during any one particular song. A song could last as long as thirty minutes, so it was important to keep a steady rhythm throughout the song.

Desert Rain took Spirit Walker's hand and entered the dance circle as the first beats of the drum were sounded. A slow, rhythmic beat announced the beginning of the celebration. Desert Rain and Spirit Walker led the procession around the fire, circling clockwise in a shuffling motion. The pace was slow, the mood solemn, as they danced the opening dance in honor of their ancestors.

There were no fancy costumes or elaborate designs worn during the social dances, but bells were tied around the ankles and legs to ward off any evil spirits that might try to interrupt the celebration. The jingle of the bells coordinated perfectly with the beat of the drum as the entire tribe—men, women and children—circled the fire three times.

After the third pass, Desert Rain led the others to the edge of the fire circle, faced the fire and began to shuffle to the left. Before long the entire tribe was shuffling side to side around the massive fire. As they shuffled around the fire, Desert Rain cast a loving glance at Spirit Walker. He was so full of life as he danced. Even while performing the tame shuffle step of the traditional dance, he was graceful, adding a special flare as he bent toward the ground and then straightened again, emphasizing the hard and soft beat of the drum.

The drum hit the last beats of the Memorial Dance and Chief Five Dreams stepped to the center of the circle. Raising his hands, he thanked *Usen* for the return of one of His daughters. Thanked Him for the assistance of the Spirit That Walks as a Man. Asked for deliverance for His People. Then he announced the official opening of the celebration. A whoop went up from the People and they separated to take their seats around the fire.

Most of the elders chose to dance in place on the edge of the fire circle. Though there was constant movement, it was also a time of fellowship. Many of them danced in pairs or small groups, shuffling around the fire, talking, laughing, joking with one another. It was very much a social affair. Periodically a particular song would be requested by someone. Then the one who had made the request would lead the tribe around the fire. After the third pass, the requester would dance in place off to one side. Many in the tribe would then place handmade gifts at the feet of the requester. When the song had ended, the requester would approach the chief. The gifts received during the dance were then distributed to other members of the tribe, as the requester saw fit. During the evening, gifts changed hands many times until the needs of the poorest among them were met. It was a lovely display of camaraderie and compassion.

Desert Rain smiled as she watched the children dance around

the fire. They usually chose positions closest to the center and danced with enthusiasm and energy unequaled by their elders. She noted the improvements some of the older children had made in their technique. The small ones were somewhat jerky in their motions, still fumbling at imitating their favorite dancers among the warriors. Beaver Tail was just a miniature copy of his father Black Beaver. He mimicked his father's scouting motions as he bent low to the ground, shuffling forward as if tracking. Every so often, the drummers would sound four loud, strong beats in the song. On each of the four beats, Beaver Tail placed his hand over his eyes, as if searching the horizon for game, bobbing his head with each beat before continuing his "tracking." It was so amazing how the children learned to dance, and so sweet to see them grow into maturity.

She had once dreamed of children of her own. She had dreamed that Arm Bow's son would be just like him. Her son would imitate Arm Bow's actions in the dance, strutting beside his proud father as they circled the fire. They would have been the envy of the tribe. Desert Rain hung her head. The dream would never come true now. Arm Bow was gone.

Chapter Twenty-seven

Spirit Walker stood just outside of the fire circle, watching as the young men danced to the heavy beat of the drum. It was a warrior's dance, and the children gathered around to cheer for their favorite dancers. The pace was quicker than before and the dancing more frenzied. His gaze followed the one who seemed to shine above all the other dancers—Cloud Maker.

Cloud Maker's feet were a blur of motion as he danced. He bobbed and weaved in mock battle, swinging his war club as if vanquishing a foe with each swing. His face contorted as he moved, his body sheened with sweat. Spirit Walker recognized the look of hatred, of disdain for the enemies of his People. Spirit Walker had once danced in that same manner, with the same fierce nature that Cloud Maker exhibited. It was long ago, just after the slaughter of his beloved.

After the massacre at Kas-Ki-Yeh, Juh had led the survivors from the battle site. The dead were not buried because there was no time or opportunity. The mood was solemn as they left the dead upon the fields of Mexico, but Juh kept the men moving. On the first night out, Spirit Walker had noticed Goyathlay sitting by himself, obviously overcome with grief. He had approached the mighty warrior and sat beside him.

Throughout the night, Spirit Walker talked with Goyathlay about what should be done to the Mexicans who had killed their families. Two days later, Spirit Walker joined Goyathlay and a handful of others in a revenge raid on the Mexican troops that had perpetrated the massacre.

Before the revenge raid, they had danced. They had danced with fervor. They had danced with zeal. They had danced with hatred. It was that hatred that drove Goyathlay to fight beyond his abilities the next day. Charging the Mexicans relentlessly, Goyathlay had risked his life to utterly destroy his enemies.

Spirit Walker remembered the frightened Mexicans as they retreated during the heated battle. They had begun to yell and scream in their native language, *"San Geronimo! San Geronimo!"* Years later, when Spirit Walker learned the Spanish tongue, he discovered that they were appealing to their patron saint for assistance. But Saint Jerome had not come to their aid that fateful day. Goyathlay led his warriors to victory, and the jubilant Apache took up the Mexicans' cry of "Geronimo! Geronimo!" That day, "The One Who Yawns" became the patron saint of the Apache warrior, and the cry "Geronimo!" would, from that day forward, strike fear in the hearts of Mexicans and whites alike.

Cloud Maker wore the look. He danced the dance. Spirit Walker saw that he felt the hatred. Could Cloud Maker's future be much different than Goyathlay's past?

During the round dance, Spirit Walker felt a tap on his shoulder and turned to see Broken Branch behind him. "*Shils aash*, my friend," Broken Branch began, "may I have a word with you?"

Spirit Walker nodded and followed the young warrior away from the fire's light. Once away from the others, they were joined by Cloud Maker and Black Beaver.

"We wish you to have a token of our appreciation for rescuing us from the blue coats," Black Beaver said.

"It is not necessary, *shils aash.*"

"This is why it must be done," Broken Branch said as he handed a fur-wrapped object to Spirit Walker.

The old warrior removed the fur to reveal a finely carved belt knife. The blade was a full eight inches long. The elk-horn handle bore the image of an eagle in flight.

"For you, the Spirit who sees as an eagle," Cloud Maker announced proudly.

Very seldom did an Apache warrior say thank you in words, but Spirit Walker felt he at least owed them that much. *"A-co-'d,"* he responded.

"Are you not happy, my daughter?" Wind Song asked, placing a piece of fry bread in Desert Rain's hands.

"Yes, Mother, I am happy that we dance. It's just that . . . well, it's just that it reminds me of things that are painful to remember."

"I know, my daughter."

"Mother, do you think that the people would think poorly of me if I requested a Lover's Dance?"

Wind Song searched her daughter's face for a moment. Desert Rain's eyes were bright now. Before she had left them and had been found by the Spirit That Walks as a Man, Desert Rain's eyes had grown dim with grief. Now the sparkle had returned. Wind Song would not see that light extinguished again. "No, my child, they would not. I shall speak to the chief."

Desert Rain watched her mother stand and walk toward Five Dreams. She turned to look for Spirit Walker. She saw him standing in the shadows of the dim moonlight, alone.

"My Spirit," Desert Rain said as she approached the solitary warrior. "My Spirit, will you dance with me?"

"Dance with you?"

"Yes, my Spirit. I have requested a Lover's Dance. Will you dance beside me?"

Spirit Walker took her hand in his. It was small in his big hand as he turned it over and examined the smoothness of her skin. "My Flower, you are the most beautiful woman I have ever known. There is no one who can match your beauty and grace. It would be my honor to dance with you."

Desert Rain smiled as she heard Five Dreams announce the Lover's Dance. With glee she turned and dragged Spirit Walker toward the fire circle.

All eyes watched as they entered the circle and the first drum beats began to sound the Lover's Dance. Murmurs rose and fell as they danced. Wind Song could hear the gasps of surprise as some of the older women expressed their displeasure. Some felt that it was too soon after the death of her husband for Desert Rain to be considering another man. Some argued that she was young and should take another quickly. Some said that the Chokonen was not one of them. Others reminded them that, though he was of a different band, he was Apache and therefore worthy of one of their daughters. His age meant that he would be able to supply a good home for the younger Desert Rain. He would give her stability. Still others argued that he was an infamous warrior and that he would only bring grief to the young woman. Wind Song listened to the discussions around her, but her heart smiled for her daughter.

Facing the fire, the pairs danced to the left in a shuffling gait. The men, standing beside their women, waved different objects in the air above their heads. Some waved feather fans, some headdresses, some shields or articles of clothing. Each warrior made sure that the arch of the wave covered his own head as well as his woman's head. It was symbolic of the joining of their spirits.

Desert Rain held tightly to Spirit Walker's hand as she danced. His right arm waved overhead and she looked up to see the object he held. The object was covered, but she could see a knife handle protruding from the fur. "A knife?" she whispered.

"My vow of protection always, my Flower."

It had been a joyous time, but as midnight approached, the people began slowly to return to their individual dwellings. The drum was silent now, the singers had departed, the night was still. The people spoke in low tones as the evening came to a close. Wind Song sat alone, watching her daughter walk slowly toward her. "Where is Spirit Walker?"

"He has gone with Broken Branch. He will sleep in his tipi tonight."

Wind Song stood. "We should retire also, my daughter."

"Yes, Mother, I am weary. But it was a lovely dance."

The smile on Desert Rain's face told her mother that the young woman had truly enjoyed herself. Her daughter's joy brightened her own spirit and she placed her arm around her as they walked toward their tipi.

The night was dark, the air barely stirring the leaves. Spirit Walker walked along the edge of the water bordering the rancheria. He had slipped out of Broken Branch's tipi as soon as he was sure the young warrior was asleep. He walked now, deep in thought, conscious only of his immediate surroundings.

He drifted aimlessly along the edge of the fast-running stream, listening to the water roll across the rocks. Listening to the night birds sing to the wind. Listening to his heart. There was no doubt in his mind that he loved Desert Rain. There was no doubt that he ached for her touch, longed for her arms. The only thing he didn't know for sure was what to do about it.

He wandered onto a trail and continued his walk, rising now

191

above the valley floor. He couldn't stop thinking of Desert Rain's bright eyes. She trusted him so much, he could see that. She looked to him with wonder and respect, but was she mistaking that respect for love? Could she really be happy with him? After a while, she might become disillusioned, discovering that he was not the man she thought he was. After all, he was a warrior, a renegade from his People. He was a man who had fought and killed, sending the sons of mothers into the After World. He was a man of war, feared by his peers, honored only by those who sought revenge against the white man and the Mexican. What did he have to offer such a tender young maiden?

The night winds moved the trees as he approached the top of the trail he was walking. He remembered Desert Rain telling him that her husband was buried in the valley below. He remembered the sorrowful look in her eyes as she spoke of her loss. Her husband had been a noble warrior, a man of respect, a man of good judgment. Her husband was not a man like himself—a man of sorrow, a man of violence, a man shunned by his People.

Spirit Walker stood overlooking the valley. It's alive, he thought as he watched the dim moon shadow move across the terrain below. Suddenly a movement overhead caught his eye. Looking into the night sky, he could barely make out the form of a large bird. The bird flew directly over him, then passed over the trees behind him. He turned as the NightHawk sent forth her cry.

Quietly, Spirit Walker slipped in among the trees bordering the cliff. He wove his way through the pines and oaks, not knowing nor caring where he was going. He followed the sounds of the hawk as she cried time and again as if calling for him to follow her.

He stepped out of the trees onto a soft patch of grass in a small clearing. The hawk hovered overhead, circling the clearing in a wide, lazy arch. Spirit Walker felt a warmth begin to spread through his body. He had never been here that he could remember, yet everything seemed familiar to him. It welcomed him like an old friend. He moved to the center of the clearing. Sitting in the dewy grass, he looked up at the NightHawk.

One last time the hawk cried and flew off toward the mountains. Spirit Walker's coyote howl echoed on the wind as he lay back in the soft grass.

Chapter Twenty-eight

In the graying light of early morning, Desert Rain slipped from her mother's tipi. Silently folding the door flap back into place, she headed for the outskirts of the encampment. She had been too tired to walk the high trail last night, but she had also feared the darkness. She hadn't been afraid of anything physical, nothing that could be seen. She had been afraid of the mental images, afraid of the thoughts and emotions that would be able to assault her in the night, for the night belonged to the dark side of the Spirit World. For that reason, the warriors of the People would not fight after sundown. The fear was that if a brave passed into the After World in darkness, his spirit would be led astray by the dark spirits and wander, forever lost. She knew that if she had walked the high trail last night, the dark memories of her life would have run roughshod over her heart. She was sure her defense would have crumbled. Now, in the light of day, she felt the courage to face the giant of sorrow that awaited her. She had to face her past, she had to see her secret place. She had to fight the fight, and she had to do it alone. She was a warrior now. She had to be strong.

Topping the ridge at the end of the high trail, Desert Rain cut right and entered the woods. It had been almost a moon since she had last visited her secret place. She had found the spot when she was just a child. Having been one of few female children in the clan as she was growing up, she had often sought places of solitude away from the more rambunctious boys. Though her mother had told her that the high trail was dangerous to walk alone, she had climbed the trail one summer afternoon. The boys had been picking on her, as they so often did, and she had simply walked away down the edge of the creek. Before she had realized it, she was at the top of the high trail, looking out over the wonders of the valley. She remembered the solace, the serenity of that afternoon of long ago. It brought her comfort to this day. She had sat there for some time, thinking, pondering her future, but shortly she had stood and began to walk through the woods. When she first spotted the lush green grass of the small clearing, she felt as if she belonged there. It became her secret place, her fortress against the cares of the world around her. The only person she had ever shared it with was Arm Bow.

She had gone there many times in her young life. Whenever she was sad, it brought her cheer. Whenever she was upset or confused, it brought her stability. Whenever she was lonely, it brought her companionship. Though she wasn't sure exactly what was troubling her now, she knew the remedy lay in the middle of that small clearing.

The morning light was doing its best to penetrate the foliage as she passed through the trees. Dew caressed her skin as she brushed against the thick bows of cedar on the edge of the clearing. She gasped as she stepped from the tree line. Someone had found her secret place. Quickly she ducked behind a tree and peered out at the prone figure.

It was a man, lying face down in the grass. At first she thought he was dead, but upon closer observation, she could see his body rise and fall with each breath. She strained her eyes to see anything about the man that was recognizable to her. His back was heavily muscled, but there was something more than that that caught her eye. It was the scars that marked his back and legs. She crept quietly toward the sleeping warrior.

He lay with his head resting on his forearms. His breathing was deep and peaceful. She knelt beside him, admiring the shape of his shoulders, his arms, his upper back. He was a magnificent specimen of an Apache warrior. Her hands were attracted to his broad shoulders, partially covered by his long black hair. She reached forward and began to massage the muscles which tapered down from his neck. Working her way down over his shoulder blades, she began to knead his upper back, feeling her way along the back of his ribs. Even in sleep, his muscles were tight. When she reached his lower back, her fingers slipped inside the top of his breechclout. Suddenly, he began to stir.

Desert Rain pulled away, sitting back on her heels, as Spirit Walker rolled over onto his back. She smiled as she watched him stretch in the early morning sunlight. Arms splayed wide open, he looked up at her.

Reaching forward, she began to run her hands over his wide chest. "Good morning, my Spirit," she whispered.

The sleepy warrior never said a word. Instead he released a sigh of sheer pleasure.

A giggle escaped Desert Rain's throat as she worked her hands over the warrior's rib cage and onto his stomach. Slowly she bent over and pressed her lips to his massive chest. Playfully, she began to flick his nipple with her tongue. Spirit Walker wrapped his strong arms around her and pressed her to him.

Like a grizzly bear playing with a cub, Spirit Walker rolled her over in the soft grass. Pinning her to the ground, he kissed her. Deeply. Hungrily. Passionately. It took her breath away, but she held him tightly, lovingly running her hands along the length of his back.

Pulling his mouth away from hers, he looked down into her beautiful face. "Marry me, Desert Rain. Be my wife."

"Am I worth six ponies?" she asked playfully.

"You are worth twice that," he said with a grin.

She pushed him away and rolled to her feet. "That should make Mother very happy. Let's go tell her!"

Spirit Walker sat up quickly and began to adjust his breech-clout. "Wait. Wait."

She smiled as he tried to hide the evidence of his passion.

"Let me sit a moment. I am not yet awake," he said as he crossed his legs in front of him.

Desert Rain laughed and bolted for the encampment.

Spirit Walker entered the rancheria slowly, not knowing exactly what to expect. He wasn't sure where Desert Rain had gone after she ran from the clearing, but from her last words, he was pretty sure she would be at her mother's tipi.

"My Spirit, over here!"

Turning at the sound of Desert Rain calling his name, he spotted her standing with Broken Branch. He approached the couple, not sure what to expect.

"I wondered where you had gone so early in the morning," Broken Branch said.

"I had many things to consider in the night," Spirit Walker told him.

"So I hear." Broken Branch smiled.

"Come, my Spirit, we must speak with Mother." Desert Rain took Spirit Walker's hand and led him toward Wind Song's tipi.

"*Shima*," Desert Rain called from the door flap. "*Shima*, may I enter with Spirit Walker?"

"You may enter, my daughter," Wind Song cried from inside the tipi.

Spirit Walker followed Desert Rain into the dwelling. Wind Song was sitting on her sleeping robes brushing her hair. She smiled up at her daughter. "I wondered where you had gone so early in the morning. Now I see why you hurried off."

Desert Rain sat down opposite her mother. Spirit Walker remained standing near the center of the tipi. "*Shima*, Spirit Walker has something to tell you."

"Oh?" Wind Song said, looking to the swarthy warrior.

Spirit Walker shot a stunned glance at Desert Rain, who merely sat smiling up at him expectantly. He wasn't prepared for it to happen in this manner, but he composed himself and began slowly. "Desert Rain and I have been talking. . . ."

"So I can see," Wind Song interrupted.

Spirit Walker realized it was not going to be easy. He cleared his throat and began again. "We have decided . . ."

"Yes?" Wind Song looked him squarely in the eye. She knew exactly why her daughter had brought the man into her tipi. She had sensed it from the time she had first talked with Desert Rain about this Chokonen warrior. Wind Song intended to make him get to the point. She wanted to know his heart of hearts, not listen to him convince himself of his love for her daughter.

Spirit Walker's gaze locked with Wind Song's. "I wish to have your daughter for my wife," he said plainly, straightforwardly, no hesitation.

Wind Song smiled. "She is worth at least three horses."

Desert Rain laughed. "I told him six, Mother."

"Six?" Wind Song laughed along with her daughter.

"I will give twelve," Spirit Walker said boldly.

"Twelve? Where do you plan to get these twelve ponies?" Wind Song asked in amazement. Twelve ponies was an unthinkable dowry.

"I will leave tomorrow. I know of a valley, just north of here. A few summers ago some of the horses of my people were left to graze there. There is a supply of wild ponies that still roam the hills. I shall bring twelve for your daughter."

Wind Song stood and approached the Chokonen. "Spirit Walker, you have saved my son's life and the lives of his friends. Besides this, you have saved the very life of the one you now wish to marry. I could ask no greater thing of you."

"No, *shima*, I will keep the traditions of my people. I will bring the horses."

The next morning found Spirit Walker readying an Appaloosa mare for the journey to the valley of horses. The pony belonged to Broken Branch, who had loaned it to Spirit Walker for the quest. Draping a blanket over the horse's broad back, Spirit Walker swung easily into place.

"Wait, my brother!" Spirit Walker turned to see Broken Branch riding toward him. The younger warrior sat the back of an Arabian gelding. "I am going with you."

"You need not, my brother, I can travel faster alone."

"I will not slow you, Spirit Walker, but I cannot say the same thing for them."

Spirit Walker glanced in the direction Broken Branch was pointing. Cloud Maker and Black Beaver each waved a greeting. They were mounted and ready to ride.

Spirit Walker shook his head and groaned. "Let us ride, then," he said at last.

Chapter Twenty-nine

Spirit Walker traveled quickly across the plains and into the woodlands. Broken Branch, Cloud Maker, and Black Beaver put some space between themselves and the Chokonen, knowing that he was used to traveling alone. It wasn't hard for them to figure just exactly where and when he would stop to eat and drink, the springs in the area were familiar to all of them.

Keeping mostly to themselves, the three Jicarilla warriors followed Spirit Walker at a distance until he stopped for the night. As they made camp, they talked among themselves. They tried to speculate where exactly the valley could be. They knew that some of their People often kept horses in valleys as a reserve. They had heard stories of Goyathlay and his exploits. Many times the renegade would travel on foot from southern Arizona to the heart of Mexico. He would steal horses and ride back to his People. Sometimes the horses were put into immediate use, sometimes they were held in reserve. Was it horses acquired in one of these raids that they now sought?

After the last meal of the day, Broken Branch asked the warrior if some of the stories they had heard about him were true. He told them of how he acquired the sash and of many battles fought beside his chief, Cochise. The one thing Spirit Walker could not bring himself to mention was the incident at Kas-Ki-Yeh.

"My uncle," Cloud Maker said at last, "is it true that you fought beside Goyathlay?"

Spirit Walker searched the young warrior's face. What he found in Cloud Maker's demeanor was what he expected to find—the look, the voice, the spirit of the *Netdahe*. "Yes, I once counted Goyathlay as a friend."

"You speak as though it is not true any longer," Broken Branch noted.

"It is not that I do not now count him as such," Spirit Walker continued. "We follow different paths now. But it is true that two spirits may walk side by side, though they walk different trails. I can live the *Netdahe* life no longer."

"Netdahe?" The word rolled easily off Cloud Maker's tongue. It was strange to his taste, but pleasant to the ear. "Death to all intruders."

"Yes, it is the vow taken by some of the younger warriors who vow to fight to their final breath," Spirit Walker explained.

"This is not such a bad thing, uncle," Cloud Maker said.

"No, it is not. But one must remember that there are consequences for one's actions. Many times, these consequences result in more harm than good."

Cloud Maker suddenly leapt to his feet. "And what good came to our People after Cochise made peace with the *Pinda-Lick-O-Ye?* Where is our great chief now? And where are the others who have sought peace with the blue coats, only to be cut down and left for the birds to feast upon? Where are they? Can you tell me the consequences of peace? Can you say that they are good and the consequences of war are bad? Where is Goyathlay and the *Netdahe?* I will tell you where they are—they are free! They are free to taste the wind, they are free to roam wherever they wish, and the white eyes cringe at the sound of their names. They ride freely while we hide like snakes under the rocks of the white man's threats. You speak of consequences, yet your words fight among themselves as they leave your mouth. There are no good or bad consequences, there is only life and there is only death. I choose life!"

As Cloud Maker stomped off into the darkness, Broken Branch turned to Spirit Walker. "My friend is troubled, uncle. He is not upset with you, only with himself. I have seen a change in him since Desert Rain's husband died. He is angry and bitter. He does not know what he is saying."

Spirit Walker glanced at Broken Branch. "There is also resentment, resentment that I am the one seeking to replace his fallen brother. He cannot bear it that I am to marry Desert Rain, that the horses he is helping to find are to be the dowry. His heart is torn. He knows not what to do with his feelings."

"I will go speak with him," Black Beaver offered.

"No," Broken Branch cautioned, "Spirit Walker is right. He is torn. He fights with himself and he alone must resolve the conflict. Leave him alone. Perhaps the morning will bring him peace."

The morning may not have brought peace, but it did bring a calmness to Cloud Maker's manner. He rode in silence when the four men moved out in the early morning light. Broken Branch tried to make casual talk as they rode, but Cloud Maker did little more than grunt in response.

It was early afternoon when they rode into a well-watered valley, lush with green grass. A small stream split the valley, several willow trees lining its banks. A few rabbits were seen immediately, but there was no sign of the horses.

"Could it be that there are no horses left in the valley?" Broken Branch asked.

Spirit Walker slid from the back of his mount and examined the ground near the edge of the water. "No, they are here," he said pointing to a distinct hoof print in the soft earth.

Black Beaver sat tall on the back of his black pony, searching the hills around them. "Where should we look first? At this time of day, I would say that they are along the hillside seeking shade."

"True," Spirit Walker said as he swung easily onto his horse's back once again. "Their tracks lead to the west. Let us prepare to take them in the hills. They will not be able to evade us there."

The four men rode off quickly in the direction of a small stand of pines on the edge of the western hillside.

Spirit Walker knelt to examine the hoof print at the edge of the rocks. It was clear and deep. Suddenly a sprig of grass in the middle of the track sprung straight up. "They are close," he said over his shoulder to the others.

"How close?" Broken Branch asked.

"Close enough to know we are here," the old warrior said.

Hooves thundered from a small opening cut in the side of the steep hillside. At least a score of wild ponies fled into the pines, making their way for the open canyon.

The three mounted warriors immediately set out in pursuit. Their heels drumming their horses into action, the men entered the tree line just behind the running herd. Spirit Walker leapt onto his Appaloosa, but instead of entering the trees, he began a circular route around them in an effort to cut the herd off as they exited the other side.

The wild mustangs were quick. Riderless, they maneuvered through the trees with ease. Cloud Maker's mount gained on one of the running ponies. Pulling a rawhide thong from his waistband, he gripped it in his teeth and bent low along his horse's neck. As he approached the nearly grown mouse-colored colt he was chasing, he attempted to slip the noose over its head. The colt bucked, jerked to the left, and headed for a tree. Barely able to guide his horse away from the tree, Cloud Maker realized that he would have to make his move on the open plains. The pines were just too thick to attempt a capture. He kicked his horse onward and rode hard.

Broken Branch and Black Beaver also realized the folly of trying to capture the horses inside the cover of the pines. Their best chance was to stay in close proximity to the herd, hoping to be within range to make a grab when they exited the other side.

When Spirit Walker first saw the coal black stallion crash through the trees and out onto the plains, he knew it was the leader of the herd. It was a magnificent animal whose coat shone in the afternoon sun, giving off hues of blue. The horse was big, his flanks heavily muscled. The stallion looked in Spirit Walker's direction, flared its nostrils, and bolted across the open field.

Spirit Walker kicked his mount into a full run. He knew that he could not hope to catch the stallion immediately. It would be a hard and long chase. The stallion was too fast to catch quickly. It would be a war won by attrition. The Appaloosa had endurance, and Spirit Walker could only hope that it would be enough to catch the leader of the herd.

Cloud Maker made his move on the mouse-colored colt he had chased through the pines. As he broke into the open, Cloud Maker lunged to his left and slipped the noose over the colt's head. Keeping stride beside the wild pony, Cloud Maker did not seek to stop the colt, but merely to keep pace and let the colt slow of its own volition. Suddenly Cloud Maker's own mount stumbled and the Apache was pulled violently from his seat. He hit the ground hard, but managed to hold onto the cord that attached him to his quarry. Cloud Maker's weight was too much for the colt's neck to bear, and the noble animal flipped head first onto the hard-packed soil of the plains.

Cloud Maker, bleeding from abrasions on his arms and back, struggled to his feet. The colt kicked wildly trying to right itself, but Cloud Maker was ready. Before the colt could roll over and gain its footing, the Apache threw himself across its neck, pinning it to the ground. Try as it might, the wild colt could not stand. It lay in the dirt, panting. Exhausted.

Broken Branch, unable to keep pace with the running herd, broke onto the plains well behind Cloud Maker. He reined his horse to a halt and slid from its back. "Do you need help, my brother?"

"No. Ride on. We must trap them now. We cannot hope to catch many in the open field unless we work as a team to capture them one at a time. I'll tie this one to a tree and be right behind you."

Broken Branch looked out over the prairie. He could see Spirit Walker riding hard after a big black, but there was no sign of Black Beaver. "Where is Black Beaver?"

The colt began the struggle anew and Cloud Maker wrestled to keep control. He did need help. "I don't know," he said. "Broken Branch, tie this pony's feet together. I don't wish to lose him."

Broken Branch smiled and rushed to secure the animal's hind feet.

Cloud Maker stood as Broken Branch finished lashing the horse's front feet. The colt struggled against the bonds, but quickly realized the futility of its actions. Broken Branch wiped sweat from his brow. "Black Beaver!" he exclaimed, as he spotted the older tracker exiting the tree line. A bright red streak across his forehead oozed blood down the side of his face.

Broken Branch ran toward him. "Black Beaver, are you hurt badly?"

Black Beaver smiled down at his worried friend. "It would seem that I am unable to duck as fast as I once could, but I am not hurt badly."

Black Beaver's smile was reassuring and both men laughed out loud. Even Cloud Maker smiled.

Chapter Thirty

"He'll never catch it," Cloud Maker said as he watched Spirit Walker race across the plain in pursuit of the herd's leader. "It's a fruitless chase. Let us round up some of the others."

Broken Branch sized up Spirit Walker's situation. The warrior was riding hard, but his mount couldn't hope to stay up with the powerful black stallion. Broken Branch turned to Cloud Maker. "You and Black Beaver try to cut another one from the herd. I'm going to help Spirit Walker." With that he kicked his mount into a run.

Spirit Walker's Appaloosa was tiring. His horse's breath was raspy, its pace slowing. The black was pulling farther away, tossing its head in defiance.

They circled the field, making a wide arch along its edge. Out of the corner of his eye, Spirit Walker could see Broken Branch coming on hard and fast. "Cut him off! Turn him back toward me!" Spirit Walker yelled.

Broken Branch ran straight at the stallion. The huge black dug in its hind legs, sliding to a brief stop, then whirled and headed back toward Spirit Walker. The wily warrior cut the stallion toward the rocks of the closest hillside.

While Spirit Walker and Broken Branch chased the stallion, Cloud Maker was busy trying to corner a mare and her young colt. Thinking that catching the colt would bring the mare to him, he maneuvered closer to the smaller horse. Cloud Maker glanced back to see if Black Beaver was in a position to help, but the older warrior was preoccupied with watching the action at the edge of the canyon. "Black Beaver!" Cloud Maker called.

Black Beaver cast a quick glance in Cloud Maker's direction, then pointed to Spirit Walker and Broken Branch. "I believe they will catch the leader!" he called back. "If the leader is caught, the rest may follow."

Cloud Maker had to admit that that was a good possibility, but his pride kept him from saying so. "I have no faith in the old man. He is no longer a warrior. He is weak. I will show him how to catch a horse." He kicked his mount into a run and headed straight toward the herd leader.

Spirit Walker carefully moved his mount to the left, matching his movements to counter Broken Branch approaching from the right. Obviously he hoped to trap the stallion between them. Finally, they were able to back the black stallion up against the eastern wall of the canyon. The only possible escape route lay between the two warriors. Spirit Walker motioned for Broken Branch to slow his horse's pace, trying not to spook the wild stallion into running again. The black turned, its chest heaving as it faced Spirit Walker.

Suddenly Cloud Maker burst through the middle of the two warriors and headed straight for the frightened stallion. Cloud

Maker held a rawhide rope in his right hand as he lay against his mount's neck.

"No!" Spirit Walker yelled, but it was too late. The stallion reared, lashing out with his forelegs.

Cloud Maker's mare jerked to a halt. The stallion's forehooves barely missed the tip of the mare's nose and she jumped quickly to the left. Cloud Maker flew from the mare's back, landing with a thud on the ground. As the air left his lungs, Cloud Maker looked up at the deadly hooves slashing overhead.

The scene was ripe for disaster. Broken Branch watched as Cloud Maker lay dazed on the rocky ground, the stallion cutting the air with his sharp hooves. At any moment, the wild horse could lunge downward and cut him to pieces. Broken Branch felt helpless to intervene in time.

Suddenly, Spirit Walker slid from the Appaloosa's back. *"Che-lee!"* he cried. "Horse!"

The stallion tossed its head. Nostrils flaring, it whinnied proudly, pawing the air. Its eyes flashed like lightning, but Spirit Walker met its gaze and walked steadily forward.

Broken Branch sat astounded at the sight. Cloud Maker rolled up against a large boulder.

"Chelee, no!" the Chokonen shouted.

The big black set its front hooves heavily on the ground and stared at the warrior. Spirit Walker kept a steady pace. *"Chelee."* The stallion stomped. *"A-pa-chu,"* Spirit Walker cried, slapping his chest as he walked.

Broken Branch could have sworn that he saw a flash of recognition in the stallion's eyes. The horse stood still, cautiously observing the warrior's approach. Spirit Walker stretched out his hand and slowly touched the stallion's nose. The horse lurched slightly, but didn't bolt. Spirit Walker ran his hand up to the broad area between the animal's eyes, rubbing in small circles. The stallion seemed hypnotized by the warrior's touch. Spirit Walker scratched an ear, then, before the horse realized what had happened, he sprung onto its back. The stallion bucked once, then began to run, the Chokonen clinging to its mane.

Broken Branch dismounted quickly and ran to Cloud Maker's side. Cloud Maker struggled to his feet as Broken Branch arrived. "Are you hurt, my brother?" Broken Branch asked.

Cloud Maker brushed the dirt from his arms and legs. "No. I'm not hurt." He glanced up. The black stallion was running at top speed, but was making no attempt to buck.

Black Beaver rode up and brought his mount to a halt before the two warriors. "Spirit Walker rides the black as if they are old friends," he observed.

"Something tells me that is not far from wrong," Broken Branch agreed.

Spirit Walker rode low across the running stallion's back. It was a familiar feeling. Though he hadn't been sure at first, there was no doubting now—this was the young colt he had placed among the herd four years ago.

The memory flooded back as the wind whipped his hair. He had accompanied Goyathlay and three other warriors into Mexico on a raid for horses. They had entered Sonora on foot and it wasn't long before they spotted six vaqueros driving a group of horses across the flats.

It was obvious that the vaqueros were herding the horses toward a hacienda located nearby. It was also obvious that the vaqueros were completely unaware of the awaiting ambush. Crouched behind boulders on the edge of a narrow pass, the five Apaches had watched their victims enter the draw.

Spirit Walker wasn't sure who fired first, but he had turned in time to see Goyathlay shoot the last rider from his saddle. The firing was rapid, the scene chaotic as the vaqueros scattered. Four riders were down, the other two nowhere to be seen. The horses were running in all directions, unsure of what to do or where to go.

The other four Apaches had gathered the herd from the backs of the downed riders' horses. Spirit Walker had waited. Alone, he sat watching for any *soldatos*, the Mexican army soldiers that roamed Sonora.

As he sat guard, he heard a whinny from the rocks below. Climbing to the valley floor, he spotted a shiny black colt standing next to the cliff face. Beside the troubled colt lay the body of its mother. The mare had been shot once through the head, the victim of a stray bullet. The colt was confused, frightened.

When the others returned, Spirit Walker had chosen one of the gathered horses to ride back to Apachería. He led the small colt on a strong rawhide cord. The colt had been too young to be of any use at that time, so when they reached the horse canyon, Spirit Walker had released it in among the others.

That was four years ago. Before Cochise left for the After World. Before Spirit Walker left for a life of solitude. Perhaps the reunion could bring those days back. Perhaps, just perhaps, the colt he had simply called *Chelee*, the Apache word for horse, could take him back to a time when he was still a warrior of the People. Perhaps.

Everything progressed just as Spirit Walker had planned. Once the black tired of running, Spirit Walker guided it expertly back into the rest of the herd. The other horses began to fall in behind their leader. Slowly, Broken Branch, Black Beaver, and Cloud Maker rode in among them as well. With the herd's leader captured, it was relatively easy to rope the others. There were twenty-two wild horses in all, but Spirit Walker requested that they take only fourteen, leaving the others in reserve in the canyon. He chose a feisty golden brown filly for Desert Rain, the black for himself, and twelve others for a dowry. The chosen horses were roped together and led out of the canyon.

Cloud Maker never said a word.

★   ★   ★

Two days later, the four men rode into the rancheria with the captured horses. Spirit Walker slid gracefully to the ground in front of Wind Song's tipi. "*Ya a teh!* Hello!" he cried.

Desert Rain rushed through the door flap, literally flying into his arms. "My Spirit, you return!" Hanging on his neck, she looked over the string of horses standing behind the Chokonen. "Oh, my Spirit! Mother will be so happy!"

With the acquisition of twelve ponies, Wind Song would become one of the wealthiest people in the clan and would gain prestige and honor among her people. There was one other thing that would bring her mother more respect even than these horses—she would be the mother-in-law of the Spirit That Walks as a Man—and Desert Rain would be his wife.

Spirit Walker took Desert Rain by the arm and led her to the horses. He pointed to the golden brown filly. "This one is for you, my Flower."

Desert Rain smiled as she looked into the large brown eyes of the pony. "It is so beautiful, my Spirit!" Slowly she reached out and stroked the horse's head and ears. "It is the best gift I have ever received."

"I'm afraid she is not ready to ride yet," Spirit Walker warned.

"Will you help me break her?"

"Of course I will. We shall do it tomorrow."

Desert Rain cast an impish look at the warrior. "We cannot, my Spirit. That will not be possible."

Spirit Walker was puzzled. "Why not?" he asked.

Desert Rain laughed softly. "We are to be married tomorrow. I cannot wait."

Spirit Walker balked for only a second. He had been impetuous when he had asked her to marry him. He had wondered many times since why he had asked, why the words just seemed to have jumped into his throat, then rolled effortlessly off his tongue. It must have been the passion he felt at the time. She deserved a young warrior, a virile warrior. He could never satisfy her desires. He gently brushed a lock of hair from her forehead. It was too late now. He wanted her too badly. He smiled. "We will break the filly the next day then," he said, trying to sound serious.

Desert Rain pulled back and punched his shoulder. "No, we shall not," she exclaimed in mock anger. Laughing with joy, she once again leapt into his arms and kissed him.

Chapter Thirty-one

Broken Branch and Black Beaver spent the afternoon of their return preparing a tipi for Spirit Walker and Desert Rain. They chose a small green clearing at the edge of the creek and began to erect the wedding lodge. Gifts were brought to the site by other members of the band and a three-day supply of firewood was gathered.

The next morning, Spirit Walker walked toward Wind Song's tipi on foot, leading the twelve horses. He was dressed in a new set of buckskin leggings and a cloth shirt given to him by Broken Branch. He wore a red bandanna around his head, two eagle feathers in his hair. Around his neck, he wore a choker of bird bones and leather, a copper Thunderbird dangling from its center.

The traditional Apache wedding ceremony was a very simple affair. At the appointed time, Spirit Walker approached the tipi and announced himself at the door flap. Wind Song exited and stood before him.

Spirit Walker glanced about him. To his right, Chief Five Dreams stood beside Old Stone, the shaman. To his left, Broken Branch, Black Beaver and an assembly of warriors watched from a distance. He noticed that there was no sign of Cloud Maker. He cleared his throat and handed the lead rope to Wind Song. "I have brought these gifts in exchange for permission to marry your daughter."

"And will you give your life for hers?" Wind Song asked.

"I have. I do. I will forever."

Wind Song smiled and turned to the chief. "Today, in the presence of my People, I give my daughter to this warrior," she announced in a loud voice.

Desert Rain stepped through the door flap. Wearing a buckskin tunic trimmed with squirrel tails, and moccasins decorated with tiny silver bells, she stood beside her mother. Wind Song placed her daughter's right hand into the right hand of the proud warrior.

"From this time forward," Wind Song declared, "Desert Rain shall be called the wife of Spirit Walker, the Spirit That Walks as a Man!"

Old Stone stepped forward then. He began the ancient chant of blessing, asking *Usen* to watch over the happy couple, pledging the clan's loyalty to Spirit Walker, and accepting the Chokonen into their tribal family.

It was a short ceremony, soon over, but for the newlywed couple, it was only the beginning. Spirit Walker walked toward the creek with his new bride. He had never felt so proud in his life.

The early morning sunlight danced across the surface of the water, the water danced across the rocks of the streambed, but it was love that danced in Desert Rain's eyes. The joy in her heart lent wings to her feet. She felt as if she could fly, that if it weren't for the fact that she was holding Spirit Walker's hand, she might lift off the ground and soar with the birds.

She couldn't help but watch Spirit Walker out of the corner of her eye. The Chokonen was rolling rather than walking. His gait was smooth, his shoulders square, his head high. She could see his pride. It was chiseled in the features of his strong jaw, the outline of his brow, the noble slant of his nose. Though he showed no sign of joy on his face, it was evident in the way he carried himself. It was in the way he held tightly to her hand, as if he too sensed she might fly away at any moment.

It didn't take long to reach the small tipi. Spirit Walker pulled the flap aside and allowed Desert Rain to enter first. She ducked into the dwelling and smiled at the smell of the fresh wild flowers no doubt placed in the tipi by her mother. The tipi was decorated with deerskins of various sizes and shapes. There was a bear hide lying in the center of the tipi and behind that a large buffalo robe.

As Spirit Walker ducked in behind her and closed the door flap, Desert Rain turned to face him. He is so handsome, she thought, as she tilted her head back, her eyes closing in anticipation of his kiss.

Spirit Walker had never felt lips as soft as hers. They infused him with love, strength, power. He kissed her deeply. Closing his eyes, he ran his hands over her dainty shoulders, down her shapely back, brushing her hair with his fingers. She was so warm and inviting. His body thrilled at her touch as she placed the back of her hand against his cheek. He had never experienced anything as exciting as her touch, her kiss, her love. It was overpowering, exhilarating, making him feel like a young warrior again.

Drawing back a little, Desert Rain lifted the hem of his shirt. He raised his arms above his head as she removed his shirt and tossed it aside. She ran her hands over his chest, reveling in the feel of his skin beneath her fingertips, the width of his broad shoulders, the swell of muscles in his arms.

Spirit Walker cradled her head with his hands, as she kissed her way across his chest. Her lips were flames of fire, pools of passion. Her delicate hands caressed his waist as her kisses flooded his senses with desire. He could feel the heat of passion rising in his loins. He knew she could feel it too. Her hands began tugging at the rawhide cord that secured the leggings around his hips. Soon the leggings were free and falling to the floor.

Spirit Walker stepped free of the leggings as he untied Desert Rain's tunic. She was so beautiful, so tender and sweet. He knelt and loosened the lacings of her moccasins. One by one he removed them and tossed them casually aside.

His hands were warm and Desert Rain sighed deeply as he ran them along her calves. She felt his lips on her thighs as his hands began to lift the edge of her tunic. She was burning with desire. Her heart pumping wildly, she stroked the hair on the back of his head.

Her tunic was above her waist now and she could feel his hot mouth on her hip. Kissing across to the other hip, Spirit Walker held her tunic above his head. His kisses intensified as he reached her inner thighs. She felt she would pass out from pleasure before he stood to his feet and pulled the tunic up and over her head.

Spirit Walker dropped the tunic behind her and drew her into his arms. He held her tightly and kissed her. She could feel his passion pressed against hers, but his breechclout separated them still. She reached down and released it. Pulling it away, she dropped it to the floor, and pulled his hips firmly against her own. She gasped as she felt the hardness of his desire, and kissed him all the more deeply.

Moving as one, they shuffled toward the bearskin blanket, at the rear of the tipi. Desert Rain lay back on the blanket as Spirit Walker removed his *kabuns*. They were traditional knee-high moccasins, often called Apache boots, but then he was a traditional warrior and she was his woman. She smiled as he removed his bandanna and two-feather headdress, then lowered himself onto the blanket.

Lying beside his new wife, Spirit Walker's hands began an exploratory journey. The soft curve of her breasts contrasted sharply with the firm flatness of her stomach. Her slender waist accentuated the curve of her hips. Surely there existed no woman on earth as lovely as she.

Desert Rain's desire rose quickly as Spirit Walker's hands caressed the sensitive skin along her inner thigh. Heat flooded her body as his fingers gently stroked and aroused her. Arching her back, she groaned with passion. She had never felt such ecstasy from a simple touch. It was a magic she had never experienced. She wanted him to possess her wholly, completely, knew she would die without his touch. She pulled him closer, her lips finding his.

His hair fell across her cheeks as he kissed her. She felt his weight bear down on top of her as he spread her legs with his knees. She opened her eyes, staring at him in wonder as his body merged with hers. Each movement rocked her entire body as he kissed along her neck, ears, shoulders, and breasts. She gripped him tightly, pulling him deeper into her passion. They were one now.

They had made love three different times during that first day. Desert Rain had never thought that possible until now. The Chokonen surely possessed great stamina, but she marveled also at her own hunger. She wanted him again and again. She felt as if she could not get enough of him. He was her food, her nourishment, and she meant to get her fill.

Moving outside under the darkness of midnight, they walked naked along the babbling stream. In the full moon's light, he took her once again in his arms. She gazed up at him with loving eyes. "Do you love me, my Spirit?"

"Now and forever, Little One. I shall never leave you again."

"Am I your song on the midnight wind?"

"You are forever my song on the midnight wind."

A shadow crossed the moon's light and Desert Rain looked skyward. She smiled at the sight of the graceful dance of a hawk. Instinctively, Desert Rain leaned back and echoed the call of the NightHawk.

Spirit Walker looked down into her lovely face and smiled. Then, backing away, he gave the cry of the coyote.

Desert Rain laughed out loud, then turned and ran back toward the tipi.

Spirit Walker caught her at the door and the two tumbled onto the floor, laughing and rolling in elation.

"Take me again, my Spirit," Desert Rain whispered.

Spirit Walker smiled. He was alive again and she was his breath.

Chapter Thirty-two

It was three days of laughter, three days of peace, three days of absolute bliss. Each morning they awoke to find food placed at the door of their tipi. Venison, squirrel, and ashcakes were brought by various members of the clan.

On the fourth morning, they left the tipi and walked back into the encampment. Later that day, Desert Rain and two other women moved the tipi into place among the others. It would become the new couple's permanent dwelling—a gift from Broken Branch and the warriors of the clan. They were settled and happy.

The next morning, Desert Rain rolled over and lightly caressed Spirit Walker's cheek. "My Spirit?"

Spirit Walker opened his eyes slowly and stretched as the last vestiges of sleep left him. "Yes, my Flower?"

"May we break the filly today? I'm so anxious to ride."

Spirit Walker smiled. How she made his heart soar with her sweet voice. "Yes, Little One. Today we shall break the filly."

They found the filly tied to a stake in the brush corral with the other horses. Spirit Walker had tied the filly while Desert Rain and her friends moved the tipi the day before. He had tied two bags of sand together and draped them over the pony's back to get it used to the feel of carrying weight.

"Will you ride it here until it is ready for me?" she asked innocently.

"No, Little One, you shall ride the filly. My weight may be too much for it to handle at first."

"But, my Spirit, I have never ridden a wild pony. What if I should fall?"

Spirit Walker removed the weights and untied the filly. "Flower, you will not ride it here. Come with me."

They led the small horse along the creek until Spirit Walker spotted a deep pool. "There," he said, pointing to the deeper water. "I will lead the filly into the water. Once the water is high enough to touch its belly, I will help you onto its back. It will not be able to buck very hard then. Just hang on and stay on its back."

Spirit Walker led the filly into the water. As he boosted Desert Rain onto its back, the pony jumped forward once and Spirit Walker lost his footing in the creek. Desert Rain laughed as Spirit Walker's head disappeared under the surface of the water, then popped up like a piece of driftwood. Spirit Walker shook his head. "Hold on!" he warned.

A couple of short hops and Desert Rain was sliding from the filly's back. She held desperately onto the rope bridle Spirit Walker had rigged. The filly tripped on the uneven bed of the creek and was partially submerged in the cool mountain stream. Desert Rain thrashed in the water, struggling to stay on top of the pony. Kicking her feet, she was aboard again when the filly gained its footing.

Spirit Walker waded to shore and watched with pride as his wife slipped again and again only to regain her seat after each fall. She was so beautiful, but there was another quality that had never before been so evident as now—she was headstrong, brave, determined. The filly never had a chance against the young warrior woman. Spirit Walker sat on a boulder and watched his woman work the filly.

Over the next month, Spirit Walker spent many hours talking with Chief Five Dreams in the sweat lodge. Many times they were joined by Old Stone, and sometimes by other members of the warrior clan. Broken Branch had grown closer to Spirit Walker, but it seemed that Cloud Maker grew ever more distant. Though Broken Branch had sought to include his friend, Cloud Maker always had an excuse to be away. He was either hunting or scouting and never seemed to be available. Spirit Walker could sense that Broken Branch's heart was sad for his friend. The conflict within Cloud Maker was great.

Black Beaver had also become a close friend to Spirit Walker. They would often walk through the forest together and talk of the wisdom of the Old Ones. Even the children had taken to Spirit Walker, sitting at his feet and listening to his stories of Coyote the Trickster and the adventures of Little Spirit, a small Chokonen boy who was always getting into trouble. They laughed as much at the way Spirit Walker told the tales as they did at the tales themselves.

Spirit Walker was sitting outside his tipi when Chief Five Dreams approached. "*Ya a teh*," Five Dreams greeted.

"My chief. You are well?"

Five Dreams nodded and sat beside the warrior. "I have news. Distressing news."

Spirit Walker could see the concern in the old chief's eyes.

"Yes, I saw the riders this morning as they entered the rancheria. What news did they bring?"

Five Dreams cleared his throat and looked about him. "We will hold council tonight, but I wanted to talk to you first. You know of Tahza?"

Spirit Walker nodded. "Yes, he is the eldest son of the last Chokonen chief."

Though Spirit Walker had not mentioned the name of the deceased chief, he referred to Cochise. Upon the great Chiricahua chief's death, the clan had looked to Tahza for leadership.

"You speak truth, Spirit. Tahza is the chief of the those who reside on the Chiricahua Reservation."

"Yes. I heard that they live in peace. That Taglito has secured their safety there."

Taglito was Indian Agent Tom Jeffords, who had been responsible for talking Cochise into making a peace treaty with the white eyes. Cochise had loved Jeffords, and had given him the Indian name Taglito, which meant "red beard." Unfortunately, Cochise did not live long enough to insure that the treaty was kept. It was broken shortly after his death, but not because Taglito had failed the Apache. Taglito was still considered a friend and ally of the People.

"Taglito could do nothing to stop what has happened now," Five Dreams said. "The white man has found yellow iron. They are forcing the Apache to move from Chiricahua, taking them to another place called San Carlos."

"San Carlos?"

"Yes. It has been said that San Carlos is fit only for rattlesnakes and scorpions. The white man does not want such a place, so they force our People to live there."

Spirit Walker shook his head in disbelief. It was a grave situation. Because of the close proximity of the Chiricahua Reservation, Five Dreams' small band of Jicarilla Apache were left alone by the cavalry, but if the Chiricahua Apache were to be moved it would endanger their own fragile existence in the Arizona Territory.

"There is news that Tahza has arranged for some of them to escape."

Spirit Walker sat upright. "How many? Where are they going?"

"They go to Mexico."

"Mexico!"

Suddenly the camp came alive with activity as four riderless horses burst into the camp and ran toward the horse corral. Spirit Walker sprang to his feet. "There is trouble, my chief."

Five Dreams stood and the two men started for the corral at a fast walk.

Cloud Maker and several of the warriors had spotted the running horses as they stampeded across the compound and slid to a stop just outside the corral. The horses stood restlessly in front of the gate, blowing and heaving from the hard run. The warriors ran to examine the horses.

"There is blood on this horse's flanks," Cloud Maker said as Spirit Walker approached. Standing next to a large mustang, he turned to address the others. "Our hunters have been shot."

Spirit Walker examined the blood, touching it with his hand. Holding the blood to his nose, he turned to the others as well. "No. If they were shot from the horses' backs, the blood would be on top of its back and only dripping down the flanks. And this is not the blood of a man, it is the blood of an animal."

Cloud Maker stepped forward. "How can you be sure of this? I say we backtrack them, then we will know who speaks the truth."

Spirit Walker met Cloud Maker's gaze. "Yes. Let us go at once."

* * *

It was not hard to follow the tracks of the running horses and before long four weary hunters could be seen walking toward the rancheria. They waved as the search party approached, the lost horses in tow.

Cloud Maker reined the group to a halt. "What has happened? Your horses returned to us. We thought you dead."

Spirit Walker recognized the leader of this young group of hunters as Wild Eyes. He was eager and zealous, but without wisdom. He had taken three others on their first hunt, with equally inexperienced horses.

"We downed a large deer and were trying to place it on the horse's back when it bolted and spooked the others," Wild Eyes explained.

"They smelled the blood," Spirit Walker noted. "They must be taught. Let us return to the deer and I shall teach them."

It was a large buck the group had killed. Cloud Maker slid from his mount and grabbed the deer by the horns.

Spirit Walker also dismounted and commanded Wild Eyes to do the same. Spirit Walker took the reins of the horse that had bolted and held him in place as Cloud Maker dragged the deer up beside it. Once again, the horse jerked and tried to run. "Wait!" Spirit Walker instructed.

Spirit Walker handed the reins to one of the other young men, then stepped over to a dry log. Reaching down, he broke off a rotting branch. He faced the pony and swung the branch. The horse staggered at the blow. Spirit Walker had been careful to hit the horse on the hard bony part of the horse's head. Silently, the Chokonen struck another blow. The horse sank to its knees. "Now, load the deer," Spirit Walker said calmly.

Cloud Maker hoisted the deer onto the horse's back. As the horse struggled to its feet, Cloud Maker began lashing the deer in place.

"The horse will bolt no more at the smell of blood," Spirit Walker said resolutely.

"I see you have not lost your touch!"

The voice came from behind them. They turned to see an older warrior emerge from the trees, followed by six others. They were Apache and wore leather breeches, cloth shirts, and bandannas. Each one carried a rifle. The one who had spoken smiled broadly. His face was wide, his eyes narrow.

"Goyathlay!" Spirit Walker exclaimed.

Chapter Thirty-three

"You look well, my old friend," Goyathlay said as he strode boldly forward.

"And you," Spirit Walker replied.

Goyathlay approached and the two men grasped forearms. Goyathlay smiled. "I heard you had been killed by Mexicans in Chihuahua."

Spirit Walker spread his arms out to the side, palms up. "And yet, I am here."

Goyathlay laughed and slapped Spirit Walker on the shoulder. "Yes, I can see. Tell me. Where have you been, my friend?"

"I have kept to myself, seeking peace only."

"Peace!" Goyathlay spit the word at the ground, pretending to grind it into the earth with his foot. "There is no peace. The *Nakai-Ye* brought peace at Kas-Ki-Yeh. They carried it in their guns and gave it to our loved ones freely. *Los Goddammies* bring the same peace. I am sick of peace."

"I am too," Cloud Maker declared as he stepped forward.

"Who are you?" Goyathlay asked, taking a long look at the young warrior.

"I am Cloud Maker, warrior of the People."

Goyathlay took a step back, eyeing Cloud Maker from top to bottom. "I will tell you, young man, that the way of the warrior is not an easy life."

"I do not seek ease, my chief, I seek the path of the *Netdahe*."

Goyathlay's eyes narrowed. "The way of the *Netdahe* is not an easy death."

Spirit Walker had almost forgotten how charismatic Goyathlay could be. He was a brilliant orator. He had a way of persuading men with a look, convincing them that the *Netdahe* way was one of mystery, one to be desired by all warriors. Often, in council meetings, Goyathlay would stand and give speeches to encourage the others. His charisma had resulted in many followers who trusted that he could deliver justice for the People. Many times, however, his charisma resulted in the death of those who followed him into battle.

"I will follow you, Goyathlay, if you will have me," Cloud Maker stated. "I do not fear death."

"All men fear death," Goyathlay snapped. "It is the fear of death that gives strength to the warrior's heart, guides his arrow, defeats his enemies. Though outnumbered, the *Netdahe* knows that the fear of death is his greatest ally. It is the control of that fear that men call courage."

"I shall be led by no other," Cloud Maker said flatly. "I will be *Netdahe*."

"You will eat with us tonight?" Spirit Walker interrupted, hoping to change the subject.

Goyathlay turned back to his old friend. "I have others that I must care for. We leave in the morning for Sonora."

"You go to Mexico?" Spirit Walker asked.

"Yes, Walker. You will join us?"

Spirit Walker couldn't remember the last time someone had called him by that name. It was pleasant to his ear, like a familiar blanket on a cold evening. "I cannot. I have recently taken a wife."

Goyathlay laughed. "You have taken a wife? I am pleased, Walker." Suddenly, the renegade's face hardened. "Then you must realize that you are in great danger if you remain here. The blue coats are herding our people like cattle at this time. They are taking them to a desert place to die. To save your family, you must follow us to Mexico."

"To die as those of Kas-Ki-Yeh?" Spirit Walker's eyes flashed fire as he spoke.

"This too troubles me, Walker. But I must go now. If you change your mind, follow the old trails. I shall welcome you gladly."

Spirit Walker's countenance softened as he reached to take Goyathlay's arm. "Be well, my friend."

"And you." Goyathlay smiled, turned on his heels, and walked away.

Spirit Walker watched his old friend disappear with his followers into the woodlands. Try as he might, Spirit Walker could not bring himself to hate the proud warrior. His intentions were honorable, if his methods at times ignoble.

"What is the purpose of the council tonight, my Spirit?" Desert Rain asked as she cleared away the bowls after the evening meal.

Spirit Walker sat on his favorite blanket and glanced at the sash draped over his lance at the back of the tipi. "It's about the coming trouble," he said, a twinge of concern in his voice.

Desert Rain put the bowls by the door flap, turned, and walked back to where he sat. Sitting down beside him, she took his hand in hers. "Is there to be trouble, my Spirit? Are we in danger if we remain here?"

Spirit Walker looked deeply into his wife's eyes. "I don't

know, my Flower. I know only that we must make a decision. We must carefully discuss the situation and then decide what is to be done."

"My Spirit, I care not whether we stay or go. I care only that I am with you. You are my life, I want to be wherever you are."

He grabbed her and held her close. Their lips met and his heart wept. She was the most precious gift the Great Spirit had ever bestowed upon him and he would insure her safety at any cost.

Framed by the council fire's light, Five Dreams stood before the small group of warriors. "My brothers, hear my words. . . ."

Spirit Walker listened intently as the chief spoke, telling about the news that had come from the riders earlier in the day. There were murmurs from the warriors and concerns about what effect the removal of the Apache to San Carlos would have on them and their way of life. Some suggested it would be dangerous to remain in Arizona Territory, others were resolved to keep their homeland and fight the blue coats. As Spirit Walker expected, Cloud Maker lead the group who argued to fight.

"I am ready to die to keep our homeland from being overrun by the white eyes," Cloud Maker said as he stood before the chief. "I will fight till there is no breath in my body." Turning to his fellow warriors, he struck his chest defiantly. "I will not run like a dog and hide in the mountains like a wounded animal. I am Apache! I am proud!"

A shout of support rose among the warriors. Their cries reached a crescendo as Spirit Walker stood and raised his hands for silence.

"Wait!" he shouted above the noise. "I have something to say."

As the shouts subsided, Cloud Maker walked toward the Chokonen. "What have you to say, old man?"

Spirit Walker turned to face the young warrior. Cloud Maker was taller than he, but Spirit Walker squared his shoulders and straightened to his full height. "I have much to say. You would do well to listen."

"I will not listen to old women!" Cloud Maker shouted. "Once you were *Netdahe*. Once you were a warrior who fought for the dignity of the People. Now you are weak. I will not listen to you!"

Once again a cry of support went up for Cloud Maker. Spirit Walker looked out over the crowd. They were young and foolish. "Will any of you listen?" Spirit Walker shouted.

Cloud Maker seemed to be the only one who heard Spirit Walker's question. He looked at him and laughed. "Go away, old man." His smile faded into a scowl as he locked eyes with Spirit Walker, who saw anger rise in Cloud Maker like a fire racing across the dry prairie grass. Cloud Maker's fists clinched, tighter and tighter, till the blood drained from his knuckles.

The crowd watched in amazement as Cloud Maker swung a hard right hand at Spirit Walker's jaw. The Chokonen took the punch squarely on the chin. His head jerked sharply to the right, but his feet never moved. Turning his head, he spit a small amount of blood onto the ground, then once again met Cloud Maker's gaze. "The *Netdahe* do not ride with men who hit like old women."

It was a degrading insult and Cloud Maker's face contorted with rage as he threw the next punch. With perfect timing, Spirit Walker bent at the waist. The momentum of Cloud Maker's attack carried him cleanly over the Chokonen's back. Cloud Maker landed hard on the ground. Spirit Walker straightened. "Anger is the greatest enemy of a warrior!" he shouted. "Stand up and try again!"

Cloud Maker jumped to his feet and lunged forward. Spirit Walker sidestepped quickly to the left and grabbed a handful of Cloud Maker's hair, jerking the younger man backward, face to the sky. With one smooth motion, Spirit Walker's right fist came down hard across the enraged warrior's throat. Cloud Maker's

231

feet left the ground and he landed on his back. Rolling in agony, Cloud Maker grabbed his throat and groaned, trying to catch his breath.

"My Spirit!" All eyes turned to see Desert Rain step from the night shadows. "I believe this belongs to you, my warrior," she said as she tossed a long slender object in his direction.

Spirit Walker caught the lance, then in one quick motion, buried its tip into the solid earth. From its uppermost end hung its sash. Taking the sash in his hands he wrapped it securely around his waist.

The crowd fell silent as he turned to face them once again. "I am Spirit Walker!" he announced proudly. "You would do well to listen to my words."

Desert Rain smiled and walked back into the night.

Chapter Thirty-four

"There is no future in fighting the white eyes," Spirit Walker began. "They are more plentiful than the stars in the night sky. Their weapons bring only death. Their words bring only lies."

Cloud Maker rolled to a sitting position. Holding his throat, he stared up at the older warrior. "So, you propose we surrender?" he asked hoarsely.

"No," Spirit Walker snapped. "We will never surrender."

"What then?" asked a youngster near the rear of the crowd.

"We move our encampment. We move to Mexico, into the heart of the Mother Mountains."

"The Sierra Madre?" Chief Five Dreams asked. "But we know nothing of the mountains."

"I do," Spirit Walker announced. "There we will find good water, much food, and freedom."

Cloud Maker considered the possibilities in the Spirit Walker's words. Perhaps he had misjudged him. Perhaps the wily warrior was proposing that they join Goyathlay's *Netdahe*. After all, they were heading for Mexico as well. Cloud Maker stood and faced the Chokonen. "We will join Goyathlay?" he asked bluntly.

Spirit Walker looked deep into Cloud Maker's eyes. "No," he replied. "We will not. We will follow the path of peace into Mexico."

Cloud Maker stood in silence.

"When should we leave?" Five Dreams interrupted.

Spirit Walker cast a look over the warriors. "First, we should lay in a supply of food for the journey. It will not be an easy one. We must prepare the horses, lodges, and clothing. We must take great care to assure that all is ready for the trip. If we do so quickly, we may be able to move by the next moon."

Cloud Maker turned to face his brothers. "You may stay and prepare. You may bow to the words of this outsider, but I will leave at first sun. Who is with me?"

A young warrior in the back stood up. "Where will you go, my brother?"

"I go to join Goyathlay. He rides the old trails into Mexico, but he does not run. He will fight. He will strike fear into the hearts of the white eyes, and he will avenge our people."

"Then I go with you!" the young warrior announced.

Slowly two others stood and joined Cloud Maker and the young warrior, and he led his small group of followers off into the night.

When the council was dismissed, Spirit Walker walked away with the chief, but Broken Branch, who was grieving for his friend's decision, went looking for Cloud Maker. He found his old friend making plans with the others who had chosen to follow him. Broken Branch approached slowly.

Cloud Maker faced Broken Branch as he stepped forward. "You will join us, my brother?" Cloud Maker asked.

Broken Branch stared into Cloud Maker's eyes. He had never

seen the young warrior so determined. Slowly he shook his head. "I cannot, my brother. I wish for you to stay with us."

Cloud Maker felt his anger rise again. He had grown tired of the doubts surrounding his decision. He had lost face in the sight of the warriors when he was bested by Spirit Walker, and he would not let that happen again. His back straightened, his fists clinched, he stepped forward.

Broken Branch sensed the tension, but did not step away, nor did he offer a reason for Cloud Maker to lash out at him. Instead, he smiled. "Cloud Maker, you have proven to be one of the most respected warriors in the clan. You are a leader others will follow. I look up to you as a friend, but also as a mentor. We need you. I need you."

Cloud Maker's demeanor softened at Broken Branch's words, but his resolve was strong. "Then follow us, my brother," he said softly. "We ride in the morning."

Broken Branch's smile faded as he placed a hand on Cloud Maker's shoulder. "Be well, my friend." Sadly, Broken Branch turned and walked away.

After making final arrangements with Five Dreams, Spirit Walker returned to his tipi. Placing his lance against the rear wall of the tipi, he undressed, and slid beneath the blankets beside Desert Rain. Her naked body was soft and warm. He wrapped an arm around her and cupped her breast, snuggling closer.

She turned her head and smiled. "It has been a hard evening for you, my Spirit. You must rest tonight."

"I do not wish for rest tonight, my Flower."

"No?" she asked impishly. "For what do you wish, my Spirit?"

Giving her breast a quick squeeze, he ran his fingers lightly down her stomach and between her legs. "I wish for you," he whispered harshly.

*   *   *

The next few days brought the scurrying of activity that accompanied the preparation to move an encampment. True to his word, Cloud Maker and three others had left the morning after the council was held. Broken Branch and Black Beaver discussed the idea of pursuing Cloud Maker and trying to bring him to his senses, but Spirit Walker warned them not to interfere. He told them that Cloud Maker would have to discover his folly on his own, that Broken Branch and the others had more important things to worry about. They must lead the warriors in preparing for the journey.

The women worked to patch old clothes and make new ones. The journey would be taxing, not only on their bodies but on their garments. The older men were busy making ropes, improvising pack saddles for the horses, and repairing equipment such as drags to carry supplies. The younger men were setting in a good supply of food, hunting and trapping as many animals as possible to be made into jerky for the trip.

Chief Five Dreams, Old Stone, and Spirit Walker met often, planning the path they would take into Mexico and how they would conduct the move. They agreed to follow the San Pedro river out of Arizona Territory and into Sonora. They would travel along the Agua Prieto river, then branch out into the Bavispe Canyon. Spirit Walker was sure that they could find a suitable place for the People in that canyon. There, they could farm and raise horses. There, they could trade with the small villages in Sonora. There, they could live in peace.

It had been a week since Spirit Walker had met with Goyathlay, a week since the council meeting, a week of preparation, and Spirit Walker was growing restless.

Desert Rain sat outside the tipi sewing a pair of *kabuns*. She looked up and smiled as Spirit Walker approached. "Look, my Spirit," she said, holding up the moccasins for his approval. "I am making a new pair of long moccasins for you. You will need them to ride among the mesquite in Mexico."

Spirit Walker smiled approvingly at his young wife. She was so thoughtful, so concerned with his comfort, so supportive. "Come with me, my Flower. I wish to ride."

"To ride? Where?" she asked, laying aside her work.

"Just to ride. To think. To clear my mind."

Desert Rain stood and placed her hands on Spirit Walker's shoulders. "I understand, my Spirit. Let us ride then."

Desert Rain was silent as she rode beside her husband. She was honored that he had asked her to ride with him. She knew he wanted to think about the days to come, but she also knew that he could have gone alone to ride. The fact that he had asked her to come along meant that he needed her. He didn't need her council—he possessed more wisdom than anyone she had ever met—he needed her presence. He needed her love. He needed her spirit to help guide his thoughts. She could almost feel the calm that her presence seemed to bring him.

They rode casually across the open range. He was so handsome sitting astride the proud black stallion. She watched as his eyes moved from side to side, carefully observing the terrain. She felt safe and secure in his presence and there was nowhere else she ever wanted to be.

Suddenly Spirit Walker reined his horse to a halt. "Riders," he announced.

Desert Rain followed his gaze and in the distance she could see a small band of people moving toward them. They were too far for her to make out any details, but Spirit Walker seemed not to be alarmed. "Shall we hide, my Spirit?" she asked quietly.

"No," he said flatly. "They are of my People."

It was a strange sight that met Desert Rain's eyes as the riders drew closer. It was a band of Chokonen traveling south, but there was something out of the ordinary about the procession. Traditionally, the Apache traveled with the men leading the group, the women in the rear. This small party, however, was led by a woman.

"Nod–Ah–Sti," Spirit Walker said, recognizing the woman at the front of the party.

The woman smiled and nodded her head. "Yes, it is I, Walker. You are well?"

"I am well, Nod–Ah–Sti." Spirit Walker cast a searching glance over the rest of the men, women, and children who followed close behind her. "Where is Tahza?" he asked.

"My husband leads the others to San Carlos. Surely you have heard what is to become of our People."

Spirit Walker nodded. "Yes, I have heard."

Desert Rain was taken by the proud woman riding at the head of the party. She was lovely, with her dark hair and eyes. She rode with a small child behind her, clinging to her waist. Desert Rain was anxious to meet the wife of Chief Tahza, so she cleared her throat to get her husband's attention.

Spirit Walker looked in Desert Rain's direction and smiled. "This is my wife, Desert Rain," he said in introduction. "Rain, this is Nod–Ah–Sti, wife of Tahza, chief of the Chokonen."

Desert Rain smiled and nodded a greeting. "I am honored to meet you."

Nod–Ah–Sti smiled in return. "This is Niño Cochise," she said, indicating the small boy who shared her saddle.

Spirit Walker stepped his mount forward, observing the boy closely. The child was a mirror image of the late chief. The boy's name indicated that he was the "son of Cochise," or "Little Cochise." A fitting name, Spirit Walker thought.

Desert Rain moved closer and addressed the young boy. "*Ya a teh*, Niño Cochise."

The child smiled. "We are going to Mexico," he said proudly. "We are the 'Missing Ones.' "

Desert Rain placed a caring hand on the child's head. "And you shall be their chief," she said with a smile.

Chapter Thirty-five

Spirit Walker talked with Nod-Ah-Sti at some length about the journey to Mexico. Tahza had secretly arranged for thirty-eight of his friends and relatives to escape the transfer of Apache from the Chiricahua Reservation to San Carlos. Tahza had jokingly called them "The Missing Ones," promising that their names would never again appear in any reservation's role book.

Nod-Ah-Sti spoke of Pa-Gotzin-Kay, the "Stronghold Mountain of Paradise." Pa-Gotzin-Kay was located on a shelf of red earth, approximately a half mile wide and two and a half miles long, curving north and south. It was bordered on the west by a sheer cliff that dropped off into the Nacozari Canyon and on the east by an escarpment that stretched on to a forested range in the Sierra Madres.

The stronghold was easily defensible, even by a small band such as hers. She explained that anyone entering Pa-Gotzin-Kay would have to make their way through a maze of boulders that literally pinched the entrances into winding clefts at either end. One misstep could result in disaster.

Pa-Gotzin-kay held abundant water, trees, fertile soil for planting, and plenty of game. But more than that, it held solitude and freedom. This was their destination, their only hope.

"It sounds so nice," Desert Rain said, as Nod-Ah-Sti finished her description.

"There, we will be happy and safe," Nod-Ah-Sti assured her. "Walker, you will join us?"

Spirit Walker considered the possibilities for a moment. It certainly was an appealing offer, much more so than the one he had received from Goyathlay. But Nod-Ah-Sti had a band of thirty-eight, Chief Five Dreams commanded nearly one hundred. It was doubtful that they could all survive for any length of time on a small shelf in the mountains. Maybe be was wrong, but he felt that they might be more comfortable in the Bavispe Canyon. They would not be far from Pa-Gotzin-Kay and could visit often. If his calculations were correct, Pa-Gotzin-Kay would overlook the Bavispe Barranca near the headwaters of the Yaqui River. That would be close enough for mutual support.

Spirit Walker shook his head slowly. "I'm afraid we cannot. We will move our encampment to the Bavispe Canyon."

Nod-Ah-Sti smiled. "You will be close," she acknowledged. "When my husband arrives, we will pay you a visit."

Spirit Walker smiled, but an uneasy feeling rose in his chest. Somehow, he doubted that Cochise's eldest son would ever make the journey, but he dared not voice his feelings. He nodded. "I would be honored."

Nod-Ah-Sti and her band continued south. Spirit Walker and Desert Rain branched off to the southwest and headed back toward their encampment. Spirit Walker's mood had become even more reflective. He wondered if he had made the right decision in suggesting to Five Dreams that they flee into Mexico. He wondered if it might not be better to allow the women, children, and old men to join Nod-Ah-Sti at Pa-Gotzin-Kay, and for him and the other warriors to join Goyathlay. There had been so much sadness among the People, so much injustice. Perhaps Goyathlay was right and there was no other way to have peace than to risk death.

He remembered the friendship that Cochise had shared with Taglito. Cochise thought so highly of the white man that he became his blood brother. So it was possible to live in peace with the white man, at least with some white men. He thought of the young blue coat officer, Captain James Jackson, U.S. Cavalry. He had not looked threatening. In fact, he looked amiable and ready to talk peace. Had he not agreed to leave the Apache alone and let them live in peace? Maybe he would be Spirit Walker's Taglito. What if he was to ride to the white man's fort and ask to talk to the officer? Was there yet a chance for peace?

"My Spirit," Desert Rain said, interrupting his reverie. "Do you think we will be ready to move soon? I have been thinking about Mexico. It sounds so nice. I hope we can leave soon."

Spirit Walker looked at his innocent young wife. He could never do anything that would jeopardize her safety. Of course, that meant that he could not leave her to ride again with the *Netdahe*. He had pledged his life to her. It was his word, his bond, and it bound him for eternity. Integrity was more important than vengeance. He had to take a chance on peace. "I will speak with Five Dreams. We will see, my Flower. We will see."

"You wish to go to the white man's fort?" Five Dreams asked. "You are sure?"

Spirit Walker gazed into the semidarkness of the evening. "I think I may be able to talk to the blue coat leader. I will try to make peace."

It was all too foreign to Five Dreams. Spirit Walker had proposed to go to Fort Lowell and talk to the young blue coat leader who had previously captured Desert Rain and the others. It was

241

a strange request. Spirit Walker had asked the old chief to hold off moving the encampment until he had had a chance to make peace with the soldiers. Was it even possible to make peace at this point? Five Dreams doubted it, but Spirit Walker seemed intent on giving it a try.

Five Dreams took a step away from the old warrior. He considered the options set before him. Maybe it was worth a try, but he could ill afford to delay their departure. He turned back to Spirit Walker. "We will continue our preparations. If you do not return to us, we will have to leave without you."

Spirit Walker nodded. "I can ask for nothing more, my chief."

Five Dreams held up his right hand. "Go with peace, my brother."

"If you are going to the white man's fort, then I am going with you," Desert Rain said firmly.

Spirit Walker rolled over to face her. He had returned to the tipi and crawled beneath the covers, sure that telling her he was leaving for Fort Lowell would be simple. He would just say that he was going and that would be that. He could see now that her mind was set on going with him. "I cannot risk your safety, my Flower. You will be in danger."

"In danger!" She sat upright suddenly, the blanket clinging to her firm breasts. "I was in danger when the trappers attacked me. Yet you were there to save me. I was in danger when the mountain lion leapt at me. Yet you were there to save me. I was in danger when the trapper sought to kill me in the night. Yet you were there to save me. Now you say that I cannot go with you because I will be in danger? Yet I will be in danger as we flee to Mexico, running from the blue coats, and you will not be there to save me. No, my Spirit, if I am to be in danger, I would rather be in danger with you than without you."

Even in the darkness, Spirit Walker could see the tears welling up in her eyes. He could hear the worry in her voice, sense her fear. How could he leave her behind? But how could he take her into the mouth of the cat and hope to protect her? He wrestled with his own mind—was he confident enough in himself to ensure her safety or should he leave her well-being up to her People?

Desert Rain wrapped her arms around the prone warrior, her lips next to his ear. "Please, my Spirit, do not leave me again. I need you so."

It was more than he could bear. He reached up and took her into his arms. She was soft and warm. How could he deny her? "I will not, Little One. You may ride with me in the morning. Together, we shall do what can be done."

"Oh, Spirit!" She kissed him.

It was an overcast morning as Spirit Walker made his way to the corral to ready the horses. Not many people were stirring in the encampment, just a few of the young boys playing around the fire circle. They yelled a greeting as he passed, and he waved a friendly hello.

Desert Rain was busy packing supplies for the trip. She was careful to include plenty of jerked meat for the days ahead, not sure exactly how long they might be gone. It was almost as if she and Spirit Walker were simply going for an outing. There was no fear in her heart at all. How could she feel fear? She would be traveling with the bravest and most capable warrior she had ever known.

Spirit Walker had brought the horses and was about to load the supplies when he heard a movement behind him. He turned to see Broken Branch and Black Beaver approaching, each carrying a Mexican saddle.

"*Ya a teh*, Spirit Walker," Broken Branch said with a smile. "We bring gifts for the journey."

Spirit Walker took a quick look at the two saddles. They were typical Mexican saddles, with their narrow seats, high cantles, and large saddle horns. The Mexicans never used a lot of leather on the saddle tree, but the stirrups were completely enclosed and came to a point in the front. This insured that the rider was able to move freely through heavy brush without getting a foot caught by a branch. It also insured the rider didn't place his foot too far into the stirrup. That way, if the rider were thrown, his foot wouldn't hang up in the stirrup and break his leg, or worse, cause him to be dragged to death. The white cowboys had developed boots with heels that made it impossible to get their feet too far into the stirrup for the same reason, and the sharp toes on the cowboy boots cut the brush well enough to not need the sharp point.

"I hope it is not too small for me," Spirit Walker observed. The seat looked only to be about fifteen inches from the back to the horn. It would be a tight fit. Desert Rain would fit easily, but Spirit Walker wondered if he would fit comfortably.

Black Beaver smiled. "We shall see. Perhaps you have grown broader from Desert Rain's cooking."

Spirit Walker cast a sideward glance at Desert Rain as she drew near. "And perhaps she has kept me from getting broader after each meal."

Broken Branch did not quite understand, but Black Beaver laughed. Desert Rain could only blush.

Chapter Thirty-six

Lieutenant Colonel Graffe shuffled through the papers on his desk and sighed. Why did the U.S. Army insist on so many forms? The company clerk had reminded him that headquarters was still waiting on requisition forms for equipment that had already been issued. Earlier in the month the colonel had finagled some much-needed supplies for a detachment he was ordered to send into the Dragoon Mountains. Known as somewhat of a scrounge, Colonel Graffe had managed to borrow the supplies from nearby Fort Bowie. Now he had to fill out the necessary forms to make the transaction legal. He released another long sigh as he settled in and tried to recall the list of supplies he had received.

He had barely started the laborious paperwork when a knock at the door broke his concentration. "Yes?" he shouted toward the closed wooden door.

"Sir, it's Trooper Wilkinson. Permission to enter?"

Graffe remembered that it was Trooper Wilkinson's day to be the colonel's personal orderly. "This had better be important, Trooper!" he shouted irritably.

"It is, sir."

"Then get in here and get it over with!"

The tall, lanky trooper opened the door and stepped into the room. He shut the door behind him and stepped smartly to the front of the desk. Exactly two paces away from the desk, the trooper stopped and came to attention, popping a sharp military salute. "Trooper Wilkinson, reporting, sir."

Colonel Graffe sat back in his chair and returned the salute halfheartedly. "What is it, Trooper?"

"Sir, we have visitors at the gate wishing to talk with Captain Jackson."

"Visitors? Son, you know that Captain Jackson is out on maneuvers. Hell, I'm just now getting the paperwork done for the supplies I gave him. Why are you bothering me with this?" He swept his hand over the mound of papers littering his desk top. "Can't you see I have more important things to do here? Just tell them to hole up for the night in Tucson and come back tomorrow. I'll talk to them then. Do I have to make every little decision around here myself?"

"But, sir, you don't understand."

Colonel Graffe stood to his feet. "And just what is it that I don't understand, Trooper? Why don't you tell me exactly what that might be?"

"Sir, the visitors . . . they're Indians, sir. Apaches. A buck and a squaw. They're riding Mescan saddles. The buck is carrying a spear, but other than that, they're not armed."

Colonel Graffe threw open the door that lead into the compound. Placing his hat squarely on his head and attempting to buckle the broad belt that held his command saber, he strode confidently toward the front gate. Trooper Wilkinson followed closely behind, almost running to keep up with the colonel's long stride.

"Where's my interpreter?" Graffe demanded.

"Sir, Trooper Sosa is with Captain Jackson," Wilkinson informed him.

"You mean there's no one here who speaks Apache?"

"No, sir. But . . ."

"But what, Trooper? What?"

"They seem to speak English, sir. At least the buck does."

Colonel Graffe stopped in his tracks. "I want to know why these Apache weren't arrested on sight, Trooper. You understand that we have orders to make sure all hostiles are removed to San Carlos, don't you?"

"Yes, sir, I understand that, but they seemed to know Captain Jackson. I thought maybe Captain Jackson had sent word back by them, at first. But then they asked to see him. I thought you would want to talk to them first, sir."

Graffe hesitated a moment before making a decision on how to handle the situation. "Trooper, I want four men ready to arrest them on my command. Is that clear?"

"Yes, sir." Trooper Wilkinson snapped a salute and hurried off toward the guard house.

Colonel Graffe walked briskly toward the front gate.

Spirit Walker watched the guards move cautiously along the top of the fort's outer walls. A feeling of trepidation overcame him as he waited patiently in the afternoon sun.

"My Spirit, do you really think the blue coats will make peace with us?" Desert Rain asked.

Spirit Walker shifted the bandanna that encircled his forehead in an attempt to arrest the sweat that threatened to trickle into his eyes. "The only hope we have is that he will return the kindness we have shown to him and his men."

"I have heard that the blue coats do not behave as we do.

247

They do not understand that one returns kindness for kindness."

"We shall see, my Flower. Follow my lead and be ready to ride hard if we should have to flee."

Desert Rain nodded. She and Spirit Walker had camped overnight at a place the Indians called "The Sweet Water." It was a spring about a half day's journey from the fort. There, they had cached a few supplies and agreed that if they should have to split up to escape the blue coats, they would rendezvous at that point. She'd said she could find it again, but Spirit Walker knew she desperately hoped it would not be necessary.

Suddenly the large wooden gate swung open. Spirit Walker examined the austere-looking man standing tall in the center of the opening. His uniform was dusty but neatly pressed. His hat fit tightly over his graying hair. The stubble of a beard made his face look rugged, and there was no trace of a smile beneath his salt-and-pepper mustache. His left hand rested casually on a long saber, his right hand draped over the holster of his revolver. "I hear you're looking for Captain Jackson," the officer said flatly.

"Yes, Captain James Jackson, U.S. Cavalry," Spirit Walker said in English.

"I'm Lieutenant Colonel Graffe. Captain Jackson is not here. You will have to wait for him. I have prepared lodging for you inside."

Spirit Walker couldn't place the feeling, but he knew something was not as it should be. There was no welcome in the blue coat's voice. Spirit Walker noticed four men moving toward the gate. They were armed with carbine rifles, walking side by side. "When will he return?" Spirit Walker asked quickly.

"Tomorrow," Graffe said. "They'll be back tomorrow. Why don't you come on inside and we'll make sure you're comfortable till he returns."

That all sounded like lies to Spirit Walker. He glanced over his shoulder at Desert Rain. "Get ready to ride," he said in

Apache. He stepped his horse forward. "Where has Captain Jackson gone?" he asked Graffe in English.

Colonel Graffe glanced nervously at the approaching guards. "He's . . . he's gone to the Dragoon Mountains on a routine patrol."

Spirit Walker kept his mount moving forward as he spoke. "Ah, he seeks Geronimo?" Suddenly the old warrior stopped, turned in his saddle and addressed Desert Rain in Apache. "When I break left, you ride right. Meet me at the Sweet Water."

Desert Rain nodded.

Spirit Walker turned back to the Colonel. "If you want Geronimo, I know where you can find him."

Colonel Graffe stared long and hard at the barrel-chested Apache. There was no sign of deceit in the Indian's voice. Could he be telling the truth? If so, it would be a feather in the Colonel's cap. Graffe smelled promotion. He had to get the Apache inside the fort's walls. "Really? Let's talk about that."

Spirit Walker nodded. "We shall talk, but first . . . we shall run." Spirit Walker jerked his horse's head to the left and gave it one swift kick. The horse was a streak of black as it bolted away from the gate toward a nearby rimrock.

Colonel Graffe stood stunned as Desert Rain took off in the opposite direction. "Catch him!" Graffe shouted.

The four troopers who had thought to capture Spirit Walker when he entered the gate turned and ran toward their horses. "Forget the squaw, catch the buck!" Graffe shouted as they thundered past him. Then they were out the gate at a full gallop.

Trooper Delaney lead the pursuit party. He knew that the Apache had a pretty good head start, but figured they could catch him when they entered the rocks. It would slow the Apache down and they could close the gap. "Keep your eyes peeled for a trap," he shouted to his men as they approached the rocks.

The black's hooves churned up the ground as Spirit Walker leaned low over its back. He felt so alive, so rejuvenated, and he knew exactly why. It was Desert Rain. She had awakened the sleeping warrior inside of him. She had revived the energy that made him Spirit Walker. He rode with confidence now, every sense in his body piqued for action. He glanced over his shoulder. Only four riders. This would be fun. A game.

At the rimrock, Spirit Walker urged his mount up the steepest grade he could find. He knew the soldiers would expect to catch him at the top. If he could reach the top quickly, he could observe their movement and choose an appropriate counter to their actions. His eye caught a movement on top of the rimrock. It was a mountain lion and it had spotted him.

"Aieeeee!" Spirit Walker yelled as he pressed his horse up the grade. The cat jumped and ran quickly away from the oncoming warrior. "Run, my friend! Run! I shall need your help." He headed straight for where the cat had last appeared.

As he topped the ridge, Spirit Walker cast a backward glance. The riders were coming on, their horses scrambling for footing on the steep slope. He searched the area to see if he could find any sign of the large cat. He saw it as it ducked into a crevice in the rocks and he kicked his mount forward.

It was a little more than just a crevice, more of a small cave, and the mountain lion was safely inside. Spirit Walker stepped his mount around the opening carefully, not wanting to arouse the large beast before it was time. It was a game he had played as a child many times. He quickly took his horse around some boulders and looked for a path that would take him above the cave.

"He went this way!" he heard the lead trooper shout as he spotted the scuff marks on the rocks left by Spirit Walker's horse.

Spirit Walker knelt calmly above the small cave. Having hunted the large cats since he was a child, he knew there were several ways to flush the animals from their dens. Often brush was set on fire and then thrown into the opening, smoking the cat out. But he had a simpler and less time-consuming plan in mind this time. He pulled the bandanna from his head and put it to his nose. The smell of his sweat was strong on the piece of cloth. He had counted on it.

The men were approaching cautiously, unsure of the direction their quarry had taken. They searched the ground for tracks, but found few, just enough to keep them moving. They searched the rocks around them for hiding places, but so far had found none. Then they spotted the cave.

"He might be in there," one of the troopers suggested.

"Could be, let's check it out," their leader said. Sliding from his saddle, he pulled his pistol.

Spirit Walker smiled and dropped the bandanna near the cave's opening.

Their leader had just looked up to see where the bandanna came from when the mountain lion leapt from its lair. The man screamed in fear, his finger instinctively squeezing the trigger of his Colt revolver. He shot only air.

Spirit Walker smiled as he rode steadily through the night. The scene he had left on the rimrock was chaotic, but amusing even so. The troopers were surprised by the mountain lion, and their horses had bolted immediately, tossing the blue coats in all directions along the rocky outcropping. Spirit Walker had taken his leave quickly after the cat sprang forward. They would be too busy to chase him now. He rode on toward the gathering place, anxious to see that Desert Rain had made it safely to the Sweet Water.

*   *   *

The night was waning as he approached the area where he had cached his supplies. He approached cautiously, carefully listening for any signs of trouble. Desert Rain should have been there much earlier and would probably be asleep. He slowed his mount to a walk and move slowly forward.

There was the cache rock he had placed over the shallow pit that concealed his supplies. He looked about him in the semi-darkness. Desert Rain was nowhere in sight. His heart sank.

Chapter Thirty-seven

It was a matter of discipline. Desert Rain was missing and she had to be found, but the sun would not be up for a couple of hours and there was no use in trying to find her tracks until then. Spirit Walker would have to push the worry and concern to the back of his mind, discipline himself, and sleep while there was an opportunity. He could only guess when he might have this chance again.

He stripped the gear from his horse and hobbled the animal so it could graze. Lying back on the ground, he covered himself with the horse's blanket. He knew if he was to be of any help to Desert Rain, he had to rest.

The song of the morning birds aroused him just as the early gray of dawn breached the sky. He rose quickly and moved to saddle his horse. "I am sorry, Chelee, but we have no time for further rest. We must find Desert Rain."

Try as he might, he could find no sign that Desert Rain had returned after the confrontation at the blue coat fort. Why had he left her to ride alone? How would he rescue her again if she had been captured so close to the fort? His stomach churned at the thought. There was only one thing that he knew at this point. If the white eyes had captured her, if they had hurt her, he would make them pay. Without thinking about it he ran his hand over the sash that crossed his chest. The *Netdahe* life was closer now than it had been in years. It was within reach and his hand was steadily moving toward it.

He was almost clear of the woods, the sun almost at its peak, when he spotted the filly's tracks coming from the direction of the fort. His heart skipped a beat as he saw the tracks veer off, away from the rendezvous point. Where was she going? Surely she knew the right direction. He scanned the ground for any sign that someone was chasing her, but there was no indication of a pursuit.

He dismounted and checked the tracks carefully. Her horse wasn't running at this point. The tracks were too close together. The rear hoof prints were overlapping the front hoof prints, indicating that the horse was walking. She could have had no sense of danger then. Following the tracks on foot, leading the black behind him, he noted where the horse had stopped for a moment, nervously shuffling in place. What had she seen? What had she heard? Something had caused her to stop. Something had caught her attention at this point. He looked around carefully.

Seeing nothing of importance, he moved along her trail with caution. The filly had walked off after the brief stop, and again, there was no sign of haste.

He covered quite a bit of ground when something red caught his eye. A leaf, low on a branch of a poplar tree, bore the stain of blood. He checked the ground. The filly had stopped here. Desert Rain had dismounted, and walked around the tree. The ground cover was too thick to make out her light footprints, but many of the ground leaves were upturned and some of them held drops of blood. He was sure she had gone in that direction and that she was injured. He had to find her quickly.

All indications were that she had dismounted and walked toward the poplar, but he could see no sign that she had remained there. He went back to check her horse's tracks. It was indeed a puzzle. The horse had been led to the other side of the poplar. Spirit Walker circled the tree and found the underbrush crushed beneath his feet. Someone had lain there. Someone who was bleeding badly.

The filly had moved away, but the blood sprinkled on the ground proved that the rider was trailing blood with each step the horse took. His heart sank deeper into despair. The rider was losing a lot of blood and losing it quickly. He had to find her, and fast!

He moved more quickly now. The blood trail wasn't hard to follow and he had no time to check the filly's tracks. He followed the blood and listened for anything out of the ordinary.

The late afternoon sun shone brightly through the trees. The going had been slow, because he had to be careful not to miss anything that might indicate a change in direction. It was tedious, but necessary. He had to find her, couldn't chance overlooking her. Suddenly, a sound from the air reached his ear. He looked up. A hawk circled the tops of a stand of pine trees to the west. It cried to him. Was it Desert Rain's spirit guide trying to lead him to her? He was sure of it. He swung into his saddle and quickened his pace.

He heard the filly whinny even before he saw it standing tethered to a large pine tree. Desert Rain's Mexican saddle was still in place, but even from a distance Spirit Walker could see the blood that ran down the saddlehorn and onto the cantle. Had she been shot while riding away from the fort? He had not heard a rifle's report. Perhaps it had happened later. He slid to the ground, tied the black to a tree, and grabbed his lance. Like a ghost in the darkness, he crept forward.

He could see the filly clearly now, but there was no sign of Desert Rain. Where could she be? He looked around for any area where someone could hide. Spotting a small thicket, he inched closer. She had to be in there, but who else might be around, watching and waiting to spring in ambush?

It was the edge of a piece of cloth that caught his eye in the thicket. It was on the ground. In fact, it seemed to be coming out of the ground. On cat-quiet feet he moved forward. It was clearly part of Desert Rain's tunic. The cloth was not coming out of the ground, but was covered by a thin layer of leaves and debris. As he moved closer, he could see the form of his wife, spread out under the thicket. She was perfectly still, face down. He couldn't tell, from this distance, if she was breathing, but there was the definite smell of blood. He kept moving. Closer. Closer still. Did he dare call her name? Did he really want to know if she was dead? He had to know.

Her tunic was stained with blood, her breathing shallow, but at least she was breathing. She lay with her right arm extended and seemed to be covering something with a piece of buckskin. He reached out and touched her arm. "Oh, my Flower, what have they done?" he whispered sadly.

He heard a low moan, but it couldn't have come from his petite wife. It was low, guttural, manly. Slowly he pulled the buckskin aside. There, partially covered by the leaves and buckskin was an ashen face. Cloud Maker. The young warrior moaned again.

"Rain," Spirit Walker whispered, shaking his wife gently. "My Flower, you are hurt?"

Slowly Desert Rain rolled over on her left side. Sleepily her eyes opened and looked up into Spirit Walker's face. "My Spirit! You have found us!"

"Yes, my wife, I have found you." Taking her in his arms, he squeezed her tightly. Relief flooding to the depths of his spirit. He had found her and she was alive. "You are hurt, Little One?" he asked again.

"No, my Spirit, I am not, but Cloud Maker is badly hurt." She sat up and pointed toward a pile of pine needles a few feet away. "Looks Twice is dead."

"No!" Cloud Maker screamed, and struggled to sit up, looking as though he somehow believed he could revive the dead warrior.

Spirit Walker placed a calming hand on Cloud Maker's forehead. "No, my brother, you must lie still. There is nothing more you can do."

Desert Rain settled back on the leaves and brushed Cloud Maker's hair away from his forehead. "Rest, Cloud Maker. Rest."

It was obvious that Desert Rain was desperate for sleep. Spirit Walker could only imagine the kind of night she'd had. Cloud Maker was breathing laboriously, but seemed to be resting as well. "You sleep now, Little One," Spirit Walker instructed. "I will care for the horses. In the morning, we will plan what to do."

Desert Rain nodded slightly, then closed her eyes. She smiled, seeming to know that now everything would be better. "I love you," she whispered weakly.

"And I love you, my precious Flower."

Spirit Walker was awakened only twice during the night. On both occasions Cloud Maker moaned loudly and tried to rise, but Spirit Walker calmed the younger warrior enough for him to drift into unconsciousness once again. The night was too dark in the heart of the woodlands to examine Cloud Maker's wounds. It would have to wait till morning light. Spirit Walker slept as much as he could.

Spirit Walker sat upright with a start. He could hear someone moving near the horses. Rising to his hands and knees, he saw, through the trees, that Desert Rain was gathering firewood in the early morning light. He took a quick glance back at Cloud Maker. The young warrior was still sleeping. Spirit Walker rose and walked toward his wife.

"My Spirit, you are awake," she said with surprise.

"Yes."

"You were tired, my warrior, so I left you to sleep while I prepared a meal for us."

She was so sweet, so considerate, always thinking of his comfort. "I will hunt for some food," he said, starting back toward where he had laid his lance.

"There is no need, my husband," Desert Rain said with a smile. "I have killed a rabbit."

Looking in the direction she was pointing, Spirit Walker spotted the large rabbit impaled on his own lance. He smiled. "You have done well, Little One."

"Well, it was just sitting in the brush when I awoke," she admitted. "It was nothing."

Spirit Walker took her hand gently in his. "You are a warrior, my Flower. A warrior does what is necessary to survive. You have done well."

She beamed with pride, dropped the firewood on the ground, and kissed him. He lost himself in her tenderness. Even under the stress she must be feeling, she was able to free her heart and love him. There was no woman on earth who could equal her spirit, her dedication, her devotion to her husband. *Usen* had truly blessed him.

The kiss was cut short by Cloud Maker's groan. "I'll see to

his wounds," Spirit Walker said as he released his hold on Desert Rain's waist.

"I'll cook the rabbit," she volunteered.

Carefully Spirit Walker pulled back the buckskin jacket that concealed the warrior's wounds. It was bad, there was no doubt of that. In fact, Cloud Maker should have died long ago from such wounds. Only his strong constitution had allowed him to live this long. It was clear that he had been shot in the back, the bullet opening a large gaping hole in his ribs and right chest. The blood oozed around the makeshift bandage, soaking the ground beneath him. Nothing could be done. Spirit Walker hung his head.

"It is bad?"

Spirit Walker looked into Cloud Maker's dim eyes. "Yes, it is bad."

Cloud Maker nodded weakly. "So it should be. I deserve the death of a fool."

Spirit Walker placed the jacket back over the wound and sat heavily on the ground next to the young warrior. "What happened, my brother? Tell me. I must know. We must know, for we must pass this way."

Chapter Thirty-eight

Cloud Maker explained that he and the other three who followed him from the encampment had barely met up with Goyathlay and his band when they were attacked by mounted blue coats. They were taken completely by surprise, mostly because of Goyathlay's feeling of safety. The battle raged hard against the Apaches. Cloud Maker and Looks Twice were separated from the main group and tried to make their way to the cover offered by the trees.

Cloud Maker had been shot while running away from the soldiers. Looks Twice had stopped to help the fallen warrior when he too was shot. Riddled with bullets, Looks Twice had dragged Cloud Maker into thick brush and lay on top of him, hoping not to be spotted by the white eyes.

"I lay on my back beneath my brother when I saw a man on a horse towering above us," Cloud Maker continued. "He raised his rifle to shoot us again, but hesitated. He looked into my face and could not shoot."

Spirit Walker nodded. It was often that way in battle. To kill a man at a distance was easy, to look a man in the face and kill him was infinitely harder.

Cloud Maker took a long, deep breath, gathering his strength to continue. "It was the blue coat leader who had captured us at the waterfall."

Captain James Jackson, U.S. Cavalry? Spirit Walker blinked with surprise. "He did not shoot you?"

"No. He only nodded and rode off in pursuit of Goyathlay."

Spirit Walker thought for a moment. Perhaps there was yet a chance for peace. "Is Goyathlay dead?"

"I know not. Looks Twice and I escaped and made our way toward the rancheria. Unable to carry me any farther, my brother left me under some brush and continued on. When Desert Rain found him, he was able to lead her back to me. I remember her coming to me, but nothing else."

"You must rest now, my brother," Spirit Walker said passionately.

"Yes, I must rest, but in a moment. I have somewhat to say to you, old man."

Spirit Walker glanced at Cloud Maker's drawn face. Cloud Maker was no longer the proud warrior who had defied him at the council meeting. He was not the same young man who bore the reproach of the blue coats and managed to hold his head high even in captivity. He was weak. He was dying.

Cloud Maker's eyes blinked rapidly a few times, then opened. He took a deep breath, knowing he didn't have long to live. "I was wrong," he said weakly. "I should have stayed with my People. You were right. I should have listened."

Spirit Walker stared at the dying warrior. It was hard to see a young warrior die, especially one with as much potential as this one. Cloud Maker would be sorely missed and mourned among his People.

Cloud Maker reached out with his left arm and began to fumble beneath the leaves beside him. Spirit Walker watched carefully as the wounded Apache pulled up a finely carved bow covered with red and black designs.

"This bow," Cloud Maker said weakly, "belonged to my best friend, Desert Rain's husband. It means more to me than anything else I have ever possessed. When I fell in battle, all I could think of was holding onto to this valuable weapon. I would not turn it loose. I wish for you to have it now."

Spirit Walker reached out and took the bow. "My brother, I shall take good care of this bow. Know that it will defend Desert Rain from this time forward, as it has in the past."

Cloud Maker's voice came in a rush as blood issued from his mouth. "Tell Broken Branch not to follow my path." He reached up and grabbed Spirit Walker's arm, squeezing it tightly. "He must not become *Netdahe*."

Slowly Cloud Maker's eyes closed, his grip relaxed. He exhaled once and breathed no more.

"Go with peace, my brother," Spirit Walker said quietly.

Captain Jackson sat opposite Sergeant Beyer at the small round table in the command tent. Jackson pointed at the military map between them as he talked. "This is approximately where we are now, Sergeant. Over here is the Mexican border. I'm afraid Geronimo may have taken this route into Sonora."

Beyer scratched his head, adjusted his cap, and dragged a dirty hand across his week-old beard. "I know we don't have permission from the Mexican government, but if we cross here," he pointed, indicating an uninhabited area of desert, "we may be able to cut Geronimo off before he gets into the Sierra Madres."

Jackson stared at the route the sergeant had proposed. The

captain had to admit that it might be possible. He would like to return to Fort Lowell with Geronimo in tow. Capturing the Apache war chief would mean a promotion at the least, and surely a commendation from President Grant. Geronimo was the prize that many sought to win. But the crafty Apache was as hard to catch as a tailless lizard in this rocky terrain. General Howard had made a treaty with Geronimo at Fort Bowie, but it was not long before the Apache quickly disappeared.

"Sergeant, I'm afraid Geronimo may be lying in wait just inside the border."

"That's a possibility, Captain. I've thought of that myself. That's why I suggested that we cross the border at this open area. Not much chance he could pin us down with no more men than he has with him."

Jackson nodded in agreement. If only the captain's sentry hadn't fired a shot to alert them of Geronimo's presence when he had first been spotted! What a stupid thing to do, the captain thought. It was just a routine patrol that had discovered the Apache camping near a small spring. When some of the Apache outriders suddenly appeared behind the patrol, one of the young troopers fired his weapon, fearing they were under attack. Captain Jackson rallied his men and had barely been able to reach his patrol before Geronimo had completely organized a battle strategy. Though Captain Jackson had never actually laid eyes on Geronimo, Jackson was sure it was his band.

The fighting had been sporadic, taking place in several places at once. It was so different than the mock battles the captain had commanded at West Point. In training, the battle lines were clear, well defined, the enemy on one side, the "good guys" on the other. Out here in the deserts and mountains of Arizona Territory, it was not so cut and dried. The Apache had obviously never attended the orderly battles of Command School. They were not acquainted with the "rules of war." Some called the Apache "guerrilla fighters," a name taken from the Spanish word *guerrilla*, which meant warfare. To the white man, the word had come to signify a particular style of warfare—fighting in small groups with no definitive line of demarcation. But wasn't that the way America had won its independence from Britain? When the British marched shoulder to shoulder across the plains in their fancy uniforms, the Colonists were hidden behind rocks in their buckskins. It was the unorthodox style of the patriots that helped defeat the British and now it was the unorthodox tactics of the Apache that were baffling the cavalry. Jackson had to change his strategy. He had to improvise, but were his men ready?

"No," he said finally. "I don't think we want to do that, Sergeant."

Sergeant Beyer straightened. "Why not, sir?"

"I don't think we're ready to meet Geronimo on his own terms. Not just yet anyway."

Suddenly a shout came from the outer perimeter. "Riders approaching!"

Jackson and Beyer stepped from the shelter of the tent into the afternoon sunshine. "It's the scouts, sir," Beyer noted.

Two troopers rode into the camp and slid to a stop before Captain Jackson. "Sir, we're pretty sure they've crossed the border," one of the men said, popping a salute.

"I see." Jackson turned to his first sergeant. "Sergeant, rest the men. We leave for Fort Lowell in the morning."

"Yes, sir." Sergeant Beyer snapped a salute, did an about face, and walked briskly away.

Desert Rain cried when she learned of Cloud Maker's death. How could she not? He had been a family friend. She remembered well the first time she had met him. Arm Bow had introduced them at one of the gatherings. He and Arm Bow had been inseparable.

Since the Apache bands changed camp sites year to year, Arm Bow and Cloud Maker had often camped where Desert Rain's band was now camped. When she and Arm Bow married, Cloud Maker had chosen to follow his best friend and live with the Jicarilla. She had not minded their friendship. In fact, she had encouraged it. They were both new to the band, so it had made them feel comfortable to have a familiar face to greet them each day.

Arm Bow had been accepted readily as a leader among the hunters, but Cloud Maker made his mark among the warriors. He had quickly found esteem in their ranks. He was a natural leader. Now he was gone. Just as Arm Bow before him, he had left an emptiness in her heart.

Spirit Walker prepared the bodies. He had no means with which to bury the men, so he constructed four-foot platforms to keep the animals away from the remains. When the bodies had been set on the platforms, he began a chant of blessing to speed them on their way to the After World.

Desert Rain watched and wept.

The rabbit was eaten in silence and then they moved on, hoping to get closer to the rancheria before night fell.

It had taken Captain Jackson's men three days to reach Fort Lowell and now the bone-weary captain stood tall in the commander's office. "Sir, Captain Jackson reporting as ordered," he said with a salute.

Colonel Graffe returned the salute. "Sit, Captain. You look tired, man."

"Thank you, sir." Jackson sat wearily in the chair opposite the desk.

"So," Graffe said, easing back in his chair and folding his hands across his stomach. "Where's Geronimo?"

"He escaped into Mexico, sir. I have no authority beyond the border, so I did not pursue him."

"I see." Graffe leaned forward and placed his folded hands on the desk. "Did you see him? Do you know this for sure?"

"We had a skirmish, sir. I believe it was his band."

"Did you see him?"

"Well, no, sir. I can't say that I actually saw him."

"So you don't really know if Geronimo is still in Arizona or not, do you?"

Jackson was becoming irritated. Who did this bombastic fool think he was? In the year the colonel had been at Fort Lowell, he had not once set foot out on the plains. He didn't know an Apache from a coyote, and probably never would. Jackson stood to his feet. "With all due respect, sir, I think I know enough to report that Geronimo has crossed into Mexico. Will that be all?"

Colonel Graffe pushed his chair back against the wall and stood, pointing a disgruntled finger in Jackson's direction. "I'll tell you when it is 'all,' Captain. I'm the commander here and let me tell you that Grant is breathing down my neck right now. He's got an agent—a John Clum—climbing in and out of every crevice in this area, rounding up Injuns like they were cattle. Now, you had better be right when you say that Geronimo is not going to pose a threat to that mission. 'Cause if you're wrong, I'll hang you for treason myself! Is that clear?"

Jackson could feel the surge of anger rising in his throat. It was foul-tasting, but he swallowed it slowly. Jackson knew his report was correct. "Yes, sir, it's clear."

"Good! Now get out of here!"

Jackson popped another salute and turned to leave. As he opened the door, he turned back to address the colonel one more time. "By the way, sir, I lost no men in the battle. You needn't worry. Goodnight, sir."

It had been a long trip. Desert Rain rode wearily in her saddle as dusk hung heavily in the air. They were close enough to the encampment that they should be seeing the cook fires at any moment.

Spirit Walker slowed their pace as they had entered the woods surrounding the rancheria. For some reason he had an eerie feeling as they rode on. Something was amiss. He had heard no voices, no indication that anyone was looking for riders approaching in the late evening. Why weren't they hailed by the perimeter scouts? Why had he not seen smoke climbing above the trees?

As the encampment came into view, Spirit Walker reined his horse to a halt. Desert Rain looked around in astonishment. The camp was gone, but only partially. A few of the tipis and wikiups were still standing, but there was no one in sight. Not a sign that anyone was still there.

Chapter Thirty-nine

The village was deserted and deathly quiet. Spirit Walker moved carefully around the abandoned shelters. He entered a few of them, but found only odds and ends.

"They have left for Mexico?" Desert Rain asked as Spirit Walker stepped out of one of the dwellings.

In his right hand he held a quiver of arrows. "Would they have left behind arrows that might be of use if they had left for Mexico?"

Desert Rain stared at the small quiver with its six willow arrows. They looked to be in good shape. Why would anyone have left perfectly good arrows behind when they would have been needed for hunting? "What, then?" she asked nervously. She wasn't sure she wanted to hear the answer, but she had to ask the question.

Spirit Walker looked about him, obviously turning the question over carefully in his mind. "They left in a hurry," he observed. "Something or someone has caused them to leave. They did not leave on their own."

"But, my Spirit, where would they have gone if not to Mexico?"

Spirit Walker approached her quietly, wrapping his arms around her shoulders. "My Flower, we shall have to wait till morning to know for sure. I will track them at daybreak. We must sleep now."

She knew he was right, knew the wisdom in his words. What good would it do to sit and wonder in the darkness? She nodded and fell into his arms. Still, she couldn't help but worry about her mother and brother, about the children. Where were they?

It was obvious in the light of day that there were more than the tracks left by Indian ponies scattered around the encampment. Spirit Walker had not seen one Indian horse wearing horseshoes and yet the ground all around him bore such shoeprints. There was only one conclusion: the rancheria had been invaded by mounted soldiers.

"My Spirit!" Desert Rain shouted from beside a partially downed tipi. Spirit Walker ran to her side. "Look," she said excitedly.

On the side of the tipi, drawn in charcoal from the fire, was the symbol for *Pinda-lick-o-ye*. White eyes.

"I know," Spirit Walker said in a low tone. "I have found tracks left by the white man's horses."

"They have taken my People!" Desert Rain said, tears dimming her eyes. "Have they been killed?" she asked.

"No," he protested. "If it had been a slaughter, there would be blood. Even bodies. There are none. They were not killed. They were taken. Five Dreams would have been smart enough to keep his warriors from fighting the white eyes. He would look for a chance to escape later, when the women and children could be protected."

"But where would they have been taken?"

"Where the others have been taken. San Carlos."

"No!" she cried. "The thought of my family being forced to live in that desolate area strikes sorrow in my heart. What can we do, my Spirit? We must help them escape."

Spirit Walker knew they had a big task ahead of them. How could they hope to overcome an army of white eyes? If they hurried, Spirit Walker and Desert Rain might catch the blue coats as they reached the Gila River, but what then? There was no time to plan right now, they would have to think on the run. They didn't know how much of a head start the soldiers had on them. Time was ebbing away.

"We shall see what we can do," he said finally. "Let us prepare to leave at once."

It was not easy, traveling at a fast pace over such rugged terrain. Spirit Walker was lucky enough to kill a rabbit while out on the plains. It was hastily cooked over a small fire the first night out. But the second day brought no game, no food, only hunger and weariness as they rode on as steadily as possible.

At least water was plentiful. Any good Apache knew that that was more important than food. A person could survive for many days without food, but very few without water. He might grow weak, but he would not soon die from lack of food. Even the pangs of hunger subsided after the first few days. Water was far more important to survival. Spirit Walker had seen the bodies of men who had died within sight of a river, unable to reach the water that might have saved them. He and Desert Rain drank frequently.

Broken Branch's feet dragged heavily along the hard-packed Arizona soil. Dust rose from the horses in front of him, almost choking at times, settling on his clothes, in his hair, along his eyelids and nose. But he walked steadily on.

The warriors and some of the younger women walked beside the horses that bore the older men and women and the smaller children. The fit walked, the infirm rode. He glanced at his chief. The old man plodded on like an ancient buffalo. He was slow, but he kept moving and that was all that was demanded of him.

Only a couple of times in the last few days had any of the Apache fallen from fatigue. Each time a young warrior rushed to the side of the fallen elder. Then someone who was riding would leap from the pony's back and change places with their brother or sister who could no longer keep up on foot. The soldiers would smile and sometimes wager on whether or not the person who had fallen could continue much longer, but the Apache were a proud People and resilient. They moved on. Undaunted, they would survive. It was their way.

Broken Branch reflected on the happenings of a few days ago, when the blue coats had come running into the encampment. Chaos flooded the camp and children ran in all directions. The warriors made for their weapons, but they stopped when Five Dreams stepped from his tipi and ordered them not to resist. At first, many of the braves thought him crazy, but it hadn't taken long for them to realize that surrender was preferable to death. It was a lesson Broken Branch recalled well.

None of the blue coats were able to speak the Apache tongue, but there were two Mexican scouts accompanying the soldiers. Five Dreams was able to use what little Spanish he had learned to negotiate with the white soldier leader through these *Nakai-ye*.

Broken Branch eyed the blue coat officer as he rode along the line of captives, checking to make sure all was secure. His red hair curled beneath the edges of his blue cap, setting off the blue in his eyes. The two silver bars on each shoulder reflected the afternoon sun and brought a look of majesty to the officer as he paraded beside his troops, head high, spurs jingling. He looked confident, almost cocky.

When Five Dreams had first begun his negotiations with this blue coat leader through the Mexican translators, the leader had not wanted to listen. Though Broken Branch could not understand the details of the negotiations, and had had no time to discuss it with Five Dreams since, it seemed that the old chief had explained that if they were to reach San Carlos alive, they would need to take certain supplies with them.

Finally, the blue coat had agreed to let them bring along a few of the drags they had constructed earlier. They were allowed to take many of their personal belongings, but all of their weapons were either confiscated or destroyed. Broken Branch shook his head at the thought of the once proud Apache subjugated to the level of prisoners.

He began to reconsider the lesson he had learned. Perhaps it would have been better if he had joined Cloud Maker.

Cloud Maker. The thought of the young, cocky warrior somehow made Broken Branch smile even in the discomfort of the forced march. He could picture his friend, wind whipping through his hair, as he rode into battle beside the great war chief Goyathlay. Cloud Maker would be the picture of the perfect Apache warrior—strong, brave, unwavering in his determination. Just like always, Cloud Maker would be popular among the other warriors. He would be a leader, invincible in war, proud in victory. Why hadn't he ridden with Cloud Maker?

Broken Branch looked around him. The terrain was familiar to him. He had visited the Apache bands who regularly camped along the Gila River many times. If he were on horseback and traveling with a band of warriors, they would have already reached the winding river. But this group could travel no faster than those who were walking. It would take at least another day to reach the Gila.

He bowed his head against the dust and kept moving.

*　　*　　*

It was full dark before Spirit Walker felt that he and Desert Rain should stop for the night and rest. They had been riding hard for two days. It had been easy following the tracks left by so many riders. The iron shoes of the soldiers' horses had chewed up the ground in a wide swath, even kicking up the rocks as they walked one behind the other and side by side.

Spirit Walker knew he was making good time in catching the white soldiers. The only thing he had to work out now was what he would do once he had caught up with them. He couldn't very well overwhelm them with numbers. He was woefully outmatched when it came to weapons. The only thing in his favor was surprise. They wouldn't expect him, but then again, it wouldn't scare them much for one aging warrior to swoop down upon a troop of mounted blue coats.

He had just removed the tack from the horses and walked over to where Desert Rain sat laying out their blanket roll when he heard a noise in the brush. Desert Rain heard it too and froze in place. She looked over at Spirit Walker, who placed a finger to his lips. "Shhh," he signaled quietly. Then, pointing at the ground, he indicated that she should stay put. Like a wisp of smoke he eased into the darkness.

Desert Rain sat quietly, clutching a skinning knife, watching the shadows of night shift with the moving leaves of the trees around her. Where was her warrior? He had vanished some time ago and she was beginning to get concerned. What if some of the soldiers had doubled back and picked up their trail? What if Spirit Walker had been captured by them? What would she do? How would she continue on her own and where would she go?

Suddenly a noise jolted her back to reality. The noise was close by. Someone was moving toward her. Her eyes widened, her grip on the knife tightened. She was ready. If it was a blue coat, he was as good as dead. She rose slowly. She was ready to lunge forward or run away, whichever was necessary.

Then someone stepped into view directly in front of her. He was too tall to be Spirit Walker, but not by much. He was thinner, his shoulders not as broad. She strained her eyes to make out as many details as possible. He had long hair. His chest was bare. He must be Indian, not a blue coat, but what tribe? Comanche? He held a war club in his right hand and slowly began to raise it.

As the stranger began to speak, Desert Rain saw a flurry of movement just behind him. Suddenly the intruder pitched forward violently. Someone was on his back. The two men rolled in the dirt, then scrambled to their feet. She immediately recognized the attacker as Spirit Walker.

The two men squared off, circling each other, looking for an opening. The stranger lunged forward, swinging his war club in a vicious downward motion. Spirit Walker caught his arm and lifted him up and over his back, slamming him hard onto the ground behind him. The stranger rolled to his feet, but Spirit Walker leaped into the air like a cat. Spirit Walker's feet landed firmly in the assailant's stomach and she heard the air explode from the man's lungs. Both men landed hard, but Spirit Walker gained his feet and sprang onto his downed opponent. Spirit Walker hit him, once, hard. The enemy moved no more.

Desert Rain breathed a sigh of relief. "Who is he?" she asked.

"I don't know, but there are others. They are camped very close."

"What tribe is he?"

Spirit Walker pulled some moss from a pouch and began to prepare a small fire. "I will have to take a closer look," he said over his shoulder.

Desert Rain stepped up beside Spirit Walker and gazed down at the unconscious Indian. As the spark flew from Spirit Walker's flint, a small flame began to grow in the moss. The small yellow finger of light began to illuminate the stranger's face, slowly chasing away the shadows.

Desert Rain gasped. "Yellow Dog! It's my brother, Yellow Dog!"

Chapter Forty

Desert Rain patted a little water along Yellow Dog's cheeks and whispered his name softly. She didn't want to startle him after the punch Spirit Walker had given him. She surely didn't want him to come up swinging. Spirit Walker had stepped away so he wouldn't be seen immediately when Yellow Dog came to.

Slowly Yellow Dog opened his eyes and look up at Desert Rain. The light from the fire was now bright enough for him to see her face, framed by its yellow glow. "Desert Rain? Desert Rain, is that you?"

"It is, my brother."

Confused, Yellow Dog looked around him. "Where am I?" he asked, halfway expecting to see his mother and her People standing near him.

"You are near where you and the others are camping for the night," she said sweetly.

Yellow Dog sat up slowly, his head throbbing. "How did you find me, my sister? I was attacked."

"I know. We thought you meant us harm."

"You? It was you who faced me in the dark?"

"Yes, my brother. I did not recognize you. It has been some time since you moved away, and much has happened. I am sorry."

Yellow Dog had always been a good-natured person. The oldest of the three children of Wind Song and Sees The Way, he was the most like his father. Both of them could laugh at nearly any situation, and that's exactly what Yellow Dog did. He laughed, rubbing his jaw. "Well, whoever the warrior was who protected you, he is quite a fighter."

Desert Rain smiled and threw her arms around her older brother. "Oh, Yellow Dog, I am so glad to see you. I would like for you to meet the brave warrior who protects me."

Yellow Dog struggled to his feet with Desert Rain's help. His sight was still a bit blurry, but he could make out the shape of a man standing close by. "I am called Yellow Dog, son of Sees the Way," he said, extending his right arm toward the shadow man.

Spirit Walker stepped forward into the flickering firelight and took Yellow Dog's arm in friendship. "I am Spirit Walker," he said simply.

Yellow Dog could feel the strength in Spirit Walker's grip, the power of a warrior. "I have heard of you, my uncle." He looked toward his sister who was beaming with pride. "My sister, you have much to tell me?"

Desert Rain placed a gentle hand on her brother's shoulder. "Yes, my brother, we have much to discuss."

Yellow Dog sat and listened as Desert Rain filled him in on the happenings of the past few months. Beginning with Arm Bow's tragic fall, she expounded on the adventures that led to her meeting Spirit Walker. She told of the captivity she, Broken Branch, and the others had endured with the blue coats and how they had been rescued by Spirit Walker. She went on to tell of her tearful return to her People and her joyful marriage. Her mood changed to sadness as she told of Five Dreams' decision to move their encampment into Mexico. The sadness grew within her as she recounted her and Spirit Walker's failed mission of peace at the soldiers' fort and the death of Cloud Maker and Looks Twice. Barely able to continue, she told of returning to the rancheria and finding that soldiers had taken her family and friends and were at this very moment, no doubt, herding them toward San Carlos.

It was a story hard to be told, but it was obvious that it was also hard to hear. Yellow Dog's head drooped in grief, but there was more to his sorrow than just the words she had spoken. When at last he looked up, there were tears in his eyes. "My sister, I also must tell you of sorrow."

Desert Rain held her breath. How much more pain could she endure? Surely she had suffered enough for a whole lifetime. She looked solemnly into Yellow Dog's eyes. They were dark, not unlike Spirit Walker's, deep and brown, but it was the sadness in them that made her heart sink.

"I too have lost my family to the blue coats."

She gasped. Spirit Walker stepped forward and placed a comforting hand on her shoulder. "Tell us what happened," he said softly.

"We were camped along the Gila, our usual camp. Most of our People, including our chief, had been gathered to the reservation. They were taken in a raid almost one moon earlier. Four days ago, I left the camp with twelve others. We rode to the San Pedro to hunt for deer and elk. When we returned, we found sign that the blue coats had taken our families. We tracked them for a short distance and finally caught sight of them. But we were too few and the blue coats too many. I decided that we should travel to my mother's People and seek more warriors. Now even that plan has failed."

Spirit Walker looked deeply into Desert Rain's soft brown eyes. He hurt so much for her, felt her deepest pain. He had promised to protect her, to let no one hurt her. But he had failed. It wasn't physical injury that pained her now, it was worse. It was sorrow of heart that now inflicted the only person he truly loved. It was the white man who had hurt her, not with weapons of war, nor with swords and guns. No, it was with words that she had been hurt. False words, lying words, deceitful words. Words of peace that transformed themselves into words of betrayal and brought destruction to the Apache way of life. They tore apart families, took children from their loving mothers, took husbands and fathers from their wives and young ones.

Spirit Walker's countenance hardened. "There are thirteen of you?"

Yellow Dog nodded.

"Let us go to your brothers. We have work to do."

Yellow Dog looked up and met Spirit Walker's gaze. "What can so few do against so many?"

"We can stand. We will never be slaves as long as our minds are free. They may capture our bodies, but they can never bind our spirits." Spirit Walker stepped closer to Yellow Dog and placed both hands on his shoulders. "We are Apache."

Yellow Dog felt a surge of energy as if Spirit Walker had released a lightning bolt into his very soul. He felt hope. He felt courage. He glanced at Desert Rain. Strangely, she was smiling now. What power did this Chokonen possess?

The stillness of the morning air exploded with shouts from Sergeant Beyer as he roused his troops in his usual manner. On the trail again, but this time heading north, the sergeant's men were becoming more and more frustrated with the routine.

Captain Jackson consulted his map, as he did every morning when they were on patrol, but this time it was all different.

Anger gripped him every time he thought about the morning

before. Colonel Graffe had called him into the office just after reveille. As the colonel had passed before the troops, assembled for roll call, he had squared off with the tall captain. "I want you in my office in five minutes, Captain," he had snapped. Captain Jackson had only nodded, but he was sure the colonel must have seen his jaw tense.

The colonel had barely returned the salute when Jackson reported, but it didn't matter. A salute was a sign of respect and the captain knew that Graffe respected no one. Jackson, on the other hand, respected every one, even the Apache, and no one was going to change that.

"I'm sending you and your men out again. I want you ready to move out by noon."

"Noon? But, sir, my men just returned only two days ago."

"Captain, let me remind you that you are an officer in the United States Army. We take orders and we obey orders. We don't question them and we don't ignore them. Now, I just received a message from Fort Bowie. The message said that an all-out roundup of hostiles is taking place in our area."

Colonel Graffe picked up a wrinkled piece of paper and handed it to the young captain. "This is the dispatch. It says that a captain . . ."

"Garrett," Jackson filled in, reading the name from the sheet of paper.

"Yeah, Garrett. This Captain Garrett has reported finding a small group of Apache camped along the Gila. He rounded them up and sent word to Fort Bowie that he was taking them to San Carlos."

Captain Jackson looked wonderingly at the colonel. "I thought there was an Agent Clum, or someone like that, sent from Washington to do that sort of thing."

Graffe walked over to his coat rack, reached in the pocket of his jacket and pulled out his favorite pipe. "Captain, you have a lot to learn about the military."

"Tell me about it, Colonel," Jackson said, as Graffe made his way back to the desk.

Graffe opened the middle drawer of the desk and retrieved an ivory cigarette lighter and a small pouch of tobacco. "You see, in this man's army you have to beat the man in front of you to the door."

"I don't quite follow you, sir."

Graffe packed the pipe's bowl with a generous amount of tobacco and placed the stem between his teeth. He eyed the young captain standing before him. "No, I didn't expect that you would." He placed the lighter near the bowl and struck the flint. After two long draws on the pipe, he set the lighter down and blew out a cloud of white smoke. "Washington sends Clum into our territory to do business for the big man."

"By big man, you mean President Grant?"

A smile traced Graffe's lips. "Yes. Good ol' Ulysses S. You know I served with him during the war."

"No, sir, I didn't know that."

"No, guess you wouldn't. Anyway, Grant sends Clum, indicating that he doesn't think we can handle things down here. I take that personally, Captain. Very personally. So does Colonel Rimes at Fort Bowie. So, he sent out troops to round up some of the strays. No sense in Clum coming out of this with all the glory."

"You're going to grab some glory also, is that it?"

"Well, I figure there's enough glory to go around for all of us, young captain. I'm sending you."

"I take my men to round up Apaches, endure the hardships, and risk their lives, just so you can get the glory?"

Jackson smiled as he thought back on the colonel's response. The old man had been beside himself with rage. He had flown into a tantrum. His face had flushed red as he launched into a tirade, accusing Jackson of insubordination and treason. Looking back on it now, Captain Jackson found it humorous. He had apologized, though halfheartedly, and agreed to ready his men for departure at noon. He had done just that.

Now, as he faced the first morning of this new mission, he wondered if he shouldn't have pressed for more time. He wondered if he should be interested in accomplishing anything at all. His orders were to sweep the area from Fort Lowell to the Gila River. Strangely, he wondered what he would do if he happened upon the warrior who had tricked him out of his prisoners.

He smiled at the thought of that single encounter. He had wondered many times about the clever warrior. It was when he thought of the Apache brave who had been gunned down in the attack on Geronimo that his smile faded. He remembered the young man as one of the prisoners he had captured at the falls. He was the one who had attempted to attack them with only a knife. There was a fine line between bravery and stupidity, and surely that warrior had crossed that line many times.

As he stood in the early morning light, Jackson wondered how the young warrior had come to join up with Geronimo. He also wondered about the other two men who had been his captives back then. Had they been a part of Geronimo's band that escaped into Mexico? Where was the beautiful Indian woman? Was the old warrior riding the warpath also?

Suddenly, a voice brought him back to reality. "Sir, the men are assembled and taking breakfast. We'll be ready to move in thirty minutes."

"Thank you, Sergeant Beyer. You're doing an excellent job."

"Thank you, sir. Captain?"

"Yes?"

"Do we have a plan, sir? I mean, where exactly are we going? I mean, I know we're sweeping toward the Gila, but do you have a definite method in mind?"

Captain Jackson looked at his brawny first sergeant. "Yes, Sergeant, I do. We're going to find that spirit warrior."

"Spirit warrior?"

"The one who stole the Indian woman from us in the night."

"Yes, sir. The spirit warrior," Beyer whispered. "I understand, sir."

Chapter Forty-one

Captain Garrett hated riding long distances on hot summer days, and this one had proven to be almost unbearable. The sun overhead seemed to burn a hole right through the brim of his hat, scorching his eyes, burning his nose. Yet on he rode. He fancied himself a noble knight among the usual rabble who wore the blue uniforms of the U.S. Cavalry. His red hair and blue eyes had always attracted the ladies, only adding to his feeling of self-importance. He rode back straight, head high, shoulders square, the perfect model of a United States Cavalry officer. Colonel Rimes had ordered him to round up hostile Apaches and, by God, he meant to do just that.

He looked out across the sea of Apaches stretched before him, some walking, some riding, but all under his command. He smiled as he thought of his West Point hero—George Armstrong Custer. Custer was bombastic, cocky, confident—not unlike himself. During the war, Custer had been given the rank of Brevet General. It was all politics, Garrett told himself. A dashing figure, with his immaculately trimmed goatee and mustache, Custer had been sparking the General's daughter and kissing up to Lincoln at the time. Garrett had to admit though, Custer was one hell of an Indian fighter.

A couple of months ago, Garrett had heard that Custer had ridden off with his illustrious Seventh Cavalry, bound for the Black Hills of South Dakota. When he'd heard the news, Garrett knew that ol' "Yellow Hair," as the Indians called Custer, was seeking the advantage he needed to impress President Grant. Let's see if Custer can round up Sioux as fast as I can round up Apaches, Garrett thought to himself. "Keep those 'Pache moving!" he yelled to his men as he stroked his week-old goatee and mustache.

Spirit Walker rode hard at the head of the group of warriors, Desert Rain at his side. They had decided on a quick plan the night before. It wasn't going to be easy to stop a troop of soldiers, especially when they were holding Apaches hostage, but Spirit Walker had done it once before. He rode with the proud spirit of his ancestors. The same spirit had led those before him to accomplish great deeds of daring and skill. The same spirit had enabled them to see visions, then go on to reach new heights of insight; to conquer, defend, and acquire new lands. The same spirit had preserved the Apache way of life. He rode with determination. He rode with power.

Yellow Dog rode directly behind his baby sister. How she had changed since last he saw her! As a child, she had always been introverted, shy. He remembered fondly how she would jump at any sudden movement or loud noise, always depending on her older brothers to defend her, keep her safe. He and Broken Branch had doted over her, always careful to watch out for her well-being. Now, she rode at the head of a war party. She rode with her head high, her hair trailing in the afternoon breeze. How she had changed!

It wasn't hard for Captain Jackson to figure out what had happened. The signs were too evident on the ground around him. Many troops had ridden this way. The prairie grasses were crushed by the hooves of cavalry horses, well shod, carrying riders. Along with the tracks of the horses were the unmistakable prints left by moccasined feet. They were heading north, toward the Gila.

"Won't be hard following these tracks," Sergeant Beyer said as he approached the captain. "That is, if we've a mind to."

"These riders are accompanying prisoners," Jackson stated resolutely.

"Yeah, I kinda got that impression. I couldn't tell for sure though."

"Oh, it's evident, Sergeant. See, when a horse walks through tall grass, it presses the grass down *opposite* the direction it's traveling. When a man walks through tall grass, he presses it down *in* the direction he's traveling."

"Yeah," the sergeant said, taking a closer look at the prints. "I see what you mean."

"There's no doubt about it, Sergeant. Whoever these soldiers are, they've got prisoners afoot."

"Could be that captain we heard tell of from Fort Bowie."

"That was my thought exactly, Sergeant."

Sergeant Beyer looked back over his shoulder, following the back trail with his eyes. "Reckon where they came from?"

"I don't know, but I know where they're going."

"San Carlos?"

"Yep." Jackson took a few steps along the back trail, then looked out across the prairie. "Sergeant, I've an idea that they've taken the clan we're looking for."

"Why's that, sir?"

"I don't know. Gut feeling, I guess."

"What do you want to do, Captain?"

Jackson turned to face Beyer. "Let's follow 'em, Sergeant. Double the pace, we'll cut them off and catch them somewhere along the Gila."

"Yes, sir." Sergeant Beyer turned toward his mount, then suddenly stopped short. "Sir, didn't you say that this Captain Garrett had been sent out along the Gila?" He turned back to face Jackson, a puzzled look on his face.

"Yes, I did, Sergeant. That's what the colonel told me."

"I don't understand. Why would he be this far south?"

Jackson hadn't considered the question before, but the sergeant made a very good point. Jackson had seen the dispatch himself. It clearly stated that Garrett's men had rounded up a clan of Apache "along the Gila." So, if Garrett was "along the Gila," whose tracks were these? "Sergeant, prepare the men quickly. I want to know whose tracks these are."

"Yes, sir. At once, sir."

"Sir, the rendezvous point is just ahead," the young corporal said, sliding his mount to a halt beside Captain Garrett.

"Any sign of the others?" Garrett asked.

"No, sir, not yet, sir."

"Very well, then. Let's prepare a camp and wait. Secure the prisoners."

"Yes, sir." The messenger swung his horse and began issuing orders.

Yellow Dog strained his eyes against the darkness. He tried to stay close to Spirit Walker as they moved through the dense forest. It wasn't easy. The warrior moved like a ghost in the night and appeared to see everything as clearly as he did in the daylight hours. He moved with grace, quickness, but most of all, silence. It wasn't long before the two men could see the reddish glow of a campfire. They had found the blue coats' camp.

Spirit Walker held up a hand, halting Yellow Dog in his tracks. After a short pause, the Chokonen motioned for Yellow Dog to move up beside him.

As Yellow Dog stepped forward, he could see the blue coats around their fire. The Indians were gathered together around a smaller fire, and encircled by well-armed guards. It appeared that only the warriors were bound. The women and children moved freely around them. They seemed to be eating. Yellow Dog had no trouble spotting his mother and brother. He released a sigh of relief. But anxiety still gnawed at him—he could not see any of his own young family among the captives.

Suddenly a flurry of activity caught Spirit Walker's attention and he signaled for Yellow Dog to watch closely along with him. There were riders approaching from the west. Spirit Walker watched as four troopers rode into view, swung from their saddles, and approached a tall red-haired man who was standing next to the fire. They began to speak quickly in the white man's language. Spirit Walker listened intently.

"I wish I knew what they were saying," Yellow Dog complained.

"Shhhhh," Spirit Walker cautioned, placing a finger to his lips.

After a while, Spirit Walker began to slowly move away from the encampment. He motioned for Yellow Dog to follow him.

"They await the arrival of more prisoners," Spirit Walker said as soon as he was sure he had placed sufficient distance between him and the soldiers.

"More prisoners?"

"Yes. Did you see any of your band at the blue coats' camp?"

"No."

"Then perhaps it is your people they wait for."

"Yes." Yellow Dog was elated, but it only took a few seconds for his elation to turn to concern. "That means more blue coats. It will not be easy."

Spirit Walker kept moving. "It will not be easy, but all is not lost either. We must return to the others and plan our next move."

Sergeant Hoyle was resting comfortably after his long ride. In his dreams he relived his adventures of the last few days. He had been sent out by Captain Garrett to look for hostile Apaches along the Gila River, while the captain took some of his men south. Hoyle'd had only a dozen men when he spotted the small village of Mescalero encamped along the river's banks. It was a good thing that most of the young men were absent from the camp when Hoyle decided to take the village hostage. It had gone very well and his men had taken the women and children easily. The others had surrendered shortly thereafter. It was clear that the Indians had no heart to fight. He'd sent word back to Fort Bowie immediately, touting his victory, then hurried to the rendezvous point to meet up with Captain Garrett's troops.

Now he slept soundly, knowing that the combination of his men and the captain's offered safety in sheer numbers. The prisoners were well guarded. Everything was peaceful.

Suddenly shouting woke him. Guns fired. He bolted to his feet. Instinct took hold of his legs and he began to run toward the gunfire.

Drawing his pistol as he ran through the darkness, he could see the flashes spit from the barrels of Winchester rifles. He ran toward the action.

"The horses!" He heard someone shout. "They're stealing the horses!"

Chapter Forty-two

"It's a fine herd of horses," Yellow Dog said, stepping up to stand beside Spirit Walker. The horses were hobbled, left to graze on a large grassy plain.

"Yes." Spirit Walker smiled as he remembered the last night's events. The white eyes had been caught quite off guard. He had been able to sneak up on two of the soldiers who had been left to watch the horses. A sharp blow to the back of each man's head had dropped them to the ground, unconscious, no longer a threat. He had bound and gagged each man, careful not to hurt them seriously, knowing that a wounded animal would fight to the death. He knew that if he killed one of them, the others would be relentless in their pursuit and might take out their frustration on their captives. It hadn't taken long for Spirit Walker's helpers to release the rope line that tethered the horses together, mount a few of them, and ride off into the darkness with the whole lot of them.

Desert Rain

It had been a first for Desert Rain. She'd never stolen a horse before. She understood now why the warrior societies honored those who could accomplish such a deed. It was indeed a brave act to sneak into the enemies' camp and steal their only means of transportation, without killing anyone. To kill the sleeping camp and then take the horses was a cowardly thing to do, not worthy to be praised. Of course there was no shame in stealing someone else's horse. After all, no one could truly "own" another living thing, so it was free to be used by anyone who could employ its services. If you couldn't safeguard it, it was free for the taking. The greatest danger in entering the camp and taking the horses of a live enemy was detection and all-out warfare between the two parties. They'd avoided it this time, but the blue coats were mad as hornets.

Yellow Dog shifted restlessly in the early morning sunlight. It had been a long night. He'd had no sleep, but neither had Spirit Walker. He couldn't help but wonder where the older warrior got his energy. He seemed tireless, almost inhuman. His eyes were sharp and alert, even after hours of planning and actually stealing the horses and hiding them. He was still quite a warrior.

Yellow Dog took a cursory glance around him, wondering how long it would be till the blue coats showed up to reclaim their stolen horses.

Spirit Walker looked at Yellow Dog, reading his thoughts. "Do not worry, the white eyes will not come looking for the horses."

"You are sure of this?"

"Yes. Not being sure how many warriors were involved, they will not be eager to fight. Also, they will not expect us to be close by. They will think that we will put much distance between them and us."

The Chokonen glanced over his shoulder at the sleeping form

of Desert Rain. She rested comfortably under a large pine tree, on a bed of pine needles. Most of the others slept also. Only a couple were stirring around in the graying light of day.

"What are we to do now, Spirit Walker?" Yellow Dog asked.

"We watch and wait for an opportunity to take our People back." Spirit Walker's eyes roamed over the younger warrior. Yellow Dog's facial features were so similar to Desert Rain's. They were truly brother and sister. Spirit Walker smiled. "I have an idea."

Sergeant Hoyle stalked a path in front of his men. He seemed to take each step as if planting his foot into the ground and jerking the earth behind him in anger. "What the hell happened last night? How in the hell did a band of 'Paches sneak in here and steal eighty cavalry horses and sixty Indian ponies? I want answers! I want 'em now!"

He was greeted with silence. Hoyle exploded. "By God, you will talk to me! I promise you will talk to me, you sons of bitches!" He walked quickly toward his saddle. Pulling a long riding quip from beneath it, he laid a hard slash across the tree of his saddle. "You will talk to me, goddammit!"

"Sergeant, slow the pace a little."

"Yes, sir." Sergeant Beyer held up a hand and reined his horse to a fast walk.

"We won't even be close until tomorrow evening. There's no sense in killing the horses," Jackson said.

"Yes, sir. We'll need to rest them soon."

"Agreed, Sergeant. I don't want to exhaust them. I do, however, want to make good time."

"Yes, sir. We are, sir. It's not hard to follow the tracks of so many horses."

"That is lucky for us, Sergeant."

"Yes, sir. Lucky."

Desert Rain

*   *   *

Captain Garrett watched as his tough-talking first sergeant ranted, raved, and threatened the men, but to no avail. Not a single man was talking. "Sergeant!"

Sergeant Hoyle spun in place, his face redder than the bandanna that hung around his neck.

"Sergeant, perhaps the men would like to talk among themselves for a little while. You come with me."

"Yes, sir," Hoyle said in frustration. He turned back to his men. "You talk amongst yourselves, but when I get back, you will talk to me. Is that understood?" Getting no reply, he turned and walked quickly toward his captain.

As soon as the sergeant had walked away, the men huddled together.

She lay somewhere between waking and sleeping, where darkness and light become one, somewhere between dreams and reality. She was aware of the hard ground beneath her and the voices of two men speaking in the distance. It was Spirit Walker and Yellow Dog talking together, planning, tossing around ideas that would save her people. She smiled. Spirit Walker was the warrior of her heart, so kind and selfless. He had taken her higher than she had ever thought she could go.

He spoke her name, with his soft gentle voice. He needed her. Slowly she opened her eyes and immediately felt the cool breeze as it brushed across her cheeks. "Yes, my Spirit?"

Gently he reached down with his large hands and lifted her to her feet. The wind whipped his hair, swirling it around his face. He is so handsome, she thought as she stared into his dark eyes.

"You are weary, Little One?" he asked softly.

"Yes," she sighed. "I have labored in climbing, my Spirit."

He wasn't looking at her now and she followed his gaze. They stood now on the side of a high mountain and Spirit Walker was looking toward its peak.

"It is the mountain of your dreams and desires," he whispered.

"I know." Tears began to form in her eyes as she spoke. "My Spirit, will I ever reach the summit? Will I ever know the joy of standing on top of the mountain?"

"Yes, Little One." Smiling, he reached up with a gentle hand and guided her face away from the peak. "Look how far you have come, my Flower."

Looking down the mountainside, she could see the tipi where once she and Arm Bow had lived. In their brief time together, she thought surely that she had reached a higher spot on the mountain of her dreams. Had they not been happy together? Had she not then felt more on top of the mountain than at any earlier time in her life? How had she risen to a higher plane?

She looked back at her warrior. "How have I come so far, my Spirit? How have I come so far from where you found me?"

He smiled. "I have carried you, my Little One."

"Oh, my Spirit!" Weeping, she fell into his waiting arms. Sobbing against his strong chest, she wrapped her arms tightly around him. "Will you not carry me to the top, my warrior? Will you not let me see the peak?"

Spirit Walker placed his hands on her shoulders and pushed her from him. "I cannot, my Flower."

"Why?" she cried. "Do you not love me?"

"My Flower, I have carried you as far as I am able. I can but take your hand and walk with you to the summit. Together, only together, can we reach the peak."

"You mean," she said, choking back her tears, "that I can reach the top of the mountain if I take your hand and we climb together?"

He stretched forth his hand and combed out her hair with his fingers. Then running the back of his hand along her cheek, he spoke. "Yes, my Flower. When you lose sight of your dreams, you can follow me."

At times, as they climbed, she felt she could go no farther. Her legs were weary, her heart heavy, her breathing labored. Each time she held tighter to Spirit Walker's hand and he helped her over the boulders that stood as a barrier against her. There were times when she gained strength and seemed to be unstoppable. During those times she helped pull Spirit Walker along the path that led to the peak.

Finally they stepped onto the highest plateau of the mountain. Overlooking the beautiful valley below them, they both stood tall. There it was! Her perfect happiness, her ultimate peace. She had reached it at last. Turning, Desert Rain leapt into Spirit Walker's arms and embraced him. "I am so happy!" she cried. "It is everything I thought it would be and more!"

He held her so tightly that she wished never to be released. "Is it, my Little One?"

"Oh, yes, my Spirit. You have brought me what I have always desired. Love, peace, contentment."

"There is more here, my Flower. Much more."

She pulled away from him and looked around. He placed a hand on her waist and turned her about. "There is the stone of success. You will be a great warrior among your People. A woman who holds the respect of many for your accomplishments, your courage, your devotion to your People.

"Over there is the tree of motherhood. Many children will call you mother and will follow in your teachings. You will be as a tree in fruitfulness, filled with the freshness of love, the fragrance of laughter.

"And over there are the flowers of light and love. You will forever bring that love to the man you choose to be with forever."

Stepping away from him, she walked to the lovely field of flowers. She did not recognize them, perhaps she'd never seen them before, but they were so beautiful. They were rich in shades of red, yellow, and green. She picked a handful and held them to her nose. They smelled so sweet and filled her heart with such happiness.

She turned and handed them to Spirit Walker. "I wish to be with you forever, my warrior. They are, and always will be, for you."

As he took the flowers from her hand, something flashed behind him. In amazement Desert Rain noticed a large pair of eagle's wings begin to sprout from Spirit Walker's broad back.

"Let us fly, Little One. I will take you higher than even this."

With wonder, she climbed onto his strong back as he flexed his wings and took to the air. Was it true that she could go higher than the peak of her dreams and desires? Yet now she was soaring. Flying. He had taken her higher than she ever thought she could go.

She was filled with such wonder and joy. It was great to be alive. Great to be his woman! She felt her own wings begin to grow. Laughter rose from deep within her and leapt from her throat. It was a laughter so deep and pure, a laughter she had never experienced before, a laughter she could not help but release. Slowly she relinquished her grip, felt Spirit Walker sink beneath her, but she was not falling. She was flying.

He beat his wings faster and faster, harder and harder, causing a strong updraft to keep her aloft. He was the wind beneath her as she soared on high.

The eagle and the hawk flew as one.

Chapter Forty-three

Captain Garrett's stride was a testament to his height, and Sergeant Hoyle found it hard to keep pace. The roundish sergeant pulled the bandanna from around his neck and dabbed at the sweat beading on his forehead. "I don't know what to tell you, sir. Not yet any way. But, I will. I swear I'll know who's responsible for letting our horses get stole right out from under us."

Garrett cast a sideward glance at his shaggy first sergeant. "Hoyle, there are more important things than who was on guard. Right now we're in a hell of a mess. We have close to a hundred and fifty captives and eighty troopers. Now, eighty mounted cavalry troops can handle that many Injuns. But, we have one major problem, Sergeant." Garrett stopped in his tracks and whirled, face to face with Hoyle. "We haven't one damn horse among us!"

"I understand, sir."

"You don't understand anything, Sergeant! If those Injuns decide to come back here, riding our horses, mind you, and attack us, we're sitting ducks. Do you understand that, Sergeant?"

"Yes, sir."

"Then I suggest that you stop playing games with those men. Forget who was on guard and get us the hell out of here. Is that understood?"

"Yes, sir."

"I want a show of strength, Sergeant. You let those captives know who's in charge here. You let them know that if they try anything, anything at all, we'll kill the whole lot of 'em."

"Yes, sir."

"I want every buck tied. I want every one of them hobbled. I want all of our tack and saddles buried so they can't be found. We'll retrieve them later. We press on to Fort Bowie in one hour. Got that?"

"Yes, sir."

The sun was coming on mid-morning when Spirit Walker settled into the tall grass to sleep. It had been a long night. He smiled as he passed his gaze over the green valley before him. One hundred and fifty-five horses stood, lazily grazing on the open range. It was a fine herd and more than enough to carry Desert Rain's clan and Yellow Dog's clan safely into Mexico. But first, both had to be rescued from the soldiers. As Spirit Walker closed his eyes in an attempt to chase sleep to its secret chambers, he thought on the matter.

Yellow Dog had awakened a couple of his younger warriors and placed them to watch over the animals while he tried to get a little sleep as well. He had been up with Spirit Walker, watching the horses and talking through much of the morning. As he lay back in the morning sun and closed his eyes, he thought about the man who had chosen to marry his sister.

Desert Rain

Spirit Walker was a calm yet cautious man. His eyes were deep with wisdom beyond his years. At first, Yellow Dog had gazed over the warrior's face, wondering at the attraction Desert Rain felt for an older man. Now, after having ridden with him, after having experienced his compassion and love for his People, he understood. Spirit Walker was still a warrior to be feared and respected. Yellow Dog smiled as sleep claimed him. He was proud to know that his sister was in good hands.

Spirit Walker's breathing was deep and even, his body wrapped in sleep, bathed in the sunshine of noon. Though his body rested in sleep, his mind was racing like the stallion. He had made his plans to infiltrate the cavalry camp and free the People without too much fighting. He had to use the element of surprise to its fullest advantage. The plan was simple, but it wasn't his alone. He drew from past experience. It was this experience that invaded his dreams.

In his dream, he stood at the foot of the Sierra Madre foothills, looking out over the freight trail running north and south along a two-thousand-foot plateau. Before his eyes, he could see the Mexican fort town of Nuri. Beyond the ten-foot high walls lay three hundred Mexican troops under the command of Colonel Luis Gomez. It was this force that he and his brothers were about to engage in a fight to the death.

The day before, two young Apache women had been abducted. One was Lucia. At the last full moon, she had been given her womanhood ceremony, though she was only now a week away from reaching the age of sixteen. Her best friend was Mathla, eighteen and already engaged to be married.

The girls had been picking mescal plants when they were taken by the *Nakai-ye*. Luckily for the girls, they were followed by Lucia's nephew, five-year-old Noshe. When little Noshe saw the men leap onto the girls and carry them away, he'd hidden under a protruding rock ledge. Later, he'd crept back to camp and presented himself before the tipi of his chief, Juh. Not only was Juh the chief of the Nedni Apache, but Lucia was Juh's younger sister. Noshe knew Juh had to be told first.

That night, at midnight, Juh, Goyathlay, and the Walker stood, overlooking the fort, formulating a plan. It was Juh who first came up with the plan, but the others agreed that it could work. They set the plan in motion the very next day. If the Mexicans wanted female slaves for their labor camps, that is what they would get.

Spirit Walker remembered entering the gates of the walled fort, walking between mounted Apaches on all sides. The mounted warriors were dressed like Mexican *guerrilleros*. Captain Gomez had often used these bandidos to acquire Apache slaves. When they had slaves, the bandidos were given a free pass to report directly to the *Capitan*, and these *guerrilleros* had plenty.

The dust was a choking cloud as Spirit Walker walked with the others. He was flanked on both sides by twenty mounted Apache, all dressed in bits and pieces of cast-off army uniforms and pantaloons, with wide sombreros on their heads and crossed bandoliers of cartridges on their chests. Each one carried a rifle, draped casually across his Mexican saddle. They looked like any other band of *guerrilleros*, but this group was different. The wide sombreros only assisted in hiding the stern, hard faces of the Apache war party.

At the head of the column of mounted warriors rode the two prominent leaders—the huge and powerful Juh and the squat, square-shouldered Goyathlay. They would spring the trap once inside the city walls. Spirit Walker's part in the plan was to control and coordinate the actions of the "captives."

As they entered the fort, Spirit Walker could barely see the lines of cages that framed the street. Between the jostling horses all around him, he caught only glimpses of the four-foot-square cages that were used to house *los diablos*, the devils, as the Mexicans called their Apache slaves. There was no sign of the two captured Apache girls. The street was lined only with Mexican soldiers and a scattered array of citizens.

Captain Gomez approached the group, a grin tracing his lips. Suddenly the crowd broke into a cheering shout, echoing across the compound with a thunderous roar, *"Bravo soldados! Vivan los soldados de Mexico! Muerte a los Diablos!"* The charade had worked. Spirit Walker could only reflect on the sight that the captain thought he saw before him—twenty mounted *guerrilleros*, flanking a line of more than a dozen captive Apache women.

Spirit Walker and the other "captives" had made their disguise as complete as possible. They wore long calico dresses, torn and muddied, to present the illusion of a fight with their "captors." Each man wore his hair in the style of an Apache female. There was only one true female, and she rode in the guise of one of the *guerrilleros*. She was Ishton, wife of Juh and favorite sister of Goyathlay.

The noise from the crowd was deafening now and the grin of the captain grew broader as he approached the supposed prize of so many healthy-looking Apache women. Gomez's grin began to fade, however, as the squat leader at the left front of the column of riders slowly raised his sombreroed head. The shadow cast by the large hat had obscured one important feature of Goyathlay's face. Across each cheek were two bright stripes of yellow paint. The captain froze in his tracks as the thunder of twenty rifles flooded the fort's interior.

The mounted warriors began to ride, trampling everything in their path. Spirit Walker and the other "captives" threw aside their costumes, producing rifles and pistols that they quickly put into action. The sound was tremendous, the screams of the victims rose to a fevered pitch, as one by one the Mexicans were cut to ribbons. The crowd could only stand like sheep in a slaughter.

When the fighting was over, the entire compound had been cleared of the fort's occupants. Not a soul remained alive. The streets were littered with the dead, but there was not one Apache among them.

Juh and Ishton had rescued the girls, who were being held in a blacksmith shop. Lucky for them that Juh had entered when he did. Juh had barely stopped the sergeant who held them before he assaulted young Mathla and branded both girls with a cattle brand. Juh had snapped the sergeant's neck like a twig as Ishton released the overjoyed girls.

The last image of the battle Spirit Walker could remember was the hanging form of Captain Gomez as he swung freely in the breeze beneath the crossbeam of the town's gate. Driven in the ground at his feet was an iron cattle brand with an "A" at its tip. It was a symbol the Apaches hated more than the Spanish lance.

Even in sleep, Spirit Walker smiled at the plan that had exacted revenge at Nuri. It was a plan that would work again. He was sure of it.

Chapter Forty-four

Spirit Walker, Yellow Dog, and Desert Rain were sitting near a small fire eating when the riders approached. Earlier that evening two scouts had been sent out to keep a watch on the party of soldiers who held their families captive. Spirit Walker had risen from sleep in the late afternoon, Desert Rain shortly thereafter. They had allowed Yellow Dog to sleep a little longer before they assembled to talk about the night's planned actions. Now, they hailed the scouts as they rode in from the east.

"*Ya a teh*, Spirit Walker," the scout leader said as he slid his mount to halt before the Apache leader.

"What is the news?" Spirit Walker asked anxiously.

Both scouts dismounted and the one who had spoken stepped forward as the other warrior led the horses toward a nearby stream.

Yellow Dog stood. "What have you learned of the enemy, my brother?"

The scout's demeanor was somewhat downcast, but he tried not to show his concern. His body language, however, was not lost on Spirit Walker. "They have treated our People badly, have they not?"

The scout nodded.

"They drive them mercilessly toward the fort," Spirit Walker continued. "They are completely void of compassion."

The scout nodded again. "Yes, uncle, these things are true. They are making good time along the river. I fear we may not be able to catch them quickly enough."

Spirit Walker saw the concern in Yellow Dog's eyes. Standing, Spirit Walker laid a gentle hand on the younger warrior's shoulder. "We shall catch them, my brother. It will not be easy, the plan is a hard one, but we will succeed."

Desert Rain stood and stepped up beside her brave husband. "Yellow Dog, you must believe that it can be done. Success is in the believing. I believe in Spirit Walker."

Yellow Dog looked deep into Spirit Walker's eyes. His eyes were piercing, his brow furrowed in resolve. "I believe, my sister. I believe," Yellow Dog said with resolve.

"At the setting of the sun," Spirit Walker said as he stepped away from the others, "we will dance. We will evoke the spirits of the mountains."

"The *Gan?*" Desert Rain asked incredulously.

"Yes, the *Gan*. We will seek their assistance in this matter. We will enter the enemy's camp tonight. Under the cover of darkness, we will surely need the mountain spirits' help."

"The *Gan*," Desert Rain whispered to herself. This was truly an important event.

The evening was filled with activity in the small Apache camp. Warriors hastily prepared costumes from branches, feathers, bits of cloth, and rawhide. There would be four dancers who would impersonate the *Gan*. One dancer would impersonate Coyote, the trickster, who would try to ruin the important mission they had planned for the nighttime foray into the enemy's camp. Spirit Walker, the shaman, would sing the songs of victory and ask the blessings of the mountain spirits upon their quest. Yellow Dog was assigned the task of fashioning a crude drum from a hollowed-out pine log. He would keep the steady rhythm, Spirit Walker would sing, and the dancers would dance. Together, they would rain down the blessings they needed to be successful in their goal. The People must be saved.

At early dusk, the dancers entered the dance circle around a sacred firelay. Yellow Dog began a steady cadence on the drum as they entered from the north. Spirit Walker sang a song of remembrance, a song dedicated to the spirits of long-gone ancestors. The dancers left the arena, only to return from the south and repeat their movements around the fire. Fading back into the night, they would return again from the east, then from the west. After the fourth passing, the blessing of the circle was complete and they were now free to dance in earnest.

The drum beat quickened and Spirit Walker's voice rose to a higher pitch as he chanted and swayed to the rhythm. The dancers were free to dance as individuals now. There were no pre-arranged steps, only the rhythm and the emotions that translated from each dancer as he moved in short, jerky, angular movements around the glowing fire. Each time "Coyote" entered the fire circle, the *Gan* dancers would chase him back out into the darkness.

Desert Rain watched as the dancers postured and gestured with their swordlike wands of yucca stalks. It was a beautiful sight to behold. Closing her eyes, she thought back to the first time she could remember seeing *Gan* dancers perform.

Her mother had spent many moons in preparation for Desert Rain's womanhood ceremony. It was to be a lavish affair, the turning point for a young girl who was on the verge of coming of age. Wind Song would sit for hours with her daughter, telling her the story of White Painted Woman, mother of the People. Desert Rain understood that her role was to follow White Painted Woman's pathway and to become a mother to her People as well.

On the first day of the ceremony, a tipi was constructed from four spruce saplings. Desert Rain would stay in this shelter throughout the four-day ritual. She would be attended by an older girl, who would stay with her for the duration. Desert Rain smiled. In her mind's eyes, she could see clearly the face of her childhood girlfriend. It was Little Hand, daughter of Wind Song's oldest sister, Spotted Deer. It was less than a year later that Little Hand fell ill and died, but for the four days of Desert Rain's ceremony, they were inseparable.

Desert Rain remembered the buckskin dress her mother had prepared with love and care. It had been painted yellow, the color of sacred pollen, a replica of the dress that White Painted Woman wore. It was decorated with symbols of the moon, sun, and stars, with long fringe representing sunbeams. It felt so smooth against her skin. She could almost feel it brush against her body as she swayed to the beat of Yellow Dog's drum.

Her father had acquired the shaman and *Gan* dancers for each of the four nights. He had gone to another clan and asked for advice in procuring the very finest shaman of the People, the very best dancers. He had traveled far to find them and bring them back, just for her. No one in her clan knew them. This made their impersonation of the *Gan* even more mysterious and special.

She remembered well the sound of the drum as the dancers danced. It was not unlike the sound she was now hearing. The dancers at her ceremony used the same steps as the ones before her now—at times short stepping or high stepping, even leaping and spinning. The shaman who blessed her along the "pollen path" with lengthy chants had the same smooth voice as the shaman she heard singing now. The exact same voice, she thought. She opened her eyes quickly, straining against the darkness to see where Spirit Walker was sitting.

He was sitting near the fire, silhouetted by the bright orangish glow from the flames. The yellow and red of the campfire cast an eerie aura around his face, highlighting his profile. As his lips moved in singing, it seemed like the fire itself emanated from his mouth with each exhalation of the chant. His eyes, even in the light of the fire, were merely deep pools of darkness, bottomless pits of coal. But it was his voice that held her mesmerized. It was that voice, she was sure of it, that she had heard for four straight nights. It was that voice who blessed the dismantling of the tipi and her own purifying five days thereafter. It had to have been *this* shaman. It had to have been.

After the dancing had ended, Spirit Walker had disappeared for a time, moving into the darkness to make final preparations with the others. Desert Rain sat alone by the fire, stirring the smoldering coals with a stick, thinking. She knew her part in the rescue effort. It was a simple thing she had been asked to do. But how she wished to be going with them instead of staying behind. She knew the mission was a dangerous one, but had not Spirit Walker told her that she was a warrior?

Now, all she had been instructed to do was wait behind for the women to be released. Once Spirit Walker and the others had freed the women captives, Desert Rain would lead them to safety, taking them as far from the soldiers as possible and starting them toward Mexico and into the Mother Mountains, the Sierra Madre. It should be an easy thing to do, compared to walking into the midst of the enemy's camp and freeing them, but she wondered how she would find the courage to accomplish it without Spirit Walker beside her. She would miss him so much, and worry about his welfare. She would pray each night that he would return safely to her.

The darkness was thick around her and the fire dying quickly.

Looking up, she smiled at the muscular form striding out of the blackness. "My Spirit," she said softly.

Spirit Walker held out his hand to her as he passed. She rose and followed him to the other side of the circle and into the night.

Spirit Walker was silent as they walked together under the starlight. Only a quarter of the moon peeked at them through the clouds as they walked, winking at them as they settled down on a patch of soft grass by the creek.

Desert Rain sat facing her warrior. Reaching up, she cradled his face with both hands, looking deeply into his eyes.

"The time has come for us to leave, my Flower."

Desert Rain could feel the tears welling up in her eyes as he spoke, but she didn't want to cry, not now, not here. "I know," she said simply.

"I love you, my Desert Rain. You must believe that I always will."

She nodded. "I love you so much, my Spirit Walker." She wondered if she should ask him about her womanhood ceremony. She wanted to ask if he was the one. It was something she just had to know, yet at this particular time, it didn't seem to be the most important thing at hand. She leaned forward and kissed him. Sweetly, gently.

Spirit Walker took her in his arms and deepened the kiss. She was so soft and warm. Wordlessly, they stood, facing each other. It was as if they were of the same mind, sharing the same thoughts. Desert Rain slipped out of her tunic as Spirit Walker removed his breechclout, then they both turned and entered the flowing water of the creek.

Wading into a deep pool, they embraced again as the water flowed just above Spirit Walker's waist. Desert Rain could feel the passion rising in the man she loved. Reaching down, she cupped water in her hands and bathed his chest, shoulders, and back. He tilted his head back, face up at the moon, as her hands played over his body like the soft stroke of a feather. Her lips caressed his neck, slid down onto his chest, then lightly brushed his stomach. Her hands played along his ribs. On their journey over his hips they moved back onto his firm buttocks, squeezing ever so lovingly before sliding around his thighs and meeting at the pinnacle of his desire. He sighed deeply as she cupped him in her hands.

Straddling his hips and wrapping her arms around his shoulders, Desert Rain eased onto him. Her muscles contracted and expanded as she gripped him tighter and tighter, massaging him with a constant rhythm.

Carrying her to the opposite bank, he laid her back gently in the grass. She could feel his weight press down on her, feel his strength engulfing her, trapping her against the ground, yet she was not crushed, nor was she afraid. She was merely swept away by passion, the freest she had ever been.

Chapter Forty-five

It was just before midnight when Spirit Walker and Desert Rain joined the others around the small fire. Yellow Dog stood as they approached.

"Is everything ready?" Spirit Walker asked.

"We are ready, my uncle."

Spirit Walker turned to face his wife. "Rain, you will stay near the horses. When we have freed the women, we will instruct them to come to you."

Desert Rain nodded in agreement. "Go with speed, my husband. Our People need you."

Spirit Walker gave Desert Rain a quick kiss on the forehead, nodded to the men, and disappeared into the night. The others followed in silence.

Desert Rain had spent the night lying on a small pile of pine needles at the edge of the pasture. She watched the dark shape of the horses as they milled about. She knew that the horses would have a better chance than she had of sensing anyone or anything that might come upon them in the night. They were so restful that often times she found herself nodding off, then suddenly snapping awake and finding everything still peaceful and quiet.

The graying light of dawn was peeking through the trees, playing among the mist of morning that lay along the meadow. She watched as the infant sun's heat steamed the dew from the backs of the horses, enveloping them in an eerie glow of vapor and light. It was beautiful to behold. She would have enjoyed it more, were it not for the task at hand. Were it not for the enemy that might be lurking among the morning shadows. She kept her eyes on the tree line at the opposite end of the clearing.

All of a sudden the hairs rose on the back of her neck. She listened closely, keeping absolutely still beneath the boughs of a spreading pine. The morning birds had stopped singing. The horses were stirring, moving away from the opposite tree line, obviously wary. Using her peripheral vision, she swept the edge of the meadow for any signs of movement. It didn't take long until she found it. Movement, slow, but steady.

It was just a dark shape among the lighter colors of the foliage beneath the trees. The shape stopped moving and crouched behind a small grouping of underbrush. She could make out a head and shoulders, the distinctive shape of a person. The person was smallish, but was hidden too much by the brush to make out any other features. Was it a man or woman? Was it an enemy or a friend? Desert Rain didn't dare move—that would only give away her own position. She watched and kept her breathing shallow.

After a while the person moved, low and bent over, to another position behind a mesquite bush. She saw another movement, then another. In a few short moments, she counted at least a half dozen ghostly shapes moving among the brush. Slowly, she gathered her legs under her, prepared for flight.

At first the noise sounded far away, but grew in intensity. It was the call of a crow. Desert Rain tilted her head skyward, looking for the silhouette of the soaring bird. The sky was lighter now, the sun peeking above the trees. She scanned the air above the field, but saw nothing. There was still no sign of the winged creature, yet the distress call seemed to grow louder.

When her gaze fell again to the tree line, the figure was standing, clearly outlined against a background of shrubs. Desert Rain strained her eyes to make out as many details as she could. Eventually, she could make out the facial features. It was Crow Woman. When she called again, Desert Rain answered with the call of the NightHawk.

Desert Rain watched as the women made their way across the open prairie in single file. She knew that this would have been the way they had marched all the way from the enemy's camp. If they walked in single file, anyone seeking to determine how many of them had passed that way would be thwarted. Even an experienced tracker would have trouble telling for sure if more than three people were on the same trail. It was a trick as old as time, so much so that it had become instinctive for the People.

There were only six women. Crow Woman led the party, and as they made their way across the meadow, Desert Rain tried to make out the faces of the women behind her. She recognized the two directly behind Crow Woman as younger women from her clan, but the next two were not familiar. Desert Rain strained her eyes to make out the face of the last woman in line. The woman was bracing herself on the shoulders of the one in front of her and shuffling her feet as she walked. At last she could see the woman plainly.

"*Shima!*" Desert Rain shouted with glee. Wind Song looked up and smiled as her daughter ran to her side. "Mother, you are hurt?"

"No, my daughter, but the last few days have not been kind to my legs and feet."

Desert Rain placed her mother's left arm over her own shoulder. "Let me assist you, my mother. Lean on me."

The woman Wind Song had been leaning on moved under the other arm and the two women braced her up as they continued across the field.

Desert Rain had not paid much attention to the unknown woman, focusing mostly on her mother's needs, but now the two women glanced into each other's eyes. "Chloe? Is that you?"

The young woman smiled. "Yes, my sister."

Desert Rain smiled in return. It was Chloe, Yellow Dog's wife. Yellow Dog had left home to live with Chloe's people along the Gila River. It was a small clan called the Gileños because of their camps along that river, but they were all Apache. They were all kin.

It was a bittersweet reunion and Desert Rain had many questions. The six women sat down wearily under the trees, well away from the edge of the clearing so as not to be seen easily.

Desert Rain spent some time inquiring about her mother's welfare. The older woman was tired, but seemed to be in good spirits.

"Are my husband and brothers safe?" Desert Rain asked anxiously.

"Brothers?" Wind Song asked with surprise. "Broken Branch is among the prisoners and it was Spirit Walker who freed me, but Yellow Dog was not among his people who were captured."

"No, *shima*, Yellow Dog is among those who entered the camp last night."

Wind Song searched the face of each woman, looking for any sign that one of them had seen her oldest son.

When at last her gaze found Chloe's, the young woman smiled. "Yes, it was Yellow Dog who set me free," Chloe agreed. "He is a very brave warrior. He will save our People."

"Yes. He and Spirit Walker have formulated a plan and led the others off to free the People," Desert Rain added. "They will take the place of the women they have freed and lay an ambush for the blue coats. They are armed and ready to fight."

"How many warriors entered the enemies' camp?" Crow Woman asked anxiously.

Desert Rain thought for a moment before answering. "Fourteen . . . yes, fourteen in all."

"This is distressing news, my daughter," Wind Song said. "If fourteen entered the camp to take the place of the women, why were only six of us freed?"

"Perhaps there were others freed who have not yet arrived," one of the women suggested.

Desert Rain scanned the far tree line where the women had first appeared, hoping to see other shapes moving among the brush. "If so, I hope they arrive soon. We haven't much time before we need to be on the move ourselves."

"Where are we to go?" another woman asked.

Desert Rain knelt on the pine needles beside the other women. "It will not be an easy task ahead of us, my sisters. We have a very important job to do in assisting Spirit Walker in freeing the others. You must summon the warrior spirit in each of you. We cannot fail our People. Let us talk of our mission."

Broken Branch rolled over slowly as the first rays of light struck his face. He knew that at any moment, the sergeant would be around to rouse the sleeping prisoners.

It had been a rough few days since their capture, but yesterday had been by far the worst. After the horses were stolen, the soldiers had tried their best to drive the prisoners hard toward the white man's fort. The children, women, and older men were having a hard time keeping up with the others, and they were mercilessly struck with whips and gun butts in an effort to quicken their pace.

Broken Branch remembered thinking that some of the women, who were taking the worst of the lashings, could have moved a little faster if they had wanted to. It didn't take long to realize that some of them were simply buying time, making the trip take longer than it would normally have taken. He wondered if they sensed something that he did not. As a warrior, he was expected to be cognizant of his surroundings. But in this case, it seemed that the women could feel something about to happen better than he could. They were lagging behind, some of them suffering terrible blows, just to slow the column down. Why? What had he missed?

Broken Branch raised his head and looked over at his mother. She was lying on the ground, her back to him. The bonds that held his feet together had been tied to a mesquite bush. Broken Branch's hands were bound behind him too, but he managed to raise himself a little and look around. He wondered where the men were who had secured him so tightly the night before. He would surely be watched closely today, for now he was branded as a troublemaker.

He hadn't meant to rile the soldiers the day before, but he couldn't stand by and watch his own mother take a gun butt to the back either. Wind Song had tried different tactics the day before to slow the group's pace. In the early evening, she had feigned a stomach problem and had fallen to the ground. A rough-talking soldier had approached her and evidently ordered her to move on, though none of them understood his boisterous language. When she had remained on the ground, holding her stomach, the blue coat had raised his gun to strike her. The blow would have landed squarely in the middle of her back had Broken Branch not thrown himself between her and her attacker. The rifle butt had caught him just behind his right ear.

Broken Branch tilted his head to his right shoulder, brushing the blood-matted hair from his ear as best he could. It was tender, but he would live. He smiled to himself. It had been a hard blow, but he had taken it like a warrior. No blue coat was going to break his spirit, not now, not ever.

Looking around, he could see some of the soldiers beginning to gather around the fire circle. He glanced once again at the sleeping form of his mother. She had changed clothes during the night, he noticed, and somehow her hair was a little different. He blinked his eyes a few times to clear his head of sleep.

She was sleeping deeply, breathing heavily, but at least she wasn't hurt. *"Shima,"* he whispered softly. She didn't move. *"Shima,"* he repeated, a little louder than before.

When she didn't move the second time, he rolled over and picked up a small pebble with his lips. Sucking the pebble into his mouth, he took a deep breath and puffed up his cheeks. With a quick, short exhalation, the small stone shot from his mouth striking the old woman in the back. *"Shima,"* he called once more.

The old woman slowly rolled to face him. The clothes were his mother's, the hair style was that of an Apache woman, but the face that smiled back at him belonged to Spirit Walker.

Chapter Forty-six

"Check the ropes on the prisoners!" Garrett ordered, "Make sure everyone's secure before we set out!"

A dozen or so troopers began to weave through the captive male Apaches, making sure the ropes that bound their hands and hobbled their feet were tight around their wrists and ankles. Broken Branch winced as a soldier pulled on the rope around his wrists, already rubbed raw from the friction, swollen, and sore. Though his body was chafed and bruised, hope soared in his heart, for Spirit Walker was among them now.

As the soldiers marched their captives along the Gila River in the direction of Fort Bowie, Broken Branch tried desperately to make eye contact with Spirit Walker, but it was an almost impossible task. Spirit Walker played the part of a captured female Apache well. He was unimposing, seemingly shrinking his large frame into a submissive posture, head down, never attempting to speak or look directly at his captors. Broken Branch noticed that the wise Chokonen had even managed a shuffling step that mimicked Wind Song's almost exactly. Even in pain, Broken Branch had to smile at the charade.

"The noon sun's hot enough to scorch a hole in my hat," a young trooper said as he took a seat beside his four friends. Captain Garrett's men had been marching their captives along the river for hours and they were ready for a little hardtack and coffee. Gabriel Sanders always enjoyed being with his friends. He felt safe with them, even in this hostile environment.

There were buddies here, men like Ty Gardner. Only a couple of years older than Gabe, Ty had proven himself to be a good man to ride with and quickly became Gabe's best friend. He was always willing to lend a helping hand when someone was in a jam or otherwise encumbered with a task.

Randy Green and Jerry Lee had been friends since they were kids. Growing up in the Texas heartland, they had moved west and joined the cavalry together. They were inseparable and if you befriended one, you were obligated to accept them both. There was just no way to come between them.

Then there was Jesse Evans, by far the roughest of the lot. He was somewhat of a rogue. After enlisting at Camp Grant, the rumor spread that he was merely joining up to avoid the law. Word was that he and a vagrant from Santa Fe, a William Antrim just called "The Kid" by most people, were accused of stealing some supplies from a dry goods store in town. Nothing ever came of the accusations and it seemed that Jesse was home free. That is, until now. For all his bravado, Jesse seemed as vulnerable as the rest of them.

"It's sure a hot one," Ty agreed. "I reckon Sergeant Hoyle must be feelin' it too," he said as he pointed toward the river.

Sergeant Hoyle had removed his heavy cavalry boots and waded into the river. Standing knee-deep in the red water of the Gila, he pulled a chewed cigar from his pocket and plopped it in his mouth.

"Wonder what he's thinkin' about?"

"Ah, Gabe, you know what he's thinkin' about," Ty said with a grin. "He's wonderin' if he's ever gonna see that pretty senorita he left back at Ft. Bowie again. Hell, he's wonderin' if he's even gonna see tomorrow, what with towin' a passel of captured 'Paches 'cross Indian land like this."

"Yeah, I've been wonderin' that myself."

"Don't worry 'bout that none, Gabe," Ty said. "There ain't nothin' gonna stop us from reachin' that fort. Hell, if'n the 'Paches swoop down on us, I'm ready to give 'em the whole lot and hightail it into the brush."

"That's treason, ain't it?" Gabe asked.

"That's survival, my friend, merely survival."

"I'll tell you one thing," Randy said in a low tone, "whoever it was that took our horses did us a huge favor."

"How do you figure that?" Ty asked with amazement.

"C'mere and I'll tell ya."

The five men huddled closer together as Randy began his explanation. "Me, Jerry, and Jesse were on guard that night when the horses got took."

Jerry and Jesse nodded.

"Yeah? So?" Ty prodded.

"So . . . they coulda kilt us all, but they didn't. They coulda slit our throats where we stood, but they didn't."

"Ah, how do you know that?" Ty asked. "They just wanted them horses. They weren't nothin' but thieves."

"I'll show you how I know that!" Randy reached for the knot that held the bandanna in place around his neck. Slowly, he loosened the knot and pulled the scarf away from his chin. A thin red line ran from just below his left ear to his Adam's Apple. "See that mark? That there's where a knife was pressed against my neck. The Injun that held it had me dead to rights."

Jerry and Jesse had obviously known about the incident, but it was news to Ty and Gabe. Ty craned his neck for a closer look. "I'll be damned!" he remarked. "Why'd he let you live?"

Randy covered the mark again with the cloth and retied the knot. "I don't know exactly. He said that he didn't want to hurt anyone. That he just wanted the horses and his people."

"He said that?" Gabe asked anxiously. "You understood him?"

"Of course I understood him," Randy said. "He spoke English to me."

"English? A 'Pache spoke English to you?" Ty asked.

"I figure it was an Injun. It smelled like an Injun, but it moved like a ghost."

"Well, I'll be hanged!" Ty said, looking around. "Do you reckon they're watchin' us right now?"

"You betcha," Randy answered. "I damn sure guarantee it, Ty, and I ain't a fightin' no ghosts."

"I'll tell you a thing," Jesse said as he rose to his feet, "when this is over, I'm headin' for New Mexico. I can't get shed of this country fast enough."

"Sergeant! Sergeant!"

The call brought Sergeant Hoyle out of his reverie. He turned toward the nearest bank. "Yeah, Trooper, what is it?" he asked the skinny recruit.

"Sergeant, we seen some horses atop that ridge yonder."

"Damn!" Sergeant Hoyle waded quickly toward the soldier. "Get them Injuns up and encircle 'em. We'll have to make a stand at the river's edge."

The orders were followed and soon the prisoners found themselves herded like cattle and surrounded by armed cavalry men.

"This creek bank won't afford us much protection if'n they decide to rush us," Sergeant Hoyle told Captain Garrett.

"That's true, Sergeant, but if they do attack, we begin killing the captives. That will make them Apaches think twice before they attack us in force."

Hoyle smiled. "Feeling a little bloody, huh?"

"It's a bloody country, a bloody business, Sergeant. Tell the men."

"Yes, sir."

Broken Branch struggled against his bonds as he maneuvered his body in an attempt to get a better look around him. He found himself being crushed by other men, also bound hand and foot, who had been bundled together and pushed to the ground in front of the soldiers.

He didn't know exactly what to make of the situation. A few minutes before he was thrown on the ground, he had heard the blue coats begin to scramble for their weapons. One man had blown on a metal horn, obviously telling the others that there was danger. The blue coats had gathered all of the men first. They had made sure that the ropes around the men's feet and hands were tight, then forced them together at the edge of the river's bank. Women and children were placed in front of them and told to lie down in the dirt. Then, the men were pushed over the top of them, forming a bulwark for the soldiers to hide behind. Broken Branch could hear the readying of carbines and pistols behind him. He knew that the blue coats were expecting an attack. He also knew that the first to die would be the prisoners.

The mass of Indian prisoners was like a living, writhing blanket of flesh. Men were rolled and turned by the soldiers in order to give some of the less experienced men a place to rest their rifle barrels. Beneath the men, the children squirmed and crawled. Some of them cried silently, but all of them sought the protection of the older men and women. The women quietly held their children and supported the men from below. Tension was strong and panic tugged at their hearts, but they knew that if they were to survive, they must keep their wits about them and assist in any way possible.

There was movement beneath Broken Branch and he felt as

if he would fall in among the women and children. His hands were tied behind his back and there was no way for him to support himself if a hole was created under him. He felt the person move under his left shoulder and he began to pitch forward and to his left. He closed his eyes, sure that he was about to tumble forward onto his face. Suddenly, a strong hand pushed his shoulder back into place and righted him once again. When he opened his eyes, he was face to face with Spirit Walker.

Chapter Forty-seven

"Spirit Walker, you are here," Broken Branch said excitedly.

"Yes, my friend, and I have brought others with me."

"Others?"

"Yes, from your brother's band."

"My brother? Yellow Dog?"

"Yes, Yellow Dog is among them."

Broken Branch looked about him for any sign of his older brother. He had not seen Yellow Dog in a long time. Just knowing that Yellow Dog was among the infiltrators brought him more comfort than he had imagined. Surely now there was hope.

"Listen, my brother, we must prepare for our escape," Spirit Walker said softly.

"Yes, how many of our people will attack and what are we to do when they come?"

"I'm afraid there will be no attack."

"No attack? But the blue coats ready themselves to fight,"

Broken Branch whispered. "They must have knowledge that the remainder of our People are approaching to rescue us."

"I wish that it were so, my little brother. What they have seen is merely some of the women on horseback along the ridges. Desert Rain leads them, making the blue coats believe that they are being followed."

"So there are no warriors?"

"None. The warriors that are with me are here, some among us, some still hidden. They dress as I do, as women. In this way, we can move about freely, unfettered. Though the warriors act as women, their dresses conceal weapons. We have begun to set some of the women free to join Desert Rain. I know that some of the women who have no small children here escaped last night. We will free others as the opportunity arises. Your sister brings the horses and gathers the women with her. Soon we will begin to free the warriors from their bonds. Slowly, we will prepare to make an escape by night. We will join Desert Rain and the horses and make our way to Mexico. We cannot let the blue coats get much closer to the white man's fort. That is why Desert Rain has caused this diversion. She had to give us time to work."

"How are you communicating with Rain?"

"I cannot, my brother. Not by words, that is. But, rest assured of this, Broken Branch—The Eagle and Hawk fly as one."

"Captain, look!"

Captain Garrett stood, straining his eyes in the direction of the first sergeant's pointing finger. Dust billowed through a draw that emptied onto the river's bank. There was a large force moving through the canyon, heading toward them at a fast pace. "And so they come! Prepare to execute the prisoners!" the captain barked.

Swiftly, Garrett grabbed Chief Five Dreams by the hair of his head and jerked him to his feet. Placing a pistol to the old chief's temple, Garrett whispered a stern warning. "If they attack, you die first. They'll change their mind when they see your brains splattered all over their women and children."

The chief seemed to understand perfectly the captain's threat. He never moved. With a face as cold as iron, Five Dreams began to sing, "Only the rocks live forever. . . ." It was his death song, and his eyes were on the mountains that he had called home—his beloved Apachería.

Sergeant Hoyle bent over and grabbed Broken Branch by the back of his belt. Leaning forward, Hoyle placed the tip of his Winchester rifle to the back of the young buck's head. "I been itchin' to put a bullet in you for some time now, Injun. Looks like I'm gonna get my wish."

"Sergeant, hold your fire until I give the order. We don't want to tip our hand too soon."

"Yes, sir," Hoyle said reluctantly.

The moment was not lost on Spirit Walker. Slowly, the Chokonen slipped his hand beneath his garment and slid a long-blade knife from its sheath. It was the very knife that had been given to him by Broken Branch, Cloud Maker, and Black Beaver. Spirit Walker's eyes focused on his target, the area just above the sergeant's belt. Tensing his stomach muscles, Spirit Walker prepared for action. He was ready and determined, but he knew he couldn't tip his hand too early either. If the captain gave the order to fire, Spirit Walker figured that with one powerful lunge, he could knock the barrel upward and slit the sergeant from stomach to neck with one smooth motion. It wouldn't be much different than gutting a deer. He hoped that the other warriors who brandished weapons would be as wise. He waited and listened.

"They're comin' on fast, Cap'n!" a young trooper yelled from the perimeter closest to the draw.

"So I see. Hold your line, men. We want them to see the

danger they're putting their people in. Maybe that will stave off the attack."

"And if not?" Hoyle asked.

"If not, we kill the prisoners first, then use the women and children as a battlement. That ought to give them something to think about."

"I can see the riders in front through the brush, Cap'n." the trooper shouted.

"Hold still, men. Wait for my order. It shouldn't be long now."

All along the bank, the men waited, each one gripping his rifle or pistol, intent on the Indian at the other end of the barrel. Some of them wiped sweat from their brows. Quite a few of them had never pulled the trigger on anything more than a squirrel or a snake. Captain Garrett knew that he had to instill a killer's rage in the younger soldiers. He wondered if today might be the last day for many of them.

"Men, now is the time to choose life!" he shouted, his voice building to a crescendo. "These murderous redskins won't take a bit of pity on you if they take you prisoner. We've treated our prisoners with only the respect they deserved, but for our humanity, they give us the threat of death. Do not think for a minute that they will treat you as well. There will be no surrender! We'll return only death for death. Men, ready your arms with confidence, we shall prevail!"

"Cap'n!" It was the young trooper again, shouting from his vantage point, closest to the mouth of the draw. "Cap'n, they're not Injuns!"

Captain Garrett stared in disbelief at the scout. "Not Injuns?"

"No, sir. They appear to be cavalry."

Suddenly, around the corner of a patch of mesquite, near the entrance to the draw, four riders burst forth. They wore the blue uniforms of the United States Cavalry. The sun glittered off the insignia worn on the cap of the lead rider.

"Secure the prisoners!" Garrett ordered. "We've been reinforced!"

Captain James Jackson held a hand skyward, halting his advancing troops. The rest of his unit cleared the draw and pulled in behind the lead four. Jackson had hoped to catch up with Garrett's force along the river, but the sight that met his eyes was something he had never imagined. All along the banks of the Gila, soldiers were pushing, shoving, and beating their male prisoners with the butts of their rifles. The women and children were piled one on top of the other like cordwood. It was a sickening sight.

Jackson watched through narrowed eyes as a tall, red-haired captain stepped forward and addressed him, "Boy, am I glad to see you."

Jackson could hardly contain his ire. "What the hell is going on here, Captain?"

Garrett looked about him as casually as if he were surveying the activities of a country picnic. "Just taking care of some dirty business," he said with a wave of his hand. "We thought you were the rest of the tribe coming to save them."

"And you were going to use the women and children to stop the bullets?" Jackson asked with indignation.

Garrett's blue eyes flashed fire as he removed his hat and beat the dust from its brim with a bandanna. "I'll tell you something, Captain, if you'd been Geronimo, there ain't much I wouldn't've done to save my men."

"I suggest you take a little care with those prisoners, Captain. Geronimo just might be watching." Jackson handed his reins to his first sergeant as he stepped down from his mount. "Or someone even more dangerous," he added as he stepped around his horse and started toward the captives.

Placing his hat squarely on his head, Garrett kept stride with Jackson as he walked. "Captain Garrett, Fort Bowie," the tall captain offered.

"Captain Jackson, Fort Lowell," Jackson returned.

"Ah, I've heard of you."

"And I, you."

"Really?" Garrett asked, his arrogance showing on his face. "What have you heard?"

Jackson stopped and faced his counterpart. "I've heard that you seek glory. Some say you have the brains and talent to find it. Personally, I think you're just another bootlick, looking to make points for promotion. And I think you'd sacrifice the lives of all of your men to get it."

Garrett's lip curled in anger as he pointed his finger at Jackson's chest. "I don't give a damn what you think, Captain. All I care about is getting these redskins back to Fort Bowie."

"I've a good mind to lash you to a pole and drag you back to Fort Bowie myself."

"Let me remind you, Captain Jackson, that this is my command and these are my prisoners."

Jackson looked around him. "Where are your horses, Captain?"

"They were stolen in the night."

Jackson pointed to his mounted troopers and smiled. "Then let me remind you, Captain Garrett, that this is my command and these are my horses."

Chapter Forty-eight

Jackson's men had dismounted and begun to form a rope corral for their horses as Jackson surveyed the situation. It would be tricky indeed to march this many captives all the way to Fort Bowie, which he figured would still take two or three days at the slow pace they would have to set with this many women and children. He shook his head when he thought of Garrett losing his horses to the Indians. Then he remembered that he, too, had been tricked in much the same way.

As he thought, he watched as the male captives were huddled together and linked to each other by a long piece of strong rope. The women and children were being gathered as well, but one trooper seemed to be having trouble with an old woman. The old squaw had fallen to the ground and a young trooper was being none too gentle in helping her to her feet.

"Get up, you old squaw! Get up!"

The woman seemed to be bent over in pain, holding her stom–

ach and barely able to reach a kneeling position before the trooper slapped her across the face with a gloved hand.

"Get up! I'm tired of foolin' with ya!"

Jackson stepped up and grabbed the trooper's arm before a second slap could be landed. "That'll be enough, son. I think she gets the point."

The captain reached down and grabbed the woman's shoulder. It was firm, the muscles firmer than he would have imagined a squaw's muscles to be. Slowly, the old woman rose to her feet, facing him. Jackson instinctively reached out and touched the woman's stomach, feeling for the wound he thought her to be protecting. It wasn't a wound he felt, however, that met his touch. It felt like a knife.

Startled, Jackson looked up into the face of the woman. It was the eyes that immediately caught the captain's attention. They were deep, extremely dark, penetrating, yet smiling. They weren't the eyes of a squaw. His mind began to race as he peered into the dark pools. He had seen those eyes before. A shiver danced up his spine. It was Spirit Walker.

"She comes!" Crow Woman cried.

"Is she alone?" Dancing Waters asked from the shallow valley below.

"Yes, she rides alone!"

Dancing Waters turned to the other women gathered with her. "Desert Rain comes. We will have news soon."

Wind Song watched Desert Rain ride into the draw with the confidence of a warrior. She sat tall and proud in the saddle. Wind Song could not remember having ever seen her daughter display the leadership qualities she had observed on this day. Desert Rain had organized the women, fed them, comforted them. As more women had found their way to the group, Desert Rain had convinced them that the plan, created by Spirit Walker and Yellow Dog, could work, would work. She had instilled in them all a sense of pride. They were *Teneh*, the People, and they would not be easily defeated. Spirit Walker would see to that, but there was also much for the women to do. For the first time in Wind Song's memory, the men's lives would depend on the swift actions of the women. Wind Song looked on in wonder at her approaching daughter. She rode like a hawk in flight.

Dancing Waters watched as Desert Rain reined her pony to a halt and swung deftly from its back. The horse stepped away to a patch of green grass and began to graze as Desert Rain addressed the women.

"I'm afraid I have some bad news," she said, her face showing her concern.

"What is it, my daughter?" Wind Song asked anxiously. "Have they killed some of our People?"

Desert Rain shook her head. "No, *shima*, they have not."

"What could be worse than that?" Dancing Waters asked.

"More blue coats have arrived. They bring horses and more men than we can possibly hope to fight."

The draw fell silent. Dancing Waters looked at Desert Rain. Surely this presented an insurmountable problem.

After a long pause, Dancing Waters spoke again. "What do we do now? I cannot bear the thought of losing my husband and son."

Desert Rain stepped up beside the older woman and placed a caring hand on her shoulder. "I know you have risked much in leaving your son behind."

For the first time, Dancing Waters allowed herself to cry. It had been difficult to make the decision to leave Beaver Tail behind with her husband. When she had been given the opportunity to escape, she had not been given much time to make such in important decision. If she had stayed to care for her son, she would yet be a prisoner, helpless, at the mercy of her captors. She had decided to escape, to be free, to possibly help rescue not only her son and husband, but her People. The result of that decision weighed heavily on her heart as she wept.

"Dancing Waters, we will do everything we can to see that all of our People have their freedom again," Desert Rain assured her.

"But, what . . . what can be done?" Dancing Waters asked through her tears, "What can we possibly do against even more blue coats?"

The same question was on the lips of every woman present and the buzz of their concern rose in Desert Rain's ears.

"My sisters," Desert Rain said loudly, quieting the crowd, "My sisters, we can and will do what our people expect us to do. We will not give up, we will fight. But the first enemy we must conquer is fear.

"You fear that there is nothing we can do that will help our people. Let us slay that enemy now. There is something we can do. First, we can trust our men. Among those held by the White Eyes, there are warriors. Warriors who, though bound, are not enslaved. I tell you that it is impossible to capture the Apache heart and mind. They will plan, they will not be discouraged. Spirit Walker . . . Yellow Dog . . . Broken Branch . . ."

"Black Beaver . . ." Dancing Waters added.

"Yes, Black Beaver . . ."

"Chief Five Dreams . . ." Wind Song said, her spirit beginning to rise.

Soon every woman in turn was naming the men who were still held by the soldiers. With each man named, the women's voices rose in excitement. Desert Rain could feel the energy of the names. It was like lightning jumping from one heart to the other.

"They are all worthy warriors!" Desert Rain finally concluded.

"Yes! They are warriors!" the crowd began to cry.

"Then we cannot let them down with our worries and fears!" Desert Rain shouted.

"No. We cannot," came the reply from the women.

Desert Rain raised her hand to silence them once again. "We must help them. We will appeal to the *Gan*. We will ask for help from the mountain spirits."

The women quieted and looked in wonder at Desert Rain. Finally, one of them said, "We have no shaman among us. Who shall make the appeal?" The questioner was Crow Woman, who had arrived from her scouting point atop the rocks. "Without a shaman, how can such a thing be done?"

Wind Song stepped forward, every eye on her as she spoke. "My sisters, we have a shaman among us."

Again, the women began to murmur, looking around in hopes of seeing the shaman to which Wind Song had referred.

"Who? Who is this shaman you speak of, Wind Song?" Dancing Waters asked anxiously.

"It is my daughter—Desert Rain."

"Desert Rain? How can this be?" Crow Woman asked.

"It is true, my sister," Desert Rain explained, "I have accomplished my vision quest. I have been blessed by a shaman—my husband, Spirit Walker. He has told me that I will be a leader of my People, a shaman as he is."

"This may be true, little sister," an older woman interrupted, "but do you know how to appeal to the *Gan?*"

Desert Rain had to admit to herself that she had not been completely prepared for that task. It had not occurred to her that such a thing might be required of her this soon. She wondered, silently, if she could perform a ceremony that would accomplish anything at all, much less actually appeal to the powerful mountain spirits.

She paused for only a moment, realizing that, if nothing else, she had to fan the flames of hope among the other women. "I do," she said, holding her head high. "I will do so tonight. I will take my journey to the top of the rocks at midnight. I will sing there 'The Song on the Midnight Wind.' I will take with me the names of our warriors. I will make my appeal and I know that I will be heard."

"Let it be so, my daughter. May the Great Spirit be with you." Wind Song embraced her only daughter as her tears fell upon Desert Rain's tunic. "I am so proud of you."

Desert Rain lifted her gaze to the clouds overhead. From among the floating puffs of white, a darker shape emerged. It was a small, V-shaped object soaring on the breeze. When she heard the call of the hawk, her heart raced. "I hear you, my messenger," she whispered. "I will be brave."

Chapter Forty-nine

Jackson had his men pull back from the edge of the river to make camp for the night. Garrett had agreed that it was a good idea for at least three reasons: The trees would provide cover for the men if they were attacked during the night; the trees would also keep their campfire from being seen at too great a distance; and the ground cover would make it very difficult for someone to pass without notice.

As the campfire began to die and the men began to bed down for the night, Captain Jackson strolled casually to the outer perimeter of the temporary encampment. He was immediately spotted by one of the perimeter guards. "It's just me, son," Jackson said in a calm voice. "Just taking a walk to clear my head before I turn in. Continue on your rounds, I'll be fine." The guard nodded, turned and walked away.

The darkness had always had a soothing effect on Jackson. He thought back to his childhood. He would often take long walks in the night after his chores were done. His father owned a nice piece of land along the Colorado River in Texas. They weren't poor, but they never had much to boast of in the way of material goods. Jackson remembered his walks along the river with the greatest fondness. It was while walking and listening to the rhythm of the water on the rocks that he had decided to join the United States Cavalry.

He had joined the cavalry because he wanted to help people. He knew that the West was expanding and with every settler heading West, the army would need more troops to protect them. And now, here he was in Arizona, the heart of Apache territory. It wasn't the dream he had expected.

Sure, he had seen atrocities perpetrated by the Apache, but he had seen the same kinds of things perpetrated by his own people. It seemed that there were no clear-cut lines between good and evil out here on the plains. It was getting increasingly difficult to tell the good guys from the bad guys. If the Apache wanted to live in peace, in their own mountains, farm their own lands, raise their own horses, kill their own food, could that really be so bad? Why not just leave them alone and insure the safety of their lands in the same manner as the lands that the white settlers were homesteading?

Jackson pondered these things as he stood in the darkness. He glanced back toward the firelight, but it was dim now, barely visible through the trees. A heavy cloud cover hid what was left of the waning moon. Everything was black.

"I knew you would come," Jackson said softly. The words he spoke surprised even him, for he had heard nothing, seen nothing, but he had definitely felt a presence.

Slowly, a figure rose from the ground. The ghostly, dark figure grew up from the underbrush in front of him until the shape of the man was recognizable.

"Captain James Jackson, U.S. Cavalry," a familiar voice stated. The words caused Jackson to smile. He wasn't exactly sure why, but he smiled. Perhaps it was the tone of the voice, calm, unafraid, not in the least bit intimidating.

To Jackson, the most interesting part of this encounter was that he felt absolutely no fear. He had felt the knife Spirit Walker concealed beneath his disguise. He knew that if the wily Apache had wanted to kill him just now, he could have done it. Why was there no feeling of danger on his own part? Why had he smiled?

"Spirit Walker, my friend." he said calmly. "I knew you would come."

Spirit Walker stood motionless in the darkness.

Almost a full minute passed before Jackson spoke again. "We have a serious situation here, Spirit Walker. I would advise you to let us take you peacefully on to the fort. I can assure you that your people will not be harmed. I will personally insure your safety."

"Are these your new words of life?"

Jackson hesitated for a moment before answering. "They are the only words I can offer," he said slowly, wondering within himself if, in fact, they were the only option.

"I hear in these words, Captain James Jackson, U.S. Cavalry, only death for my People, no life. Without freedom, the spirits of the young men will die. They will forget what it was like to ride freely, hunt freely, live freely. The elders will yearn for the past that the young will never know. Our language, our history, our heritage and culture will die with the old."

"No, Spirit Walker, you will pass it down. Generation after generation will hear of the bravery of Spirit Walker, Cochise . . ."

"Geronimo? Will they hear the truth about these men or just what the white eyes choose to tell them? Will they be proud to be Apache or will they bow their heads in shame, cut their hair, speak the white man's tongue and forget their own? Will they live like cattle and grow to love it?

"The warrior heart will die and within the young will beat only the heart of a slave who will depend on the white man for his very existence. He will look to the blue coats for his food, shelter, and clothing. When hungry, he will extend his hand to his captors, begging for a piece of their meat, instead of extending his hand to his bow and hunting his own. He will forget his ways, become idle. When cold, he will beg to be covered by the white man's cloth, instead of preparing hides to make his own blankets. He will forget these things and become lazy. I see no life in these new words, only death."

"It doesn't have to be so, Spirit Walker. Your people will have schools. They will be educated, learn to read."

"I have heard that in these . . . schools . . . they must speak the white man's language only. Is this true?" Slowly, Spirit Walker sank into a crouched position as he awaited the captain's reply.

"Yes," Jackson whispered.

"Yes, what, Captain?"

Jackson whirled at the sound of the sentry's voice. Turning, he saw the young trooper standing only a few yards behind him and to his left. Quickly, the captain looked back toward where he had last seen the Apache, but there was no sign of him. "Nothing, Trooper, I was just talking to myself."

"Oh, I see. Well, Captain, you might want to be getting to bed soon. It looks like the cloud cover's going to keep it pretty dark tonight. You might not have much light to see with, seein' as how the campfire's dyin' so fast."

"Thanks, son, I'll keep that in mind. Just tryin' to work out a few things first. Tossin' some ideas around in my head. We want to make it safely back to the fort, you know."

"Don't I know it," the trooper said, his voice a bit shaky. "I'll be glad to put these woods behind me. I keep hearin' things."

"Hearing things?"

"Yeah. I hear things, but never see nothin'. Captain, do you believe in spirits?"

"Spirits?"

"Yeah. If I didn't know better, I'd think the woods were full of 'em."

"Well, son, you walk your rounds and don't you worry none about the spirits."

"Yes, sir. I'll come back in a little while and make sure you're all right."

"Thanks, son."

Jackson watched as the perimeter guard walked slowly off into the darkness. The air was still, the night quiet. Jackson strained his ears for any sound, anything to indicate that Spirit Walker was still in the vicinity. He heard nothing.

Figuring that the Apache had left, Jackson turned back toward the main encampment, but jumped at Spirit Walker's voice.

"What will you do, Captain James Jackson, U.S. Cavalry?"

Jackson froze in place and spoke into the darkness, not knowing exactly where Spirit Walker was standing. "I don't know," he admitted.

"Yet you know that I cannot let my People be taken to the white man's fort."

Jackson turned in the direction of the voice this time, finding the warrior standing only a few feet away from where the trooper had once stood. "I know."

"And you know that I could have killed the blue coat just now."

"This, I also know. Why didn't you?"

"Because I, too, bring you my words of life. Just as before, I will harm none of your men if you will let my People go."

"Can you be sure of this?" Jackson asked.

"Yes."

"Are the 'spirits' the trooper is hearing your people moving through the woods?"

"Do you believe in spirits, Captain James Jackson, U.S. Cavalry?"

It was an odd question, Jackson thought. He had avoided the question once before, but he felt compelled to answer it now. "Yes."

"All around you and your men are the spirits of our ancestors. I walk with them, talk with them, we are one. They protect and advise our People. The old ones listen to this advice, the young ones sometimes hear only their own voice and ignore the spirits. This causes bad things to happen to the People. We must listen and be brave enough to believe them."

"And what are they telling you, Spirit Walker?"

"That we must live . . . freely."

"Where? It is not possible to live as you once did. There are settlers moving into this area. Settlers will bring more soldiers, more forts for protection."

"We will move south."

"South?"

"Yes. We will move into Mexico. We will make our peace there."

"When?" Jackson asked anxiously.

"Tomorrow we will follow the advice of our ancestors."

"How? How will you free yourselves, Spirit Walker?"

"Tomorrow, Captain James Jackson, U.S. Cavalry, the Desert Rain will fall upon you and you will know."

"What? What does that mean?" Suddenly, a twig snapped somewhere to Jackson's left. He turned quickly to see the sentry once again approaching, but this time the trooper was running.

"I saw him!" the guard yelled as he stopped and leveled his gun at his shoulder. "Hold still, Captain, I'll get him!"

"No!" Jackson yelled as he made a lunge for the soldier's weapon. Knowing he was too far away to reach it, Jackson flinched in anticipation of the gun's report.

"Damn," the trooper exclaimed as he lowered his rifle. "He moved too fast. I can't get a clear shot through the trees. Sure would've been good to have fresh meat in the morning."

"Fresh meat?" Jackson asked in wonder.

"Yes, sir. From the deer, sir. Didn't you see him? He was standin' right there, plain as day."

Jackson laughed nervously. "Yes, son, the deer. I saw him."

"Why didn't you want me to shoot 'im, sir?"

"Oh, well, I . . . I just didn't want you to wake everybody up. If you'da fired that shot, the rest of the company might have thought we were under attack."

The trooper looked back over his shoulder at the encampment. "Oh, right. I didn't think about that, sir. I was just thinkin' about that fresh meat."

"I understand, son." Jackson walked up to the trooper and patted him on the shoulder. "You're doin' a fine job, son. Keep up the good work. I'm goin' to bed."

"All right, Captain. Goodnight."

"Goodnight, son."

•

Chapter Fifty

Desert Rain walked alone along the top of the rocky ridge. The night was dark. A heaviness hung in the air, but it was not just the dampness of the coming rains that embraced her, it was the weight of the situation that pressed upon her heart.

Stopping at the northernmost edge of the finger ridge, she peered into the darkness, trying to make out the outline of the river. She remembered the many times that she and Arm Bow had stood on the high trail overlooking the valley near their village. She could almost hear his voice as they watched the valley shadows play beneath them, "It's alive," he would say. He had also never tired of watching nature spring to life each morning, bringing with it the promise of a new and glorious day. She wondered what he would say to her if he were with her now. Tears began to trickle from the corners of her eyes, but there was no time for such things. Not now. There was much to do.

Wiping her cheeks with the sleeve of her tunic, she turned

her face toward the eastern sky. "What must I do?" she asked. "Where do I begin?"

There was no audible answer, but her hand immediately went to her medicine bag. She had carried the bag ever since her vision quest with Spirit Walker. He had helped her to collect some of the items in the bag; others she had gathered on her own. It was an odd mixture of powders, feathers, beads, and bones. She had placed some of the things into the bag not even realizing why. Somehow she just knew that they belonged there.

She sat on the ground, crossing her legs in front of her, and opened the bag. Taking out a small pouch, she untied the cord around its top. Closing her eyes, she again lifted her face toward the heavens. She tried to clear her mind, let her heart tell her what to do next. Her finger dipped into the pouch, then touched the outside corner of her right eye. She continued the process of dipping and touching her face in various places. She could feel the hodentin cling to her skin with each touch. It felt like raindrops covering her face.

Eyes still closed, she rose to her feet. Instinctively, she turned to the north. She didn't have to guess which way to turn. Somehow she just knew. She retrieved a pinch of the powder from the bag and sprinkled it before her. She turned and repeated the action to the south, then east, then west.

"I appeal to the spirits of the four winds," she said out loud. "Bring the *Gan* to the aid of the People. We are in need. Without them, we shall perish."

The night winds began to blow from the north, rising from the river below. It was a warm wind that brought a sound to her ear. She wasn't sure but it seemed to say, "We shall not perish."

Turning to the north, she opened her eyes. Rising from the rocks before her was at least one shape, but maybe more. "The *Gan*," she gasped. Falling to her knees in reverence, she bowed her head toward the ghostly shape approaching her. She knew that she must make the appeal with a humble spirit, she must not insult them at any cost.

Suddenly, there were hands on her shoulders, lifting her to her feet. They were warm, large, caring hands. She rose, head still bowed.

The arms enfolded her and she wrapped her arms around the bare back of a strong man. It was comforting . . . and familiar. She nestled her head against his chest and drank in his strength. She felt that she could stand there forever. It was exhilarating.

After a while, she lifted her face and smiled. "Spirit Walker, you have come to me."

"Yes, my Little One, I have come."

"Do you hear it?" Crow Woman asked as she rolled over and tugged on Wind Song's tunic in the night.

Wind Song shifted on her bed of pine straw and brushed her long hair away from her ear. "Yes," she said with a smile. "They are the voices of the *Gan*. They chant to the four winds."

"It is a chant of protection for our People," Crow Woman added.

"Yes, a chant of protection."

"Desert Rain has done a great deed here tonight."

"Indeed she has."

"All will be well in the morning," Crow Woman concluded as she rolled onto her back and tried to resume her sleep.

Wind Song's heart was full for her daughter. Tears of joy flowed freely as she listened and laughed silently. "Yes, all will be well in the morning."

"What the hell is that?" Beyer asked, sitting upright on his bed-roll.

Captain Jackson came awake immediately, raising himself to his elbows. He listened intently for a moment before he answered quietly. "Sounds like chanting."

"It sounds like hundreds of chanting Injuns," the sergeant said with alarm.

Jackson looked around him. The rest of the camp was still. Not one soldier stirred, including Hoyle and Garrett. "Are we the only ones hearing it?" he asked with wonder.

Beyer also took a moment to look around. "How can they not?"

"I don't know, but it seems no one else has noticed it."

"Surely the sentries must be hearing it."

"If so, they would be rushing in to wake Garrett and he would even now be doubling the guard."

"Yes, sir, that he would be. Maybe you should wake him."

"No, Sergeant. I think not. That's why we're the only ones hearing it."

"I don't understand, sir."

"Never mind, Sergeant, get some sleep. Looks like the rain's coming; there won't be much sleep after that."

"Do you understand what is to be done?"

"Yes, Spirit Walker, I understand."

Spirit Walker brushed Desert Rain's hair back from her face. She filled his heart to overflowing. In the dim light offered by the partially hidden moon, he could make out the spots of hodentin that flecked her soft cheeks. They looked like small raindrops on her skin. "You are my Desert Rain," he said softly, lovingly.

"And you are my warrior," she replied.

Bending forward he kissed her softly, felt the passion rise in his loins. The matter of planning was over. The mission was a dangerous one; now was the time to show his wife just what she meant to him, for there might never be another time.

Holding his lips tightly to hers, he reached down and grasped her tunic at the waist. As he pulled back, he lifted her tunic over her head and dropped it to the ground at his feet.

*   *   *

The night wind caressed her skin as Desert Rain stood naked before her husband. He was the perfect figure of an Apache warrior. In his youth, he had ridden with the best and most noble warriors of the People. He had saved the lives of many, taken the lives of others. He had fought and loved with equal determination. It was just such determination she saw reflected in his eyes now. It was the look of a man who wanted her to know the depth of his love.

He had worn only a loincloth to the encounter with her on this night. She reached for the cord that secured it around his waist and released it. The breechclout fell easily to the ground and he stepped toward her, enfolding her in his arms once again.

Their bodies molded into one form in the dim moonlight as they held each other. Spirit Walker broke the embrace long enough to spread Desert Rain's tunic on the ground beneath them. Laying her back gently on the calf-hide garment, he began to kiss her neck tenderly.

She moaned as his lips moved down onto her shoulders, working down onto her breasts. She ran her fingers through his tangled hair as he kissed along her stomach. She writhed in pleasure beneath him as he carefully picked out each and every spot he knew would cause her to giggle with delight. He knew her so well. He cared for her so much.

She pushed him playfully back into a kneeling position and sat up to cover his lips with her own. Curling her legs under her, she kissed him deeply, wanting him to feel the same sensations that she was feeling. His lips were firm, yet soft. She ran her fingertips over his biceps, felt his muscles quiver at her touch as she ran her hands down his arms and over his chest, causing him to release a sigh of pleasure. She kissed down his chin, wrapped her arms around his back and let her lips play over his broad shoulders and chest.

Her hands passed smoothly down his lower back and around

his waist to his thighs. She felt the tense muscles of his legs, so powerful, so strong. Just touching him thrilled her as much as when he touched her. He was all man. Her man.

She kissed and nuzzled every inch of her husband until he could take it no longer. He pushed her back onto the tunic once again and she felt his weight press her firmly to the ground. The love they would make on this night would be the sweetest of all. The eagle and hawk became one.

Chapter Fifty-one

The rains came a couple of hours after midnight. At first it was just a light drizzle. Some of the men stirred, but the trees' thick foliage kept most of the rain from disturbing everyone's sleep. Everyone, that is, except Captain Jackson.

Jackson had awakened when the first drops of rain began to pelt the leaves of the trees overhead. That had been hours ago. Leaning back against his saddle, he now sat in the dimness of early morning. Checking his pocket watch, he figured that the sun should just now be beginning to throw an orange glow over the horizon. It would be, that is, if there wasn't so much cloud cover. Through the branch canopy above him, he could see that the rains were increasing and weren't about to burn off by midday. He grumbled to himself. It was already a nasty day and apt to get nastier.

The rains came harder less than ten minutes later. The camp was beginning to stir now as soldiers rolled out of their blankets, cursing the weather and everything else about being out in the field. Jackson smiled to himself, somehow comforted by the fact that they were suffering even more than he was.

Stiffly, he pulled on his boots and walked toward the river. At the edge of the tree line, overlooking the banks, he stopped to relieve himself. The morning light was grayish, the clouds thick and dark overhead. Visibility was only about a hundred yards, but he could see the edge of the river clearly as it ran along the banks.

The rain was falling harder now and the noise of the raindrops striking the trees masked any sounds that one might make if walking through the underbrush. Jackson noted that this would be a perfect time for Spirit Walker to make his escape. If he hadn't already.

He was just about to turn and check on the prisoners when a flash of lightning lit the area around him, followed by a crash of thunder. For a brief moment, his eyes caught a movement in the river. There was, no doubt about it, someone riding along the water's edge. He crouched behind some sagebrush, sweeping the shoreline for any other signs of activity.

Suddenly, at the very edge of the river, the rider appeared. He was broad shouldered, long haired, and covered with mud. He sat astride a black Indian pony. Jackson had to look closely to identify the features he knew so well now. It was Spirit Walker and he was painted for war.

The warrior sat still, surveying the tree line. Jackson watched and waited. He wondered what the wily Apache had in mind. It would be the perfect time to attack the sleepy camp, if there were enough warriors and if they were better armed than the soldiers. But Jackson knew that wasn't true. Jackson remained out of sight, but somehow he could feel Spirit Walker's gaze rest on him. It was an unsettling feeling, the feeling that Spirit Walker was touching his very soul. After a minute or so, Jackson could sit still no longer. He stood to his full height. The two men locked eyes.

Neither man moved a muscle until Jackson heard movement behind him. With catlike quickness, Jackson spun around, jerking his Colt revolver from its holster.

"Hold on there, Captain. I'm friendly."

It was Garrett. Jackson relaxed.

"But it don't look like he is," the red-haired captain continued. "How long's he been there?"

Jackson turned back to find Spirit Walker still sitting on horseback, still waiting. "He just rode up."

Garrett gazed up and down the river as far as the rains would let him see. "Can't be sure how many are out there, can we? Damn rain."

"Yeah. It doesn't rain often, but when it does it means it."

"What do you think he aims to do?" Garrett asked.

"I think he aims to get his people back."

Garrett turned and yelled over his shoulder. "Sergeant! Sergeant, ready for attack, I need some men up here! We got company!"

In a few minutes Hoyle and Beyer were standing beside their leaders, peering out from among the trees at the lone rider. Spirit Walker still had not moved.

"This is the eeriest damn thing I've ever seen," Beyer remarked.

"Yeah," Jackson agreed.

"I have my men all along the tree line. If he issues an attack, we'll be able to cut them down before they can get to us," Garrett said with pride. "Ain't no Injun gonna make it this far without a couple of bullets in 'im."

Jackson heard the plan, but wasn't sure it was the best one. After all, Spirit Walker must know that that's exactly what they would do. He would know that they could defend themselves almost without danger from their position inside the trees. There had to be something they were missing, something Spirit Walker knew that they didn't. The warrior had to figure that he had the upper hand in some way or he wouldn't risk his life and draw their attention.

It took only a second for Jackson's mind to react. He jerked his head in the direction of the prisoners. They were being held in a circle of trees, behind him and to his left. Since the appearance of Spirit Walker and the attention given to him by Garrett, no one had thought much about them. There were guards stationed around them, but everyone's attention had been drawn to the tree line. He could see the warriors, hands behind them, standing and watching also. It took only a moment for him to realize that they were all men. There were no women. No children.

"Captain Garrett," Jackson said softly, almost afraid to draw attention to his discovery.

"What?"

"You better look. . . ."

"Aaaaaaaaiiiiiiiiiiiiiiiiiiii," Spirit Walker cried.

It was a bloodcurdling yell and with it Spirit Walker set his pony in motion. He was running straight for the tree line.

Jackson had no more time to inform Garrett further that the attack, if that's what it was, was on.

Garrett gave the order, "Fire!"

Jackson's eyes widened as he anticipated the carnage to come. He could almost hear the crack the rifles would make as the bullets tore Spirit Walker's body to ribbons right in front of him. But the only noise was the sound of metal striking metal—hammers falling on empty cylinders. The clicking of empty weapons.

Spirit Walker reined his mount to a halt fifty feet from the tree line. Grinning, he tossed a handful of objects on the ground. Not one of the soldiers could make them out, but Jackson knew they were bullets.

Garrett cursed. "Reload your damn weapons!"

Spirit Walker turned his black horse and galloped off to the west as the surprised troopers began running for their saddles.

Suddenly the sounds of running horses invaded the forest all around them. Soldiers shouted and jumped for cover as a herd of bareback ponies thundered in among them. Jackson watched in wonder as the sentries who had been guarding the prisoners threw off their jackets and hats, revealing their long hair and tanned bodies. The "bound" prisoners tossed their ropes on the ground as they deftly swung aboard the running animals. One by one, they disappeared into the murky morning, yelling and whooping.

Not a single soldier managed to reload in time. Not one shot was fired. Somewhere among the running animals, Jackson caught sight of one lone rider. It was a woman, her face painted with bright yellow spots that resembled drops of rain. In her hand was a lance. To Jackson's surprise she pulled up for only a moment and sent the lance soaring in his direction. It embedded itself in the ground at his feet. The shaft bore six eagle feathers and was covered with yellow raindrops. In a moment, she was gone, disappearing into the rain-shrouded mist.

The tether line that had secured the horses Jackson and his men had ridden in had been cut. A few of the animals, not caught up in the stampede, were rounded up and brought back to camp. Garrett sat dejectedly on his bedroll. He had lost his horses, his prisoners, and surely his promotion.

Jackson, who had coordinated the effort of retrieving the horses, had recovered his own and about half of the others. He was sure that he would find even more as he made his way back toward Fort Lowell. There was no reason now for him to continue on to Fort Bowie.

"I demand that you help me recapture those Indians!" Garret screamed as Jackson approached.

"You demand nothing from me, Captain. You made enough blunders to last a lifetime already."

Garrett jumped to his feet. Puffing out his chest, he stood toe-to-toe with Jackson. "I demand satisfaction, Captain."

Jackson unbuckled his holster and let it drop to the ground. "If you mean that as a challenge, Captain, I'm ready when you are."

Garrett lunged forward and threw a vicious right hook at Jackson's jaw. Jackson ducked and countered with a punch to Garrett's midsection. The fight was on.

The soldiers gathered around the two men as they punched and grappled in the wet foliage. Cheering their respective leaders, the men watched as first one and then the other landed blows and kicks that would have dropped most men. When the fighting was done, Jackson stood wearily. Garrett lay face up in a puddle of water, his hair matted to his head, face bruised and bleeding. Garrett gasped for breath, inhaled a little water, and began to cough.

"Sergeant Hoyle," Jackson said softly, "when he recovers, I suggest you start your men back to Fort Bowie. We're going after the prisoners."

"Yes, sir."

Chapter Fifty-two

The wind whipped her hair and the rain stung her face, but still she rode on. Clear of the tangle of trees that offered protection from her enemies, Desert Rain raced toward the gathering point she had set for the People.

Before her rode the warriors she had helped free. They rejoiced in their newfound freedom, whooping and yelling, weaving their ponies in and out of the running herd like little boys on their first buffalo hunt. Their attitude was one of jubilation, yet there was one concern that held her own celebration in check. Where was Spirit Walker? Was he all right?

The ground before her running horse was being torn apart by the animals' hooves as they ran. The rains were falling hard and she realized that the muddy ground would hold their tracks for a long time after they had passed. It would not be hard for the blue coats to follow them. These thoughts added a sense of urgency to the situation. They would have to ride long and hard or risk capture once their enemy began the pursuit. She wondered how long it would be before the soldiers recovered enough to begin the chase. She wondered if the forced march to the white man's fort had only been prolonged.

Rounding the edge of a finger ridge that led away from the river, she drummed her heels on her pony's flanks, picking up the pace a little. She knew it wouldn't be long before she was at the rendezvous point. There, they could regroup and plan the rest of the escape.

She rode through canyons walled with cliffs streaming water from the hard desert rain. Throughout the summer, the sun had baked the ground into a solid floor of rock-hard dirt. Each year, as the rains began, signaling the coming of autumn, the desert floor was unable to soak up the water in order to prevent flash flooding. She knew it would be dangerous to stay long in the hilly draws.

As she rounded the last bend that would lead her to her destination, she heard a chant rising among the People. The chant made her heart leap. "Spirit Walker! Spirit Walker!"

The sight that came into view was a joyous one. The Apache, still chanting, were milling about, some catching the horses that were not yet ridden, some still on horseback pumping their fists in the air. Women and children were gathered on the rocks surrounding the small canyon, chanting loudly. Spirit Walker sat proudly on the back of his black stallion. Making his way to the front of the throng, he rode up beside a large rock. Halting the horse, he stood on its proud back and stepped off onto the boulder.

"Spirit Walker! Spirit Walker!" the chant continued.

Spirit Walker raised his hands. It took some time before the chanting stopped and the People calmed down enough for him to address the crowd. "My People," he began, "we have seen a great deed done this day."

"Yes, we have seen the wisdom of Spirit Walker and the defeat of our enemies," someone called out. Again, the crowd erupted in the chant.

Desert Rain, still sitting astride her pony, felt pride in her husband well up from deep within her. She couldn't help but think of the Spirit Walker she had first met. He had been a warrior who thought that his time was gone, that he was of no further use. Now, the People chanted his name, a name that would live on in legend.

When her eyes finally rested on her husband's face, she saw the beckoning look in his eye and the wave of his hand. The crowd parted as she rode toward Spirit Walker. Taking her hand, he assisted her onto the boulder beside him.

"This," he said as the chants faded once again, "is the one who has delivered the People!"

A hush fell over the valley, only the sound of the water falling upon the rocks could be heard as Spirit Walker continued to speak.

"It was Desert Rain who appealed to the *Gan* for your deliverance. She gathered and protected your women and children. She arranged for them to meet us in this place and assured that they were safely secured in these rocks. She stampeded the horses through the heart of the enemy's camp. As the only rider among the herd, she placed herself in grave danger, but risked no other life. This is not my day, my People. This day belongs to Desert Rain, for she has fallen hard on our enemies this day."

Desert Rain couldn't believe her ears. She stood proudly beside her husband as he led the chant, "Desert Rain! Desert Rain!" Her eyes welled with tears of joy as she noticed her mother and two brothers chanting even louder than the rest. It was a great day for them all.

"Captain Jackson, there just simply aren't enough horses for all of us," Beyer said.

"Noted, Sergeant. We have no choice but to divide our forces."

"Divide? We couldn't hope to recapture the prisoners with only half of a regiment. That would be suicide."

"Sergeant, I don't intend on recapturing them."

"Then what is your intention, Captain?"

"Surveillance. Simple surveillance. I will take a force of men and we will follow their trail, tracking them to their final destination. Once we have established their location, we'll report back to the fort. You will take the rest of the men, who must ride double, and lead them back to the fort immediately. Make a formal report to Colonel Graffe and prepare for my arrival."

The idea didn't set well with Beyer, but he had to admit that it was probably the only choice they had. Reluctantly, he agreed and set about selecting the men who would ride with Captain Jackson.

Within the hour, Jackson rode out with eleven men. He had no trouble following the Apaches' trail and headed into the rough hill country.

"There are more than enough horses to carry us into Mexico," Spirit Walker informed the People. "Desert Rain will lead the women and children to the mountain fortress of Pa-Gotzin-Kay. There, she will join with Tahza's band and await our arrival. For protection, half of the warriors will ride at her flanks, at a distance, yet close enough to render assistance if needed. The other half of the warriors will ride with me. We will lead the blue coats away from the main band heading for Mexico. We will join them later at Pa-Gotzin-Kay."

It was a good plan and the People accepted it wholeheartedly. Plans were set and the warriors prepared for the journey.

Everyone was busy with the preparations for the long trip to Mexico. Desert Rain was finally able to get Spirit Walker away from the warriors to address her private thoughts. "My husband, it will be no small thing to get past the white man's forts and into Mexico."

Spirit Walker looked deeply into her eyes. "This you can do, my Flower. Take the old trails. Travel in single file; it will be harder to determine the number of horses passing in that way. Though you will have many riders, it will appear to be a small force. The warriors who ride with you will warn you of any approaching danger, but you must ride as quietly as possible."

"And you will be along shortly to meet us at Pa–Gotzin-Kay?"

"Yes, my Flower, I will meet you there."

Desert Rain wrapped her arms around her warrior. "I can't bear the thought that something might happen to you, my husband. I would not be able to live without you."

Spirit Walker held her tightly to his chest. "Nothing will happen, Little One. I will return to you," he said, stroking her hair gently.

Slowly, she tipped her head upward and kissed him.

It was just before noon when Jackson's men came upon the rendezvous point the Apaches had used. The ground all throughout the canyon was chewed into a muddy mess by the multitude of horses that were now in the possession of the Indians. Jackson had taken it slow in following his prey, figuring that they might have had warriors waiting for them in the passes, set for an ambush. They had seen nothing, not so much as a scout upon the rocks. It was clear to Jackson that the Apaches sought only escape, not combat.

"Captain, we have a decision to make."

Jackson turned to face the trooper who had addressed him. "Tell me about it, Monroe."

"Well, sir," the young corporal began, "we've picked up sign that they've split into two bands."

"Two bands?"

"Yes, sir. A few have started into that draw yonder." He

pointed to the southeast. "A larger group has headed into that other one," he finished, pointing to the southwest.

Jackson cast a glance skyward. "This rain's still going to last for some time, Corporal. It's let up some, but it's not about to quit any time soon. We need to make a decision and get on with it. We can't stay long in these canyons—they're bound to fill with water soon."

"Yes, sir. Which way should we go?"

"I think we follow the larger group, Corporal. The smaller group may be just a diversion."

"Yes, sir."

Corporal Monroe had turned to go when Jackson suddenly called him back. "Corporal, I'm curious. How did you determine that one group was larger than the other?"

"It was easy, sir. The smaller group followed too closely one behind the other, couldn't be more than five or six ponies as far as we can tell. The other group is all spread out, riding at high speed."

"I see. Carry on, Corporal."

"Yes, sir." Monroe turned and walked toward the rest of the men.

Jackson stood for a moment, his eyes scanning the rocky ledges around him. "Spirit Walker, you are a crafty one. I hope we meet again."

Chapter Fifty-three

For two days, Spirit Walker's warriors had cut a wide swath through Arizona Territory. The rains, which had lasted throughout the first day, had allowed them to spread out and chew up more ground than they would normally have done. This made them appear larger in number and easier to follow. This had been the plan all along. With Desert Rain keeping her band in a thin narrow column, they would appear to be a smaller force and make it impossible for the white man to determine an exact number.

Several times over the past couple of days, Spirit Walker had strayed away from his main group of warriors. He had taken the time to double back, loop around the flanks, and observe the area around them from the highest point he could find. It was early on the third day that he had spotted Jackson and his men. A dozen blue coats, well-mounted and armed. Spirit Walker knew that he and his men were still at least one day from the

Mexican border. He had to slow the captain's approach. He set on a plan.

Jackson stopped to take a rest around noon. He had been three days tracking his quarry. The going had been easy, but he knew he couldn't let his guard down. He appreciated the cunning of the man he was tracking. He had sent two scouts ahead of him and watched closely as they returned.

"Sir, we have a small group of warriors disappearing into the trees about a mile ahead."

Jackson studied the scout's face. "How many?"

"I'd say a half dozen at least."

"Well, looks like we're close enough. Better check your weapons."

The tracks showed no more than seven or eight ponies traveling close together. Jackson figured it must be a scouting party for the main group. He had his men move carefully through the trees, sure that at any moment they would spot the warriors.

Jackson had informed his men that they were not to shoot if they encountered the Indians. "I just want to observe them. Find out where the main body is headed," he had told them. "There's no need for us to risk our lives or theirs at this point." His men had readily agreed. They were in no hurry to risk being captured or killed themselves.

One of the scouts held up a hand, motioning that he had seen movement through the trees. Captain Jackson halted the rest of the men. They sat quietly on horseback, listening intently for any sound that might give away the enemy's position.

Jackson watched as Monroe dismounted, tethered his horse to a sapling and crept forward through the underbrush. A few minutes later, he slipped back into view, pointed to his eyes and then in the direction he had gone, indicating that he had seen something up ahead.

Jackson pointed at the ground and swung his leg over the back of his saddle. The others followed suit and soon they were all on foot.

As they inched forward, moving tree to tree, they stayed low and kept their heads down. Jackson gave the silent signal to stop when they approached a small clearing.

In the middle of the clearing, a lone figure stood. He was dressed only in a breechclout, his forehead painted red with yellow lightning bolts on each cheek, his gray-streaked hair flowing freely. Around his waist was a dingy white sash connected to a lance, which was firmly embedded in the ground. In his hand was an elk-horn–handled knife. It was Spirit Walker.

Jackson stood and motioned for his men to stay down, "Don't move, men, I'll handle this one."

"But, Captain, he's armed," Monroe protested.

"Yes, Corporal, he is. If anything happens to me, you get the men back to the fort, pronto. You're the next ranking man. You're in charge, but don't, by any means, make contact with the Indians."

"But, sir . . ."

"Don't argue with me, Corporal. That's a direct order!"

"Yes, sir."

Jackson removed his hat, drew his gun, and stepped forward into the clearing.

This time, Jackson was the first to speak. "Spirit Walker, my old friend."

"Captain James Jackson, U.S. Cavalry. Have you come with words of death this time?" He nodded toward the gun Jackson held in his right hand.

"Spirit Walker, many things have changed since we first talked."

The Apache warrior cocked his head to the side and searched the captain's face with a wary eye. "What has changed? The blue coats still take the People and imprison them in their forts of wood. They still take our hunting grounds and give them to the white settlers. They still desecrate our sacred burial grounds. They still drive the People from the lands of their ancestors. What has changed? I see nothing."

Jackson stepped steadily forward, raising his pistol, leveling it at Spirit Walker's head. "I have changed, Spirit Walker. I have changed. When we first met, you dared me to shoot you. You begged me to shoot you. But that was when you had the advantage. You knew the gun was not loaded. I raised the gun then, because, somehow, I trusted you. Now, I have the advantage. Do you have the same trust?"

Spirit Walker's hand tensed on his knife. He had learned to throw a knife with deadly accuracy when he was just a youth. He knew that with one jerk of his wrist, he could send the blade directly into the young captain's heart. He'd done it before, in a similar situation. He could do it again. But this time was different. He looked long into the captain's face, saw Jackson's finger tighten on the trigger. He raised the knife and spun it into the ground at Jackson's feet. Jackson pulled the trigger. The gun was empty.

Jackson nodded as he brought his left hand out in front of him, palm up, fist closed. He turned the closed fist over slowly and opened his hand. Six bullets fell to the ground in front of him.

The situation was almost surreal, Jackson thought. He sat opposite Spirit Walker across from a small fire. Behind the captain sat his men, behind Spirit Walker sat about a dozen warriors. There were no arms. Both groups left their weapons with their mounts.

Spirit Walker had taken a pouch from his belongings and retrieved a small pipe. The substance he stuffed into the bowl was unknown to Jackson, but it had a sweet smell when the Apache lit it with a firebrand.

The warrior set the pipe to his lips and drew a deep breath. Blowing the smoke into the air, Spirit Walker waved his hand over his head, wafting the blue cloud over his face and hair. He handed the pipe to Jackson, who repeated the actions he had seen Spirit Walker perform.

They smoked until the pipe was empty, then Spirit Walker placed the pipe on the ground between the two of them. "Captain James Jackson, U.S. Cavalry, will you let my People live in peace?"

It was a direct question, and a fair one, Jackson thought. It was one that deserved a direct answer. "Yes, Spirit Walker, *I* will let your people live in peace. But it is not up to me, my friend. I alone cannot ensure their safety forever."

"I understand these things. There are white chiefs above you who would see the People wiped from the earth."

"Unfortunately, that is true. But I will guarantee you that I shall do whatever is possible to bring you peace."

"I believe your words, blue coat. My People are on their way to Mexico, there we will stay."

Jackson released a sigh of relief. At least he wouldn't have to worry about defending them in Arizona Territory. He knew his commission would be on the line for letting them go this long.

Spirit Walker read the young captain's reaction with ease. "Yes, we will live in Mexico . . . in peace."

"I wish you well, my friend." Jackson paused for a moment, looking deeply into Spirit Walker's eyes. "You know, Spirit Walker, I wish things could have been different. I feel that we could have become friends if it weren't for our cultures."

Spirit Walker tilted his chin forward, ever so slightly. "You are a noble warrior," he acknowledged, head high, "I would have been proud to ride with you."

"And I, you, Spirit Walker."

"You are welcome in my camp any time."

"When things calm down in the Territory, I will send word for you, Spirit Walker. I will invite you to visit me and we shall talk of a lasting peace."

"Let it be so," Spirit Walker said solemnly. "I wish it to be so."

"And I." Jackson extended his hand, Spirit Walker wrapped his hand around the captain's wrist and gripped it tightly. Jackson did the same.

"I will call you, 'He Who Shoots No More,' " Spirit Walker said.

"Let it be so," Jackson returned. "I wish it to be so."

As Jackson led his men onto the trail that would take them back to Fort Lowell, Monroe rode up beside his leader. "Sir, are you sure we did the right thing back there?"

"Son, there's one thing I've learned in my years of riding with the cavalry."

"What's that, sir?"

"An officer may not always make the right choice, but he can always live with a choice he makes from his heart. Not once, in all the time I've dealt with Spirit Walker, did he ever put any of my men in danger. I can't say the same about any other man who has had my company's fate in their hands. Many times, he could have killed me and my men, yet he always chose peace. I was glad to be able to make the same choice for him. He purposely placed himself in my hands. I made the choice from my heart. It's a choice I can live with, regardless of the consequences."

"Do you believe that they will go to Mexico and not cause any more trouble in Arizona Territory?"

"I believe it, Corporal. Only because I believe in The Spirit That Walks as a Man."

Chapter Fifty-four

It had taken longer than expected, but finally Desert Rain and her people crossed over into Mexico. As she surveyed the Mother Mountains, she couldn't help but wonder what her life would be like in the next couple of years. Would she have children? Would they even know or visit their homeland? Would they live in peace?

The warriors who had flanked Desert Rain's group throughout the arduous trip came riding in closer, reveling in the safety that Mexico afforded them. They no longer had to fear the *Pinda-Lick-O-Ye* and their blue-coated soldiers.

"We have arrived, my sister," Broken Branch said as he and Yellow Dog rode up beside her.

"Yes," she said, almost afraid to relax her guard and let the joy of the moment overtake her. "But we are not yet finished. We must continue on to Pa-Gotzin-Kay and the safety that Tahza can give us."

"Ah, yes, Tahza," Yellow Dog interjected. "I have met him. A few years ago, he came to visit our band. He is a man of peace."

"I have not met him," Desert Rain admitted, "but, I have met his wife Nod-Ah-Sti and their son Niño Cochise."

"Yes, he is named for his grandfather," Yellow Dog added.

Desert Rain looked about her, searching for Chief Five Dreams. She realized that now that they were in Mexico, and no longer concerned with the blue coats, he would want to take the leadership position once again. It was customary, during a dangerous situation, for a clan chief, like Five Dreams, to relinquish authority to a war chief, such as Spirit Walker. Once the situation returned to normal, the clan chief would once again take charge of the well-being of the People.

Desert Rain excused herself from her two brothers and approached Five Dreams. "My Chief," she began, "you will lead us to the mountain stronghold?"

Five Dreams recognized Desert Rain's attempt at diplomacy. Spirit Walker had placed a great honor on her when he announced that she would be the one to lead the People to safety. He knew that she felt out of place and was now trying to indicate that she had no desire to usurp his civil authority. She was indeed an honorable and humble woman. He smiled. "Desert Rain, you have greatly served your People. I thank you for your part in our survival. You will always hold a high standing in our clan."

"My chief, I could do nothing else. I only sought to see that those who had served me throughout the years were taken care of. I could not stand by and let my People be taken into captivity. Not at any cost."

Five Dreams cast a weary eye to the mountains ahead. "That will be our home now, Desert Rain. I will need help getting the People established, making them feel at home in our new surroundings."

"You can count on me and my family to help in everything."

"Do you think that Spirit Walker will stay with us? Do you really think that he will settle down?"

Desert Rain looked back over her shoulder as though wishing Spirit Walker were riding with them. "My chief," she said, "though I cannot answer directly for my husband, this I know: He loves me and he loves my People. He will do what he feels is best."

Five Dreams nodded. He knew that was a fair answer and he would accept it. After all, hadn't Spirit Walker risked his own life to save theirs? It was more than Five Dreams could ask of anyone. "We will find a place for the night," was all he said as he kicked his horse into a gallop. Once again, he was the chief.

Spirit Walker and his braves rode into Five Dreams' encampment on their second day in Mexico. The reunion brought great rejoicing among the People. It would not be long before they reached the mountains and began to take the switchback trails that would take them to Pa-Gotzin-Kay. Though Spirit Walker was anxious to see his wife, he knew that his first order of business was to meet with the chief.

He found Five Dreams standing on the banks of the Aqua Prieto. It was this river that they would follow into the Bavispe Canyon. Once in the canyon, they would surely be spotted by those already dwelling at Pa-Gotzin-Kay. Contact would be made and they would be welcomed.

Spirit Walker and Five Dreams exchanged salutations before settling down to discuss weightier matters. Sitting on the rocks at the edge of the river, they talked of life at Pa-Gotzin-Kay. Mostly they discussed matters such as lodgings, planting and harvesting, hunting, and other decisions that would have to be made in order to accommodate the People's needs.

It wasn't long, however, before Spirit Walker felt a need to discuss his main concern. "My chief," he began slowly, "you know that we desire to live in peace, but there are those who may make it difficult. I refer to the *Netdahe*."

Five Dreams nodded. "This I know."

"You know also that Goyathlay will not cease his efforts to exact revenge on the Mexicans as well as the whites."

"Yes."

Spirit Walker paused before continuing. "We cannot let such things interfere with our peace, my chief. I have ridden with Goyathlay. I know him and he knows me. I ask you to allow me to deal with him should he visit Pa-Gotzin-Kay."

Five Dreams turned his head slowly and looked deep into Spirit Walker's eyes. "I believe you have the heart of an Apache, Spirit Walker. But, I also believe you have the cunning of a fox, the strength of a bear, the wisdom of an eagle. I will trust you with this thing."

After meeting with the chief, Spirit Walker went immediately to his wife. Desert Rain leapt into his arms. Locked in the embrace which gave them both strength, they were surrounded by Wind Song, Yellow Dog, and Broken Branch. The family was together at last.

The warriors sat around the small fire that night and retold their part in the escape. One warrior told how he had caught the horse he used to ride from the blue coats' makeshift prison. He laughed at how he was almost rubbed off when the pony came too close to a tree. He showed the "badge" he had received in his effort—a long deep scratch on his left shoulder. Everyone laughed.

Broken Branch recounted his "meeting" with Spirit Walker while tied and piled on top of others at the river bank. With great dramatic flare he pantomimed being pulled by the hair and feeling the gun barrel pressed against his head. He admitted that he had been concerned. He said that he had been more than ready to die for his People, but that he knew it would not happen that way, because Spirit Walker lay beneath him—that when he looked into those dark eyes, there was never a doubt in his mind that they would escape. Everyone cheered.

Yellow Dog was prompted, at that point, to tell the story of his first meeting with Spirit Walker, though he admitted that he didn't remember much about the initial "introduction." The warriors laughed when he told of being knocked unconscious by the older warrior.

"Yes," Broken Branch interrupted, "we have all seen his fighting ability."

Some of the warriors began to nod and murmur, remembering how he bested Cloud Maker at the council meeting long ago.

Broken Branch laughed the loudest. "I remember the look on Cloud Maker's face that night," he said. "Cloud Maker always thought that no one could defeat him face to face. I bet even now, he tells the story differently. I bet, as he rides with Goyathlay, that the others believe, as well as himself, that no one can defeat him."

Though the others laughed, Spirit Walker fell quiet. Slowly he rose to his feet and pulled something from his blankets. It was a bow.

Broken Branch recognized it immediately, as did several of the others. "That is Cloud Maker's," he said, astonished. There was no mistaking that it was the bow that had originally belonged to Arm Bow and had been given to Cloud Maker after Arm Bow's death.

Spirit Walker knew that it was his place to tell the story. To speak the name of the dead was taboo and it was time they all knew the truth.

"Cloud Maker gave it to me," he announced. "He was killed by the blue coats before he was able to make it to Mexico with Goyathlay. Desert Rain found him. I tried to heal his wounds, but they were too severe. He died in my arms. We must now put to rest the name of Cloud Maker."

It was done. It would be the last time they would hear his name spoken.

The moon was almost full as Spirit Walker and Desert Rain walked along the banks of the Aqua Prieto. It was the first time they'd had the opportunity to be alone since Spirit Walker returned from his meeting with Captain Jackson.

Spirit Walker had related the meeting to all who had sat around the fire earlier that evening. He had told of the peace agreement between him and the blue coat leader and expressed his trust in the captain's words. He explained that he had based his trust on Jackson's actions in the clearing. Five Dreams had announced that his clan would stay in the Sierra Madre and live in peace.

Desert Rain walked beside her husband, watching the moon reflect along the strands of silver that streaked his hair. "My Spirit?" she asked softly.

"Yes, my Little One?"

"Do you believe that the blue coat leader will keep his word? Do you honestly believe his words of life?"

Spirit Walker stopped and took his lovely wife into his arms. "Yes, my Desert Rain, I believe him. I must believe. The life of everyone I love depends on his words of life."

Desert Rain looked up into her husband's dark eyes. "Spirit Walker, will our children know this peace? Will we be able to take them back to our beloved Apachería and show them the places of the Old Ones? Will they know anything of our past, our culture, our life before the white man?"

"We shall make it so, my Flower."

"When? How?"

Spirit Walker smiled, pulled her close to him and buried his face in her hair. "When our first child is born, and for each one thereafter, we shall journey back to our homeland. We will begin the instruction early for each one of them. Each summer we will make the journey so that they will know and learn and appreciate the deeds done by their mother."

"And their father," Desert Rain added.

Spirit Walker kissed her then. As she melted into his embrace, she felt her knees weaken. It was not weariness that possessed her, it was passion, the passion of love for the one man who had taken her higher than she could have ever imagined.

In the moonlight, with the river speaking the mysteries of the ages, they made love as they had never before. It was a deep, possessing love that flowed through each of them like a river of warmth. To Desert Rain, it was a life-giving warmth, one she would never forget.

Chapter Fifty-five

"It is alive, isn't it?" Desert Rain asked softly.

Spirit Walker smiled and nodded. "Yes, my Flower, it is alive."

Spirit Walker draped his arm over his wife's shoulders as they sat on the rocks at the edge of the high trail overlooking the familiar valley below. His thoughts wandered back over the last year. It had been that long since they had last visited this very spot.

They had remained with Tahza's band at Pa-Gotzin-Kay for only six months after their arrival in Mexico. It was at Spirit Walker's request that Five Dreams moved his band into the Bavispe Canyon. The small ledge of the mountain fortress had proved to be inadequate for such a large group to survive together comfortably. That was not to say that the two bands didn't get along—they were especially close, but they needed their space.

The two bands came together to rejoice as well as to grieve. The most tragic event had been the death of Tahza. It was reported that he had died of pneumonia while visiting the Great White Father. It had been a devastating blow to Nod-Ah-Sti. Many braves had tried to take his place, but Spirit Walker had sensed that the next leader to emerge would not be ready for a few years yet, though he already showed the promise of being a great leader. His name was Niño Cochise.

Goyathlay had ventured to Pa-Gotzin-Kay, but only to visit his relatives and friends. Mostly he kept to himself, though he and Spirit Walker had talked on occasion. At their last meeting, Goyathlay had admitted that he could not continue to raid both sides of the border for too much longer. It looked like the life of the *Netdahe* was destined to end soon.

Captain Jackson had visited with Spirit Walker as the last snows of the winter had melted in the foothills. He told the Apache warrior that he had been promoted to major and there was some talk of him becoming an agent at one of the reservations in Arizona Territory. Though the blue coats called him Major Jackson, Spirit Walker called him Shoots No More. The major had invited Spirit Walker to visit him at Fort Lowell. The town just outside the fort's walls, Tucson, was growing rapidly. It was a lawless town, for the most part, and only the presence of the cavalry kept peace in the surrounding area. Jackson had even mentioned that he might consider becoming its sheriff.

Spirit Walker's reverie was interrupted by the lonely howl of a coyote.

"The Trickster is calling for his mate," Desert Rain said with a laugh. "He has always loved the full moon."

Husband and wife cast a glance at the white orb that illuminated the night sky, when a silhouette floated into view. Desert Rain giggled with delight when the hawk gave its shrill cry.

"And there is his answer," Spirit Walker remarked.

As Spirit Walker pulled his wife closer into his arms, another sound breached the night. It was a baby's cry.

Desert Rain pulled gently away from her husband and placed her hand into the small willow basket on her right. Laying her hand on the small infant's chest, she spoke softly, "Do not be a afraid, my son, you shall hear many tales of the Trickster."

Spirit Walker laughed. It was the most pleasure he had known in his life—watching his wife and son interact.

"Why do you laugh?" Desert Rain asked, slugging him lightly on the shoulder. "You will tell him the stories, won't you?"

"Yes, I will tell him the stories. He will know everything, I promise you."

Desert Rain reached into the basket and picked up her son. Cradling him in her arms, she began to sing:

You give the moon its light, you give the stars their shine.
The sun cannot rise without your smile.
The wind whispers your name to the pines, and they bend to your will.
The leaves dance at the sound of your voice, and the deer leap for joy.
You give the birds their song, they sing of your beauty.
You are the song on the midnight wind.

As she sang, Spirit Walker watched the hawk soar on the winds. It wasn't long before she was joined in flight by a mighty eagle.

Spirit's Song

MADELINE BAKER

She is a runaway wife, with a hefty reward posted for her return. And he is the best darn tracker in the territory. For the half-breed bounty hunter, it is an easy choice. His was a hard life, with little to show for it except his horse, his Colt, and his scars. The pampered, brown-eyed beauty will go back to her rich husband in San Francisco, and he will be ten thousand dollars richer. But somewhere along the trail out of the Black Hills everything changes. Now, he will give his life to protect her, to hold her forever in his embrace. Now the moonlight poetry of their loving reflects the fiery vision of the Sun Dance: She must be his spirit's song.

___4476-5 $5.99 US/$6.99 CAN

Chase the Wind
MADELINE BAKER

Elizabeth Johnson is a woman who knows her own mind. And an arranged marriage with a fancy lawyer from the East is definitely not for her. Defying her parents, she sets her sights on the handsome young sheriff of Twin Rivers. But when Dusty's virile half-brother rides into town, Beth takes one look into the stormy black eyes of the Apache warrior and understands that this time she must follow her heart and not her head. Before she knows quite how it's happened, Beth is fleeing into the desert with Chase the Wind, fighting off a lynch mob—and finding ecstasy beneath starry skies. By the time she returns home, Beth has pledged herself heart and soul to Chase. But with her father forbidding him to call, and her erstwhile fiancée due to arrive from the East, she wonders just how long it will take before they can all live happily ever after. . . .

___52401-5 $5.99 US/$6.99 CAN

Theresa Scott
Eagle Dancer

Bound and helpless, the blue-eyed prisoner is an enemy of her people. One who is going to die. But his powerful gaze tells Hope his spirit is strong, and suddenly she knows this man has a part in her future.

Baron's will to live had fled during the Civil War, during an act so unforgivable he's been punishing himself ever since. He doesn't want mercy at the hands of his captors, but he is granted a second chance by an old woman and a beautiful Lakota girl. Can a sacred ritual and a loving heart make him whole again, give him the right, at long last, to take Hope?

___4899-X $5.99 US/$6.99 CAN

Velda Sherrod

Lord of the Plains

To save her sister, saloon singer Kate Hartland plays the hundred-dollar whore. Trembling in her innocence, she seduces a handsome outsider who appears safe, kind, and Irish. But the virile stranger turns out to be anything but safe. He awakens a dangerous passion, incites torturous longings, and worst of all possesses hated Comanche blood.

As Sean O'Brien he takes her virginity, claiming her in the most primitive sense. As Grayhawk he saves her life, making her his wife in the eyes of the Comanche. As he risks death to unite the white settlers and the Indians in peace, he also risks his spirit to unite body and soul with the lass who has captured his heart.

___4901-5 $4.99 US/$5.99 CAN

WHITE DOVE

SUSAN EDWARDS

White Dove was raised to know that she must marry a powerful warrior. The daughter of the great Golden Eagle is required to wed one of her own kind, a man who will bring honor to her people and strength to her tribe. But the young Irishman who returns to seek her hand makes her question herself, and makes her question what makes a man.

Jeremy Jones returns to be trained as a warrior, to take the tests of manhood and prove himself in battle. Watching him, White Dove sees a bravery she's never known, and suddenly she realizes her young suitor is not just a man, he is the only one she'll ever love.

___4890-6 $5.99 US/$6.99 CAN

Look for these titles
in October 2001 from

APACHE DESTINY
HOLLY HARTE

Abby Madison has maintained the Flying M ranch ever since her husband's brutal death at the hands of raiding Apache warriors. So when an Apache man wanders onto her land, fury boils within her. But the feisty redhead can see he means her no ill will. In fact, his simmering brown gaze and lean body arouse longings she thought she'd banished long ago. Chino Whitehorse seeks vengeance for the murder of his family by a gang of white men. But when he comes upon the white woman under the hot Arizona sun, he is drawn to her with an intensity that threatens to distract him from his mission completely. After one searing kiss, they realize they are meant to share a love tempestuous enough to sweep them into a happier tomorrow.

___4930-9 $5.50 US/$6.50 CAN

MADELINE BAKER
Chase the Lightning

Amanda can't believe her eyes when the beautiful white stallion appears in her yard with a wounded man on its back. Dark and ruggedly handsome, the stranger fascinates her. He has about him an aura of danger and desire that excites her in a way her law-abiding fiancé never had. But something doesn't add up: Trey seems bewildered by the amenities of modern life; he wants nothing to do with the police; and he has a stack of 1863 bank notes in his saddlebags. Then one soul-stirring kiss makes it all clear—Trey may have held up a bank and stolen through time, but when he takes her love it will be no robbery, but a gift of the heart.

___4917-1 $5.99 US/$6.99 CAN